# S. R. EMONTS

# THE SANDCASTLE
# IN
# THE RAIN

# THE SANDCASTLE IN THE RAIN

# 1
# Knossos

Joan's mother lost her identity on June 26th, 2153.

She looked at the only private hologram she had of her mother and sister smiling, thinking of the day they might be reunited.

Rays of the rising sun sliced the floating memory. She pressed a button on her cuffputer, and the hologram vanished.

The seat rattled and she gripped the grab handle as turbulence shook the hovercar. Thru the door's window a line of artificial trees raced by, briefly obscuring endless acres of rotting forest. On the horizon the steel skeletons of skyscrapers cast long but thin shadows over countless kilometers of abandoned urban ruins.

In the window's reflection sunlight passed over the badge on her assault armor. *MOTH* embossed underneath, adjacent to a ring of 12 stars and her full name, Joanna Lyon. Reversed letters in the makeshift mirror. The reflection of her partner, Peter, adjusted elevation with the collective lever, his attention fixed on a topography hologram over the throttle. The green tracker ring wrapped around his wrist glowed next to the cuffputer strapped to his forearm. He's still human, she thought, rolling up her sleeve and checking her own green wrist-tracker. And so am I.

Their reflections vanished with the rising sun as Peter cleared his throat over the loud engines. She returned to the tactical hologram projected from the dashboard. Vague, variegated lines of light fell on each hand and details pierced both eyes.

One of the many dilapidated prewar buildings outside of Settlement Five, 100 clicks beyond the perimeter wall. A reverse pinching gesture zoomed out to a single-story, T-shaped house. Four bedrooms along a narrow hall. A kitchen and great room in the front completed the modest labyrinth. Outside, two dead trees in the front lawn that could be used for cover.

Pulses tickled each fingertip as she swiped to a live holographic projection. Human-shaped outlines vibrantly colored in red and green. 500 meters short of the structure, two dozen police robots flashed blue as they disembarked a carrier drone and formed a column.

The dashboard countdown beeped. Six kilometers. Two minutes. She reached back to tie her hair and turbulence shifted taut body armor against her diaphragm.

"Equipment check rookie," Peter said.

The carbine painfully pressed down on her lap as she balanced the barrel towards the passenger door. 30 in glowing-red digits. In her hip holster, a loaded Solara-120 blaster. Twisting the grip to the RA-battery readout, a dotted circle full and blue above the ammo readout. Three gas grenades on her bandoleer.

A medical kit on her belt. One fingernail tap turned the red and white medical cross top transparent. Inside, the nanobot injector and plasma balloon tumbled around as she shook it in a circle until the green tip of the gas repellant tube popped up. Lifting it to her nose and squeezing sprayed a foul mist into each nostril.

The combat helmet in the backseat was beyond her shoulder's range of motion and it kept jolting up and down with the turbulence, which forced her to twist around and bump into Peter's holstered blaster. An M400 disruptor. A hand canon as subtle as him.

Eventually Peter noticed her staring. "Okay Lyon. Take it from the top."

She scratched her head. Is this the fifth hostage rescue this week? "12 outcasts, three hostages."

The dashboard beeped. One minute to target. The digits of the timer rapidly flashed, like that's going to help anyone manage anxiety right before entering combat. She wiped sweaty palms on one knee while tapping one foot on the floorboard. Her shaking fingers rotated the mood twister attached to her cuffputer until the sphere read Enforcement-Numb, 20%. One by one, each finger turned steady.

Peter pulled the throttle back along the colored bands, into the black stripe labeled *Stealth Mode*. The blaring turbines slowed until they were about as loud as a hair dryer. "Don't Forget, there's a camp of outcasts two clicks from here. In and out. Three minutes." He sighed. "And don't run out of ammo this time."

Easy for him to say when he never shoots anything. In the side mirror a distant transport drone moved up and down, its blinking lights visible as dots in the orange sun. "Same plan as last time?"

"Right. We meet in the middle." He clicked the dashboard transmitter, "Pollux, are you ready?"

"Da Peter," Ivan Pollux said in a thick Settlement-Nine accent. No trace of anxiety in his voice as he coordinated their mission 130 kilometers away, safe and sound in the Hall of Justice Command Center.

She pointed to her hologram and said, "Peter, drop me behind them dead trees."

"Right." His eyes moved between her and the controls. He smirked. "Don't die rookie."

Horizontal motion slowed until the hovercar earned its name. A flick of her finger dismissed the hologram and the target building appeared thru the windshield. An old residence abandoned years ago when radioactive dust claimed the neighborhood. The roof had lost some shingles, flaking like a dead snake. Intact windows obscured by smears of dirt. A lawn of tires, aluminum siding fragments, and dead tree branches.

A button above the door dropped a cable from the car ceiling into the back of her armor.

Strapping on her helmet, she opened the door and jumped. The cable and gravity played tug of war with all 55 kilos of her, one side winning a meter per second. Her boots hit the ground. She quickly disconnected the cable and ran behind a nearby tree. A tornado of dust surrounded her until the black hovercar disappeared with growing turbines, replaced by crickets too stubborn to die from background radiation.

"Peel your eyes," Ivan said into her ear communicator.

She squeezed both lids shut and after silently counting to five opened them with activated retina implants. The Wall-Thru function downloaded satellite scans and drew images into her eyes. Bounding boxes and human-shaped outlines around all 15 building occupants, their distances in meters. Heat signatures and vital signs. The closest thing to x-ray vision she could get without black market eye drops and headaches. A mission timer started on another eye function in the corner of her vision, three minutes counting down.

Thru a bored hole in the dead tree, dust settled on the littered yard of split boards and broken bottles. Parched dirt with more cracks than a failed pottery class. Wall-Thru flashed a dozen red shapes under the surface. Spider mines. Too many to defuse.

20 meters behind her, the expendable squad of robots. Grey, two meters tall and as wide as bodybuilders. Human shaped, except for their small cube-shaped heads. Blaster rifles in their skeletal-metal hands. She curled up behind the tree while pointing at a single bot and making a hand signal. It ran past and towards the house, now visible in the tree's hole. Chunks of soil crumbled around the emerging spider mines that lunged at the robot.

An artillery-sized explosion threw her onto her back and decimated the tree's branches while raining dirt everywhere.

Each finger turned white as she pulled a cone-shaped gas grenade and fumbled with the child-proof pin until an increasingly pitched tone rang. Standing caught an outcast's attention. Blasts elevated bursts of dirt by her feet and thumped against the tree.

The grenade whirred and spun as she threw it, the tip of the cone flaming as it rocketed towards whatever shattered window she stared at. The five second fuse counted down on another function over the mission timer. At her hand signal the rest of her robotic squad charged at the house, and she pointed at the front door as the rally point, where a function drew a blue circle on the ground.

A brilliant flash with a loud burst. Delirium gas flowed from the windows with coughs and screams. The bots battered down the front door and entered a fray of blinding blasts as she sprinted past still-smoking craters and over the threshold.

Darkness. 10 seconds until the Cat-Eyes function brightened the dark house. The police robots lined up in silence. Floorboards squeaked under her rubber soles. The kitchen. Faint bubbling from a Russel-brand tea pot between a simmer and boil. Lingering gas fought the repellent in her nose with an odor kind of like glue and cinnamon.

On the right. Tables, chairs, and couches overturned and blasted into splinters and foam. Above a mantle and two crossed swords mounted on the wall, bits of dust fell thru bullet-sized lines of penetrating sunlight. Blaster scorches painted the walls in patterns like Rorschach tests. Four bloody bodies on the floor. A step landed in the red pool between them. Damnit. These are new boots.

Confirmed kill chimes rang on the audio channel, each corpse crediting her account with a $30 bonus in flashing green.

The mission timer beeped: two minutes.

A growing-high electronic pitch followed by a function alarm: *Energy surge detected.*

"Plasma charge," Ivan said.

On Wall-Thru, one outcast rapidly moved towards the front of the house. Her robots rushed the hallway to intercept. A function drew a blue dot like a laser sight as she aimed the carbine.

Her heart rate flew like the Jupiter Express. The tea pot whistled. The outcast came into view for half a second. A dirty-faced man with holes in his clothes and anger in his eyes.

Joan managed one trigger pull, which missed. "Oh F—"

The charged blast burned like the sun, vaporizing the robots and her carbine before propelling her into crumbling drywall with the force of a sledgehammer. Orange embers drifted to the floor thru a cloud of white powder.

She yelped when she tried to move. Sharp edges of charred and broken armor curled around her stomach, cutting deeper with every breath. A function flashed a message about her cuffputer auto-releasing painkillers into her bloodstream. Vital signs somehow still in the green. Both ears rang and something trickled on her forehead which she checked with a finger. Blood.

A high-pitch alarm beeped in both ears, synchronized with red function text. *Shield Failure.*

"I'm entering. Grid one," Peter said, his voice sounding distant on the wireless.

"There is no door there, Peter," Ivan said.

A second charge warning. Sunlight flooded the room with a bright blast that sounded like something heavy falling over.

Eye movements dismissed the shield alarm and an automated message played: *Thank you for choosing Hoplite armor. We hope you survive long enough to become a repeat customer.*

When the smoke cleared Peter had blown Joan's attacker into a collage of bloody bones and organs that slid down the nearby wallpaper. Peter turned to fire down the far hall, producing a kill-chime before the crossfire struck him down and he fell out of sight. An officer-down klaxon boomed.

"Peter!" Attempting to stand resulted in her rolling over and vomiting inside her split-in-half helmet. She spat, the gross variety with gooey saliva falling from the edge of her mouth.

The kitchen's island laid in waste, reduced to a marble archipelago. Though the Russel-brand tea pot remained perfectly intact. Wedged between rubble.

The mission timer beeped: one minute.

"Joan, is Peter K-I-A?" Ivan asked.

"Standby," she said between spits, eventually reaching her feet with her blaster drawn. Around the corner, Peter laid against the wall. Wounded in the gut and unresponsive. She stopped short of the blood pooling under him and pressed two fingers against his neck. "Negative."

On the wall next to Peter, faded marker notches measured height with various dates, all of them pre-war. *Jessica, age 8* written at the top. She'd be 22 now. Older than me, Joan thought. She probably didn't survive the war. Even if she reached a fallout shelter, she probably starved like all the others, dying with a parched throat and a hole where her stomach should be. Bullies would have taken her food while everyone else pretended to not see, forgetting it even happened, or that she existed at all.

Wall-Thru illuminated the room at the end of the hall. Three hostage-indicators standing still in the far corner. The red outline of an outcast behind them, using one as a human shield. Another ducked behind an overturned table. The outlaws snickered, and her teeth ground together as she imagined their grins. They think they've gotten away with it.

Beyond an open door, a dim lamp sliced the darkness of the room at the end of the hall. A shiny gold finish blemished by erosion. It stood on a table with a missing leg that leaned against the wall. Something shiny next to the light. A memory disc blinking rainbow-colored lights. Maybe it's her, the disc with her lost memories.

30 beeping red seconds left on the mission timer.

"Joan, you're out of time. Abort," Major Lansing, her commanding officer, said on the mission audio channel.

The extraction point blinked on a function 100 meters to the left.

She turned her mood twister to 70%. Fear and anxiety fell away as her consciousness lagged reality by several seconds, and the hallway glistened with semi-luminescence. "Ivan, reposition the transport for extraction." Her own voice sounded external, a few centimeters in front of her.

She fired at the outcast behind the relic-wood table, splitting it in half and instantly spray-painting the far wall red. A kill-chime credited her $30.

The remaining kidnapper returned fire and she ducked behind the door frame. Two chunks of wall above her blasted into clumps of dust. The sight of the falling cloud froze. With the mood twister consciousness lag, you don't experience your own death. Just the one or two seconds before it. I'm already dead, she thought.

Sneezing broke the spell as the mission timer reached a line of flashing zeroes. Firing ceased. A metallic thump. Maybe a blaster magazine hitting the floor. He's reloading.

She jumped up and ran into the room.

He had already reloaded and raised his blaster. Damn lag. A hostage between her and the outcast. Pairs of eyes scared and furious.

The targeting function drew a red X. *Excessive Collateral Damage Risk.*

Me or the hostage, she thought while aiming at the enemy's neck and pulling the trigger.

Blood splattered the wall behind the outcast as a scream fled his mouth. He fell backwards, discharging his weapon and shooting the hostage.

Smoke rose from her blaster barrel. The other captives gave muffled screams from gagged mouths and bulging eyes. A kill-chime credited her $30.

"Hostage *down*," Ivan said incredulously.

Major Lansing screamed inarticulately over the com as red text blared on a function: *PRIMARY MISSION OBJEC-TIVE FAILED*.

"Fuck."

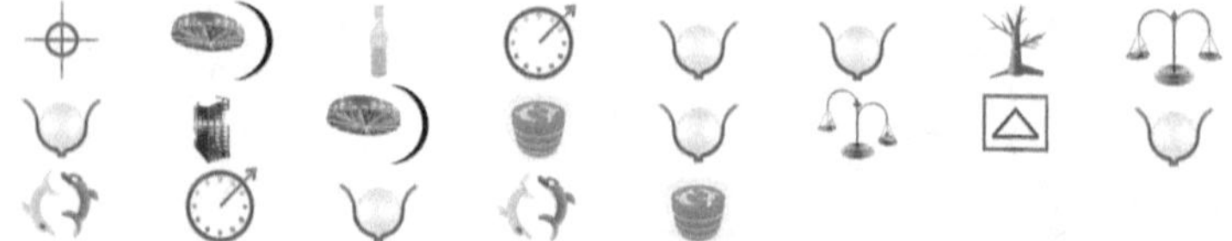

# 2
# Aletheia

Joan bit her fingernails while *PENDING SUSPENSION* blinked in holographic letters. Brightness from the skylight far above her polished desk, but the floating cursor automatically grew brighter, blinking at her every second like Major Lansing impatiently tapping his foot. Thankfully, he wasn't here.

Up in the corner of the raised mezzanine, a cleaning bot squeaked a polishing pad along the glass walls of the CO's dark office. The MOTH slogan in spinning text over his door: *TRUTH LEADS TO JUSTICE.*

Bullshit. Major Lansing does not want the truth. He doesn't care that getting that hostage killed was unintentional. Or that unrecovered hostages in the wastelands get brainwashed by Dr. Wasserman and when they return, they commit acts of violence and terror. Mercy for the guilty is death for the innocent.

And all Lansing cares about is the words *excessive force* in big red letters on some auto-report. Too many suspensions and you're fired. And if you're not a cop you're weak. A target.

She sighed and tied her hair back while slouching in the padded desk chair. Comfy. Especially after changing from assault armor to a nylon blouse and pants.

With a falling finger the computer hologram sank into the desk, revealing the massive room. A multimillion-dollar renovation budget couldn't disguise that the Hall of Justice was an aircraft hangar before the war and a failed fallout shelter after that. Though the seemingly endless ocean of desks manned by constables constantly yelling at their phones, computers, and each other sometimes did the trick. The blended chatter echoed along the tall arching roof end to end.

The command center's gigantic holo-map, which tracked crimes in the Settlements with a chickenpox-like infection of red report dots, was a reliable landmark. The globe slowly rotated from the Atlantic Marshes to the North American Wastelands, then the green dot of Settlement Five, the Pacific Tide Pools, finally the Desert Australis.

Two desks to the left, Morgan Sullivan's workstation. She was there, navigating holograms floating over her lamp-top computer.

Joan stood and walked thru the grid of desks, briefly pausing for an officer running by with a web of holographic documents floating around him.

"Mornin'."

"Hi Joan," Morgan said with a smile. Seated, she was nearly as tall as Joan, who unconsciously smiled back at her friend. The air moved calmly around her. Safer. Like she was the only other dolphin in the police shark tank. "Are you okay?"

"Mmhmm." She nodded.

"Ivan told me things got a little heated this morning," Morgan said.

"More like melted." She sighed. "I took a risky shot and a hostage died."

"Oh sweetie. I'm sorry."

"I thought I had a clean shot. The computer warned me. But it was the only way to get that disc." She sat in Morgan's extra desk chair. "Please tell me it was worth it."

"I was just about to come over." Morgan swiped thru an evidence file to a *Memory Playback* button that threw a floating collage of animated memories into the air.

A lab with a table of filled flasks. Blinking lights and beeping from a datacore in a corner. A memory of sitting in the passenger seat of a ground car that drove thru the entrance of a corporate campus. Delphi Datacore etched on a stone sign.

"It's not her memories." She exhaled and landed her chin on the palm of her hand.

"I'm sorry," Morgan said.

"Damnit. I'm gonna get suspended for nothin'." She leaned back in the chair, tapping one foot on the floor.

Morgan rubbed Joan's shoulder and leaned in so she could whisper. "Troy was telling me that local radiation spikes can interfere with the targeting function." Her eyebrows elevated for a few seconds.

A simple fib to keep my job, she thought. A sensible fix. "You long-legged genius." She held her cuffputer over Morgan's desk to load her report. Fingers met the holographic keyboard, slow clicks to a quick lie.

The computer flashed the globe logo of the DOLOS system. Digital Omniscient something-something System. There was some question about it on the final academy exam. It prompted her to validate her mind. Can't have officers filing reports if they've been brainwashed by mental hacks.

She handed her blaster to Morgan and connected a wire from the desk to the tracking ring wrapped around her wrist. "If I turn out to be a meat robot, shoot me twice in the head. Just to, you know, be sure."

Morgan laughed. "Did you hear about—"

The light falling on Morgan's desk disappeared, and with a rumbling noise the hologram vibrated. They looked up. Thru a skylight, the Zeus weapon platform eclipsed the sun for several seconds. The bottom edge faced the Earth. A colossal circle with a dark void in the center.

"I heard the anti-matter cannon is going online tomorrow," Morgan said. "Did you hear about Greta?"

DOLOS beeped green: validated as human. After pulling the wire she took back her blaster and holstered it. "No. What happened?" Clicking submit sank the After-Action report into the desk with a green check mark.

Morgan leaned in close with a grin and whispered, "A mutant rat clawed into her apartment. And she shot it 24 times." Which means she shot thru her entire magazine. "On her 24th birthday." Morgan discretely navigated to the police social media feed, where Greta's name had been replaced with a nickname: Rapid-Fire.

After they snickered, Morgan nodded up towards a bulb-shaped interview room 100 meters away. "So, who are they?"

Inside the far room, the two surviving hostages sat chained to the table. A young boy and an adult woman. The woman's feet tapped rapidly under the table. The boy played with strands of her curly hair, straightening them out. What the law would soon be doing with the rest of her.

"Not sure." She leaned back in the chair and covered her mouth while yawning.

"I hope the child will be okay."

"I gotta get 'em processed so I can get back out there. Start searchin' again."

"The station computer will like that. And I'll keep an eye out for your mom's lost memories too. Once I return to field duty."

Skatá. Should have asked earlier. "How's your hand?"

"I need another week of plastia-paste to regrow my wuttle finger. It doesn't hurt anymore though." Morgan lifted her injured hand and rotated it back in forth. A cone-shaped tube filled with blue fluid wrapped around her pinkie. "Can you stop by when your shift ends?"

"Okay."

After sitting and landing a cup of coffee on her own desk, Joan watched Peter pace in front of the two-way mirror of the bulb-shaped interview room with a mug that was un-doubtedly filled with coffee, and a flatputer. He was Peter-splaining something to Captain O'Connor. The tall and beautiful officer who laughs at all his boring jokes. How can they be this happy when he almost died a few hours ago? He's never jovial around me, she thought.

Maybe it's dangling boogers or bad breath. No, Morgan would have said something. Hopefully. She exhaled on the back of her hand and sniffed it. When no one was looking, of course. Smells okay.

Peter's distance could be a good thing. The people closest to you are the ones that can hurt you the most.

O'Connor finally stopped flirting with Peter. Her heeled boots tapping as she looked over with a smile and raised eyebrows before disappearing among the horde of station foot traffic.

She walked over and took a seat at a nearby table, where her crossed legs dangled with no hope of reaching the ground. Peter didn't notice her. He just stood there, like a robot waiting at pre-programmed intervals to consume a liquid formulated to lubricate its inner machinery. His wound hidden under business casual. "You feelin' alright?" she asked.

He took a sip from the white mug, which lit up with a holographic logo of the Grand Titan Hotel, before he looked over. "Did you take an anti-radiation tablet?"

"Yeap. And I even managed to tie my own shoes."

"Perfect." Ceramic pings rang as he tapped the scratched-dull wedding band on his fourth finger.

Is he going to say thanks for dragging his heavy ass 100 meters to the extraction ship and pressing a nanobot injector into his neck? Joan inhaled steam from her mug and silently counted to 10. Nope. Dropping a cream and sugar tablet into the cup produced a black and white vortex of foam.

With a grimace Peter wedged the flatputer against his side and scratched his face with the freed hand.

"Still waitin' on that lab?" she asked.

He shook his head with some sort of gruff old man sigh. "Yes, waiting for DNA."

Loading a hologram on her cuffputer, she navigated to the casefile evidence page. Still no results. Poking the refresh button, it beeped. Still nothing. Refresh. Refresh. Refresh. Oh, come on already.

Behind the two-way, the boy left the woman's lap and began surveying what appeared to him as a curved mirror. He stopped a meter from Peter, pressing a fingertip against the glass. Peter mirrored it with his index finger. The child departed after a few seconds.

Joan's attention evaporated into the familiar sound of the old shelter air filtration system. The spinning-up ceiling fan sent warm air and chills down her spine. Neck and arm hairs stood on end. Both hands embraced burning squeezes around the coffee mug. Time moved on its knees, with its hands gripping memories of being trapped underground. Claustrophobic. And hungry.

Peter's flatputer vibrated and broke the spell. He lifted and looked at the bright screen. "Well, shit."

# 3
## Camera Obscura

The chrome chair clattered loudly as Peter dragged it across the concrete floor and sat at the large table in the small interview room. The subject sat beyond the line of shadow from the single bright light hanging overhead, where her nervous breaths echoed as though they would rattle the distorted reflections smearing every curve of the mirrored walls.

Red digits on the wall clock pulsed every second, as though the small chamber was the heart of a large police organism. Twisting his mood-dial to Interrogation, he wondered, how much of the past does someone have to forget to become an entirely different person? How could that make a person any less human?

He leaned back in his chair as Lyon sat down next to him. The rookie managed to do it silently. She always seems to be sneaking around, even in plain sight. Her generation is too young to comprehend the old world, and how much was lost in the war.

A baby-faced officer led the subject's child out and the interview-bulb door closed with the hiss of a vacuum seal.

He reached for the control panel under the table and an ocular subroutine rendered the text of each textured button, until he found *Holo-Recorder*.

A square contraption descended from the ceiling, painting his reflection blue and slashing red glare across Lyon's cheek as though it were a bleeding scar. Initialization parameters scrolled across his eyes as the interrogation response matrix and behavior-cylinder linked to a subroutine. With exchanged glances, Lyon kept tabs on the cylinder while he monitored the matrix, an aggregation of interrogation techniques from the memories of long-deceased detectives.

He smiled at the subject and said for the record, "Hello. I'm officer Peter Ramsey with the Monitoring Organic

Trespassing Hazards Cadre. We require information in order to confirm your human status. You'll then be entitled to legal representation for any further questioning."

"Do you understand?" Lyon asked. The woman subject leaned into the light and gave a slow, fixed-gaze nod, and Lyon said for the record, "This is Joan Lyon. It's eleven eleven AM on September twenty-third, twenty-one sixty-three."

The woman's eyes pulsed with recognition. "Lyon? Are you related to Forest Lyon? The golfer?"

"No, I'm not," Lyon said in a rural-sounding twang, the accent that infected the unsavory corners of most fallout bunkers. Her eyes narrowed like a targeting laser. The gleaming blue rims thinned, as though nearly all of them had crossed the event horizons of the black centers. "Please state your name."

"Andrea Aeneas." Andrea looked at the floor, her body language and vitals priming the baseline cylinder.

"Who's the boy?" he asked.

"Luke. He's my son." Andrea forced a smile.

Andrea's profile loaded on his wrist-computer. No son or husband listed under her bio. Sometimes it only takes one question. Brainwashed with false memories or perhaps imprinted with another consciousness entirely. Andrea was turned into someone else. Undoubtedly without her consent, so punishing her for that doesn't seem fair. But orders are orders.

Lyon read from a flat-panel under the table. "You're twenty-eight years old? And you emigrated from the settlements on March twenty-eight, twenty-one fifty-three?"

"The settlements weren't chartered then. But yes, that's when I left."

"That's one week after the all-clear," he said.

"After being confined to a bunker for so long we wanted to live somewhere that was still green."

"What's your current address and occupation?" Lyon asked.

"One-five-nine-eight Doyle Street, Aphrodite Terra, New Eden. And I work as a memory manager for Recollection Fountain."

Lyon nodded. Andrea's original identity isn't completely lost.

"You create minds? Based on memories?" he asked.

"We do dream-strips now too."

Lyon crossed her legs under the table. Her low-tech signal for baseline completion that spared him from running an additional subroutine.

He scratched his nose. "What brings you to the settlements?"

"We were abducted," Andrea said.

"Where?"

"On New Eden."

"By whom?"

"I didn't recognize them."

Short, rehearsed answers. The matrix subroutine blinked a recommendation: *Conversation Reset*. "Could you start at the beginning?"

Andrea hesitated and took a deep breath. "We were at Trailblazer Marketplace. There was an explosion. The Banshees were shooting at something. I moved Luke behind a stone tree planter. Then two shadows suddenly appeared, two men standing over us. Something bit my leg. A stun pincher, I think. After that I don't remember anything until we were here. In the settlements." She scratched her cheek and nose.

Lyon kicked his leg under the table. Her signal that the behavior cylinder detected a profound lack of truth. "What happened after that?" she asked Andrea.

"When I woke up, we were both thawing in stasis tubes onboard the *Salamander*. We had already landed here. On

Earth." Andrea fidgeted with her hair. "They—the Outcasts, turned us over to a tall woman.  She took us far into the wastelands in a stealth hovercar."

"Did you get her name?" Lyon asked.

"Melinda.  Dark hair.  Blue eyes."

Peter leaned back, sinking into his thoughts as well. Something on the tip of his tongue.  Though not a name or a face.

Lyon leaned forward.  Her clasped hands halfway across the table.  "Did the Outcasts have any memory disks?"

"No."  Andrea shook her head.  "Not that I saw."

Lyon sat up straight and crossed her arms.

"Where did she take you?" he asked.  "The tall woman?"

"Some place they called the grove."

"The place we found you?  That's the grove?"

"No.  They moved us around a few times."

No blinks or kicks from Lyon.  She typed away on a volumetric keyboard under the table.

"Did you try to escape?" he asked.

"We wouldn't last two days in the wastelands.  And we didn't have re-entry visas.  Signaling for help could land us in even more trouble."  Andrea crossed her arms.  "But we ended up here anyway."

His wrist-computer vibrated with a tune.  A typed message from Lyon.  *The Salamander docked on September eleventh at gateway four of the set-5 spaceport, after a 300-day voyage from New Eden.  According to the manifest it was transporting livestock and produce for the Green Star Trading Company.  Ship inventory has a dozen stasis tubes listed for crew use only.*

Lyon twisted her mood-dial and leaned like a cat ready to pounce.  "Are you familiar with this device?"  She switched the volumetric representation to a bird's eye view of a briefcase-sized device with a corded crown attachment. A slowly rotating schematic.  Glaring blue lines outlined regions of the device with explanation-filled clouds. *Dolus*, the brand, etched on the surface. Fine print on the side, automatically magnified by the computer, gave the company's guarantee: *A full mind wipe in 30 minutes or less. You'll forget how much you paid for it, or you'll get your money back.*

"Of course. It's a memory-printer." Andrea rubbed her eyes, and abruptly paused to squint at a scar on her hand, as though she had never seen it before. Whoever brainwashed her took the memory but not the mark.

"Your employer reported one of these models as missin' from their warehouse in the Waset prefecture, on November eleventh of last year," Lyon said.

Andrea's mouth and eyebrows twisted in a puzzled expression.

"If you brought one here, but help us find it, we can help you," he said.

"I didn't," Andrea said.

Lyon kicked him hard enough that he said, "ow!"

Andrea leaned back in her chair, returning her face into darkness until the room computer adjusted the light levels. "I didn't take it."

Lyon kicked him again. He grunted and rubbed his shin. She looked over with a coy smile. Her eyes wandered for a few seconds and returned to Andrea. "The Outcasts would love to get their hands on a mem-printer. They could brainwash someone in twenty minutes instead of the three days it takes 'em with a black-market re-sequencer. Plus, you're a printin' expert."

"It's a legal line of work in the colonies. There are billions of clones and they each can't wait two days for a new mind." Andrea's eyes drifted left, and she shifted her weight. "I don't know anything about any memory-printers here on Earth."

The matrix subroutine lit the subject's responses across the deception spectrum. More red flags than a colonial trade summit. Making false statements to constables. Violation of memory protocols two and eleven. A list too long to bother scrolling to the end.

Andrea sat still and silent with the blank eyes of an imprint. It's impossible at this point to know who she was originally. Outcasts hollow out the human shell and inject a living ghost. Purged of any compromising memories in case of capture. Which means uploading her mind will result in memory sequences as coherent as a Jovian bootleg of the holo-film *Norse Dakota*. A mishmash of blurry visuals and gibberish dialogue.

He looked over at Lyon and she returned a nod. Nothing she wants to add. Nada. Zip.

It would be trivial to tell Andrea everything's fine and to just sit tight while we verify its information, and let it cling to a chance of walking out of here. To allow it to experience shock and panic when the recyclers come to retire it.

After clearing his throat, he said, "Unfortunately, your pre-frontal checksum doesn't match any of the neurological baselines the Colonial Confederacy transmitted, so we have no way to prove that your mind hasn't been compromised by fake memories, or reprogrammed behavior."

Its head rotated instantly like a robotic owl. "What? Can't you run it again?"

"On Earth you are classified as an unregistered organic and are trespassing in violation of protocol eleven, subsection C."

"What happens now?" It asked.

"Organic nullification," he said.

The imprint pleaded with grinding teeth and a twitching head that flung its loose hair in random directions. "They were arguing over something. I don't know what exactly, but they stole it from Delphi."

"Right," he said. "Delphi. The company that predicts the future. The Outcasts stole something from them. I'm sure they wouldn't anticipate that." He pointed at Lyon. "You can try fooling her with that."

Lyon kicked his ankle as he reached over to the table's large red button to end the interrogation. But there his finger hesitated and, using Wall-Thru, his gaze drifted to his desk outside the room and several rows away.

Behind a privately rendered tableau of Peter with his wife and daughter, a volumetric globe of the lush green surface of Titan spun on his desk. A quiet colonial world, far from trouble. Where a person can forget their past without being condemned as less than human. Where someone like Andrea wouldn't be an artificial lamb sent to a real slaughter. Another countless casualty in this hero-less war.

Fifty days. Fifty days and I can shove off this dying rock. If Lyon doesn't get me killed first, he thought.

Lyon's ten fingers flew over a hundred and one volumetric keys to punch two death sentences. A pair of floating documents flattened with a green check mark, and she clicked the red button to terminate the interrogation. Case closed.

"Nullification," Andrea repeated to itself with a thousand-meter stare. "What about Luke? What happens to him?" Tears fell past its upper lip.

# 4
# Carcerem

A pop song played low as Peter watched Lyon grin while taking bite after bite of a burning, disgusting, delicious Martian-style soft taco. Ground pork, melted cheese, onions, and some kind of pepper. Viscous red-Ceydonian sauce formed a steaming puddle in the wax wrapper she held underneath like an inverted tent.

Through the booth window, the holo-dome on the opposite corner of Rolling View and Idlewild. Within gaps of traffic, the spinning neon sign of Kropveld's diner reflected in the dome's glass.

Kropveld's interior was a bright, open space. Done up in the retro style that was common in Settlement Five. Floor to ceiling glass formed into several curves. Bright-white tables and booths with glossy-red imitation-leather cushions. Lines of pink and blue neon bordered the bar and ceiling. A few early lunch patrons. Fewer robot waiters.

A volumetric news feed played in a ceiling corner. A trial of someone labelled a war criminal. Some poor sap who was just doing his job fifteen years ago. His wife and children weeping in the courtroom gallery. Widows and orphans in the name of ex post facto justice.

The feed morphed into an advertisement of two dolphins' swimming on opposite ends of a circle, followed by a montage of happy people and a voice over of a woman who must have been smiling while speaking: *Will your daughter be an astronaut when she grows up? Is your life partner going to be true to you? Buy the future with Delphi Datacore prediction packages. We already know you're going to buy it.*

There's no need to use Delphi on someone like Lyon. Most of the twenty-somethings today had survived a childhood in fallout bunkers with minimal food rations. They were always pleading for food, he thought, wrapping themselves around my ankles and begging. Hard to say no, until the only food I had wasn't enough to sustain an adult.

Thankfully my daughter will never know that struggle. Won't be transformed by it into someone as cynical and jaded as Lyon. Although Lyon would occasionally make some expression or gesture that reminded him of his daughter. And they're both blonde. But that's where the similarity ends.

"What?" Lyon asked.

"Nothing."

He looked away as Lyon loaded the Narcissus routine on her wrist-computer and checked her face while still simultaneously eating. Once her stomach is full, she'll be easier to reason with. These risky missions of hers are truly pointless.

Glaring light from the window as a hovercar flew by at low altitude.

"How's your hovercar training been?"

"I keep crashin' instead of landin'," Lyon said between bites.

"Fortunately, you don't die in the simulator."

Lyon raised her eyebrows and nodded while eating.

Clanking utensils from a booth across the diner drew his attention. A family of three enjoying ice cream sundaes topped with whipped hover-cream. Two strawberry and one caramel. Caramel. Carmen's favorite. She's probably doing one of those floating puzzles right now. And Ariadne must be watching one of those docu-dramas and helping with the harder puzzle pieces during commercial breaks. Although lately she's been watching some cop show set on Mars. I kept pointing out how inaccurate it was regarding police procedure, until she stopped letting me watch it with her.

His burrito vanished before Lyon was halfway done. She frequently wolfs down her food like she's starving but had somehow paced herself. Spinning ice around in his glass didn't melt it into water any faster. Damn Ceydonian sauce.

Taking a deep breath to move air over his tongue only seemed to fuel the burn.  None of the dozen napkins on his lap were clean, so he placed his open palms under the hand sanitizer by the window.  It accelerated its cleansing light to maximum, but his spice-stained hands did not return to a fleshy color.

Lyon chortled bits of laughter at him.  Her personality must be cracking through her mood-dial.

"Ya gonna finish them fries?" Lyon asked.

"Help yourself."

While Lyon pulled his plate away and dug in like a Tasmanian devil, his wrist-computer played a pingtone, a melody from an old song not heard on public audio channels in years.  He clicked a button to load voice messages.

A private audio playback of his wife's voice. Ariadne. "I know you can't talk right now.  But, I, um, I had a bad dream about you.  So, I just, um, wanted to hear your voice."  She exhaled deeply and continued, "I hope you're okay.  You know how when you're at sea, and the water just goes out farther than you can see?  That's how much I love you.  Be safe out there."

"Is that work?" The normally self-conscious Lyon asked with her mouth full.

"No."

"Shouldn't we send out an alert?  That memory-printer sounds awful dangerous."

Alerts lead to witch-hunts.  Not unlike the one that caused the war. "No. Once those imprint memories are uploaded to Delphi, they'll predict if any more crimes are pending."

Despite both her hands being occupied, Lyon somehow navigated a private subroutine on her wrist-computer with an occasionally free finger, appearing as though she was playing an invisible musical instrument.  Her wrist-computer reflected the diner's neon light each time she alternated between eating and reading.

"What are you reading?" he asked.

"Wildlife Measure Seven."

"Oh, the thing about the, uh, wolf-mind modifications?" His stomach tightened and he found a rattling pill bottle in his coat. A quick dose of instant antacids. Better. Much better.

"Yep."

"How are you going to vote?"

She licked her lips with a glowing-red tongue. "I don't like it. They've attacked humans. They're dangerous."

Peter gripped his chin. "Isn't that the point? Editing their minds so they don't attack humans? Otherwise, they only have their instincts, like any other animal."

She scoffed. "They still have the teeth of a carnivore." She took a sip of her drink. "And once the Outcasts figure it out, they'll reprogram 'em to attack us. Same as they do with people."

"So, what's plan B then? Shoot them when they limp into the settlements, when they're starving and desperate enough to attack someone? They could go extinct. There aren't many wolves left."

Halfway to a bite, she said, "There are fewer sheep."

If a wolf is conditioned to never use its teeth, is it still a wolf? Lyon bit into her burrito. She certainly wouldn't be the same without hers.

A robot waiter walked by, and he mouthed the word "water". The bot tilted its head and kept walking.

"There's a new Delphi liaison. Some guy named Moira," Lyon said.

"David Moira?"

"Yeah. Why?" Lyon finished her food.

He hesitated. "I knew him a long time ago."

"From the Navy?" Lyon licked her lips. "Morgan said, well she heard you were in the Navy."

He hesitated. "Yes, I was."

"Really?" Her eyes scanned him as though he were a Rubik's cube. "Water or interstellar?" Her head sank into the plush booth without turning away from him.

"Water," he said. It would be nice to have some. The ice cubes in his glass still refused to melt.

"Wow." Lyon erupted with laughter. "You are *ancient*." She drew the word out verbally, and with a finger used the volumetric table-computer to spell it out with floating letters, which she pushed into his face until he swatted it away.

He lifted the glass, and a few drops reached his mouth, and after returning the rattling glass of ice he straightened his back. "So, I was thinking about this morning."

Lyon's smile slowly leveled to serious, and she tucked some hair behind one of her ears. "Targetin' computers malfunction all the time. It's true. Just ask Troy."

"Yes, they do." She must feel guilty over that hostage. The station computer could flag her for a memory treatment, and she could forget the whole thing. But for some reason she never takes them. As though forgetting anything is against her personal religion. "I had a chat with Captain O'Connor, and she told me that most senior officers select low-risk missions while training their rookies."

"We take turns selectin' missions. That's the deal we made. Remember?"

"Yes, I remember. B—". He placed both palms face down on the table. Don't say but. If you say but, then she knows to put her guard up. "Do you remember the Carters? Three weeks ago. No priors, yet one day they break into a greenhouse at four AM and take all the plants, growth hormone bottles, and soil purification gels that will fit in a box and a bag. And flee into the wastelands."

"Yeah. Weren't they already brainwashed?"

"The Outcasts coerced them into stealing that food. And they rarely take prisoners." He scratched a spot on his face where his razor missed. The cutting beam needs recalibration. "The Delphi odds on these missions you're selecting are not quite ideal."

What could her selection criteria be? She could be one of those adrenaline junkies.

"So, we should just forget about 'em? What if it was someone you knew?"

"Despite what they thought, those two clones weren't even related to each other." Clouds circled outside, until their reflections turned solid in the darkening window. "There are people we can help, but we are not selecting those cases."

Lyon quietly sipped her drink and seemed lost in thought for a moment. "Where do Outcasts get their memories? The ones they're brainwashed with."

Oh, perfect. Just change the subject. Can anyone reason with this stubborn little creature? "Some are smuggled from the colonies. From real people or fabricated memory segments. Supposedly there's a black market here on Earth."

She said, "Black market," to herself as though someone as cynical as her was not already familiar with the term. "Have you ever—" She stared past him, towards the diner entrance.

He looked back. Major Lansing paused within the diner's rotating door until radiation vacuums lifted pale yellow dust from his coat. Police-issue peacoats allegedly maxed out at size forty-eight, which created a small mystery as to where the portly CO got his.

"Major." Peter said. He started to get up but aborted at Lansing's gesture, which transformed into a handshake when the distance closed. "What brings you here?"

The major smiled, but the grin was exaggerated beyond sincerity.  His eyes remained motionless.  His movements, robotic.

Thunder growled outside the window and the sky darkened.  Before the interior lights automatically adjusted, light glowed under Lansing's sleeve.  A red glow.

# 5
# Athanor

Joan's head slammed into the window with a crack. Diners shrieked and a strong grip crushed her left wrist. Another squeezing her windpipe. Thru squints, a large hand strangling her. A bright red tracker ring. Lansing's face with soul-scorching, psychotic eyes.

She reached for her blaster. Her hand didn't move. Screams of pain from her mind but her lungs barely managed a hiss. Text popped on an automatic function: *Stimulant Injection Initializing.*

In the corner of her eye, the booth table wedged into Peter's waist. One of Lansing's legs pressed against the lifted edge, pinning Peter's hands and blaster under it.

Twisting enough to free a hand, she pulled her blaster. The barrel crushed her grappling fingers against the window as Lansing the meat robot slammed her hand into the glass. Pulling the trigger blasted the window into sharp chunks. Napkins danced across their faces as the building depressurized. Lansing's hand fought for the blaster. The sweaty struggle knocked it into the bush outside.

Its choking hand released, and it pulled its own blaster, aiming at Peter's head. Something toppled the table and knocked the meat robot back. On the ground Peter and it struggled over a blaster, which discharged in random directions with rattling bangs and shattering glass.

She hopped thru the window's dangling shards. A function flashed the outline of her blaster between thorny bush branches. One reaching fingertip landed on something metallic. She lifted the blaster thru the piercing branches and aimed thru the broken window.

The meat robot stood over Peter with the blaster. It said with a robotic grin, "Dr. Wasserman sends his regards."

Pulling the trigger blasted blood over the pink and blue neon bar top. A second shot came from the floor as Peter drew his own weapon. The meat robot fell over, its blaster rattling on the tile in a twitching hand.

The kill-chime sounded distant in each ringing eardrum. A function credited her $30, an even split with Peter. She lowered her blaster and rain ran down both shaking arms. Nausea, until she found the button on her cuffputer to disengage stimulants.

Walking around to the revolving door and re-entering the diner painted a messy picture. A brush with gravity slid blood along the walls towards the tile floor. Rounds must have punctured the refrigeration tubes and appliances in the kitchen since they hissed gasses and blinked malfunction-beeps. Empty booths. No diners. Maybe they fled thru the emergency exit swinging back in forth in the far corner with a strobing light. Holographic radiation alarms spun from the ceiling with instructions to *cease consumption*. The text blurred with shrinking smoke trails rising from the fuming blaster barrels. Ozone and death overpowered the smell of coffee and caramelized onions.

Peter lifted his upper half off the floor by two elbows, panting air in and out. He staggered to his feet and kicked the dead meat robot a few more times. Maybe he didn't hear the kill chime.

"Are you hurt?" she asked.

Peter checked his injury from earlier this morning. "No. Are you?"

"I'm good."

"You're bleeding." He pointed to a line of red on her arm.

That thorny bush. My mood twister must be masking the pain, she thought. "Why didn't the satellite functions warn us?"

Peter rolled Lansing's body over and spread its coat open. After rifling thru interior pockets, he lifted a flatputer wired with a small antenna. A still-smoking hole in the screen. "Satellite jammer." He padded down the corpse. "Damnit. His access card is missing."

"His station keycard?" she asked. Morgan. Before Peter could answer, she grabbed her coat and ran thru the revolving door. Raindrops tapped her head as she rushed thru the parking lot, threw on her coat, and pulled the passenger-side doorknob. Locked. "Hurry Peter. We still have time to—"

Peter stood at the far side of the parking lot, a few meters from where the rusted gutters of a decaying brick building spilled small waterfalls of stinging rain onto the chipped sidewalk. "We have to follow quarantine procedure. Which means no communication. Which means we initiate lockdown until everyone validates their minds."

"You're just gonna leave 'em?" She sneered.

"Think rookie. We need to contact command and wait for orders."

"What if some of them aren't brainwashed?" She frantically pressed buttons on her wrist to call Morgan, but the icon flashed red. Offline.

"Lyon. Stop. Lyon!"

She looked up and froze. That bastard Peter had drawn his blaster. "Don't point that at me." Peter didn't budge. He stood still, like a pillar at one of those temples crazy people visit. "I validated half an hour ago."

"Wasserman could have imprinted that memory. How do you know if we're even having this conversation right now?"

"If I wasn't me, I'd know."

"Wrong answer." With one hand he tossed his validation-tube towards her, close enough it rattled and rolled the rest of the way into her steel-toed boots. "Prove that you're still Lyon."

"We don't got time for this."

"Wrong again. It's the only thing we have time for." Rain pebbled on his coat. "Plug it in."

She reached down and attached the tube's cord into her cuffputer with a beep. It emitted a flashing green light and ticked like a clock. A small display on the tube flashed images of her brain being compared to her last validation check via satellite, neuron by neuron. Followed by an image of a double helix unraveling into a four-letter DNA sequence and matching against the previous DOLOS record. *Tick-tock.* Still green. "What about you?"

He raised his free hand and made a gimmie gesture. "Throw me yours."

She parted her coat and threw him her own validation-tube. As he knelt and connected the validator to his wrist, she quickly drew her Solara-120. The rain accelerated. The clouds darkened. *Tick-tock.*

He stood up and somehow steadied his heavy M400 with one hand. His face was blank. Like one of those cheap holo-cards you send to someone when you don't really give a shit. He didn't make a sound either. Only stinging raindrops and the cutting-cold wind that screeched in each ear and slapped cold across her face. It tossed the validation tubes side to side, their green lights bouncing back up from a dozen puddles.

*Tick-tock.* The validation tube clicked with another green ring. It tickled slightly, having neurons uploaded.

Might as well shoot him now. If he fails validation, he'll harm someone. Her index finger brushed up and down the cold trigger. Just squeeze it. The soles of her boots squeaked as she shifted weight. A function popped up a warning. Elevated heartrate.

Another gust swung green luminescence in the dim parking lot. The cylinders gave out one final sound. All *tick* and no tock. Solid green.

KROPVELD'S CAF

She lowered her weapon. "Jesus."

Peter re-holstered his blaster, and they exchanged cylinders.

Halfway thru a deep breath she shook her head. "I'm not leavin' them to die." Running 17 blocks will take too long. And no luck getting an auto-car this close to noon. She stuck out a hand. "Give me the keys."

***

She floored the accelerator while skidding thru the tight corner on 7th Street, nearly hitting a yellow coupe and an autonomous utility-truck. In the rear-view mirror, a shiny aluminum weapon case bounced up and down.

A confident voice spoke over the dashboard wireless, "All units, this is Kyudo. Robot roadblocks are being established on Figuero and 5th, and North Flower and 6th. Setup a perimeter and await further instructions."

Tires screeched among a horde of beeping horns as she weaved thru traffic and messaged Morgan for the fifth time. Still no response from her. Where is she?

The Hall of Justice came into focus on the right so quickly that she slammed on the brakes, launching the weapon case from the rear seats into the gear shift. Gripping the case with both hands and opening it revealed only a Styrofoam outline of where a fully automatic blaster should be. She threw the case into the passenger seat. Think damnit.

Peter sometimes keeps a weapon under the driver's seat. She reached under and felt a barrel of some kind, pulling it until it bumped into the brake pedal. A scatter blaster with a bandoleer. It clicked with a metallic crunch as she pumped a shell into the chamber and toggled the ejector side.

Her boots rang loud clops on the concrete steps leading into the station, and on the marble floor of the two-story lobby. Passing the suspiciously vacant front desk, her echoed movements continued to carry the only sounds in the eerily quiet station.

In the large hall, she gasped and froze. No officers at any desk. Blinking lights on every phone. Nothing on Wall-Thru. No one. No Morgan. But she said she had jail duty.

Past the armory, the brick room positioned like a room-sized chimney, a descending stairwell led to a hallway, where the sharp teeth of a lifted blast door pointed downwards like a hungry animal waiting to devour its prey.

Central booking. The fortified entrance to the station jail. Surface-level windows pierced the top of the tall walls, reinforced by a lattice of iron bars. No one's head or hair protruding from the booking desk. Walking up to it and leaning over the edge revealed an empty chair, a game of holo-Sudoku, and a can of blueberry iced tea. The stuff Morgan drinks by the gallon. The holographic fill line animated waves near the twist top.

A deafening klaxon accompanied flashing ceiling lights. Screams and gunshots echoed from the floor above, where red outlines appeared. Wall-Thru is finally back.

Both arms shook as functions totaled 40 meat robots. They clumped into a red tumor on the ground level. Cold sweat captured her sides as the brainwashed congregation spread into a centipede-like line and crept towards the armory.

Underground and trapped. Like living in a fallout shelter all over again. Someone called her name on the wireless, but the rest of the words didn't form. Need to stop freaking out. She turned her mood twister to Stoic-Calm. After a few seconds of tingling, it was like a shadowed hand reached up from some sort of underworld and shut itself like a clam over her. Calm. Stay calm.

A static voice on the wireless. "Joan. Joan, are you there?"

"Troy? Is that you?"

"Joan. Major Kyudo is ordering Officer Hamilton to remotely arm the explosives in the station armory to self-destruct. She'll blow up half the station before she lets Wasserman's minions get their hands on heavy weapons."

"Where's Morgan?"

"Did you hear me? You need to seal the blast door to booking. Now."

Deep breath. "Troy, is the memory bank in the blast radius?"

He took forever to answer, "Affirmative."

She looked up on Wall-Thru, then along the barrel of the scatter-blaster, counting the shells on the bandoleer. "I'm gonna need a bigger gun."

"I'm sorry Joan," Troy said. "Delphi just predicted Morgan can't be saved."

Allowing something to happen is as bad as doing it yourself.

The armory lit up on Wall-Thru, 50 meters ahead and one floor above. She ran for the corner stairwell. Her elbow struck the railing and she cursed while running halfway up the stairs.

"Joan, what are you doing?" Troy asked. "Go back. Now."

"All units standby for detonation. Fire in the hole," Kyudo said on the wireless.

One red outline at the top of the stairwell. Joan lifted the scatter-blaster as a meat robot appeared and opened fire with a blaster. A tall woman. Captain O'Connor. On the outside, anyway. One of her bullets grazed the skin between two knuckles, creating enough pain to forget about the elbow.

Joan leveled the scatter-blaster and fired, splitting O'Connor into two lean halves. A kill-chime rang, and a function credited her account, $60. A second meat robot emerged from a corner. The name McGuire flashed on eye functions.

She fired again, shattering the target's head into marble-sized bits. This time the recoil flung her onto the railing. A cleaning bot fled with screeching beeps, abandoning the bloody mess on the wall and floor.

At the top of the stairs, she accelerated into a full run. Lungs burned. Ankles cracked.

Meat robots shuffled into the armory 40 meters away, their feet marching in unison. Bound hostages in tow. One of them Morgan. Joan called out to her as the armory's blast-door slowly began to close.

The shock wave knocked her flat on the ground. The back of her head slammed into the floor and throbbed. A fire alarm strobed above probably at maximum volume, but it sounded far in each popped ear. The scatter-blaster bounced a few meters away.

A muffled sound of breaking glass above. The memory bank looked larger. And larger. She franticly rolled out of the way as the memory bank struck the floor, crashing into countless, glaring flickers of light. Thoughts and dreams shattered on the floor and into darkness.

Smoke plumes rose from the cracked-brick walls of the armory-turned-chimney.

She brushed off dust and rose to her feet, limping towards the armory. One hand slowly slid the smoking door, hot enough to burn her fingertips, until it broke and fell into the room with a vibrating thud. Her racing eyes widened into what felt larger than old dollar-coins, scanning the armory's fresh coat of blood-red paint with rapid breaths.

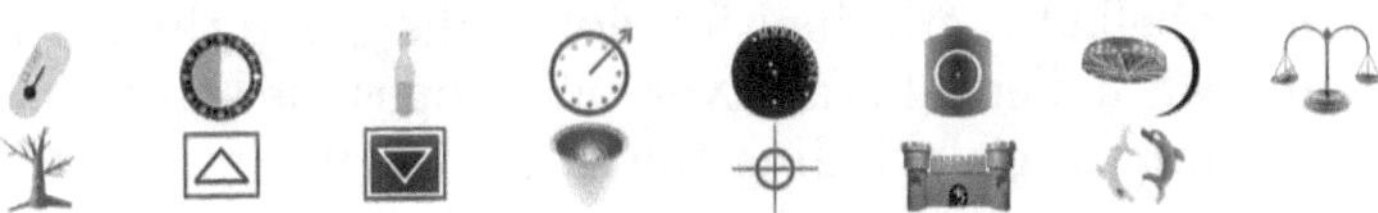

# 6
# Kareishu

Peter huffed and heaved labored breaths up each concrete step. At the top he stood at the entrance to Major Lansing's corner apartment while sweat fell into his eyes. Shouldn't have given the car to Lyon.

His hand hovered over the metal door's button until he realized it was already ajar. Storming into the residence he looked through five rooms in a blur, quickly finding a utility closet with a laundry press. And a shelf of items that fell between his fingers as he rapidly rummaged through them. In Lansing's living room a cabinet on the floor. Its two doors spread open.

He fell to one knee and ran his fingers along the shelves. Bare, but something on his fingertips. Lifting his hand, he found dust on his fingers, as well as along each shelf, thin lines at regular intervals. Something on the floor, bright for a moment. A memory disk, blinking red for empty. Zip. Nada. Nothing. Picking it up and rotating it allowed for a perfect fit between parallel lines of dust.

Damnit. I should have run faster. Now someone's taken every backup of Lansing's memories.

Quickly standing shot pain through a calf muscle and his face formed a grimace. "Son of a bitch cock ass mother-fucker." A cramp. Walk it off.

He entered the bedroom to pace. It held the odor of un-washed bedsheets, which laid in a rolled-up pile in a corner. A tableau on top of the dresser by the window.

Lansing with his wife and two children. He was dressed in his air force uniform and considerably thinner. A pre-war image capture that would never be seen in the major's office.

War crimes. That's what they're called today. I'm sum-marily labelled a criminal for doing the same thing I did when I was hailed a hero. Everyone judges the war because of the aftermath, including the ones that wanted it in the first place. Especially them. Just as the future ceaselessly judges the past.  Because those in the future were never there.

And whoever took the major's memories will find out my past, he thought.  Which means judgement day.  The war crime tribunal.  Then execution.  Do not pass go.  Do not collect two hundred dollars.

At most, I have a day to find them.  Who would have taken Lansing's memories?  Perhaps someone else who is ex-military.  Though everyone has secrets, and Lansing knew everyone.  The silver lining is that him being brainwashed means corrupted memories uploaded from his corpse are inadmissible as evidence.

The screen on his wrist-computer beeped.  An image of his cramped leg and a message about hydrating.

Lansing kept his drinking glasses in the cabinets below the countertop instead of above.  The premium water button charged the major's account and not Peter's.  He had deactivated all ocular recording and ghosted his wrist-tracker after he left the diner.  Little suspicion in logging a long bathroom break after eating a Martian burrito.

Between gulps an earie silence gripped the apartment, similar to his home on rare occasions.  Another glass on the countertop, in a corner by a toaster.  Drops still at the bottom.

He set down his water and quickly pulled his scanner, flipping the mode to fingerprints and running the scanning light over every edge. Nothing. Nada. Flipping to DNA gave partials on the rim, nothing identifiable. A red smear. Lipstick perhaps.

Whoever was here earlier needed water.  But there's no smell of sweat and she took enough time to clean up her prints.  Perhaps she ate something and was thirsty afterwards.

Lansing's refrigerator was a maze of expired meals and beer bottles.  It smelled worse than his own though something else lingered in the air. He leaned his head into the fridge and sniffed. Algae. Mixed with another odor. Jasmine? Lilac? Hard to remember which is which. The plants went extinct on Earth. A woman's perfume then.

No prints on the refrigerator door, or any other surface he scanned while walking to the living room. Spartan furnishings for someone drawing a major's salary. He picked up the blank memory disk, on the laminate floor by the empty cabinet. Mnemosyne brand.

Laminate floors. Fake wood. No footprints.

The second bedroom was setup as a home office. A white desk flush against a large window overlooking the street below, with enough sliding raindrops to scatter sunlight. On the desk, a palm-sized projector lit with volumetric artwork. King Arthur's round table and a volumetric stylus off to the side. Gripping the stylus and tapping the edge on Lancelot's shiny armor dripped white strokes. Peter virtually painted a lighthouse. An ugly one. There's some command to load the color palette but he forgot it. And the painting.

Stacks of holo-films, *The Lights of Marfa* on top. Three rows of those cheap sleeves that black-market merchants use for bootlegged movies. A small volumetric emitter, about the size of a shot glass. The red button on the side activated a volumetric rolodex.

A business card without a label. An image of two weights equally distant from a metal pole, balanced despite one having a feather. A connection sequence underneath. Flicking the volumetric edge animated the scales tipping, and a drop of ink fell from the feather. Huh. Possibly the company Lansing bought his virtual paint from.

A vibrating beep on his wrist. Major Kyudo scheduling a debrief about what happened at the Hall of Justice. Fifteen minutes. The Chrono app automatically started a countdown, given current weather and traffic conditions.

Damn. Lansing's corpse isn't even cold and Kyudo is making her move to replace him. It takes two days for the Outcasts to brainwash someone with their primitive, makeshift memory crowns of soldered circuits and duct tape. The very reason the council amended protocol eleven several years ago. DOLOS validation is mandatory every forty-eight hours to maintain legal status as a human.

To take Lansing's mind, the Outcasts must have used a colonial memory-printer on a MOTH commander. Ergo, Kyudo and the rest of the brass will lose their minds until it's found. When it finally is, she'll have a press conference, where the confiscated device will be placed on a finely polished table, so she can smile, get her picture taken, and advance her career. Same as the old boss.

He parted his coat, resting both hands on his belt while he looked around. On the wall a framed tableau. Major Lansing shaking hands with Councilman Warner, the legislative champion of protocol twenty-seven. The right to mental privacy for living humans. The reason DOLOS stores the checksums of memories and not the content.

Lansing was careful. If this happens to him, it can happen to anyone. And the major could have retired years ago and lived like a king in the colonies. Clone his dead family there. But he lingered too long and woke up one day to find midnight. So, he clung to memories shared only with the dead, long gone halcyon days that lived on only in memory. And tried to find meaning in his day job to fill the dark void life left for him. Or perhaps he just didn't know what else to do. Like a lone wolf wandering the wastelands with no purpose.

He circled through the apartment again in a vain search for more clues. Each room formed a mental puzzle-piece in the story of someone's life. A solitary existence of no discernible meaning. Furniture fated for auction or doomed for recycling. Then this place will be leased to a new tenant.

An entire life carpeted over and buried, as though it never existed.

Toggling the bathroom light switch, the square bulbs flickered for a second and the room returned to darkness. After a few seconds, his eyes adjusted enough to see the mirror, and his own shadow staring back.

Another beep from his wrist-computer. He lifted the bright screen to find the Chrono app flashing. I'm out of time. Just like Lansing.

Another shadow joined his reflection. He turned around.

Through the tandem doorways of the bathroom and bedroom, a tall woman stood at the opposite end of the apartment, by the now open balcony door. Dark hair, blue eyes, and a smile of straight teeth. In denim and a sleeveless shirt. Somehow familiar, though he couldn't place a name.

"Pete," she said. He walked half the distance between them. "Don't go to the spaceport or anywhere downtown this week. And actually listen this time, okay?"

"Who are you?"

Her smile widened and she approached.

He recoiled.

She stepped back with a frown. "Once your family finds out your secret, they'll leave you. They don't really love you." An alarm sounded. Through the nearby window, an organic monitor mounted on a building across the street. "Remember what we talked about Pete."

"You're an Outcast?" He drew his pistol.

The woman lunged towards him, gripping the pistol long enough to thumb the mag release, dropping the magazine onto his foot with a painful thud.

"Sorry not sorry." She ran onto the balcony and leapt over the railing.

He hastily picked up the magazine and reloaded his pistol while hobbling onto the balcony and peering over the edge of the railing.

Nothing below but the sidewalk.

# 7
## Archer's Bullseye

Volumetric retirement papers moved up and down on Peter's bouncing knee as he sat in the third row of the packed briefing room at the North Valley substation. Adjacent to a congregation of third shift officers, easily identified by their bloodshot eyes with bags under them. At the back of the room, Lyon leaned on the wall by one of the doorways. Arms crossed and scowling, though she gave a wave which he returned.

A news feed played on a large stream at the front of the room. Doyen Councilman Warner in a suit and tie talking to a reporter, inaudible against the room's chatter.

Eye movements loaded a subtitle subroutine and the text scrolled: *The Hall of Justice is currently closed due to some unexpected renovations, but Commissioner Dignam has assured me that this won't impact any police patrols or response times.*

It's a good lie. A great one really, considering the truth would cause panic and unrest. Both of which would make finding Wasserman and this printer impossible. When forced to play the odds, choose the best dice.

The room turned to hushed silence and the news stream abruptly vanished. Major Selene Kyudo walked past the room's podium, with each bootstep clopping as loud as a hammer driving a nail. She stood as straight as a Mercurius Blink-ship by one of the large windows and cast a tall shadow upon the nearby wall. Her steady gaze through the glass lasted for half a minute, seemingly oblivious to the army of subordinates quietly waiting.

She turned and walked to the polished-wood podium. Her black hair tied behind her pale face and above a perfectly pressed wool uniform. She was older than him but looked younger. In the colonies they call her the Venusian Butcher. No one knows why, but most imaginations fill in the blank with red letters.

Kyudo cleared her throat. "Thank you all for coming. Fifty-six Officers were either brainwashed or killed in action today. In the wake of Major Lansing's passing, I am assuming command of the Settlement Five MOTH Unit."

The room's volumetric emitter spun back up, and an arrangement of pictures of the recently deceased fell like leaves from a tree. One of falling faces was familiar. The brown-haired girl Lyon is always chatting with. He looked back at his partner. Her eyes were down and averted. Poor kid.

"The man responsible, as you all have guessed, is Dr. Wasserman," Kyudo said. The doctor's ugly face rendered largely in three dimensions. "Delphi has confirmed our logical conclusions, which is that the doctor has a memory-printer in his possession, and he is using it to brainwash and indoctrinate more fanatics." She leaned on the podium with her hands at the edges. "Finding this printer is our highest priority." She stood up straight again. "I want results. Dismissed."

Peter stood up with everyone else. He pushed, as politely as possible, to navigate the rabble and commotion until he caught up with Kyudo.

"Major. Do you have a minute?" he asked.

***

"So, early retirement?" Kyudo asked in her dim office. The medals on her uniform gleamed as she opened the bottom drawer of her mahogany desk and set a glowing-teal bottle on the polished surface. After pouring two fingers of Ganymede-Sake into two small tumblers, she handed one towards him.

"No thank you ma'am. I quit drinking." He took one of the two chairs in front of the desk.

Kyudo produced another glass and filled it with ice and water and placed it in his hand. All at a rapid pace a robot would envy. "I see. Will there be a third surprise today?" With a smile she sat in her black leather chair and tossed back the drink. Twisting the empty glass back and forth between two fingers, her grin faded, and she took a deep breath. "I'm afraid that after that incident today, our current man and woman-power situation leaves, quantitively, a lot to be desired."

Perfect. He nearly gagged on his sip of water. A hurricane spun in his stomach. Don't barf on the new CO. He swilled half the remaining water and leaned back until the cushioned chair swallowed him.

Kyudo placed her hands on her desk. "Peter, this is not the easiest thing to say, but my Delphi briefing indicates a ninety-nine percent chance that your partner Joan will be dead by the end of the week."

He paused with his drink halfway to his mouth. "Dead?"

"I'm afraid so."

Peter coughed as he swallowed water down the wrong pipe. He asked with a raspy voice, "Does Delphi know how?"

"I was not furnished with that information. But I imagine it's not an elaborate mystery." She rubbed her eyes and poured herself a refill of the pulsing-teal liquid. "Earlier today Joan violated quarantine protocol and nearly died. Reviewing her record reveals a consistent pattern of brutality and insubordination. This needs to stop before she gets herself killed."

"Yes ma'am."

Kyudo's eyes moved back and forth, scanning his face or perhaps she's navigating a private subroutine. "I want a minority outcome."

"Right. So, I just need to keep her alive for a week?"

Kyudo downed her drink, then popped a sobriety tablet from a small pillbox. "Once Delphi predicts her future is a living one, I'll release you from your service obligation."

"With benefits?"

"With full benefits." She swiveled in her chair to grab a small water bottle from a wood credenza behind her. "I know you got saddled with a lemon. Turn her into lemonade."

Perfect. Turn Lyon into anything that doesn't resemble a loose cannon. Every human being is capable of change but Christ almighty. Kyudo stared with an expression one could call amusement. Impossible to pierce those dark eyes. "Right," he mumbled and got up to leave.

"Peter," Kyudo said just as he reached the door, and he turned back. "Is your partner related to Forest Lyon? The pro golfer?"

***

A few steps from Kyudo's office he heard the heavy door slam itself shut, and he staggered down the narrow concrete hall to his temporary desk at the Hollywood substation. He fell into his chair and tugged at his collar to loosen it. Chest pain while breathing but it's not a heart attack. If it was my wrist-computer would light up, he thought.

Whoever has Lansing's memories won't need a week to find my war crimes. Fleeing to the wastelands is certain death, even for those that aren't ex-cops. Leaving the planet requires authorization. Perhaps a cargo carrier, for the right price, would look the other way. Searching casefiles for known-smugglers shouldn't be too—

A vibration and ring on his wrist with flashing text. *Incoming Call.* He clicked answer.

On a private volumetric a toddler with short blonde hair. She said in a squeaky little voice, "Daddy."

His shoulders lowered a bit, he smiled, and he adjusted his tone and volume for something toddler friendly. "Caramel?"

"Hi."

"Hi baby. What are you doing? Did you finish your puzzle?"

"Umm. Noo." Something wrong with how she said no. Stretched out like sad little pizza dough.

"What's wrong?"

She looked down. "I don't find Mommy."

"You can't find Mommy?" This is the problem with phone calls. There's a problem and you're too far away to do anything.

"Mmm." Five seconds of silence. "Noo."

"Oh. Is the front door open?" Ari must have disappeared on her.

"Mmm." She lifted her chin with one finger and looked to her right. "No."

"Okay. Wait there for Daddy and don't open the door. Okay?"

"Okay."

The call ended with a click. He grabbed his keys and coat and raced out of the building.

***

His lungs heaved and knees ached as his run reduced to a jog halfway down the apartment corridor. The keycard nearly fell out of his sweaty hands, but he grabbed it in time, and it buzzed against the lock. He threw the door into the wall.

"Caramel!" Entryway. Kitchen. Living area. Caramel's room. Her closet. Caramel. She was under the rack of hanging clothes.

He lowered himself to his still-aching knees.

"Daddy," she said.

"Hi baby. Are you okay?"

"Mhm."

"Good. Wait here. Okay?"

She nodded and he stood.

At the foyer he paused and looked back at Caramel's room before pressing his card against the utility room lock. In the darkness, beyond the laundry press, a deactivated robot, and shelves of canned food, red text blinked *Battery Low*. The house computer should reorder these when they're running low.

He opened the carbon media cabinet under the headless-volumetric emitters to grab an RA battery wrapped in plastic. And tried to pull it open. It had one of those flaps where you're supposed to turn it and pull it, with tiny white arrows pointing in different directions. Too much sweat to get a good grip. It kept slipping. Son of a bitch.

Relenting, he pulled out his pocketknife and cut one corner. The new battery had that freshly manufactured smell. After swapping the batteries, the emitter activated with a hum. Two spinning rings of twisting rods glowing with blue light, resembling large eyes staring at the ceiling.

Within the cabinet, stacks of Mnemosyne memory disks, each of them the size of an outstretched hand and yet filled with enough digital neurons to house a human mind. Black ink on white labels, scribbled dates barely legible in the dim light. Backups he made in case something goes wrong.

He bumped his knee and winced as he reached around the emitters and cursed before reaching the flat computer wedged against the wall. The screen flickered a few times as he double checked the wires. Newer devices don't need batteries. This tech is getting old, and much harder to replace since the passage of protocol two hundred. Neural technology that can modify artificial minds can also modify real ones. Delphi secured most of the license exemptions. At this point anyone walking into a Neuron Store and asking too many questions can quickly find themselves forced into giving answers. Hell, I arrested someone for doing that last week.

He hastily thumbed text on the flat keypad:

*lazarus memdsk -integritychk -sectors 1:N -verbose*

Click-back. *Parity check: one hundred percent.* He sighed with relief as the light from the entryway ceased.

A black silhouette gripped each side of the doorway. A woman's hourglass. "Petey," she said. Her beautiful eyes glistened in the dark. Like the first time he caught her looking at him decades ago, across a bar in Okinawa. Or looking up at him while cradling their newborn. Her hair frazzled and sweaty but the light in her eyes burned like the only stars in the night.

"Honey, I'm home?"

"I didn't hear you." One of her hands moved from the frame to her hip. "My battery died again?"

"Yes. Were you compiling another neuron model?"

Ariadne sighed. "Well, I was updating my CV, and everything I've done is so out of date."

"Neuro-engineers are in high demand in the colonies. They would kill for someone with your experience."

"Well good, because I would die to be organic again," she said. He followed her into the kitchen, where his holographic wife merged with the house robot to move some boxes on the dining room table. "Don't worry about these. I'll have everything packed up by tonight. I'm so excited!"

"Actually, it's going to be a few more days."

"What happened?" Ari closed a box of family tableaus.

"Nothing too big. A small case came up that I need to work out before we can go."

"Will you be getting your pension?"

"We have enough saved for a cloning procedure or two." Which was closer to the truth than a lie. He paused in front of the fridge and thought of the instant pizzas stacked inside. It's weird to eat in front of my wife. She can't eat anything herself.

"Admiring our little Picasso?" Ari's eyes glanced to the surface of the fridge. A volumetric drawing by Caramel of a giraffe and lighthouse of equal height.

"With her voice, she'll make an even better singer."

"Mommy!" Carmen said.

"Carmen." Ari walked into the living room and sat down on the couch next to their daughter, who inspected her mother's volumetric cello. Part of a two-hundred-dollar black market software package that enabled her to hold and play an instrument, sophisticated enough that she once claimed to be out of breath after a long solo. Merging with the house robot and using a physical instrument proved impractical. Even with Manos Premium she broke every string.

"Want to play?" Ari grinned and lifted her eyebrows in the direction of the piano.

"I should get back to work."

"Happiness is a choice," his wife continued.

"Just one song." He smiled and unbuttoned his coat, twisting his elbows until the sleeves fell off his arms and the wool crumpled on the floor. Ari and Caramel frowned in unison, so he reached down, picked it up, and draped it over a chair. The sound of a heavy bump. Lansing's broken memory disk peeked over the edge of a pocket. Something could be on it. Something a diagnostic tool could perhaps decipher.

"Daddy?" Caramel asked.

He walked over and sat on the bench, running his fingertips along the black and white keys.

"Pachelbel's Canon in D."  Ari smiled, then focused on her instrument.  Her taste in music hadn't changed in years.

Caramel sat on the floor, leaning against the front cushion.  Only a few centimeters from her mother's legs, yet they could never hug or even touch.

He flattened a key.

# 8
## Gemini's Dilemma

Joan was the only warm body in the cold morgue. Four walls and eight tables covered in jars filled with organic remains. One was holographically labeled with slowly spinning text: *Sullivan, Morgan.* A projected line of letters lit up the table's edge: *Due for delivery to: Organic Recycling Facility Five.*

Next to a chair in a corner, green dots lit on two memory discs within a polymer bin. Two fragile discs were all that remained of Morgan, and maybe the only chance to bring her killers to justice. For evil people to succeed, the world need only forget.

Neither disc was labeled or timestamped, so she picked up the rightmost one and connected it to her cuffputer. Parallel memory streams sprung to holographic life, alternating sequences that curved above her head and below her feet, like she was inside a sphere of someone else's thoughts. "Lazarus," she said to her cuffputer, which morphed the memory streams into a holographic representation of Morgan a few meters away.

Hologram Morgan wore black pants and a white tee. Her brown hair was longer, and her arms and neck seemed thinner.

"Hi Morgan."

"Hi," Morgan said with hesitation.

She doesn't recognize me, Joan thought. This mind backup must be old. Like if someone still-living lost her memories, and no longer recognized the ones who love her. You look at her and she looks back, but with the eyes of a stranger. "I'm Joan."

"Nice to meet you." Morgan smiled. "What is this place?"

"The morgue."

"The morgue? How did I get here?"

"We're at the North Hollywood Police Station."

Morgan smiled. "Oh. I'm applying to the constable academy. Are you a police officer?"

She blinked a few times and grinned, pointing to the badge on her belt.

"Oh." Morgan snorted and took soundless steps closer. "Is the academy hard?"

"Nah. It's easy," she lied.

"Thank goodness I—wait, what is that?" Morgan pointed to the jar of her organic remains. "Is that my name?" Her jaw fell.

Joan clicked *Terminate program* and the hologram mercifully vanished, returning Morgan to peace.

She took a seat in one of the two corner chairs, next to the polymer bin. Landing in the cushion didn't seem to stop the downward motion. Like the concrete floor was permeable and the chair and her were sinking into it. She turned her mood twister to Pensive-Brooding. A bubbling sensation percolated in her brain, like someone poured a fountain soda directly into her skull. The room turned blurry for a few seconds, then refocused in muted colors. Much better, and not about to cry.

After a minute she picked up the second memory disc. Loading the memory sphere and selecting a stream with Immersion shrouded her in a room dark enough that white walls appeared grey. She saw herself holding a cupcake. A sparkling candle on top. My 20th birthday last month, she thought, but from Morgan's perspective. Weird to see yourself from someone else's eyes. Morgan's hands moved out in front and handed Joan a small, gift-wrapped box. Quickly torn and opened. A golf ball. They both laughed like it was the funniest thing in the world.

Back at the sequence sphere, *Activate Lazarus* blinked. Tapping it loaded a function with a wait cursor, an old clock that spun forever while she leaned back in the chair and tapped her foot. Come on already.

Morgan appeared again as a holographic phantom, this time in denim and a tank top that showed off her toned arms.

Joan stood. "Hi Morgan."

"Hey Golf Ball." She turned and completed a 360, her eyes scanning right and left. "Why are we in the morgue?"

This time don't let Morgan know she's dead. Joan walked over to the table and sat on the end, blocking Morgan's view of the jarred remains. "Someone turned up the thermostat upstairs."

"I'm dead." Morgan raised her hand and pointed to her intact pinky. "My finger was blasted off a few days ago."

Morgan's expression hardly changed, except a slightly resigned smile. Compared to her expressive, pre-cop version, her eyes were dim and her posture still. Maybe it's the psychological reconditioning every academy cadet undergoes to remove any remnants of childhood optimism that growing up in a shelter hadn't already stolen. The same program I went thru, she thought. Did that actually change me, or just the shell, the mask I use to protect myself in this line of work where any vulnerability is seen as weakness? Knowing most people are awful doesn't mean I am too.

"I'm sorry. You died a few hours ago. I tried to get there, but—what's the last thing you remember?"

"I snuck into the bathroom and did a remote mind-backup."

"What happened?"

"There was commotion in the main hall. I heard a woman's voice asking someone about those two hostages you recovered from the wastelands. She also mentioned something about some Delphi tech they had stolen."

"Would you recognize her from a mugshot?"

Morgan shook her head. "I didn't see her. I have no idea who she is." She walked along the table and stopped at the jar of blood and bone. "But I'd like to find out."

Joan stood and instinctively reached for Morgan's shoulder until her hand passed thru the hologram. "Maybe we can still help each other. We can find out who did this to you. After that, I need you to help me with findin' my mom's memories."

Morgan twisted her head and frowned. "How can I help now?"

"You've always been a better investigator."

Morgan nodded. "Sure. Why not?"

****

The grid of desks was nearly absent of other officers and wasn't holographically labeled, which made finding her desk at the substation a five-minute exercise. Morgan and her eventually spotted it based on the presence of Peter's leather briefcase. It was on its side, with bent discs, ammunition, and assorted old-guy stuff spilling out. That flaky slob had left a cold cup of coffee and a half-eaten donut next to it.

Flicking the computer's power button lit a wide holographic screen with the memory-printer casefile already loaded. A scan of the colonial memory-printer. The bounty for its capture lit up in green. The number two and a long list of zeros arriving far from one. Enough to never be hungry again.

Pointing joined fingers and spreading them split the display into two holograms. She swiped to the dossiers of Andrea and Luke Aeneas, both marked *deceased*, while Morgan loaded the Delphi Corporate Campus on a 3D map. Each of them dragged and dropped onto the Cross Reference app. Beep.

"Nothin'?"

"What about that third hostage? The guy?"

"The one I—" got killed.

"Maybe I can check." Morgan effortlessly swiped and palmed over documents to a dossier again marked *deceased* in red, diagonal letters. "Dr. Brooks." She poked the refresh button. Beep. Brooks's face appeared in a circle, with lines connecting him to the Aeneas's on one side and Delphi on the other. "No relation to the other hostages. He was a human here on Earth. Formerly employed by Delphi as a nuclear engineer."

"What would Wasserman need a nuclear engineer for?" Pushing buttons loaded Dr. Wasserman's dossier, which floated with a water-like ripple. *AKA The Ventriloquist*. A mugshot of his arrogant eyes and cocky smile. Somebody ought to wipe that smirk off his face. The hologram shook. She looked down to find her shaking hands clenching the table.

Making a rotating gesture with one hand, the file switched to a recent recording of Wasserman making an impassioned speech to a band of ruffians about how he was a Delphi employee from the future. He touted a giant hologram of his own, a headline from 2173 of humanity going extinct. His bloodshot eyes and scarred face burned as he recited a rebellious sermon from a hardcopy of *The Isis Manifesto*. "Humanity will not have a future until we tear down the walls of the Settlements and end Delphi's reign of terror. Until we set things back to the way they should be." The rabble cheered.

"What a heap of shit," she said while pressing *mute*.

"Wass has always targeted Delphi personnel," Morgan said. "I don't feel like Brooks being a nuclear engineer was a deciding factor."

Joan sighed. "You're right." With a swipe she dismissed the silent rant and reviewed Delphi's long list of disavows and denials, written in lawyer-speak. And how time travel was impossible. Especially since Delphi never predicted it occurring.

She pivoted back in forth, rotating the chair left and right in an endless sequence, then spun the chair in a full circle. "Hmm. Why didn't the computer connect Andrea to Delphi? She said the outcasts stole somethin' from Delphi."

"If the A.I. classifies her as brainwashed, it disregards her statements. Well, no, not disregarded. More like, it doesn't take her seriously." Morgan walked over to Peter's chair and slowly sat down while gripping the armrests, like she was worried she might fall thru.

"What if she was tellin' the truth?"

Morgan tapped on the desk hologram, beeping buttons that brought up the Delphi police portal. The main feature of the data feed: A building with the company logo engulfed in flames.

Joan double tapped to switch to a thin casefile and read aloud. "Scene report by Detective Sergeant Diaz. A fire alarm at 7:05. Investigation closed at 11:00 as an industrial accident. This visual capture, the heap of rubble, is the only one she took."

Scrolling back to the Delphi feed, Morgan also read out loud. "A B-N-E at a private residence on the corporate campus. No suspects found by satellite tracking. Nothing reported stolen, so no officer investigated. Just paperwork from the security robots."

Swiping the feed to the map view drew a hologram of the Santa Monica campus that slowly rotated. Large enough that they had to stand and step back. Which is super annoying since the chairs are comfy.

A labyrinth of residential streets and office parks. 101 acres, according to scrolling text at the edge. Two adjacent buildings lit in red among the green structures. A tower, which must be the arson. A house across the street.

She swiped back to the casefiles. "The computer didn't link these two crimes. But they're literally across the street from each other. Hmm."

Morgan briefly twisted her lips. "I know you hate using the phone, but maybe give them a call?" She hovered a finger over one of the ribbon buttons running along the bottom of the Delphi info portal. *Contact Liaison Officer.*

"Can you talk to them?"

"Golf Ball, I'm dead."

Joan's finger couldn't push the button for Liaison officer. Like a magnet repelled it. This is for Morgan. I made a promise, she thought.

She sat down in the comfy chair again. The call function rang twice as pain moved up her stomach, like she ate something rotten.

The hologram morphed into an avatar, a featureless and grey head. "Hello?" The floating head transformed into a dark-skinned, middle-aged man. His name flashed in green letters: *David Moira.* He shifted his weight, and his neck and wide shoulders entered the frame. A tailored suit and sharp gold tie. Goodness.

She crossed her legs and checked her own reflection on the desk's shiny surface. "Um, hi. This is, um, Officer Lyon. With the Set-Five MOTH unit."

"Yes, I have your information loaded on my display."

Of course. He has caller-information. Or he knows because it's Delphi and they predicted this phone call.

"Ask about Dr. Brooks," Morgan whispered. Which is silly since she's on a private hologram and no one else can see or hear her.

She sat up straight. "I'm, ah, lookin'—" He won't take me seriously unless I speak clearly, she thought. Focus. "I was, ah, looking at a report here on one of your former employees. A Nathaniel Brooks."

David scratched his chin. "Standby." He looked off to the side, like he was using eye functions. "Yes, we did previously have a Doctor Nathaniel Brooks employed here. However, in August we initiated a separation. He is not eligible for re-hire."

"Oh. Do you know why?"

"There were some issues regarding his past."

"That's corporate-speak for war criminal," Morgan whispered.

Brooks committed atrocities. I'm glad he's dead now, she thought.

"Is there anything else, officer?" David asked.

"Yea—yes. I saw two incidents reported on your campus today and was wondering if you considered that they might be related?"

"Are you referring to Hiraeth Tower and the Fischer residence?"

"Mm hmm." She turned her mood twister to Professional-Conversing. Should have thought of that earlier. "Yes."

He cleared his throat. "Major Selene Kyudo already made that inquiry. We do not currently believe the laboratory fire was intentional. We suspect a software glitch in a maintenance robot to be the source of the accident."

"Oh. I'm sorry." Shit. Of course Kyudo already thought of this. How embarrassing. David doesn't look mad but still. Maybe that's the only good thing about phones. If the other person gets mad, they're too far away to do anything.

He smiled. "That is okay. Is there anything else I can help you with?"

This David seems nice enough. "Well, um, what was in that tower?"

"I am afraid many of our activities are protected by the protocols pertaining to corporate trade secrets. But I can tell you the Glimpse program was impacted."

"I'm sorry, what?"

"The Glimpse program."

"It's how they predict future crimes," Morgan said.

"Delphi receives neuron uploads for all convicted organ-ics," David said. "That information is then partitioned thru our proprietary predictive algorithms in order to anticipate future crimes."

Alright already. "Does that include the MOTH memory bank?"

"Yes, I am certain it does. Or did, rather."

"Okay. Thank you, David. It was great to meet you."

"No problem. Goodbye." His face flickered and was re-placed by computer files.

"Think damnit," she muttered to herself while spinning in the chair.

"Delphi doesn't want the police sniffing around," Mor-gan said. "But why? And on the same morning the memory bank is shattered, the only backups are burned to a crisp."

"No way this is all a big fat coincidink. And that spider Wasserman has got to be somewhere in this web."

"They say his fortress in the wastelands is filled with memories. Ones you can't find in the Settlements."

"The Sandcastle? Is it even real?"

Morgan nodded. "Ivan told me he isolated a unique iso-tope from every footprint left by the infamous Wass. No one has found the source, but it has to come from somewhere."

A small holographic animation ran along the desk's sur-face from a holo-capture of her sister, Mary, working her first day at Triskelion Fitness. A private hologram no one else could see. "What if they stole the memories? Copied 'em and destroyed the originals."

"Sounds consistent with what Andrea said."

She turned her mood twister up a full rotation, lifted three fingers, and horizontally spread them like a fan. The hologram transformed into three side-by-side views. Cube one. Wasserman's case file. Cube two. The memory-printer. Cube three. Delphi. Leaning back, her head rested on her interlocked fingers and pressed into the chair's plush headrest.

"What's Wass's end game?" Morgan asked. "If he's brainwashing people, he can make them believe anything. So why would he lie about being from the future?"

"To cover up what he's already done. Nothin' is more dangerous than forgettin' the past." One memory, one lie, can be the difference between danger and safety. She formed a fist and rested her chin on it. "Those two hostages must have known somethin'. But what?"

Morgan loaded cube four. Brooks. The former Delphi employee and war criminal. "Something worth killing for."

She nodded towards the Delphi casefile. "Let's get a closer look." Grabbing her coat and satchel, she followed the orange holographic arrows on the floor labeled *Motorpool* while loading Delphi's address on Navi.

# 9
## Trial by Fire

Peter stood on the sidewalk reading Lyon's report on his wrist-computer. The rookie thinks that Outcasts stole memories from the Delphi campus. A crazy theory, though it can't be ignored. Not until Lansing's memories are accounted for.

Streams of people walked in and out of the substation's revolving doors, entering with white and yellow dust but exiting clean through the magnetic hum of protocol-eighteen-approved radiation vacuums. Crisp midday air, lacking the foul odors of the wastelands.

A nearby engine revved. An unmarked SUV with a Ran'na emblem on the front grill pulled up parallel and he got in. He closed the door and vacuums over the passenger side window suctioned radioactive dust off his wool coat. Before he could buckle up, Lyon accelerated like a getaway driver.

"Easy," he said.

"Where the fuck were you?" She looked over. Infinity brand sunglasses over her eyes.

"Me? I just waited twenty minutes for you."

"Not now. Before. I couldn't find ya."

"I had to take care of something." He glanced out the window at the passing lines of artificial trees, which faded into a field of plastic grass that stretched several kilometers to the metallic scaffolding of the Theodosian Wall. Its horizon-spanning energy-web glowed faintly in daylight.

Lyon looked over for a few seconds, as though she wanted more. Her vulgar vocabulary certainly leaves room for professional improvement. It reminded him that Officer Norris had sent over a subroutine he had been meaning to try. Chun's Censoring. He used eye movements to load it.

"Did you get my message?" Lyon slowed to a stop as a real-render tree at the corner flickered into a flashing stop sign. A transparent red coupe lit up on the windshield. A red X next to a right arrow and a four second timer counting down until a real red coupe passed.  Then the volumetric stop sign morphed into a green checkmark, and she accelerated.

"About Hiraeth Tower?  Yes."  He squinted at the now dead-ahead sun.

"No sign of forced entry.  And satellite coverage didn't ID anyone."

Right.  He loaded a volumetric map on his side of the dashboard and navigated to Delphi's main campus.  Eight Chronos Street.  Double clicking loaded the residence profile.  Shannon and Carl Fischer.  Senior Delphi scientists.  PhDs in quantum physics from Oxford and MIT.  Their pasty portraits lit up with green checks next to protocol eleven validation, one hour ago.  Scrolling led to visual captures of the laboratory tower engulfed in flames.

Brakes squealed.  His abdomen thrown against the seat belt and his face into the dashboard.  The volumetric file bobbed up and down as Lyon honked the horn and yelled something through her rolled-down window.

Lyon screamed, "You bleeping crazy blank-hole. Get the bleep off the street before I arrest you."

Of course, she didn't actually say bleep or blank. Chun's subroutine flashed a small dot each time it replaced Lyon's wild words with tamed language.

The man standing in the street was dust-covered but handing out clean pamphlets.  Paper ones like they used in olden times.  He wedged it under a windshield wiper and spoke without any sign of alarm.  "May the Goddess save you."

"Bleep off loser."  Lyon flipped him off and accelerated past him. The man's pleading voice faded along with his image in the sideview mirror.

"That was a little harsh."

"He shouldn't be harassin' people on the street."

Lyon shooting her mouth off could be the thing that gets her killed. Perhaps a little encouragement would go a long way. Just play the right keys and I can shove off this dying rock. "See that badge on your coat? What do you think it means?"

She raised her eyebrows and shrugged. "That I'm a police officer."

"Which means you're a professional. Say something like, 'make way sir'."

"Well, I'm unpredictable. Get used to it."

"Perfect," he said sarcastically.

***

Before Navi computers were common, the sprawling Delphi Datacore campus would have been large enough to get lost in. Only the numbers on the curbside retro-mailbox and subroutine identifiers distinguished Eight Kronos Street from the river of white houses with red doors and black roofs. He looked up after examining the postal replica.

A few meters away Lyon fixated on still-smoking rubble on a hilltop across the street. Hiraeth Tower. Quite an expensive accident.

He looked up at the police drone overhead, pointed at the residence and moved a raised finger in a circle. It flew off towards the backyard with flickering blue thrusters.

The house was close enough that the sun barely edged over the dark roof. Chilling winds rustled the leaves and branches of the fake trees into a crackling symphony. He popped the collar of his peacoat and thought of a house much like this. An old home built on a joint operations airbase in Northern California. Back when it was called that. The down payment was a fistful of gold coins his wife hid in an empty Guiness can. He sliced his hand while cutting them out and she had to bandage him up on the way to the bank. But there's nothing where it used to be. Only howling winds. Unmarked graves and ghosts.

"I am Rrrrrobbie the robot reporter," a monotone and inorganic voice said.

He turned to find a tall robot with a boxy, metal head talking to Lyon.

"Do you have a comment on the recent Hall of Justice closure?" the robot asked.

"Nah, I don't got no comments," Lyon said.

"Don't talk to him," he said loudly while walking over to them and nodding towards the house. "Let's go Lyon."

"I wish to solicit comment from you, Officer Ramsey."

"You know what Robbie? Why don't we meet at that warehouse on Prospect and Hillhurst?"

As he grabbed Lyon's arm and walked her towards the house the robot said, "But Officer Ramsey, Peter, you never arrive at these arranged meetings."

"Let go." Lyon shoved him.

"Next time tell him to get deactivated," he said to Lyon.

"Because he's a robot?"

"Because it's a reporter."

"He just wants the truth."

"It's not programmed to care about the truth, or your reputation. It will say anything for volumetric clicks." At the front door he pressed a thumb to the biometric scanner, and the bright red door briefly changed to a shade of sky blue. Opening it and entering the house, he held the door and looked back at Lyon. "Wasn't coming here your idea?"

Lyon entered and closed the door with a click. They wiped their feet on the foyer entry mat as tiny-tube vacuums slid up between the narrow gaps of the tile floor, lifting dust off them like a hydra of snakes.

A cathedral ceiling topped the foyer with a chandelier suspended from a circular skylight. A wooden plaque hung high on the wall. A carving on it of two dolphins swimming head to tail. *Shannon and Carl Forever* embossed. One lustrous piece of real wood for two filthy-rich bastards. "Hello?" he called out.

"Delphi moved them to another house."

Lyon sprinted up the first few stairs before he said, "Wait."

"What?" She stopped and turned. "Don't you want to split up?"

"No." I can't afford any mistakes. Not when the Outcasts could have Lansing's memories. "Let's take it from the top." His stomach growled.

"You forget to eat lunch again?" Lyon asked. "No wonder you're wastin' away."

"What?"

"Want me to remind ya next time? I'm always down for food."

"Right. I'll think on that."

Lyon navigated her wrist before sighing and switching to a flat-panel from her coat pocket. "Motion detectors only went off on the ground floor."

In the dining room he ran the blue light of his scan-gun up and down the walls. Where the room met the kitchen, the crime-scene subroutine rendered half a dozen fingerprint outlines. All of them green. The homeowners. "No red prints."

Lyon blinked a few times and looked over her shoulder, as though a volumetric angel or devil were whispering in her ear. The mutable painting behind her slowly morphed from the Great Pyramids to people dining Al Fresca, somewhere in Old Europe. "So, the suspect wore gloves or had their fingertips smoothed. Or maybe they just didn't touch nothin'."

"Do people break into homes in order to not touch anything?"

A light reflected in the window. He traced it to the floor by a small end table where he took a knee and an evidence bag. A diamond engagement ring by one of the table legs. It vacuumed into the self-seal evidence bag. He stood and found Lyon standing close enough he could smell her breath.

"Get back down on one knee and I'll think about it." Her lips turned in and she blushed.

"Don't get cute rookie." He placed it in her outstretched hand.

She ran the light of her scanner over it. "D-N-A. Shannon Fischer."

He squinted at the shiny diamond. "What married woman forgets her ring?"

"They must have left in a hurry. Or maybe the Fischers are separatin'?" Lyon opened her mouth again, and he was certain she was about to ask why he still wears his wedding band. But she returned the evidence with a coy smile instead. She either cares enough to not mention it, or not enough to remember.

He turned around. Dried streaks along the white walls. Running fingers along the brittle lines left a powdery residue. Rubbing a thumb and finger together crumbled dry algae onto the floor. He flicked the pale green chalky substance off his fingertip. The smoky odor smelled somehow familiar, but from what time or place? Lansing's apartment.

"Algae?" Lyon asked and he nodded. "I wouldn't figure Delphi scientists as the smokin' types."

"Right. So, what's your theory?" he asked. "Mr. Banks did this?"

"Brooks?"

"Right. Brooks."

"No, the computer ruled him out."

"Ah, right. He was killed a few hours before this went down."

Lyon opened her mouth but closed it without a word, her eyes averted. It must be eating at her. Words can't help a guilty conscious. On the way to the kitchen Lyon stopped in front of an Alacrity service robot. She whispered something inaudible to it.

"Robot, move away," he said loudly.

Lyon turned her head halfway back to him with a hand covering her ear. "Blank-hole. Don't bleeping yell in my ear."

"Raise your voice when you issue commands to them," he said.

"I don't like orderin' 'em around. It makes 'em look miserable."

Ordering them around is the point, Lyon. But he nodded in insincere agreement. The robot didn't respond. Walking back through the dining room and around the hall, they entered the kitchen from the other side. A panel on the robot's torso was flipped open. Standing next to it and peeking inside revealed empty spaces where the behavioral circuitboard and mini-reactor should be.

He walked over to the kitchen window. Leaning on the corners of the sink with two flat palms, he took in the impressive view of the campus and Galaxy Park beyond the brick patio and back lawn. But they love company. Miserable robots love company. Yes, that's what I should have said to Lyon, but it's too late for a comeback now.

Security robots passed through the backyard. "All of the security around here and an Outcast isn't detected?"

"Maybe they wore a thermal suit," Lyon said.

"DOLOS satellites also use motion tracking. That should have spotted them and raised an alarm." He looked up. Impressive Italian cabinetry ran along two sides of the kitchen.

"What about a sat-umbrella?"

"That would do the trick, though I've never heard of an Outcast managing to build one on their own. Even a hacker would need insider knowledge of the dampening frequencies needed." He scratched his chin. The black market. Something nearby beeped.

Lyon stood by the kitchen island, clicking away on the home's main computer as it floated over the marble surface.

He pulled two nearby stools over, handing one to her, though she opted to remain standing.

She put her hands together as though she were clapping and then quickly separated them to split the volumetric interface in two. They sat and stared into the binary abyss of information.

"Huh." Peter scratched his chin. "There's no food or water missing from their vault." He looked up at the locked pantry. A steel door with a biometric lock. Which means Lyon can't steal any. I only caught her doing it once, but she's probably done it a dozen more times and gotten away with it. Not that it matters in the grand scheme of things.

"Maybe they didn't need any."

"No Outcast would pass up an opportunity to drink clean water and eat uncontaminated food." He ran his eyes over the stock list again.

"It's locked up, so maybe they couldn't—oh, wait a sec. If they could hack the house security system and robot, hackin' the pantry woulda been bleeping easy." She rested her chin on a clenched fist. "I'm thinkin' after they stole memory disks from the lab, they stopped here to check what they had. Make sure they got what they came for, or I dunno, maybe the buildin' fire really was an accident?"

He sat on one of the stools. "Delphi didn't report anything missing. Those forensic computers can calculate charred remains down to the micron. So, the Outcasts must have brought their own disks and copied memories onto them. Right?"

"Hmm, yeah."

"Right. So, we got a guy," he said. Lyon raised her eyebrows. "Or gal. They use a satellite umbrella that had to have been illegally bought within city limits.  Plus, what would Outcasts want with memories? They create their own fake ones."

Lyon looked down. "I suppose."

"Let's check the black market.  I know a hacker down there who owes me a solid."

"Shouldn't we find the person that did this?"

"We can cuff whoever is in possession of stolen Delphi property and flip them in interrogation.  They'll plead out and name names."

"No, I mean we should find Wasserman."

Kyudo's intel indicated Wasserman was behind the attack on the police station.  Nothing implicates his involvement in this incursion. Lyon is stretching. Trying to tap two keys nine intervals apart.

Lyon scratched her head and her eyes narrowed. "What I can't figure is, doesn't Delphi predict everythin'? Shouldn't they have been able to like, prevent this?"

He rotated his stiff shoulders.  Maybe because Delphi can't actually predict everything rookie.  But you can bet your blank they're doing their own private investigation and—huh.  The subroutine is censoring my own thoughts too.  Well, I'll be bleeped.  Where was I?

Lyon is out for revenge as though killing Wasserman will change anything.  Wasserman has been killed several times. He'll simply clone himself again.  That man's DNA has been copied more times than a fraudulent copy of *Norse Dakota*. Even if she stopped him, someone just like him would take his place. Same game. Same players. Same outcome. Over and over. And rookie's friend will still be dead.

Revenge. That's what's driving her now. And her standard operating procedure already resembles a relentless Pacific-Coalition war robot more than a human.  Which may help locate Lansing's memories, yet if she dies then I'll be right back at square one.  Stuck on this dying rock with nothing. Nada. Blank. What am I going to do with this stubborn little creature?

"I have no idea," he said.

"Don't ya care enough to find out?"

I need to think. And without Lyon's incessant pestering. Either go to the powder room or— "I'm going to check the basement."

The door creaked like floorboards in an old farmhouse. The downward path narrowed into darkness. Halfway down he paused and looked back.

Lyon's silhouette predictably held still at the threshold.

"Are you coming?" he asked despite knowing she never would. Young people around her age grew up underground. Thankfully, Carmen will grow up with real sunlight.

"I, um. I'm goin' to check upstairs." Lyon's silhouette pointed upwards and walked away.

The lights automatically lit when he reached the last step. A finished basement. Bright white walls, gray carpet, no foul odors. What one would expect for a high-income couple with no children.

He leaned against the railing and rotated his mood-dial to Focused-Thoughts. Exhaling seemed to forcefully pull the air from his lungs, as though he were on a low-atmos-phere spacecraft. Yet inhaling was immediate and effort-less.

I need those memory disks, he thought. But chasing Wasserman in a revenge-fueled rampage could be what gets Lyon killed. Unless attempting to protect her is what inad-vertently causes it. A self-fulfilling Delphi prediction.

A prediction isn't destiny. Probable events can be pre-dicted. Like colonial riots during food shortages, or Sonoma County sinking into the ocean. But that doesn't mean a per-son is locked into a lifepath.

Banging noises from another room. A door in the utility room trying to close itself every ten seconds kept colliding with a laundry press that had fallen over. He stepped over it and into a windowless room with bright lights. Unlike the rest of the home, this room was not well kept. A maze constructed from stacks of page-books and papers. The narrow path of carpet led to a work desk against the wall topped with a computer. The Fischer's robot must be programmed to not come in here.

Something greasy on the computer's power button. He ran the blue light of his scanner over it and looked down as it clicked-back. Robot-grade machine oil.

A ring in the carpet. Not a diamond ring this time but something much larger. A thick impression half a meter in diameter. Must have been a datacore. Some work they brought home from the office, perhaps?

Horizontal lines shaped like a footprint next to it, which he scanned. The device clicked-back. Militia-surplus boots. Unisex size eleven. The scanner's radioactive icon lit up with a chime. Two hundred milli-sieverts. Huh. Forgetting to wipe their feet doesn't fit with two conscientious scientists. Plus, the Fischers are lace-curtain types with triple digit IQs. Not the type that generally own or wear militia boots.

Turning unwittingly knocked over a stack of books with his leg. A sharp pain in his knee. Blank. He examined them while rearranging them onto the stack. *Hack the Multiverse* by Brighton. *Stringless Quantum Entanglement* and *Theoretical Time Travel* by Mercer. *The Isis Manifesto* by Reylah Yorman.

Official subroutines flashed a red box and text. A protocol thirty-seven violation. The manifesto was banned on Earth a decade ago. Picking it up and flipping through it, he stopped and read the sentence closest to his thumb. *With three crowns the Goddess Hathor shall break her Earthly chains.*

The book fell from his hand, though subroutines continued to blink red criminal implications around it.  The district attorney will never press charges against a few Delphi VIPs.  Even if he did, the outlawed rag can't be burned as fast as it can be printed.

Clicking his mood-dial off, he stood quickly and stumbled his way out of the room.  A new rookie can be trained.  But even a nonsensical story can never be untold.

He rushed to the top of the stairs and slammed the basement door shut, which revealed Lyon sitting at the kitchen island.  She was looking over her shoulder, whispering in the direction of the refrigerator.

Huffing and staggering over, he leaned on an edge.

"Hey," Lyon said.  "I was thinkin' about what you always tell me.  About every crime bein' motive and opportunity."  She looked at his shaking hands.  "What happened?"

"Nothing.  Were you just talking to yourself?"  I just need to think of an excuse to leave.  Go to the black market alone and leave Lyon here.

"No."  She sat up straight.  "Maybe we're not lookin' for an Outcast.  Maybe the suspect is a settler that's been brainwashed."  Lyon rotated the volumetric display, a large bubble with a myriad of stick figures floating inside.  A photo and some text popped over each one as she ran a finger among the sea of icons.  "There was a satellite outage in sector eleven late last night.  Four hundred twelve people whose whereabouts were unknown until this mornin'.  I'm guessing one of 'em could be our suspect."

"Cookie for the rookie.  So, during this outage, Wasserman brainwashes someone, and sends them here?"

"Yeah.  He's a coward, usin' meat robots to do his dirty work."

He adjusted his tie.  Cowards manipulate others into taking all the risks.  Right.  "Did you filter out those who have since passed DOLOS protocol eleven?  In order to rule out brainwashing?"

"I know what I'm doin'."

That doesn't answer the question.  But surely there is a nicer way to phrase that.  He paused to think.  "That doesn't answer the question."

Wind rattled the kitchen window and Lyon sighed.  "I already did that.  See?"  She pointed to *Applied Reductions* on the volumetric display.  "That cut, like, I dunno, half of 'em."

"Filter by occupational and recreational access to cybernetic oil."  He fell into the adjacent stool and caught his breath.

Lyon tilted her head and looked over with both eyebrows raised before lifting a volumetric cube of buttons.  She tapped a square in the cube, typed it in, and rotated the single square forward, twisting it like a Rubik's cube.  The computer clicked-back.  Most of the floating stick figures vanished, which left the remaining ones with space between them, like buoys bobbing in the ocean.  "That reduces the number to twenty-three."

"Now filter by shoe size eleven.  Unisex."

Lyon twisted a square in the floating cube's top edge, and the interface clicked-back.  "That narrows it to six."  She scratched her chin.  "Hmm.  That's short enough that we could robo-call their employers.  See who didn't show up to work today."

"Cross reference with military records."

With a small grin Lyon looked over.  "Military records?"

"Yes.  Provincial Militia."

"*Right*," Lyon said mockingly, her impression of him.  After a few clicks her smile quickly flattened.  "One match.  Abe Carruth.  Male.  Thirty-two years old.  One-point-six-one meters tall.  Shoe size eleven."

"Riddle me this.  Is he a robotics engineer?"

"Robotics tech at Liberty Robotics."

"Someone who would know how to deactivate a robot and hack a home security core."

"Yeah.  His current address is twenty-two-eleven Hermes Avenue.  Let's go."  Lyon jumped from her seat and jogged towards the front door while he tried to keep up.

# 10
## Cold Jury

Joan rubbed her hands together in front of the tepid air blasting out of the dashboard vents while looking thru the windshield at the Grimaldi Apartment complex. A pedestrian-packed sidewalk where radioactive dust covered each textured paver in a yellow and grey mosaic. The structure's irregular-brick walls and red-roof shingles worn smooth with the erosion lines of stinging rain. One of the corner stairwells had collapsed into a heap of concrete and rust.

Behind the apartments, the sun formed a semi-circle over the base of the Western perimeter wall. Its shiny metallic base gleamed orange, a mix of sunlight and the half-kilometer energy web pulsing above it.

"What'd you say this guy's name is?" Peter asked.

"Carruth."

"No, his first name."

"Why does he ask when he can just do it himself?" Hologram Morgan asked in the backseat.

"I don't know," she said to herself and Morgan. A few swipes on the dashboard hologram loaded the suspect's info. "Abe Carruth. Male. 32 years old. 1.618 meters tall. Shoe size 11. Current address is 2211 Hermes Avenue." Grabbing the corners of the hologram, she moved them diagonally away from each other to enlarge it. "How do you say his last name?"

"Caro? He could be French," Peter said.

"Franch?"

"No, France. F-R-A-N-C-E. It used to be a country."

"Okay. Jesus." She crossed her arms and looked straight ahead to scan pedestrian traffic. Old women walked by slowly, squinting but not seeing thru the SUV's tinted windows. The windshield rendered green boxes around them as the computer eliminated any chance of them being Mr. Carruth. A tactical function streamed visual data from the two police drones circling the complex.

"Maybe it's Carrot," Morgan said.

She laughed until Peter stared.

"What?" she asked.

He shrugged. "Nothing." Mr. Creepy popped chewing gum in his mouth and started smacking loudly. Because he is so. Very. Annoying.

The hologram beeped.

"Oh, Delphi results," Morgan said.

Tapping the Delphi app lit up the corporate logo with a beep. Two dolphins swimming in a circle, head to tail. Odds beeped and blinked in large red digits. "Delphi predicts a 99% chance he's brainwashed." She stretched against the driver's seat and her stomach growled. This damn carrot better show up and get himself arrested already. "I, um, think we ought to enter his apartment now and set a trap for him."

"This guy is a robot tech. He'll have a robot, or surveillance hardware somewhere, setup to warn him if anyone enters his residence," he Peter-splained.

The sound of shattering glass on the left. Maintenance bots emptying refuse cylinders into an overflowing recycler. The trash fell back to the ground, and they swept it again into the receptible in an endless loop. A few meters away, narcotic fiends sat against a wall of cracked concrete in dirt-covered raincoats, looking outwards with thousand-meter stares.

Maybe Delphi can predict how stupid Peter is. "We gotta put him down quickly before he takes hostages or like, hurts an innocent person." She unbuttoned her peacoat and checked the blaster holstered on her hip. The blue battery light blinked 100%.

"And what about the 1% chance that he's innocent? People aren't probabilities. And if you shoot a human, you can bet your ass Kyudo will write you up. She's nothing like Lansing."

"You bet your own ass. And don't come cryin' to me if you get shot again today." Pangs from her stomach. Should have stopped for food. A warm basket of tendies or something. And some crispy golden chips. Where they crunch with every bite and the salt dissolves on your tongue. She licked her lips.

"You're right Joan. Better safe than sorry," Morgan said.

Peter's head fell back against the headrest. "Killing him could cause brain damage. If Carruth is a puppet, his memories may lead to the ventriloquist. Don't you want to find the one who killed your friend?" He lifted one of his fingers and moved it up and down while asking, "Don't *you* care enough to find out?"

She tapped her fingers against the dashboard as the sun fell. Artificial light from the wall's energy-web cast shadows and flickers across the road and sidewalk. Foot traffic increased into the apartments. Radiation laborers in sprayed-clean hazmat suits, which gradually progressed back to dirty with every gust of dust-laden wind. Then foundry workers. The Hephaestion corporate emblem was the single clean spot on their filth-covered jumpsuits. "I ain't playin' 20 questions with this damned Mr. Carrot. He's gonna be armed."

"What makes you say that?" Peter loaded a passenger-side hologram with a 3D scan of Carruth's apartment. "Satellites didn't detect any weapons."

17:39 ticked on the car chronograph. After fidgeting in her seat, she lifted her tea from the cup holder. Green turning to yellow on the radiation strip. The side of the can illuminated a holo-advertisement with a map pointing to the nearest store, where one could buy more breakfast tea in the afternoon. "I used to live in a place like this." She took a burning gulp.

"You didn't live in the academy dorms?" He lifted his own tea tin on the center console and clicked the plastic top open. Steam and the smell of Earl Grey floated over as he took a sip.

"No. They were fine."

"You never told me that," Morgan said.

"You weren't living with your folks?" Peter asked.

"Why didn't you tell me?" Morgan asked.

Why are they prying? I shouldn't have said anything, she thought. Just pretend to agree with Peter so he'll drop it. And if Carruth endangers anyone blast him. Or it, rather. A meat robot's life isn't worth a human. "You're right about Carruth. Non-lethal force." Pulling a stun-gun from the car's center console, she racked a stun-prong round into the semi-transparent slide. "Loaded for teddy bear."

"Perfect. Now—"

The car computer beeped, and the windshield zoomed in on a man 300 meters away walking towards the apartment complex's dim South entrance. A blinking-red circle around his face. Abe Carruth. A Twins baseball hat with black hair pushed out under the edges, barely visible within the hood of a brown sweatshirt. Automatic shoe-scans matched his shoes to the crime-scene impressions.

"Let's go." Peter opened his door and got out.

She paused with one hand over the driver's side door latch. I can't have Morgan asking for my biography right now, she thought. "I need you to stay here and warn me if this guy double backs," she said to Hologram Morgan. Before Morgan could open her mouth Joan disconnected the memory disc from her cuffputer and plugged it into the car's computer console.

She ran to catchup with Peter.

***

In the lobby a wall-computer buzzed and flickered with a grid-map. The echoes of something dripping far away, and foul odors almost as bad as those years spent cowering in that damn shelter.

At the top of a dark staircase that hugged three walls, a long hall of worn carpet. Stains arranged in a leopard-like pattern. If there ever was such an animal.

She checked her mood twister. Apprehend-Suspect.

Sounds at each passing door. Crying babies, streams of football matches, and a couple screaming loud enough that Carruth might have cellmates.

White letters labeled unit 2211. No biometric lock but a card reader by a knob of worn brass. Peter looked over and nodded.

She moved the stun pistol to her other hand and reached into an interior coat pocket until a fingertip bumped into the mini-computer slicer.

Holding the small apparatus against the access panel it blinked, and metal slicing-wires emerged like they were living worms, squirming into the terminals of the copper key-reader. Each fingertip turned warm, and her palm turned sweaty. 10 seconds of sizzling shocks and the red lock lit green.

A kick flung the creaking door into the wall with a thud. Behind her Peter shouted, "Police." Her stun-gun swept left and right as she walked down the apartment hall, which led to a common room devoid of occupants. A holographic lamptop. Dark but warm to the touch. A loud thump and Peter cursing.

He was gripping his knee by a neon-yellow coffee table where a lonely blue flower peeked out of a wobbling Guinness-pilsner vase.

No dirty dishes in the kitchen sink. A cast-iron pot and Russel-brand tea kettle on a powered-off stovetop. A George-Jack Shack milkshake stood on the counter. Half gone. Dots of vanilla thru the transparent aluminum.

Carruth wasn't carrying it with him earlier. But those shakes stay cold for a while.

Behind it, a teacup with a few sips of brewed tea still in it. She ran a pinky along the cold rim. Something red smeared on the curved edge. Lipstick. That obnoxious shade of red that Mary wears when she bats her eyes at boys.

Morgan mentioned hearing a woman's voice during the station attack. One of Wasserman's puppeteers. "Peter, we got a plus one here," she whispered into her com.

"Right," he said like a mindless robot.

An alcove at the edge of the kitchen led to a cramped home office, where orange light from the nearby perimeter wall poured over the desk thru a large circular window. A trench coat and sweatshirt draped over a swivel chair. Half a dozen dirty, half-filled mugs and glasses of various heights arranged like the Settlement skyline. A stack of hard-copy papers spread in a mess, next to a holodisc of *The Clementine Homilies.*

Crumpled up papers and busted electronics in the drawers but no memory discs.

Peter flipped on a light down the hall and stuck his head into another room.

"Full bath?" she asked.

"No. It's empty."

She interlocked her fingers into a sweaty grip and aimed her stun-gun towards the last closed door. "Carruth?" No answer. "MOTH Cadre. Come on out with your hands up." Silence, except for Peter's heavy breaths. His turn to kick a door into a wall. A thud and he stepped aside. Framed darkness. Her fingertip moved to the trigger. Something moved. She fired stun needles that squealed and flashed like lightning.

Silence. Cat-Eyes adjusted to the darkness and brightened the room. No suspect. No threat. Clothes piled into a mess on a corner bed. Above it a window with a clear view of a concrete pedestrian path winding thru fake grass. A Gemini baseball hat and brown hoodie on a small scrub top table. Four stun rounds clung to the wall in a vertical line, the bottom one left of the rest of the grouping.

"Kind of looks like a J." Peter's fingers ran up and down the wall and he looked back. "I've got an extra stun-mag if you want to write your name."

Her face flushed and for a moment she considered stunning him. But the fire alarm blared.

Outside the window a hooded figure ran down the paved path, casting shadows at each lamppost. He looked back as he turned towards a marketplace. Facial-Recognition popped up a name in red: *Carruth, Abraham*.

She sprinted to the apartment threshold and paused at the congested hall. Filled with pandemonium and people. She lifted her badge.

"Police," Peter shouted.

No one seemed to notice or care.

This is like being in a shelter. Like being trapped. Cornered.

She pulled her S120 and aimed it at the crowd. "Move! Get out of the way!"

With gasps and screams the bottleneck unjammed and she ran thru.

# Long Shot

Joan slowed to a walk and read the painted letters of peeling paint arranged as *Cedar Lake Marketplace* on a rotting-wood sign. Hundreds of people moved in lanes of gravel between merchant tents, their breaths floating into the cold night and blending with dancing wisps of steam and smoke rising from grills and pellet stoves. Frigid winds turned hanging LED lanterns into swaying pendulums and carried the smell of charred food and Eucalyptus chips. She fetched gloves from her coat pocket and after pulling them on, re-gripped her stun pistol.

A hundred meters to the right, Peter's blue signal turned a shade brighter as he spoke on the com-channel, "Central, 6-Moth-5, 10-43."

Troy joined the wireless with the operator icon and his fancy accent. "All units be advised. MOTH personnel are in pursuit of suspect: Carruth, Abraham."

She jogged down the left pedestrian path while scanning.

"Taco?" A geriatric Chinese vendor asked in a heavy accent next to a chalkboard menu of Martian Tacos and a line of bubbling, hydroponic growth-vats. Flashing lights of text in Russian and Chinese briefly interfered with eye functions. Firetruck sirens rang out in the distance.

"Troy, why can't we track him?" she asked on the wireless.

"He's shielding himself from satellite tracking. A thermal suit is a distinct possibility. Get a visual and your oculars can ID him. I'll reposition the drone to the far side of the market and have it work its way towards you." After clicking sounds that could have been typing, he concluded, "Okay, we're set. No hurries no worries."

A hooded male figure 40 meters ahead.

She ran as a gap in foot traffic appeared. Stun-gun raised towards the sky. 20 in glowing-red on the protruding magazine and odd stares from pedestrians. Maybe they've never seen an armed blonde before? There's plenty in that Viking holo-game Morgan plays. Played.

The suspect passed a table of polished mirrors. The reflection of his face flashed green on functions. Not Carruth.

Stopping and doing a 360, pedestrians in filthy raincoats and mink hats forked around her like ants avoiding a puddle. On the horizon a storm of radioactive-dust pelted the perimeter energy-web, sending pulses of light in the air and vibrations thru the ground.

"Joan, the drone may have found something. 30 meters to your left. Bearing 1-2-4," Troy said.

Eye functions zoomed in. A red square rendered around a man in a hoodie as he entered a merchant tent. "I got him."

*Pawn shop* lit in green neon letters one a time until the entire word blinked. Her badge glowed in the reflection of the dim lights that hung from each side of the tent entrance, above two middle-aged men. Their backs straightened and they nodded as she entered.

Inside, pebbles on the bare dirt floor crumbled with each bootstep and the smell of burning onions invaded both nostrils. I can't wait to eat something after I cap this guy, she thought.

A center path divided 30 meters of wares on stacked shelves. Patrons clustered in shadows behind shelves of merchandise. They looked over as she passed, their whispers hastily hushed to silence.

Sweat ran under her clothes and body armor chafed her skin as she scanned aisles, keeping the far entrance always in sight. Shelves of radiation-safe boxes. Canned food. Rows of semi-transparent metal bottles filled the liquor section. A hologram played *Norse Dakota: The Musical*. Vikings dancing with axes. Now available on nano-disc for $4.99. The game is better.

On the left a woman haggled with an attendant in a booth, offering diamonds for canned food. In a dark corner someone sobbed, for a reason no one cared or dared to find out.

The puppeteer is preying on the weak. He must be thinking that no one will stand up for the downtrodden folks living in literal filth. But technology isn't the only way to brainwash someone. Or to convince them they're worth nothing.

Only half of the tent left. Arm hairs rose, and her weapon grip turned moist. He's here somewhere. A small game aisle, including playing cards and poker chips. Two shelves and no dice.

She switched gun hands to wipe a sweaty palm on her coat. A beep from the Tracker function. The hooded figure doubled back, out of the tent where she entered. Turning and lowering her center of gravity she ran until a toddler cut her off and she stumbled.

Back on her feet she ran thru the other exit, shouting and pointing her gun to clear a rapid path thru the marketplace. Puddles splashing with every rapid step. Waves of hot and cold air alternated between the barrel-fires that divided the night of dark commerce with flames bright enough to blur function text.

At the pitch-black edge of the marketplace, she stopped and panted visible breaths. As they faded, a patch of dead trees. Not enough to call it a forest, but close. A paved road and a public park with raised lights by a playground. *Fermin Park* according to scrolling words from an eye function.

Something smelled of smoke. That damn market. It better not have stunk up this coat. She lowered her nose and raised the thick wool and sniffed. Nope. But something on the ground.

Blue-smoke trails rising from an un-snuffed algae cigarette between gravel rocks. A blaring siren. Two firetrucks passed the far road with spinning-red lights. For an instant, the light revealed a silhouette by the road. Marked with a red square and a klaxon by MOTH functions.

"I got him. He's headin' for Fermin Park," she said on the wireless.

"Ferming Park?" Peter asked.

"No. Fermin."

A sign announced the park was open until midnight and the paved paths were lit with those floating little lights rich bastards put on their front lawn. Benches and playgrounds surrounded the square-brick war monument. 100 meters beyond, a fake-tree line reached the bottom half of the perimeter wall, which towered above a concrete base into a glowing web. Radioactive particles brilliantly flashed into embers as loud warnings overwhelmed eye functions. Deliberate eye movements terminated the annoying Energy-Surge function.

150 meters to the right, Peter's signal flashed blue. "I'm covering Shepard Street."

Beyond the sidewalk she knelt by fresh shoe impressions in moist dirt. Two pairs, one size 10 militia boots. Evidence functions drew green tread lines and moved them overtop the footprints, a flashing 100% match with the Delphi crime scene. The other pair, size 11. Women's hiking shoes.

A button on her cuffputer pinged Peter. "Are you seein' this?" she asked.

"Yes."

A police drone flew overhead, slowing to a hover 150 meters to the left, completing a triangle with her and Peter.

With another step, the loud clop of her boot echoed like it was far away. Carruth is trapped. Like when you hear footsteps coming and inescapable dread crawls up your back, bit by bit like a giant hairy spider. A despicable way to make someone feel. Less than human. But he's not Carruth anymore. His past was taken from him, and so was his future.

It's just a walking meat shell, pre-programmed to feel nothing.

"Backup is on the way. Let's wait five for them," Peter said.

She checked the sleeve of her armor. A full green shield on the small readout. "Why would they run towards the wall where they could be cornered easily?"

"Something you'd like to share rookie?" Peter asked.

"They must have a way out. In five minutes, they could be gone." Icy wind brushed her face as she turned her mood twister to Apprehend-Suspect, 25%. Colors turned crisp, like all of them were the difference between black and white. "I'll flush him out."

"MOTH-5, be advised, there are over two dozen civilians in the park," Troy said.

The footprints led over a hill, to a playground's edge where two toddlers sat constructing a sandcastle. Parents sat on benches on the right, by the war monument. On top of the square monument base, a bright hologram of a long-gone city reached for the sky above circling text: *Never Forget*.

She walked in front of it, the side where ancient, glossy photographs peppered the brick base. A collage of those lost in the war. The lighting changed. Something reflecting among images of the dead.

Turning around to face the tree line, the section of the motion-controlled lampposts went out. More lights dimmed and faded, creeping like a cloud. A function alarm shook her to a standstill. Abe Carruth. 100 meters away in a red box within the tree line by the perimeter wall. The silhouette of a tall woman next to him. In a weaver stance. Her hair carried by the wind in slowing motion.

A pregnant woman standing by the memorial turned and said something inaudible over heartbeats pulsing in both ears. A barrel flashed from the darkness of the far tree line. Time stopped.

A shot of pain ran up her spine as her back slammed into the war monument. Chipping bricks whacked both ankles. She landed on blood-soaked pavement on all fours like a cat. Boiling blood forced both eyes shut and scalded each hand as she coughed ozone.

The frozen image of two assailants faded into yellow blasts passing thru rising smoke. Ears vibrated with the muffled pitch of each passing round. To the left, a screaming five-year-old girl stood at the playground's edge. Tears irrigating the sand.

Peter's voice echoed far away on the wireless.

The stun-gun was dripping red and left a clean outline of itself on the concrete. Next to it, a severed skull.

A second blast passed her face, close enough to burn her cheek. It landed in the monument with a deafening shatter. Uncemented bits of brick sprinkled her hair. A third blast struck her armor.

The world vanished.

# 12
# Halcyon

Peter couldn't breathe fast enough as he shoved his gripped pistol in every conceivable direction while the bright scanner attached to the barrel shot illumination through the dark forest. The shaking light reached the concrete base of the Theodosian Wall, and he scanned the maintenance hatches, finding all of them locked with no sign of forced egress.

A hovercar made a low pass, its loud turbines shaking and tossing leaves every which way. Aerial drones sliced the arboreal shadows with blinding searchlights, gradually converging on a recently felled tree, where rising ozone evaporated along with the last trace of the suspects, leaving him with nothing. Nada. Zilch.

On the wireless a repeating sound through sporadic static interference, perhaps the echo of a satellite umbrella. A signal thirteen. On an ocular subroutine the high-pitched pings flashed a red bubble over one hundred meters away, by the war memorial and adjacent to billowing smoke.

"Lyon."

After fifty meters of jogging, he could only manage a fast walk to the smoking monument. His shoes clopped on cobblestone coated in burnt blood and topped with charred splinters of bone the size of toothpicks. The foul smell of dead flesh and no sign of Lyon. These are her scant remains. She's vaporized.

"Damnit!" Kyudo's going to make an example of me, he thought. No. Lyon's outline blinked two dozen meters from the opposite side of the structure, along with a medical transponder. A dash brought pain to his knees and an ambulance hovercar into view. A silhouette sitting on a stretcher in front of the bright lights of the open hatchback.

Police subroutines clicked-back Lyon's ID. She was wrapped in a blanket with a medical robot doting over her. Her face as pale and white as an old Boston Christmas. A vitals scanner between her closed lips. She looked younger bundled up, resembling a child more than an adult. "I'm okay," she mumbled over and over while shivering. Her monologue ended and she looked up at him. "Am I okay?"

"Your vitals are stable and are indicative of a positive prognosis," the medical robot said to Lyon. "Remember to not panic and comply with the instructions of all medical Autonomots."

"I wasn't askin' you circuit head." The vitals scanner fell from Lyon's mouth.

"Oh, you sound fine." He pinched the front of his clammy shirt and pulled it away from his skin.

"My primary circuits are housed within my torso." The robot lifted the vitals scanner and shoved it in Lyon's mouth until it closed with a palatal click. "Are you related to five-time Interstellar Golf Champion Forest Lyon?"

"No, I'm not," Lyon muttered to the robot. "I didn't see the shooter in time," she said to him. "There was two of 'em."

A thump from the dispensary tube running along the interior of the ambulance. The robot lifted a clear capsule with a small, shiny pill and read from a volumetric form. "You have been selected for a memory treatment Officer Lyon. Traumatic events affect us all in different ways, and it is important to evaluate your human prerogative to forget. This right is guaranteed by protocol twenty-seven."

The landing lights of police hovercars formed a perimeter of large white circles and brushed the park's fake grass back and forth.

Lyon signed a volumetric document with her thumb and took the memory capsule, holding it up to the light between two fingers. Blue and red spinning lights split through it like a prism and her face widened with intrigue. The blanket fell, revealing streaks of dried blood staining her arms and pants.

Though her holstered pistol was polished clean. "How come the computer never tosses you a memory-treatment?"

"I don't remember." He didn't think of the response, it was simply the first thing that came to mind.

"Does any of this affect you?" she asked, in an unusual tone of kindness and vulnerability. Poor kid isn't herself. When he didn't respond, she whispered, "Lansin' was in the war. They made his records public after his death."

"Huh." He paused, unable to think of what else to say. "Take her to an aid station," he said to the robot.

The stretcher rolled Lyon into the ambulance and the hatchback slammed shut. He stepped away as it lifted off and flew over a nearby hill. Its pitched headlights illuminated a crumbling brick wall that he had seen many times before, the sight of which caused him to involuntarily gulp the aircraft's smoky wake.

He unwrapped a stick of gum and chewed while walking back to the blasted war memorial, where humanoid robots tagged evidence on a makeshift table by an evidence van. Blood-stained armor and a torn police peacoat in thick plastic. The case-file subroutine rendered a volumetric slideshow, starting with Lyon getting shot. He paused at a pregnant woman's remains, quickly using an eye movement to switch the loop of reenactments from real-render to a traditional chalk-outline. The blast's line of fire appeared as a solid red line. The source stood seventy meters away and one-point-eight meters from the ground. Someone taller than Mr. Carruth.

Officer Norris kneeled a few centimeters from dried blood. After smacking on thermal gloves, he reached into a pile of brick rubble and lifted a smoothed ball of metal, rolling it between two fingers. "Look at this. Partial thermophoresis." After scanning the evidence, he lifted his wrist to show the ballistics report. "Twelve-millimeter, Rhea-Hypersonic. More of those sulfur-shit-slugs the forsaken have been slinging.  It didn't even change fully into plasma. That's why your partner is still kicking."

"Right."

"Does she?"

"What?"

Norris stood and removed the smacking gloves.  "Does she kick?"

"Whoa, I'm not going there."

Norris chuckled for an instant before sheepishly kneeling again to examine evidence.

Peter turned around.

Major Selene Kyudo in a red dress and black heels.  A white-pearl necklace and diamond earrings that reflected the distant downtown lights.  Her glossy jet-black hair tied up elaborately.  She must have been on a date somewhere nice. "Ramsey."

"Ma'am."

Kyudo grinned, though it was less of a smile and resembled the way a shark or wolf bares its teeth.  "Imagine my surprise upon hearing Joan's ten-thirteen signal tonight.  I thought I made myself clear earlier today regarding the importance of her safety."

He raised an open hand.  "Sorry Major, but she acted on her own."

Kyudo lifted her arm to read from her wrist-computer. "Did Joan point her service blaster at a crowd of civilians?"

"Uh..."

Kyudo sighed and lowered her arm.  "The Australis Uranium Mines are always in need of police personnel.  Perhaps a transfer there would provide you ample time to improve your memory-retention skills."

"I assure you that won't be necessary."

"Good.  Because if Joan loses her future, I assure you the world will remember past events that would otherwise be forgotten, *Ensign Ramsey*."

Kyudo turned blurry, as though she were a volumetric display experiencing static. But she was physically there. Ensign. She knows. She knows what I did, he thought. Peter realized his mouth was hanging open and chewing gum was resting against the inside of his bottom teeth. He consciously shut it. His fingers twitched as he took a deep breath.

"Have a look at this." Kyudo lifted a volumetric sequence of documents from her wrist-computer. She pinched the image and dragged a copy over to Peter's wrist.

A headline from the *LA Times*, dated two days from now. A crashed hovercar by a burning train. On the side of a ruined car large letters: *Train 81*.

"This Delphi prediction hasn't been legally purchased." He zoomed to the corner, enlarging Delphi's watermark of two dolphins swimming head to tail, half the circle filled with color. "Otherwise, the logo would be fully inked. Where did you get this?"

"Carruth's ground car. A patrolman found it parked at the Spaceport."

"Perhaps he stole this from Delphi."

She landed a hand on her hips. "That's what I want to know. There must be something Delphi isn't telling us. Something they won't tell *me*." Kyudo stared with eyes that glimmered in the dark night as bright as twin thrusters. "Good night, Ramsey."

He deactivated ocular subroutines while walking over the park's hill and across the cordoned roadway. Halfway through the maze of parked police vehicles, bouncing red and blue lights converged on a large humanoid robot. "Hello Officer Peter Ramsey."

"Hi." He moved around one of the cars and the robot intercepted.

"I am Robbie the robot reporter."

"Right."

"Would you like to comment on the evenings events, Peter?"

"No."

"Come on Peter. You have to give me something."

"Right." Peter held out his hand until the robot mimicked the gesture. He pulled the chewing gum from his mouth and shoved it down on the cybernetic palm. "Here you go." He walked around the robot.

"Peter Ramsey, you need professional help."

The black bars of the hilltop cemetery's rusted gate creaked the way they always did, and in the shadows of the dead trees he navigated the graves of the deceased as though he were in a dark but familiar room, knowing by memory the arrangement of the furniture, and where he could and could not step.

Rays of the city's ambient light ended on the mausoleums that bookmarked each side of the summit, where a shallow cloud of mist rolled between them as though they marked the threshold between the worlds of life and death. Crickets composed a song for the night, though the news says those insects are extinct. Perhaps they're as artificial as the graves.

He stopped a few rows beyond the mausoleums to sit and lean against a fake tree. The trunk certainly felt like real bark, digging into his back as he looked up through a break in the leaves.

Dust heavy as snow fell against the energized barrier curving half a kilometer above, a violent storm that shook the web back and forth like the sails of an old ship. Loud enough to conceal the sound of ocean waves striking the megalithic wall, though nothing can deny the smell of the sea.

Kyudo thinks I'm a criminal. And she'll never move past that judgement, even though only the rear-view mirror of life lacks fog. Even though it wasn't my choice, he thought.

It was demanded by everyone that dehumanized the enemy and thought of them as mere numbers in need of subtraction. Once someone isn't considered human, anything done to them can be justified. A recipe for genocide.

He leaned his head back against the tree. Darkness. The sounds of the sea crashing against the Theodosian Walls. In his mind's eye he could see the waves breaking against a line of rocks and the rusted seawall. Salty drops that tasted a momentary freedom from the tyranny of the dark pool below, before yet again sinking with defeat, enslaved again by the leviathan of time, and drifting deep beneath rising bubbles, into his cold abyss. A rhythmic call of the void.

The brass believes in Delphi's smoke and mirrors. So, Lyon's supposed fate has to change and only one person knows how to do that. Someone I haven't spoken to in fifteen years.

The commander who started the war.

Both eyes finally adjusted to the pitch black, and he lowered his head to read the nearby grave from bottom to top:

*Beloved Daughter*
*Forever Alive in Our Hearts*
*Died September 20th, 2147*
*Born August 11th, 2143*
*Carmen Astraea Ramsey*

# 13
# Mare Nostrum

Bath steam lifted into Joan's angled-back nostrils. The sound of percolating bubbles behind her from the shampoo box her hair dangled in. A holographic button on the bathroom wall loaded the Narcissus mirror-function and she grabbed a grooming-wand to quell a few rebellious strands. The tub glowed green like an algae-tank from the green wrist-tracker on her arm. Her removed cuffputer stood at the vanity's far end, next to a half-empty bottle of cinnamon gel-soap and the memory-treatment capsule. The shiny pill glowed like a little eyeball that stared back, and she turned her mood twister to Chill-Relax-97.

The muted news spun on a wall-mounted visual feed. Apartment functions scrolled text under the closed captions. The monthly water bill is already $82.40? She lifted one foot above the water line and turned off the flowing water-tap with her big toe.

"Knock knock," holographic Morgan said.

"You can come on in."

Morgan walked thru the bathroom door and sat in front of the vanity, resting her head against the marble edge, both knees lifted a few centimeters in front of her chin. "I didn't know if you were decent."

"Ya plugged into the apartment computer okay?"

"Yes. I'm free to roam within your domicile." Morgan swayed her shoulders back in forth, her upper half in an adorable little dance. "Do you know if that holovision show is on?"

She focused on the *Holovision* button. "*Sing with Science.*"

They were virtually sitting among an audience within a particle accelerator. Thankfully the VR program dresses you when you're bathing or showering. Down front a singing contestant, a woman in a red skirt. Blue lights and five raised orange beams bounced up and down in the gargantuan tunnel as the woman belted out something enchanting and sad in a language that functions didn't translate.

Joan briefly opened her mouth, but thought, I can't sing. Everyone says my voice is too raspy.

Everyone clapped and cheered, but live voting awarded only a six out of 10.

"She deserves an eight at least," Morgan said while clapping.

Joan moved her eyes to the eight and blinked.

The show broke for commercials, and they exited holovision. The broadcast continued on the bathroom wall's visual feed. Images of celebrities arranged in a grid, all of them with green checkmarks next to their names. *Vote yes for Wildlife Measure Seven. Because these celebrities are telling you to.* Faces scrolled by. A famous holo-film actress. The one with a fancy accent like Troy. Then Forest Lyon. "That mother fucker."

"Heh, Golf Ball," Morgan said.

"Pfft. I'm votin' no out of spite."

Large drops fell from Joan's arm as she clicked the shampoo cage open and after a stretch, she reached out of the tub, to the floor and lifted a bottle of McNichols Hard Cider to sip from.

"Mm. Drinking alone?" Morgan asked.

"I'm not alone. You're here."

Morgan laughed. "Silly Golf Ball, I can't drink."

"Oh really?" With eye movements she loaded a shadow-web app store for artificial entities and blinked while focusing on *inebriating beverages.*

A holographic blue drink appeared in Morgan's hands. "Aw, thanks."

"You're welcome." She watched Morgan take a sip. "Will you really get drunk?"

"Totally. I'm a lightweight."

"Nah, I mean—" Hmm. There's no nice way to ask if holographic life can be intoxicated.

"When I start ranting about my ex-boyfriends, then we'll know."

They both laughed. She took a swig of hard cider and sighed. "I can't believe Carruth got away."

Morgan scooted over to the outside edge of the tub. "Sweetie, that could have happened to anyone."

"But it happened to me."

"Have you thought about, you know?" Morgan glanced at the memory-treatment by the sink.

She scoffed. "Forgettin' about the people that killed you? No fuckin' way."

Morgan's eyebrows went up. "I'm worried you'll be hurt avenging my death."

"It ain't revenge. It's justice."

"Is it justice if you end up like me? All ghost and no shell."

"What if I—ya know? Forget too much."

"It's only one pill Golf Ball. It'll be okay."

"Mmm." Looking at the memory capsule automatically loaded text on an eye function. *Memory purge option expires at 04:00 September 24, 2163.* She took a deep breath. "My Mom's overdose wasn't an accident."

"What happened?"

"I went out to get some food. When I came back, she was on her bed with the empty bottle."

"We'll find her memories. Troy told me he has a way to check memory discs, so you'll know it's truly her. He's even done it before, because of what happened to his mom. She still passes DOLOS validation."

"I wish I could hug ya right now." She took a sip of cider. "What'd ya get?"

"Australian Surfer." Morgan smiled and held up her blue drink, which was halfway finished. "Blue Curacao, rum, grenadine, and some juice. I think it's pineapple, but it could be mango."

A meow and clawing noises at the bathroom door.

"That damn cat."

"Aw, Slippers misses you," Morgan said.

"Nah he's hungry." More scratches and meows from the door. "Alright already!"

After drying off she pulled pajamas from her bedroom dresser and closed the drawer in cautious, habitual silence. Slippers rubbed his orange and white fur against her ankles. His raised tail reached a knee. She tried putting the memory-treatment in her pant pocket, but of course the pocket just had to be made too small, so it had to be left on top of the dresser next to the picture to her sister Mary working at the gym, wearing a *Triskelion Fitness* tee.

In the kitchen Slippers purred and gobbled cat food. "Eat up ya little shit." She patted his head before stroking his furry ears. "I'm tryin' to fatten him up," she said to Morgan.

"Do you have a robot? I can possess it and feed him later."

"No, I don't got one."

"Oh." Morgan blinked a few times.

"They like, can't ever say no. That don't feel right to me."

"But, um, you have an oven. Doesn't it cook what you tell it to?"

Joan smirked. "Ovens aren't shaped like people. Some of them home-bots even look like real people."

"Protocol Five says anything with an off button isn't alive. Otherwise, the red-light district would be pitch black."

"Maybe we can get one for you."

"I don't need anything too flashy." Morgan squatted down by Slippers and watched him eat. "I can't wait to pet this little guy."

Joan yawned. "I'm goin' to sleep. Do you want me to leave the news runnin' or somethin'?"

Morgan stood. "No, it's okay. You can deactivate me. Wake me in the morning?"

"Okay. Good night." Using eye functions she navigated to Lazarus, smiling at Morgan before shutting off the hologram.

After checking the three locks at the front door twice, she grabbed her blaster on the kitchen counter from its holster and carried it a room away to the nightstand. Switching-off the lights, she climbed into bed while rotating her glowing mood twister to the Sleep-Now setting. Slippers jumped up and curled into a purring ball of fluffiness by her legs. She looked at the pitch-black ceiling for a minute before closing her eyes. An image kept coming to mind.

The pregnant woman murdered at the park earlier. Most of her vaporized in the blast. The hollowed sockets of the severed skull staring back.

Endless tossing and turning didn't make it go away, it only made Slippers jump off the bed and walk over to sleep on his small cushion by the dresser.

Sirens outside. Usually, they pass by with that Doppler sound or whatever it's called but this time it stayed close.

The floor was cold as she walked over and slid the transparency bar on the bedroom wall, transforming it into a window. Downtown Settlement Five was a horizon of skyscrapers. Neon holo-advertisements floated like balloons while others straddled rooftops like bright bridges as aircar headlights raced underneath. A police hovercar landed on the suspended landing ring 40 floors below, in the center of 12 sky-paths arranged in a circle like a fraudulent zodiac.

An officer stepped out to check the civilian hovercar he stopped. A woman in a neon skirt stumbled out and vomited. No one owns tonight.

The kitchen was dark without the lights on, and her eye functions deactivated. Filling a glass with water and setting down the memory-treatment, she paced while faint lines of light moved up and down the walls. Reflections from the holo-ads visible thru the window, floating between high-rises.

Pressing a thumb against the pantry door sprang a hologram, a virtual window thru the cold metal surface. Two shelves of drinks and packaged food, naturally arranged by deliciousness. Readouts confirmed 40 days and 40 nights worth, and no radiation had found its way inside. She kept her thumb there for a minute and stared.

A high-pitched ring as she popped her mood twister and held it in a palm with rapid breaths.

Both my arms shake as I lean against the pantry door. A tightness squeezes my stomach like a ravenous snake. This is how I really feel.

I pick the memory treatment up off the counter and rattle it between my fingers. The gel falls slowly back to the bottom, like a thirsty well. I look at the glass of water and think about how trivial it is to drink today. During the shelter years people would gather around a pipe, waiting for a drop to fall. A don't-die-of-thirst lottery, sometimes without a winner. That was the same day I saw a dead cat in a dim corridor on the way back to my family's cramped quarters. Maggots flowed like running water over its exposed rib cage. I covered Mary's eyes, so she didn't see.

I wonder if it's wrong, hiding the ugliness of it all from her. What she did see, like bullies stealing my food and calling me ugly, she seems to have forgotten. Like it all happened to someone else. Like bad memories are just grains of sand or drops of water falling between her fingers.

But that's how despicable people get away with it. Everyone forgets what they've done. There's no crime if there's no victim.

I set the pill back on the counter and press my mood twister back into place with a click.

While pouring the glass of water down the drain the apartment computer beeped and she looked up at the kitchen wallputer. The screen lit with an encrypted police message from Officer Norris.

A blurry image of the shooter that tried to kill me, she thought. The station AI enhanced the image. The shooter's face wasn't clear but obscured behind the flash of her blaster barrel. Baggy sleeves around her arms. A canvas jacket. It was unzipped, the flaps were parted, and she had a shirt, maybe a tee or a sleeveless under it. An image or something on it. Zoom in. An icon of a person running on a treadmill. Triskelion Fitness.

She dropped the empty glass on the countertop.

That's where Mary works.

# 14
## Demiurge

Inside a square room of gray walls within an abandoned brick and steel structure at the settlement's edge, Peter watched the Chrono app ticking away on his wrist-computer. One would imagine a Delphi employee could predict the actions required to arrive on time. He rested his elbows on the conference room table to roll up a sleeve. His wrist-tracker emitted pale white while *Ghost Mode* scrolled along the curved surface in black text.

Pain in his cracking neck, no matter how many angles he could turn it. He stood and circled the table to look through the room's large window. Beyond the lot where he parked his marked cruiser, a woman pushed a shopping cart with a toddler sitting inside, using a twenty pack of beer as a chair. They turned into the skid-row maze that stretched half a kilometer to the East Theodosian Wall, its glowing web lost in the morning sun.

A volumetric billboard probed the sky above the slums with an animation of a man opening the top bun of a burger, with a woman asking: *Ketchup or mustard? You are your choices, so choose happiness with Delphi Datacore.*

Five past eight on the Chrono app. When he arrives, I should get him to talk right away. That would be easier with Lyon, bad cop is etched into her DNA, though she's the last person I want hearing a word of this.

He circled the oval table and sat down again. Something crinkled inside his coat. Unbuttoning the top two rows of his peacoat and reaching inside he found *The Isis Manifesto*. When and where did this come from? Fanning the pages with a thumb produced the same sound Caramel does when she makes a Bronx cheer. Thick paper, impeccable print.

With ocular subroutines deactivated, nothing marked possessing it as illegal. Tabloids often quote it. He scratched his chin. How much could they quote it before their publication is also illegal?

He flipped to a page.

*If artificial life is to ever be considered equal to natural life, than our choices must be carefully made and calculated. Just as the past witnessed our creation, the present defines our great trial, and the future will be our eternal judge.*
*For Time is a savage God, born only of cruelty.*

Huh. Machines really can think for themselves.

"What are you reading?" A voice from behind him asked.

He quickly shoved the manifesto back in his coat pocket and spun the chair around. "A book."

"Ah." Captain Moira unbuttoned his camel coat and the flaps fell away, revealing an expensive suit. From an interior pocket he produced a fork-shaped scanner, which momentarily squeaked and projected blue light. He walked around and sat in a chair by the window, at the exact opposite side of the table. His face looked different, but not much older. Anti-radiation meds slowed the aging process for most healthy people. His hair had grown out and he didn't seem as tall as Peter remembered.

But the face was still unquestionably the same one that stared him down on the bridge of the *Reliant* fifteen years ago. Seeing it flooded Peter with memories of officers staring at their stations with sweaty foreheads, others racing around in a din of panic while currents shook the submersible. Orders Ramsey. Orders. Turn your key, Ramsey. Just turn your key.

"You called?" Moira asked.

"First, prove you're Captain Moira." He tossed his DOLOS validation tube.

"It has not been Captain in a long time. And meeting here, at an abandoned substation with inconsistent satellite coverage, implies that this is far from an official meeting, Ramsey." Moira tossed the tube back.

"Official? Would you prefer that? We can go downtown right now."

"And I can bring the entire Delphi legal team, which is larger than half the colonial militias. And we would simply predict all of your questions anyway."

"Right," he said more sarcastically than usual. Peter considered turning his mood-dial to an interrogation program, but it wasn't worth giving Moira the satisfaction of seeing him sweat. He loaded a volumetric display on his wrist-computer. The arson at the Delphi campus. "Is there anything you'd like to add to your company's statement?"

"Regarding Hiraeth Tower? No."

"Nothing you'd like to add?" He forced himself to smile.

"Is this what you had me drive all the way out to Woodland Heights for?"

"What's the matter? Not what you predicted?" he asked. Moira stood up and walked towards the door. Peter took a deep breath and used one foot to rotate the chair in the Captain's direction while he continued. "Someone torched one of your labs and broke into a nearby residence. It's listed as a burglary and yet somehow, nothing was reported stolen. And this morning Kyudo had to call in most of her favors with the Janissaries to patch up the manpower shortage for the next thirty days, because for the first time in years Mars Security has an empty bench. It's almost as though someone is hiring every mercenary and private investigator on the planet."

Moira stopped at the door and turned back with a shrug. "And?"

"And this." He loaded a volumetric of the Delphi prediction found in Carruth's apartment. The wrecked train. "Gosh, what would happen if your shareholders discovered a grease monkey from the wrong side of the tracks managed to rip you off and get away. Clean."

Moira approached, squinting before dragging and dropping the image to his own wrist. "Where did you get this?"

He crossed his arms. "You tell me, Mr. Predicts-Everything. But wait, I'm just wasting your time. Right?"

Moira slowly returned to the table and sat in the same chair by the window. "Delphi is willing to compensate you. You need only provide me with the time and place this company property was found."

He turned his chair towards Moira. "Oh, perfect. All I have to do is give you confidential information from an ongoing police investigation."

Moira clasped his hands together on the table. "What do you want?"

"Why don't we make a trade? I need to change someone's anticipated future."

"A minority outcome?" Moira squinted while turning his head up and looking down his nose at Peter. "Since when do you believe in fate?"

"I don't," he said. "But someone I know does. It's important to them."

"Did you meet someone?" Moira smirked.

"Don't you want to make a deal?"

"Certainly yes. But for what you are asking, we will need more from you."

"Right."

Moira leaned over the table and whispered, "Wasserman's Outcasts stole a predictive datacore."

"A datacore?" He lifted his eyebrows. "Son of a bitch. The Outcasts didn't steal memories of the past. They stole the futures predicted from them." Moira nodded. "But how did they access the core? Did you forget to set a password?"

"No, they were quantum encrypted. We do not know how they gained access to the electronic contents, but they did. And there are thousands of predictions on that core."

He scratched his chin. "Hasn't Wasserman claimed to be a Delphi employee from the future?"

"Come on Ramsey. Do not tell me you have become one of those conspiracy theorists. Do you think a time traveler would come back here and choose to live out in the wastelands, enjoying all the mutated discomforts life has to offer?"

"Right right right. So, you need this datacore returned?"

Moira adjusted his sleeves. "Correct. We need this stolen property returned and have predicted Wasserman is hiding it at his fortress."

"The Sandcastle?" He leaned back in the chair and scoffed. "Forget it."

"We have a considerable amount of influence with the Junta. We can make things happen for you. Do you think Major Kyudo will let you retire? With what she now knows? She is going to hold it over your head until one of you is dead. You can bet your rear end on that, Ramsey."

Delphi either predicted that Kyudo found out, or Moira is tossing that argument to test my reaction, he thought. "Kyudo? What does she have to do with this?"

Moira's shoulders broadened. "Get real Ramsey. Kyudo knows about your past, and these days, a mere accusation is more than enough."

"Then she knows about you too. And if my past becomes public, it's mutually assured destruction. Sound familiar?"

"I do not work for her or you. I work for humanity's bright future." Moira adjusted the knot of his tie. "If you do not take this deal, someone else will. And it will be them, and not you, who benefits from participating in destiny."

"The last time I listened to you the human race almost went fucking extinct." The table shook, and he realized his hands were grappling the edge.

"Those were orders, Ramsey. And it was the accepted wartime doctrine at the time. Any hesitation and we would have only flattened empty silos."

One hell of a price, paid in full by faceless victims. Numbers on a page. He released his hands from the table and turned the chair to stare out the window. Where do Moira's words land on the bullshit detector? Delphi wouldn't trouble themselves with a generous offer if there was an alternative. A predictable alternative.

Moira smiled and he turned his nose up, a gesture he consistently deployed at the smell of victory.

The volumetric billboard towering over the slums morphed from an advertisement for The Red Jacket Steakhouse into an animation of a slender, nubile woman pouring martinis, shots, and cocktails for lined-up bar patrons from a single Vodka bottle. *Brighten your day with Helios Vodka.* Even without subroutines, in his mind he could hear the alcoholic streams burbling. The cuts of the liquor along the inside of his throat with each gulp. The slowing numbness that would pull him from the chaotic world and cradle him in a calm bubble.

I haven't had a drink in years. People can change. I'm not the man who launched those missiles.

But even then, I was only a cog in a wheel. A robot in an assembly line. If I had said no, I would have been thrown in the brig and Moira would have found another officer to turn the missile key. I would have been executed for treason, and it would have changed nothing. Nada. Zip.

"Cloning and neuron upload operations can be expensive in the colonies," Moira said. "We can help reunite you with your family."

"Right," he said sarcastically.

"Bring me that core and I will show you what is possible."

No matter how satisfying it would be to tell Moira to go to hell, this isn't about me. It could be the only way for Carmen and Ariadne to live again.

Moira patiently tapped his fingers on the table, not randomly like Lyon does, but in a rhythm resembling an old song, though he couldn't remember which.

Does Delphi know my answer before I do, he wondered? "Right." He swiveled to face Moira directly. "We have a deal."

"You have made an excellent and forward-looking choice, Ramsey. Do not tell anyone else in your department anything regarding this matter. One of our predictive models indicates that there is a mole within your MOTH unit."

"A MOTH and a mole. Perfect. This keeps getting better and better."

"We are not certain who it is. Wasserman molds the minds of his imprints with dichotomous personalities, crafted from real but random memories. Consequently, their behavior rarely manifests a pattern."

"If an officer was brainwashed, they'd fail DOLOS validation."

"Unless the mole is human."

"Who would willingly help an Outcast?"

"Excellent question. We do not know. But tread carefully, Ramsey." Moira stood, rebuttoned his coat, and put on a pair of leather gloves that he pulled from a large pocket. "Find the datacore before the end of the week. After that, those predictions will expire."

"Expire?"

"Once everyone knows the future, it offers no advantage. It will be too late to change anything. Too late to make a different choice." Choices. How much can change with one choice? "When you find it, use this contact card." Moira produced a serial number on his wrist, then dragged and dropped a volumetric of it to Peter's wrist.

Can I trust Moira this time, he wondered?  "I want the minority outcome now.  Before I find the datacore for you."

Moira's lips bulged slightly, as though he were running his tongue along his teeth but kept his mouth shut.  "For whom?"

"Joanna Lyon."

Moira grinned.  "Your police partner.  Are you and her—"

"No."

Moira looked down at his wrist to tap a few buttons.  His eyes briefly narrowed, and he looked up.  "She does have a minority outcome.  However, it is on the missing datacore."

# 15
## Sphinx

On the sidewalk of a busy street Joan turned her body at sharp angles to narrowly pass other pedestrians. Most of the fools were playing with their cuffputers instead of looking where they were going.

The station computer had analyzed the records of every gym member and employee whose height matched Carruth's accomplice, cross-referenced with their tracked coordinates at the time of the shooting. It couldn't identify even one potential suspect.

She yawned. Bright yellow sheets of sunlight covered the tall canyon of glass towers. Mary was standing at the corner of Selma Avenue and Laurel Canyon, bundled up in her dark blue coat. Hopefully, she'll know some detail that leads to last night's shooter, or maybe even a name. But I can't ask directly, Joan thought. Mary can't know it's important.

After exchanging hellos and a hug, they shivered and waited at the crowded intersection until holographic text stacked in a bunch of languages labeled the crosswalk safe. She checked her mood twister as they crossed with a horde of pedestrians. Subtle-Interview. Should I be using an interrogation setting on my own sister, she wondered?

An advertising autocar stalked them curbside. *Emilie's Dress Shop* in scrolling text. The car drew two Narcissus holograms, mirror images of the sisters in a rotation of dresses. They stopped, and lifting a finger revealed a scrollbar to navigate outfits.

"Maybe you can find somethin' to go with that top. You know, the one you have from work."

"From the gym? Hah. I don't think they have anything that would match."

She tried to think of a clever follow-up question but stopped at an emerald-green dress and did a 360, looking back at herself. "Does my real butt look this good?" she asked.

"No," Mary answered cheekily. Her fingers scrolled to a tight-white dress.

"You know who else wears white?"

"Don't say a call girl."

"A prostitute," she said loudly.

The autocar raced away with squealing tires towards five wealthy-looking women in vibrant dresses. Each of them in turn unclamped their leather purses and took self-images while handing paper credits to a bum holding a sign. *Please help. Delphi predicts I'm unemployable.*

"You're just jealous jam," Mary said dismissively as she continued walking.

"I'm not jealous jam." She followed.

"Lemon jam."

"Whatever."

Rapid clops drew closer, and she turned towards the roadway. Two young boys, maybe around six or seven years old, ran past her and her sister. "No runnin' in the street."

The children ignored her and ran into a nearby alley between two brick buildings. On Wall-Thru their outlines stopped behind a dumpster.

Another advertisement car passed. New Eden organic plants. The Green Star Trading company's logo over a hologram. *Own your own piece of Eden.* A basil plant twisting around a stick.

"Officer?" A man's voice asked.

She turned and found a middle-aged man out of breath, heaving and leaning on his knees with his hands. He stood and straightened his vest, a circular logo spread across it. *Kate's Go-Ceries.* "Did you see two boys? They ran over here, not a minute ago."

"Yeah."

"Can you use your True-Sight ability to find them?"

"What did they do?" Mary asked.

"They stole a loaf of bread," he said.

Memories came back around like clothes rotating thru a laundry press. She and Mary had to scavenge for food every day when they were children. Back when life was underground. This world lit by sunlight is plentiful by comparison. An LED sign a block away flashed *Soup Kitchen* every few seconds.

The little thieving bastards ought to be hung up by their filthy little khakis. But Mary looked over with pleading eyes, so Joan put on an act of looking over all the buildings up and down the block, quickly moving past the dumpster in the dark alley where the two boys were still hiding. The little guys must be shivering back there. Maybe that's punishment enough.

"I'm sorry sir, I don't see 'em."

Mary smiled as the man frowned and walked away.

***

It wasn't even eight, but the Sphinx Café was already packed. Clatter and chatter from 100 occupied tables lit naturally under the angled sunroof, like the ceiling was one big skylight. Loud voices and waving hands from a table in a corner, but everyone at the table was smiling and laughing.

She followed Mary onto the quick queue, a large green mat. After a few seconds a chiming arrow pointed to the only available table, over by where the low brick wall met the slanted edge of the sunroof. Mary practically skipped instead of walking.

It was a circular table for two with a panoramic view of Galaxy Park. They each pulled out opposing chairs and someone cleared their throat nearby. A scowling woman lowered her eyebrows for a few seconds, but she quickly smiled and pointed to the badge on Joan's black-wool coat. "Thank you for your service."

She involuntarily smiled. "You're welcome."

The woman walked away, and Mary said in a childlike voice, "Lemon. My hero."

"Not heroine?"

Mary leaped into her chair and sat in it sideways to rest her feet up against the brick wall. "No. Just say no to drugs."

"You're ridiculous." She sat while sliding her chair closer to the table.

Mary chortled. "Can you believe we got a table by the window? I love having a cop sister."

From this high up, the cars looked like those little bugs from the wastelands. The ones that chomp long-dead trees into dust. She draped her coat over her chair. Mary, now sitting upright like a normal person, mirrored her, revealing a grey tank-top with a mermaid.

Maybe asking Mary about her job will give me a chance to find out what I need, she thought. It's not a gym member or an employee, so it must be someone not in their computer records. This would be so much easier without those damn privacy laws.

The table's holo-menus composed themselves with a luminous real-render under the bright sunlight. Mary quickly flipped thru like what men do with channels on the visual feed. Joan quickly checked a floating box next to *black coffee* and turned the holographic page to find French toast. That must come from Franch, that country Peter was ranting or raving about. She slowly swiped pages, her mouth watering with anticipation as much as hunger. Waffles, syrup. Whoever thought of that combination should have gotten a medal. Maybe someone thanked them for their service. She licked her lips while checking the box and pushing the *order* button. The holo-menu morphed into a smiley face and fell into the dimming lamptop.

Mary was still taking forever, humming something to herself.

"So, how's work goin'?" she asked.

"Amazing," Mary said while continuing to swipe thru the menu. "I switched shifts so I could watch Mom last night. Are you all set for tonight?"

"Yeah, I'm gonna bring her pasta."

"Oh, I was thinking of taking her pizza for lunch."

"She likes Italian food."

"She's doing better with those stretches I told you about. When we took our after-dinner walk, I barely had to slow down." She pressed a holo-button and her menu disappeared. Mary landed both elbows on the table and rested her chin on her clasped hands. "But I had to tell her who I was three times. It's like she's reliving the same day over and over again and she doesn't even know it." Mary's gaze fell to the table.

She reached across the table and grabbed Mary's hand. "We'll find her memories. I promise."

"Did you find a case so you can search the wastelands again? Or if it's in the Settlement, could I help you like last time?"

"Umm."

"I know last time that old cop said obstruction of justice, because I'm not a cop or whatever, but I'll be more careful this time."

Joan's stomach cramped. Tell Mary no and she'll lose hope. Say yes and she'll get herself arrested. Or worse. Worrying about Mom is already a fulltime job. "I'm lookin' into a few things. I'll let you know."

A wait-bot interrupted with a round tray held high in its shiny robotic fingers. The white edges of plates and cups peeked over the rim. It carefully set down two cups, two plates, and utensils.

"Thank you."

It smiled before rolling away with whirs.

"Did you just say 'thank you' to a robot?" Mary asked.

"Manners matter." She inhaled steam puffing up from the surface of the coffee and took a tongue-burning sip. Warmth from the hot liquid spread within her all the way to her toes, like it was life fuel or something. "I was thinkin' about your gym this mornin'. I—"

Mary smiled while looking at her plate but not when she looked over. "No waffles today?"

On the plate was a croissant sandwich and a hash brown. This does not match what was ordered. Lifting the edge of the sandwich, melted cheese peeled away from a square patty of scrambled eggs and a round one of sausage.

"Did they mix up your order?" Mary shoveled a fork-full of home fries into her mouth.

"It's not a big deal." She took a small bite from one of the narrow ends. It wasn't bad.

A voice across the café raised into commotion. Screams directed at a wait-bot. Its lowered head changed to an unhappy emoji. Some screaming guy in a golf cap. Forest Lyon. He smashed a plate of waffles on the table in front of him and screamed profanity and something about a breakfast sandwich.

Joan lowered her head and wolfed down that stupid golfer's breakfast order, which suddenly went from not bad to delicious. "That mother fucker," she mumbled with a mouthful.

Mary covered her mouth, concealing laughter with one hand as she turned her plate to examine her own sandwich. It was a BLT on flat bread, cut into triangular quarters and arranged like a pyramid. Mary lifted one of the quarters and took a bite. Juicy bits of tomato fell onto her plate.

The fresh sight pulled an old image to mind. Scraps of bread floating in dirty water, years ago in that god-awful fallout shelter. When a lower level flooded and a search for food had only yielded fragmented slices, soggy and coated in mud. Who in their right mind would deliberately eat a soggy sandwich?

She covered her mouth to conceal a belch that embraced revulsion, like the croissant sandwich bounced from her stomach to halfway up her throat.

"Joanie?"

"Thought I was gonna barf," she muttered hoarsely.

"Gross." Mary munched on a fork-full of home fries.

"Gross yourself." She gulped her coffee. "Potatoes for potato?"

"Don't even."

"When your hair turns white, I'm gonna have to call you onion."

"Oh, I can't wait." Mary took another bite from her sandwich. More of that repulsive tomato leaked and splattered.

"So, I was thinkin' of tryin' out your gym."

Mary sat up straight and tossed some of her brown hair out of her face. "Oh yeah?"

"Mm hmm."

Mary continued with another quarter of her sandwich. "I thought you liked the police gym. Doesn't Troy workout at the crack of dawn?"

"I could try nights. If you're workin' and it's not busy, we can catchup."

Mary set her food down and lifted a teacup from an adorable little saucer, blowing air over the steaming liquid before taking a sip. It carried the smell of lavender. Mary has an almost-identical fragrance she puts on every morning so they kind of like, blended or something. The combination won by a nose. "Silly Lemon. Any nights I work you'll have to watch Mom."

"Oh, yeah. You're right. I just, uh, saw this really tall woman wearin' a shirt from your gym and was ya know, thinkin' about it." She fidgeted a bit and hastily took a sip of coffee. "She was taller than you, even."

"Taller than me? Hah." Mary's teacup landed back on the saucer with a porcelain clank. "I signed up a woman last week for a free two-week trial. She wore these obnoxious high-heeled boots that I swear added 20 centimeters to her height. When she came back in running shoes, she was Lemon sized."

The crime-scene scans must have missed the shooter's shoes and estimated her height incorrectly. And if she just signed up at Triskelion Fitness for a trial, the computer might not have her billing records yet. Checking satellite records again but without the wrong height data could match potential suspects. But that could be a long list. She placed her hands flat on the table. "What's she doin' with heels like that? Is she a stripper or somethin'?"

Mary chortled. "She works over at the starport." With a giant bite Mary was finally halfway done with her BLT.

"Are a lot of people signin' up? For the free two weeks?"

Mary grabbed a napkin and cleaned her face. "Yeah, but I remember her."

"Because of her ridiculous shoes?"

"No. She said she's friends with a cop, so I asked her if she knew you, but she said no." Mary bounced in her chair slightly and leaned over with a smile. "Why? Is this about one of your cases?"

"Nah." Joan shook her head and took a bite of her hash-brown while looking out the window at the cars and people far below, on the boulevard between the block of skyscrapers and verdant park.

Shit. Joan had told Mary a hundred times what operational security is and to not give out certain information. If the high-heeled woman Mary met is friends with a cop, then maybe it's the wrong person altogether. Or the cop friend is dirty. But if I don't get answers, Joan thought, then someone else might question Mary officially about this. Then she might stick her beak where it's dangerous.

The last sip of coffee was cold, and she turned back to her sister, who's food was nearly gone. A beep from the floor.

A cleaning bot the size of her cat sweeping up crumbs. When it was done its little antennae eyes lowered, sadness, so she found a few crumbs on her plate to drop in front of him.

"Is that a new coat?" Mary asked while looking at the garment draped on the back of Joan's chair.

She lifted a crisp edge of the dark wool. "Nah, I just had it cleaned," she lied.

Mary crossed her arms. "Don't tell me you got a robot."

"Of course not. Don't be ridiculous." She finished her hashbrown. "Ya got time for a turnover?"

"Were trees ever real?" Mary asked.

She smiled. "What?"

"Doesn't tea come from a tree?" Mary sipped what was left of her tea.

"I suppose it does."

Mary leaned forward. "A real tree? I mean, I can't believe you once climbed one. How can something that big that doesn't breathe, or move, be alive?"

"It's just a big plant." A hovercar passed by the window, the echoes of its trailing engine slowly fading. Tapping a finger against the table's lamptop loaded the menu and she searched again. "Where'd that come from?"

"Nothing. Just a book I've been reading."

"A book about tea?" She swiped on the holo-menu to cupcakes. Strawberry and cream. She paused at chocolate and salted caramel and her mouth watered.

"No, *The Grasshopper and the Almond Tree.*"

She stopped mid-swipe and sighed. "Potato, that's a heap a conspiracy rubbish."

"No, it's not. He found different manifests for the *Corvis*, the last ship to leave. Well, the last one before—" Mary leaned over the table, her long strands of brown hair colliding with the holo-menu, and whispered with a smile, "The manifests each had a different list of last-minute passengers who fled at the last possible minute. Isn't that weird?"

"Mary, any old fool can slap together a fake computer record with a bunch a made-up names." She swiped to turnovers. Cherry topped with a white glaze, sprinkled with dots of vanilla. Apple topped with white frosting and little golden raisins. She licked her lips.

"The *Corvis* departed from the same airbase where we lived. Well, I wasn't born yet. Do you remember it at all?"

The sun was brighter, and the air smelled like heaven, she thought. Until it all started. Screams, then the sky was on fire. Mom somehow running with a pregnant belly, one of her hands pulling me along towards the shelter. Dark and crammed with dirty people. After the heavy metal doors closed, stragglers banged on them for days, unanswered pleas to be let in. Then silence.

By the time Mary was born, decency was a slipping memory, and Dad had to beat up two beggars to get Mom to the shelter maternity ward. The only good deed that deadbeat ever did.

She bent over in the chair, pretending to retie her shoes while turning her mood twister two rotations, to Stoic-Calm. "I dunno. It was a place with houses. Sometimes a plane or ship or somethin' flew over."

Mary whispered, "Dr. Hawthorne, the author, he believes there are other universes. Different realities, even ones where the war never happened."

She sighed and used a finger to dismiss the holo-menu. "You sound like one of them wasteland rebels."

"Can you imagine what the world would be like? I know the holo dome has the *Old Earth Sim*, but still. Is that thingy even close? You know, and I think, I'm not sure, wouldn't we be different too? All of us?"

Only Mary could be so naïve. She was born younger and somehow stayed that way. Maybe because she never saw the things I have, Joan thought. She could have been more worldly at her age if I wasn't there to cover her eyes when she was a child. Or warn her to hide when— "Nah, people wouldn't be any different. The few good ones would still be good and the rest of 'em would just hide their shittyness below the surface, like that sulfuric lava that killed all them people on Io."

Mary turned her lips inward and leaned back, shrinking into the chrome chair until she seemed shorter than Joan. Her head turned away, towards an animated image hanging on one of the café's brick walls showing a bright blue sky above the domes of Martian greenhouses, surrounded by red desert.

She rested her chin on a fist. Mary's still thinking about Mom and the cupful of gels she took. A bitter taste for her children to swallow. Out the window, far down to the roadway below, ground traffic stood as still as the stone remains of the Sahara Sphinx. A name for this new gym member, and her cop friend, would be useful. But I'm the only wall between Mary and this vicious world, she thought.

***

Two clanks echoed as Joan drove over a metal grate by the holographic sign *Inglewood Intergalactic Starport* and thru the Lincoln Boulevard auto-gate. Both parallel lines of concrete walls ended and the top third of the windshield filled with the sight of four gateways that gripped the bright sky, each of them a curved-cornucopia arrangement of expanding rings from the ground to the stratosphere.

"Have you ever been to the starport before?" Morgan asked from the passenger seat. Her holographic body flickered as they passed under the shadows of the sky rings, like driving thru a tunnel with evenly spaced lights.

"Nah. What are those for?"

"The magnetic rings? They're for energy efficiency. When's the last time you had a $40 steak?"

"Never."

Cracking sonic booms shook the windows as a starship burst thru the atmosphere high on the horizon. Its burning corona faded as it decelerated from one of the highest and widest rings to a smaller one at the surface.

"Without those they'd be $80 steaks." Morgan tapped and swiped small holograms on her side of the dashboard. "So, get this."

"Did you get a name?"

"Gemma Overton," Morgan said while expanding one of her small holograms into a large one. A woman's face with dark hair over brown eyes and a resting bitch face. "She matches the height, the revised height range." Morgan turned, leaning into the seat with a shoulder. "Gemma's height is 155 centimeters. DOLOS records match her at your sister's gym every morning this week, and she was un-tracked for 90 minutes last night. A perfect overlap with your hostile encounter. And you'll never guess where she works."

Traffic in front of her slowed to turn into the passenger terminal and she braked. "Instant Stellar?"

"Green Star Trading Company. Sound familiar?" Morgan asked. Joan shrugged. "Those two you found in the wastelands yesterday, Andrea and Luke Aeneas, the stowaways on *The Salamander*."

"Which Green Star chartered."

"Precisely."

The road curved around a ring of skyscraper-sized ships that appeared to float. Each suspended inside a circle of tall, magnetic columns topped with sharp curves, like the Earth had wrapped them in claws. The cargo terminal came into view and Navi drew orange arrows and text for the Green Star Trading Company.

She pulled into the adjacent lot, between a dive bar and the Janissary barracks, parking five spaces from a dust-covered coupe. The warehouse in question stood 200 meters ahead. Morgan zoomed the windshield in on the Green Star Trading Company logo over the cargo terminal's revolving-door entryway. On the sides, the grill-plates of trucks stuck out of loading bays. Rubber docking-sleeves engulfed the back-third of them. Behind the terminal on both sides, an endless rainbow-sea of customs-sealed cargo containers obscured the rest of the starport.

The car-computer moved lines around the edges of the three-story structure, measuring 2187 square meters. But no rendered images of the interior.

"Can you setup a structure scan?" she asked.

"There's a queue," Morgan said.

Joan pushed the Satellite Bandwidth button on the console 50 times, sighed, and leaned back in her seat.

The police wireless button lit up on the dashboard console with the name Abbie Boothe. Joan turned up the volume as a voice said, "Officer Mayfleet. Officer Mayfleet. Come in, Rapid-Fire Greta."

After a few seconds, a response crackled, "This is Mayfleet. Go ahead, Abbie."

Abbie said in a sarcastic tone, "I hear a squeaking sound. I think it might be a mouse. What should I do?"

Morgan chortled and looked over. "Greta mag-dumped that mutant rat Thursday."

Joan clicked the transmit button. "You should definitely draw your service blaster and empty your *entire* magazine at it, Abbie. That's what any sensible person would do."

Laughter roared on the wireless.

"Joan, that rat was larger than your cat," Mayfleet said.

She clicked transmit again, "Jesus Rapid-Fire, did you have to shoot it 24 times? Maybe aim next time."

"Good idea Joan. Next time I'll shoot for a hole in one," Mayfleet said to another uproar of cackling and jeering.

Her face turned hot, and she slowly backed her finger away from the transmit button.

The car computer beeped with a rotating hologram of the cargo terminal. 12 human workers and over 50 robots moved up and down the corridors. Livestock on the first floor. Grains and dry goods on the second and third. Saying "Gemma" zoomed in on a human outline near the structure's main entrance. "She's in the lobby. I'm gonna go grab her." She put her hand on the door handle.

"Wait. If you arrest Gemma, she'll clam up. And since she's obviously a smuggler, all we need is evidence to flip her. She'll have no choice but to cooperate. Or—"

"Or?"

"Or the evidence leads directly to Wasserman. Then we don't need her."

She chuckled. "Okay, it's a good plan, I like it. Did the computer locate any contraband?"

Morgan used a reverse-pinch gesture to zoom out to the maze of cargo containers around the Green Star building, 12 of which were clouded on the hologram. "See those satellite-shielded containers?"

"Yeah. They must be for smugglin'. Searchin' all 'em might take a while."

"You can't go right in there. They'll remotely incinerate those containers before you get within 20 meters."

"How'd you know that?"

Morgan looked over. "I worked that undercover case in June. Remember?"

"Oh yeah, them Orion Pirates."

Morgan snickered. "One of them was cute. Too bad he'll be in prison until he's a shriveled prune."

A subroutine beeped a warning message: *Officer Sullivan, Morgan, accepted a memory treatment at 14:25 June 22, 2163. Please re-read the attached cover story regarding the Orion Pirates.* Morgan had fallen in love with her criminal target, the handsome pirate. Arresting him broke her heart.

She fidgeted and stretched her arms. "Maybe I can go in there and pretend to be a civilian or somethin'."

"She knows your name. Because of your sister."

"Oh fuck. You're right."

"Could she recognize you? From last night?"

"I don't think she got a good look at me. But she could of used a recordin' function or somethin'."

"Not at the barrier wall. There's too much radiation. Your picture isn't on any social platforms, is it?"

"No."

"Good. We can use Janus."

"Janus?"

"Yeah. Can you toggle my Lazarus visibility setting to public?"

"Okay." She checked the holographic button.

"Thank you. Now we need Troy." Morgan pushed a button and Troy's holographic face popped up next to a dial button.

"Wait a sec." She pulled down the sun visor, flipping open the overhead mirror to examine her reflection's hair, teeth, and face.

"Golf Ball, you're adorable. Can I push the button now?"

"Alright already." She slammed the visor back into place.

Morgan dialed and Troy answered. The car hologram morphed into an avatar of Troy's face.

"Joan. Hello." Troy's eyes lit up with a grin.

Joan couldn't help smiling.

"We need a Janus package," Morgan said.

"Is that Morgan?"

She looked over at Morgan and back. "Yeah."

"You're running her on an unsanctioned Lazarus hologram?" Troy stopped smiling. "Are you trying to get me fired?"

"Aw, Kyudo will never fire you," Morgan said. "All we need is for you to encode my mind so Joan can run me on her mood coin. We need to infiltrate this location." She split the hologram, Troy on one half and the cargo terminal on the other. It drew a starship taxiing onto the launchpad a few hundred meters behind the building. Thru the windshield a wing edged over the distant stacks of shipping containers.

"I've only heard of Janus," she said.

"It's like being possessed. Just don't end up like Sergeant Walsh," Troy said. "He loaded an auctioneer Janus-personality and ran it too long. It fused with his neurons. Now he's on Venus, auctioning sugar cane futures."

She shifted her weight and began tapping her foot on the floorboard.

"You'll be fine Joan," Morgan said.

"So, like, you and I merge?" she asked. Morgan died after creating her Lazarus image. But she grew up in an underground shelter, just like me, she thought. Which one of us has the more terrorizing memories to bleed into the other? The last thing you want is your best friend judging you. Joan's palms were sweaty as she let them slide down the edges of the steering wheel and onto her lap. "Maybe we should wait for Peter."

"I agree," Troy said. "If your cover is blown you will need to be extracted."

"Look." Morgan pointed to the holographic scan. Hauling robots moved Container Five off the stacks. It slowly fell towards the ground, where it hovered, bouncing and floating towards the terminal. "Don't you want to catch them?

These people didn't just shoot me in my armor and bruise me. They killed me."

"Of course I do." She pulled her blaster and chambered a round. "Troy, let's do this."

"We can't take a weapon in there. They'll scan for it. A stun stick, or a smaller caliber blaster wrapped in scan-foil could work," Morgan said. "Troy, we'll need a different outfit."

"A drone is already enroute." Troy smiled like a Cheshire cat. His keyboard clicked loudly as he typed. "Going once, going twice." He slammed a single key with a finger. "Sold!"

Morgan's hologram dissolved into cloudy wisps that sank into Joan's mood twister like they were being slowly vacuumed. The twister glowed bright purple.

Joan's eyes twitched and her head shook uncontrollably, like it was inflating like a balloon.

# 16
## Lead Lock

A large fan mounted on a high window of the police substation pushed curved lines of shadow over Peter's desk while he sipped from a bottle of orange energy-milk and stared at a button flashing *Submit* beneath volumetric documents.

He had typed up his meeting with Moira, including the claims regarding a MOTH mole. Telling Kyudo could start a witch hunt. Everyone will be guilty until proven innocent. But if I don't tell her and the mole harms someone, I'd be responsible. The mole could compromise Lyon and be what gets her killed. He moved his finger towards the volumetric button. Just give it to Kyudo. Wash my hands of it, he thought, and whatever happens is because of her and not me.

He pulled his finger away and looked up at the industrial blades of the whirring fan impatiently spinning against time.

After a sip of milk, he leaned back in his chair. What's Wasserman's angle with stolen predictions? Dr. Baloney says he's a time traveler from the future, but tricking people into believing that won't remove him from the most-wanted list. Unless he brainwashes everyone. Stealing them gives him nothing. Unless a prediction would have uncovered his mole.

Leaning back over the desk again he launched a query of MOTH personnel, filtered by the height of Lyon's unidentified shooter.

Anastasia Hamilton. A red head. A service timeline mostly blurred out except a few segments, patterned like the sharp keys of a piano. Huh.

"She's married Peter."

Over his shoulder was Kyudo.

"Major." He pivoted his chair around. Do I tell her about the potential mole?

"Where's Joan?"  Kyudo clasped her hands and rested them on the lower buttons of her dark uniform.

"She hasn't come in yet."

Kyudo cleared her throat. "Joan's at the spaceport."

His palms fell onto the chair's armrests.  That Outcast woman at Lansing's apartment warned me to not go there.  Not that the Outcasts are renowned for honesty.  "The spaceport?  What is she doing there?"

"She's not my partner.  Though if she was, I would want to find out.  Quickly."

He turned and loaded the phone routine, but Kyudo reached over and swatted the volumetric app away.

"Joan entered a warehouse posing as a merchant.  Calling her is inadvisable."  Kyudo pulled an ignition key from her pocket and dropped it into his hand.

I can tell her about Moira's claims later.  Besides, she'll want proof and I can't drop Moira's name.

***

He parked next to Lyon's parked vehicle and got out.  Sonic booms jumped up and down in his ear canals as a Mercurial Interceptor passed through the magnetic rings of the gateway, catapulted into the blue dome.

"Do you read me Castor?" he asked.

"Loud and clear Peter," Castor said on Peter's hidden ear com.  "Joan is inside the Green Star warehouse."  Lyon's location, within a concrete structure a few hundred meters ahead, lit up on the Wall-Thru subroutine.  Another location as well, a recess in the brick wall of an adjacent building.  "This position should offer concealment.  And you'll be close if Joan needs backup."

"Right."  He followed the flashing indicators but stopped by a dumpster flush against a building and tall enough to hide him.  "What is she doing in there, Castor?"

"Joan believes Carruth is involved in a smuggling operation here."

Peter peeked around the brick corner at the Green Star warehouse loading bay. Only parked vehicles in sight, though the hydraulic sounds of robotic loaders echoed across all ninety meters of the paved alleyway. Easily heard over the light drops of acidic rain.

The creaking sound of a metallic door on his right. The dive bar across from him. A pair of intoxicated clone-pilots stumbled out. Half-filled bottles of Blue Europa Gin dangled from each hand. Their one day of inebriated reprieve from a gravity-less existence of shuttling colonial food here and leaving with machine tools and medicines. The glowing-orange bands of visa trackers pulsed on rolled-up sleeves, guaranteeing a cyanide death one step past the spaceport perimeter.

He crossed his arms and leaned against the building's bricks. Blue police transponders from a dozen drones circling high overhead, far enough from Green Star that they wouldn't draw immediate suspicion.

A gust of wind passed, strong enough to flop around the bottom quarter of his peacoat. If Lyon doesn't find the Delphi cores, what then? Where would Carruth put them? Off-world and outside the jurisdiction of the settlements, though a customs scan would spot the sequence code and he'd be in cuffs within seconds. So, Lyon is probably right about him working with a smuggling ring. But smugglers would want cash up front. And after Lyon being shot last night, the heat is on, so they'd ask for a taller stack than a two-bit tech could front. Where would he hide? Not in the warehouse, but he'd want to stay close.

A creak from the dive bar's door. A man in a hooded sweatshirt and beaten-up jeans walked out and into the alley leading to the warehouse loading dock. His hood raised and no tracking ID on the subroutine, even after squinting. Could be a clone with a glitching visa-tracker.

No blinks from Lyon's position or anything else on tactical. *Offline* scrolled in large red letters. He rolled up his sleeve and checked his wrist. The green tracker faded to a darker shade. I must be in the magnetic wake of a satellite umbrella.

Peter looked back towards the man walking away. It's Carruth. Unfortunately, I can't consult with command without letting him get further away and escaping.

He took one step outside of his computer-assigned position. And another. The steps accelerated until he was gaining on the unidentified man.

As he passed the loading dock, robotic loaders as wide as pianos looked over but continued lifting metal crates with their giant claws. One kept staring though. He gave it a thumbs up and it beeped before returning the gesture.

The alleyway curved and ended with a chain-link fence. Beyond it a path, wide enough for three people to walk in parallel, between stacks of cargo containers.

A narrow opening cut into the fence with a scanner welded above it. It drew a yellow rectangle on the entry way and ran two separate white beams in random patterns inside the bounds. A sign in large red letters: *Authorized Personnel Only*.

No barbed wire over the fence. He wedged a foot into the wire and climbed. The rusted metal links cut into his fingers enough that one of them bled. At the top he realized the fence looked shorter from the ground and moved one foot over the edge to climb down. The metal wire rattled loudly as his fingers slipped and he fell.

A sharp pain in his left elbow. "Damnit," he cried out while rolling onto his back. Light rain dropped between the towering cargo stacks. Standing up slowly he gripped his throbbing arm.  A cold wetness around his left foot, submerged in a puddle.  Slightly radioactive water based upon text rendered on the toe cap, and it made a sloshing sound as he resumed walking.

At a T-intersection the path opened to a wide cargo-corridor.  It was bright with sunlight, which bounced off the beads of water rolling down the sides of the colorful containers and into thin streams along the pavement.  The hooded man was a hundred meters on the right, walking away.

Peter pulled his stun gun and quickened his pace, accelerating the crunches of tiny pebbles under his boots.

The hooded man looked back.  Carruth.  He waved at something on the left and ran towards a narrow path between stacks.

Peter aimed his stun gun with both hands. "Freeze! Police!"  He pulled the trigger, missed, and ran after Carruth.

After a hundred meters of throbbing legs his back began sweating and his lungs couldn't capture air.  A metallic thud rang from the cargo container on his right.  Something hot brushed his face.  Another thud.  The smoking ember of a blaster slug.

He skidded to a halt.  Pops and thuds landed in a line rapidly moving towards him.  He fell backwards onto the ground and rolled over to crawl, his left elbow still sore.

For thirty seconds no one shot at him, so he sat up against the nearest container to cough and catch his breath.  Where's the loose cannon?  Wall-Thru blinked *Offline* in red.  No satellite connection, no subroutines.  Huh.

After several seconds his ears were still ringing, but different.  A faint buzzing from above.  Between the vertical stacks, one of the police drones high enough in the blue sky that it looked smaller than his thumb.

Of course.  Short-wave wireless could work within the jamming cloud.  A few fiddling keystrokes on his wrist-computer and the visual feed loaded on a routine.  A bird's eye view of the cargo stacks.

A prone figure two rows over between two containers arranged as an arrow's point, with a large enough gap to fire through but close enough to provide excellent cover. A few clicks zoomed in. *MAR-SEC* on their armor and blaster rifle. The Mars Security Company. Perfect. Big guns, small brains, quick-pull triggers.

He zoomed out until he spotted Carruth. Over two hundred meters away by now and heading for a ship on a runway.

Clicking the drone com-bridge app flashed a no signal icon with an error chime. No chance to call for backup.

With the drone's weapon systems, he targeted the mercenary. Nine high-explosive, green javelins loaded. Four lines moved from the corners of the visual feed until they formed a beeping square around the prone target. He squinted. That mercenary has an hourglass figure. It's a her, not a him. Is that meaningful? He scratched his head, the short hairs wet with rain.

No.

On his wrist a red button flashed *Fire Ordinance*. What if she has children? Then she should have gotten a less hazardous job. But she's probably being jammed too. Without satellite routines, perhaps she didn't know she was shooting at a cop.

The flashing big red button. He moved his finger over it, and it hovered as though they were magnets arranged to repel one another.


6,261,997


What's one more death on top of the others? His chest constricted, a sharp pain with each breath.

He lost track of time, but it was long enough for drops of rain to pebble the surface of the screen, turning the red button blurry. Some landed in his eyes, and he blinked before raising the wrist-computer to his mouth to use the audio interface. "Cancel fire mission."

Returning to the drone's visual scan, he determined a longer path to the runway that safely navigated around the mercenary but required doubling back.

# 17
## Silver Key

High-heeled feet passed the lobby's revolving door, clunking with each step as Morgan Sullivan crossed the Green Star logo etched into the marble floor. Wrapped in a bright turquoise dress and Joan's body. It was like floating, witnessing a version of yourself that could walk in heels without falling over. Like being a passenger in your own car. Morgan stopped at the lobby's imposing front desk. Made of granite it spanned half the room.

An administrator in a business suit smiled. A scrolling hologram identified her as Gemma Overton. A flat picture of her hung on the wall behind the luminous projection. Employee of the month. "Can I help you?" Gemma asked.

"Good morning. Do you have any outbound gaps?" Morgan asked. *Whatever that means.*

*It means do they have surplus space on any outgoing transport.*

"Who are you?" Gemma asked.

"Evelyn Campbell." *That's our cover name? The police computer assigned it.* Morgan produced a holographic business card and shook Gemma's cold and clammy hand. *She's hiding something. Definitely. But she doesn't sound like the voice I heard at the station.*

Gemma turned her nose up and asked, "Have you done business with us before?"

"Not at this location. I've shipped a few thousand kilos through your other terminals."

Gemma tapped computer keys on a flat-computer behind the tall desk. "There are no records of you or the Silver Key Trading Company in our main datacore." She waved a go-away gesture. "Our Five headquarters is another kilometer down the road. Right next to the main passenger terminal."

"Yes, I know. I'd go there if I wanted to pay full price," Morgan said. Opening their purse, turquoise with an animated surface, like the flowing veins of light at the bottom of a swimming pool, she produced a small fortune in shiny-copper contracts. She used Joan's short but freshly-painted-red nails to spread them like a fan. The gloss of the untraceable serial numbers brightly reflected in Gemma's eyes. A breath drew in the odor of the textured bills, money that even smelled rich. *The more valuable something is, the better it should smell.*

Joan exerted control of her hand and snapped the purse shut to conceal her Caduceus stun baton and backup blaster, wrapped in layers of scan-shielding. A retina-function flared at a scanner above the company logo on the wall. The unmistakable light spectrum of a behavior-cylinder. Ms. Overton suspects a sting.

"Are you from around here?" Gemma asked.

"Settlement Two."

Gemma nodded with an open mouth. "How long have you been at Silver Key?"

"Six years."

"You know, you seem familiar," Gemma said. "Have we met before?"

"I'm not sure," Morgan said.

"Do you go to Triskelion Fitness? The gym?" Gemma asked.

Her throat shook, like a voice was trying to speak but couldn't. "Yes," Joan said. "I go running every day. And lifting sometimes." Her forced enunciation wove an unnatural cadence through the air. For most people, pronouncing g at the end of a word isn't a huge deal. *Why are you so hard on yourself?*

Their face flushed. Troy spoke into their hidden ear com, "Relax Joan. Let Morgan do her thing." *Exactly. We got this.*

"Any brothers or sisters?" Gemma asked.

"Only child." That's not true. Mary. A wave of emotion quickly swept under a carpet by her mood twister.

"Joan, you're doing great," Troy said.

"Parents?" Gemma asked.

A knot burned in her chest. Janus was a terrible idea.

"Joan, stop fighting her," Troy said.

*Could you think of something else? Like chocolate chiffon pie?*

With a deep but discrete breath, the muse took back over, thumbing through the copper certificates. "Died in the war," Morgan said.

Gemma performed another sequence of hidden keystrokes, and the cylinder scanner deactivated. "What do you need to ship and when?"

"Radiation wands and moisture harvesters. 400 kilograms. Today."

Gemma's mouth fell open. "400? Today?"

"Yes. Can you help?"

Gemma's mouth closed, and she licked her lips. "For $60,000 I can have it there by the 20th of December."

Morgan laughed. *What an insult.* "I could get a better deal at Instant Stellar."

"So, go there."

Joan reasserted control over her body and said, "Okay." She stuffed the currency notes in the purse and carefully turned to leave. Morgan mentally fought nearly as much as the heels, so each awkward step took a few seconds, giving the unintended appearance of negotiation theatrics. *Where are we going? Stop. This damn Gemma is unreasonable. Negotiating is the art of reasoning with the unreasonable.* Sometimes you have to put your foot down. But that's hard to do in these stupid heels. *Slow down sweetie. You have to balance more weight on the front of your foot. Like you're a velociraptor.*

"Wait. Wait. Alright alright. $50,000," Gemma said.

Morgan looked back halfway to the front door, forcing Joan to cease her attempts at tripping over herself. "$30,000."

"$40,000."

Morgan gracefully carried herself back to the desk.  It must be magic.  Morgan magic. *No magic required. Practice makes perfect.* "$35,000."

"I'll take $35,000 and 12 water purification filters," Gemma said.  After a brief stare-down Morgan smiled.  "And you have *got* to tell me where you got those heels."

"I can give you a pair.  Size eight?"

"Good guess," Gemma said.  She extended her hand, which Morgan shook.  "When can you deliver?"

"2:30."  Morgan counted out $35,000 in certificates and placed them in Gemma's eager hands.  What a mad lass.

Gemma said under her breath while checking her chronograph, "Less than four hours."  She tapped her nails on the counter and smiled.  "Please wait here."  She placed the certificates into a brown nylon envelope and sealed it with thermal staples while muttering, "Don't want anyone peaking."  Gemma disappeared into a long hall through two swinging doors adjacent to the desk.

The doors swung closed with a snapping lock.  Red lights blinking over them and an alarm blasting.

"Troy, what's happening?" Morgan asked.

"Their security spotted Peter and opened fire.  Time for plan B."

"They shot at a peace officer?" Morgan asked.

Behind the long desk, her own reflection in the polished company logo.  The mirror image winked despite no feeling that her eyes were moving and no change in vision. *Be careful sweetie.* Joan exhaled with more breath than her lungs could hold.  Morgan evaporated on the emotion orb, her clouded mind burned clear like fog in sunlight, and Joan ascended again to the throne of her own mind. She rotated her hands, cracked her fingers, and breathed deeply.

"Okay Joan, Janus is offline. Go dark now," Troy said.

A wrist-button activated the ghost function and the infiltration overlay, which flashed green arrows along the floor. A computer-optimized path to the target container 144 meters ahead. Wall-Thru rendered employees as red outlines.

"There's one foreman, two administrators, four techs, and a five-strong security team," Troy said. "Without your tracker broadcast, they'll ID you as an illegal intruder instead of a constable."

"10-4."

"I'll hack the door. Standby."

She turned her mood orb to Infiltration as the two doors unlocked with a beeping green light. Carefully pushing beyond the *Authorized Personnel Only* sign, a long, empty corridor with intersecting hallways. Evenly spaced recesses. Her two removed heels landed in one of them and on the far end of the hallway the distance function measured 89.9 meters.

Both bare feet shook on the cold fiberglass tiles. The floor vibrated from reactors and machinery humming faintly in distant rooms. Echoes of hydraulic cargo bots blended with the alarm.

Her toenails stopped short of a function-provided blue line. 10 meters from a wall-mounted security scanner.

"They're offline," Troy said.

She held her breath and crossed the threshold. After 20 meters, she peeked at an open door on the right.

A giant garage-like room with a matrix of overhead lights but dark corners. Three lanes of hovering cargo containers being loaded with boxes and barrels by teams of robots. One container on the ground in the middle lane, larger and more of a square than a rectangle.

The alarm stopped. Gemma's voice shouted orders. Two guards, armed with assault blasters and in mercenary armor, ran out thru the open loading bays.

"Scanners in that room have infrared and audio sensors," Troy said. "I have a crack for the infrared, but these audio parameters are hardcoded. Move quietly."

The infiltration function rang a klaxon in her ears. Panic as a single human outline on the left moved towards the corridor. 11 seconds until he would clear a corner 15 meters ahead.

"Hurry but stay quiet." Troy updated her functions. Arrows on the floor leading into the large room.

The line of containers offered concealment as she followed the bright lines, walking quickly but quietly. A leftover, thoughtless habit of moving each foot forward but only shifting her weight after it landed. The lines led to the near left corner. A room marked *ROBOT DIAGNOSTIC BAY*.

"How on Earth are your decibels in the teens?" Troy asked.

On Wall-Thru someone else approached the nearest line of cargo containers. She sprinted as the red outline stepped within five meters of her position. The purse started slipping. The one-meter alarm boomed as she slid into the room, banging her knee and tearing a corner of her dress. Crawling to the far side of a diagnostic terminal she curled up, concealed in the small, dark space. She looked back.

Heavy footsteps clunked louder. The human outline grew larger on Wall-Thru until it reached the doorway and she ducked back with quickened breaths. The target stood still on the opposite end of the maintenance computers, blocking the only line of escape. A sound like someone slowly exhaling, but mechanical. The slow cadence of a combat-respirator.

"Stay still Joan," Troy said. "It's a Martian mercenary."

BAY

Glancing down at her dress, something was missing. Morgan's purse. Carefully peeking right, the handbag sat on its side a meter away between two mainframes. Both straps out of reach.

Sweat poured down the sides of her torso as she laid flat and stretched out with a hand. Clawed with a fingernail barely shy of it. If I could grow out my nails, she thought, I'd have reached it already. Stupid constable regulations. She pushed herself along the floor with one foot.

The mercenary shifted their weight.

Her finger curled around a strap, and she pulled the purse back into the shadows. Her eyes switched between the mercenary's Wall-Thru outline and the wrapped J30 blaster inside the open purse. A palm-sized, single-stack blaster fitted with a cone-shaped suppressor.

After a minute Troy finally said, "I found a way in for you. When you're ready, press any key on your arm-computer and follow the path."

She tapped a key and new arrowed pathways lit up on a function. She left the diagnostic-bay with knees bent to about half her height. The tall mercenary's back was turned a few meters away. His black body-length armor tapered around the neck. A glowing-teal plasma shield embossed on his back. Don't turn around don't turn around don't turn around.

She slowly stepped away from him and towards a hovering container. The nav-lines led underneath, requiring her to crawl beneath a multi-ton object that could crush her in a second while dragging that stupid purse.

On Wall-Thru, two more hostiles between the two lanes of containers, far to the left and right. Between them, dozens of hauling robots, the big ones with tank treads instead of feet, loading pallets of metal barrels.

Following Troy's waypoints kept robots and cargo between her and the red outlines, leading her to the narrow space between two containers, one of them the sat-shielded one. The measurement function blinked 12 by 12 meters. Turning the latch caused a red light and an angry little beep.

"The door has a rotating encryption key. Just a few more seconds," Troy said.

The infiltration function rang an alarm in her ears. *Lifeform approaching.*

"And I'll be dead," she whispered.

"Shh."

*You are about to be spotted. 12 meters. 8 meters. 5 meters.*

The door unlocked with a buzz. She pulled open the heavy door with two hands and closed it behind her. Dark silence shook her until she gnawed her quivering lips and turned her emotion orb up to 20%. Some light from the No Satellite indicator blinking on eye functions. After 10 seconds Cat-Eyes adjusted.

Stacks of tied sacks in a far corner, each about the size of an anti-radiation salt bag. After taking a few steps, something blue glowed like a diamond. One offline function counted 50 bags while another lit a hazard icon and played an audio message: *Silicon-02-A. Avoid respiratory and somatic contact.* Saturn-Ice. Bounding boxes popped up around each bag and a tally of felony-protocol violations scrolled by. Possession and distribution of narcotics. All local Green Star employees are now subject to detainment and arrest. Fuck yeah.

"You gettin' this Troy?" she asked.

Only static on the wireless. Oh yeah. Why am I so stupid sometimes, she wondered? Hmm. Morgan did say I'm too hard on myself.

A disc on a table. Lifting it lit a small hologram of *Norse Dakota.* Two bearded men and one woman in medieval helmets arguing in some ancient language and making absurd hand gestures. Surrendering it to gravity, it landed with a clatter.

In the opposite corner, 12 stasis cells arranged in an outward facing circle. A web of tangled power cables connected them to a three-meter-tall reactor in the center. Young men and women in cold-sleep jumpsuits stood frozen within glass enclosures. Cryogenics sprayed inside every tube in an arranged melody, kind of like that tune Peter sometimes plays on his holo-piano.

On the circle's other side, tube five hung open. A red-haired woman with a perfectly regal face. Dead eyes and no pulse from the Ginger's neck. Maybe she's a pleasure robot. Rolling up both sleeves of her white jumpsuit exposed no tracker ring on either wrist, only room-temperature skin that felt real. Maybe she's an unregistered organic. Or was, anyway.

Two tubes beyond the redhead, a young boy and girl embraced in a frozen hug. None of the stasis cell buttons she franticly pushed released them. *Cell Locked* blinked in large-red letters on the glass cylinder. Child pleasure bots? Cloned children?

A fumbling sound came from the container door. Beeps, like someone's keying an access code.

Fuck.

She raced around the stasis tubes to the purse and pulled the wrapped J30 blaster. One fingernail pressed against the dotted *cut here* line. To no effect. She tried again, pressing harder to tear the rubbery encasement as it continually slipped between her fingers. Jesus this thing is built like a condom.

Muffled but raised voices from the door. Without Wall-Thru there's no way to know how many of them there are.

She ran around the stasis tubes and peeled the white jump suit off the comatose ginger while also undressing herself. The jump suit was baggy, but the moment she zipped up the fabric de-stretched to form-fitting. No time for socks. The matching white boots were too large and wobbled as she dragged the body by the wrists behind the stacks of narcotics, hiding it along with the green dress and purse. One of the stacked bags fell over, shooting up dust that made her dizzy and raised a function alarm. *Silicon-02-A exposure. Seek a well-ventilated area.* She dropped the still-wrapped J30 into a cargo pocket big enough for a small blaster.

The container door creaked open. She darted to the open stasis tube.

Boots clanked along the floor as lights came on, bright enough to be briefly blinding. The sound of something being rolled, like a couple of bowling balls but kind of squeaky. She remained statue-still within the deactivated stasis tube, upright but resting against the padded interior.

"Did you see the boss lady blowin' her gasket?" A man's voice asked.

"There's some blaster fire in the stacks." Another man's voice answered.

"Must be another of them clone pilots. Downed a liter of tequila and started shootin' off more than their mouth."

The loud boot steps and squeaking rolls entered her field of vision as two men pushing a fiberglass cart with a large metal box on top of it to the back end of the container. One of them old like Peter, ancient, but with a weathered beard. The younger one clean shaven and topped with short-brown hair. Their filthy-blue jumpsuits gave off the vile odor of dirty oil.

"How ya want the gravity detonator configured? Two miles ought to do it?" the young man asked.

"Make it three. I don't want my car covered in debris like last time."

The young man lifted the top of the metal box, and Joan risked a glance. A contraption of wires and a metal cylinder with *ATLANTIC ALLIANCE* in large white letters.

The ancient man squatted to reach a toolbox on the cart's lower shelf, which he plopped next to the contraption with an echoing thud. The younger man lifted a circuit board and held dangling wires somewhere within the box while the ancient one gripped a solder gun and briefly blasted a burning laser.

Beeps from the circuit board as the younger guy twisted a button or something. "The connection ain't workin'. Ya want me to grab another trigger?"

The ancient guy set the solder gun on the floor, less than a meter away from her. "Forget it. We'll use the timer."

A holo-lock popped out of the top of the metal case. The ancient man entered a sequence and the rendered light morphed into red digits. 10 minutes. Well, now nine minutes and 59 seconds. And then nine minutes and 58 seconds. Oh Jesus, it's a bomb. He pushed a button and the holographic countdown disappeared in twisting static.

The younger fellow walked over and stood in front of her. His eyes moved over her like a robotic scanner examining every centimeter of her too-tight white jumpsuit, and his grin sent noxious trash-compactor breath on an express lane to her face. She focused on a spot on the wall behind him and held her breath.

"Sure seems like a waste to blow all this to bits," the bad-breath guy said.

"Didn't you hear?" the ancient guy turned to face the other. "Miss Mot took a pot shot at five-o last night. The boss lady wants everything clear and clean by sundown."

"And an explodin' ship won't draw no attention?"

"No one's going to bat an eyelash. Sheet cakes in the colonies are octagons. The colonials cut corners on everything."

The young guy leaned in, his chin a centimeter over her shoulder. He suddenly grabbed her butt. "What a waste. She's firmly built." Fortunately, neither of them could see her blink, breathe, and roll both hands into fists. When he backed away to leer at her, she again focused on a spot on the wall while holding her breath, drawing not on an emotion orb setting but an old instinct. An undead habit. "Didn't Gemma say number five was a redhead with emerald eyes, not a blue-eyed blonde?" The asshole grabbed a few strands of her hair.

"The boss lady also said to get the fuck out of here as soon as we're done. Let's go Marty." The ancient man twisted his lips and pounded on the top shelf of the cart. It rolled over to the stacked narcotics, knocking over a bag and exposing the shiny green edge of her discarded dress.

Their footsteps faded and stopped, maybe at the door. "Damn. I forgot my toolbox," the ancient guy said.

"I'll get it. Go on ahead, I'll catch up."

"Don't take too long this time. Tick-tock."

The door creaked and for a few seconds Troy's voice came over the wireless. Too much static to piece together even one word. As the heavy door sealed shut the room briefly fell back to silence, and she refroze.

His footsteps echoed until he was in front of her with blank eyes, a grin, and foul breath that nearly fractured her stoic face. The zipper of her jumpsuit slowly moved down her chest with what could only be the man's dirty fingers. Thumps from her accelerating heartrate shook both eardrums.

I could kick him in the crotch, she thought. Make a run for the toolbox and find something heavy to bash his head in. Or try the door, but maybe it's locked. The red barrel of the soldering gun on the floor still smoked. A good shove and gravity could do the rest.

A clang rang out and the man turned his head and backed away. He walked to the corner where the body and dress were hidden and leaned over the piles of bagged Saturn-Ice in the corner.

With two careful steps she bent to grab the soldering gun while pulling the wrapped blaster from the jumpsuit's cargo pocket. Pressing the soldering barrel to a corner of the sat-wrapping melted it within a second and she pulled the J30 blaster out. The melted edges burned her fingers, and she couldn't help but say, "fuck."

The man stood upright with a piece of the turquoise dress in a hand. He turned with bulging eyes, breathing thru his mouth like a useless idiot.

"Surprised mother fucker?" She aimed the blaster at him.

"Who in the hell are you?"

"I'm five-fuckin'-o."

"Miss—Ma'am. What I—I thought you was a robot."

"You're a fuckin' creep."

The man looked at the flakes of Saturn-Ice spilled on the floor near his feet. "I got information. Valuable infor-mation."

"It's okay. We'll upload your mind before we prod your ass into the recyclin' chamber," she said. The man glanced at the marred and rusted handle of a wrench sticking out of the toolbox. "Go on. Pick it up." She cocked the blaster's clicking hammer. "Pick it up ya coward. Either way you're pushin' up basil plants this time tomorrow."

Her finger rolled along the cold trigger, and she licked her lips, tasting his fear. The mask a predator wears when it's convenient.

The container moved upwards, like an elevator, then jos-tled sideways. She lost her balance and bumped into a nearby wall. The man grabbed something and lunged at her. With a two-handed grip she pointed and pulled the trigger. A flash and a high-pitched, suppressed pop.

Blood dripped against the wall, above where the man slowly slid to the floor, his eyes slowing until still, and he fell over with a lifeless thump.

The container picked up speed as she ran to the door and rattled the latch. A keypad blinked red. Locked with math. "Troy? Troy?" she asked while tapping transmit on her cuff-puter. Static. No computer slicer. Maybe a charged shot from my blaster, she wondered. No, in here that will kill me. She ran to the ancient guy's toolbox and rummaged thru the dirty and rusty tools, quickly returning with a hammer.

Striking the lock mechanism hurt her shaking wrists more than the door. Beads of stinging forehead-sweat slipped thru each eyebrow as she relentlessly hammered the vault-like door with deafening clangs.

# 18
## Icarus

Peter found a Mercurius Blink-ship on an enormous runway beyond the maze of cargo containers. *Icarus* scrolled in large letters on the fuselage. Its four one-hundred-meter white wings extended into an X. Rumbling thrusters scattered clouds of dust in every direction, nearly concealing the vague shapes of cargo containers hovering onto the spacecraft.

He ran along the ship's length and leapt into the first open hatch, banging his knee on the bulkhead with a curse. Over the airlock threshold both boots hit the metallic-mesh deck with a clank that echoed to infinity. On the solid ceiling the outline of footprints from magnetic boots. In space the ceiling is another floor. After twenty seconds there was still no sign of anyone following him, and he walked down the corridor.

A ladder led to a catwalk high above the dim engine room, where tubes pumped a plethora of brightly-colored liquids into plexiglass balloons of foaming fuel. A tickle of static came over the wireless but no satellite connection, only the sound of pulsing reactors far below.

The catwalk led to a heavy hatch, a dark passageway, and another catwalk spanning the lit cargo bay. A stadium-sized room where an endless line of cargo containers hovered up an open ramp and into an interlocking mountain continuously growing in height and width from an ever-expanding peak. Around its base, lines of diagonal yellow and black marks volumetrically labelled *CAUTION*. A similar line under his boot at the edge of the catwalk.

On both walls, rivets the size of his head bordered panoramic windows into the cargo stacks. Two escape pods in each corner.

A banging noise from far below. From a container door shaking as though someone were striking it with a hammer on the inside.  The one Lyon was trying to sneak into. Rookie must have gotten herself trapped.

Another sound.  A clank from the opposite end of the catwalk in the dark, upper-right corner of the giant compartment.  The figure of a man looking down at the noisy container as it moved to the top of the heap.  He quickly returned to the shadows.

Carruth. Take Carruth alive.  Take his intact memories in case the Delphi cores aren't here.  Peter pulled his stun gun.  Safer to leave Lyon where she is in case Carruth is armed. Safer for Carruth too.

Peter slowly walked down the catwalk, aiming his stun-gun with both hands.  The Cat-Eyes routine adjusted his eyes to the increasing darkness.  No sign of the suspect, and without Wall-Thru, no way to track him.

The stun-gun flew from his hands, spinning away to a clatter, and someone punched him in the gut.  He lifted fists, blocking a blow.  Carruth leapt at him, sending them over the railing and onto a passing cargo container.  His back and neck throbbed as he stood.  Carruth stood and kicked his knee.  He punched back, sending Carruth over the edge, though not before the man grabbed a hold of his sleeve.

They fell onto a stationary container and grappled.  He was on top of Carruth.  An alarm from a cargo container, hovering towards them as fast as a speeding train.

Peter rolled over and the container clipped Carruth, flinging him across the loading bay, bloodied but still breathing.

Jumping to another container to escape hovering traffic, he wiped beads of stinging forehead-sweat that slipped through an eyebrow.  Random white spots appeared, as though an ocular subroutine malfunctioned, yet blinking didn't reset the field.  Instead, the spots turned into scrambled Cyrillic characters.  Other subroutines abandoned their Latin letters before rendering an arrowed path on the floor.

"Your partner is in danger. You better get to her, and fast," a woman's voice said. He looked around. No one. No flashing icon, so it's not a wireless communication. Nada. "Why don't you listen? You never listen," the woman's voice said in a defeated tone. She sounded similar to the Outcast woman he saw at Lansing's apartment.

The arrowed path flashed rapidly along narrow paths between the containers, which had stopped moving. A large dome moved overhead. The magnetic field generator that holds the cargo in place.

He reached the container where Lyon continued incessantly banging on the door. The red lock clicked-back green the moment he touched the knob.

"Peter!" Lyon flew out. "There's a bum on the ship."

"A bum?"

Distant thrusters rumbled and the ship accelerated abruptly, knocking them over. Back on their feet the craft shook up and down as the cargo stacks flew by outside the viewport, disappearing with a view of the sun over the large, curved roof of the passenger terminal.

"Go! Go! Go!" Lyon grabbed his arm and waist and pulled him with shaking biceps. He lost his balance and Lyon switched to pushing him by his slipping boots towards an escape-pod hatch in a nearby corner. Striking the flashing-red button the moment she squeezed them into the constricting pod.

The ejection mechanism launched the pod laterally through a chain-link fence a hundred meters away. Momentum-counteracting gel absorbed the bulk of the exterior impact. The less-toxic variety flooded the chamber, a viscous-pink fluid.

"What the hell Lyon?" He kicked the pod hatch open and emerged soaked, fanning his hands to shake off the globs of impact gel.

The *Icarus* raced to the end of the runway and through the gateway.  Each magnetic ring changed color as it passed through the center, the ships main engine burning brilliantly and rumbling.  Its growing distance popped up on a subroutine with a green satellite icon.

He spit pink gel a dozen times, then shook his head at Lyon.

"There's a bomb.  On the—" Lyon panted and swallowed the gel.

"You're not supposed to drink that."

She leaned forward until her hands rested on her knees. "I don't—so thirsty."

"It lowers your blood pressure."  He lifted his wrist transmitter to his face.  "Castor.  Notify Zeus orbital-defense.  Tell them to intercept the *Icarus*."  He turned his wrist to read.  "Golf-Sierra-five-six-niner-one-one-two-three."  He pulled a loose hair from his mouth, clearly Lyon's in length.

"What's it taste like?" he asked Lyon.

Her face turned from red to greenish.  "Mm.  Peanut butter 'n glue sticks."  Lyon's eyes rolled back into her head, her knees buckled, and she collapsed with a gravel-crushing flop that puffed a small cloud of gray dust.

"Huh."  He looked up at the ship shrinking through the gateway-rings.  Until it exploded with the sound of a falling anvil and a brilliant flash.  Peter slowly brought his transmitter back to his gaping-open mouth.  "Castor? Scratch my last."

***

Lyon was at the interview bulb's table, tapping her fingernails on the shiny surface.  Her crossed legs dangling short of the floor.

Gemma Overton sat at the far edge. Her eyes averted and her fingers playing with the blonde highlights of her dark hair, as though she memorized where they were.

My wife used to do that, he thought. If Overton faces charges in a trial, it will start weeks or months from now. Long after Delphi needs their cores back. What she knows needs to be entirely confessed, or enough to secure a neuron warrant.

He dialed in to Interrogation-Vulture, a new mood setting Norris had posted on the police social media feed. A faint pulse vibrated inside the small chamber, and the red digits of the wall clock ticked at a slower tempo. Bending and landing caffeinated chewing gum on his tongue, the edges sliced the insides of his mouth with every chew, though it drew no blood, it's only a sensation. This dial setting is something else.

The behavior-cylinder slowly lowered itself from the ceiling to a few meters above their heads.

Lyon clicked the *Record* button on the table's side and an adjacent screen illuminated lines that waved with her every word. "Officers Joan Lyon and Peter Ramsey, Monitoring Organic Trespassing Haz—"

"Are you sure you're Joan? Wasn't it Evelyn earlier?" Ms. Overton asked.

"State your name for the record."

"Are you related to that golfer? Forest Lyon?"

"No. I'm not. It's two twenty-two PM, September the twenty-fourth, twenty-one sixty-three."

"The subject is Miss Gemma Overton," Peter said. A button on the table's edge rendered a volumetric file. "Residing at five Avernus Street, Settlement Five."

"Has your name always been Gemma Overton?" Lyon asked Gemma while reaching over to him, making a reverse cutting gesture at the file in front of him to create a copy, and pulling it back. "Looks like you used to be Gloria

Sekhmet, but you had it changed. I ain't the only one with more than one name. Ya got somethin' to hide? You're almost old enough to be a war criminal."

Overton crossed her arms. "I'm not a reprogrammed organic. I know my rights. I don't have to say anything until my arbiter gets here."

"Fine," Lyon said. She looked over. "You could play your holo-piano while we wait."

"That depends. Are you going to sing?" he asked.

Lyon rapidly shook her head, as though he had proposed that she sing in front of the entire world naked.

"Then why don't you and I just go over the casefile while we wait?" he asked Lyon in a mocking tone.

Lyon grinned. "Oh, I'd thought you'd never ask."

He launched volumetric images of the wreckage of the *Icarus* sprawled among the waves of the Pacific Tidepools. "Oh look, it's that ship we almost died on."

"I had to shove him into an escape pod," Lyon said to Overton.

"Thank you for that," he said.

Lyon looked over and smiled. A real one that showed her teeth. "You're welcome."

"So, riddle me this. What would happen to someone who attempted to murder two peace officers?"

"Hmm, I dunno. Maybe it's attempted murder of two peace officers?"

"Right. Doesn't that carry an automatic life sentence?"

"Only if you get a plea deal. Otherwise, it's the recyclin' penalty." Lyon smirked at Overton.

Overton rolled her eyes. "I work in the cargo terminal. I don't know what happened on that ship. And it's only a recycling penalty case if a peace officer is killed. Neither of you died."

"No, but he did." Lyon loaded a volumetric image of Carruth.

"It's not murder if it's a reprogrammed organic."

"He was part of an ongoing MOTH investigation," he said. "Is that obstruction of justice?" he asked Lyon.

"You bet your ass," Lyon said, impersonating his tone and cadence.

"And what about racketeering?" He scrolled to the volumetric recording of Lyon posing as a merchant and handing a stack of bonds to Overton. With both hands he pinched frames on the preview reel underneath, scrolling until the recording repeated the few seconds of bribery in an endless loop.

"Don't forget smugglin'," Lyon said.

"Oh, how could I?"

"Have you heard of Dr. Wasserman?" Lyon asked Overton.

Overton shrugged. "Who hasn't?"

He loaded a volumetric stack of brown file folders on the table and pushed them over to Lyon.

She stood and began pacing behind Overton. "How about that bombin' at the Olympic Marketplace?" She grabbed one of the brown folders and threw it down in front of Overton with an artificial thud. "Or the shootin' two months ago. A couple a meat robots gunned down four off-duty officers." Lyon slammed down another file in front of Overton. Volumetric tableaus spilled out. Gory images of bloodied corpses on a street.

"Riddle me this," he said to Lyon. "How did Outcasts get such weaponry?"

"Them was colonial carbines."

"Huh. How do you think Wasserman is sourcing all of these colonial weapons?"

Lyon leaned over Overton. "My God, I'm just dyin' to know." She picked up the remaining stack and slammed down the folders one at a time while saying, "It's almost like someone is givin', and givin', and givin' him exactly what the *fuck* he needs."

Overton silently looked away with trembling shoulders and gnawed on her long fingernails.

"Look at all of these capital crimes," he said. "If only we had more names."

Lyon sat on the table in front of Overton and looked back. "We could spread the love, couldn't we?"

"Right. I'm getting all warm and fuzzy inside."

"Someone is aidin' the Outcasts." Lyon looked at Overton.

A shadow rapidly moved under the table. Overton tapping her feet. "I don't know anything I'm just a manager I'm not involved in anything illegal!"

"Really?" He scrolled and read through Overton's volumetric dossier. "Look at these priors. Possession of Saturn Ice. Shoplifting. And we still have your money in evidence. Civil forfeiture. Colonial cash in small denominations."

"No fancy schoolin' and you're a warehouse manager. How many neckties did you have to grease to swing that?" Lyon glanced at Overton's dossier. "Now we can add on smugglin' and murder. Ya got them dirty hands of yours in all kinds of rotten pies, don't ya, Gloria?"

Overton looked up at Lyon. Red circles around her eyes. "I don't use that name anymore."

"Wait wait, don't tell me," Lyon said derisively with a hand in the air. "You've changed? You're suddenly a different person?" She looked over. "Peter, what did we find on her computer?"

He glanced at the behavior-cylinder. No deceptive lines in the readout. Gemma is trying to move on from her past. She must have found herself caught up in something too big to stop and is now haunted by guilt. Trying so hard to forget who she used to be that she changed her whole name.

With a clicking twist he deactivated his mood-dial.

Lyon sighed. "Earth to Peter."

He scrolled to recent evidence and clicked a spreadsheet icon. Multiple pages of a volumetric ledger. Labelled columns for dates and transactions in Martian Cryptographs totaled in millions. The data descended into a collage of symbols as abstruse as an abacus. Might as well be Greek.

Lyon reached over, gestured a volumetric copy from the computer, and then pushed it into Gemma's face with an open palm, as though she were pieing her in the face. "Check this out. Dates in the future with already-negotiated prices. I wonder what this is?" Lyon clicked a volumetric column to sort and tabulate. "No wonder ya never came back for that strippin' cash. Smugglin' sure pays better." She clicked somewhere and the view changed to floating pages, like an old handwritten ledger. Inked in shiny black in the top right corner, scales, the kind used to weigh. Equally balanced with a feather on one of them. I've seen that before.

With both hands he turned his volumetric copy of the ledger, scrolling and pushing buttons to locate the page or view Lyon had. After half a minute he asked her, "Lyon, give me a copy of that?"

Lyon rolled her eyes and slid over a volumetric copy. A grid of black and red lines. The transactions were all in the future, days to weeks. Hundreds of thousands of dollars for each entry, though hovering a finger over them flashed *Anticipated Price*. Global position coordinates, which could be customer location data. Jumbled characters and numbers, probably quantum-encrypted checksums. Thousands of transactions according to the navigation buttons on the bottom.

He scratched his chin. This is too much volume for a three-man smuggling operation. Even with robotic aid. Son of a bitch. Delphi predictions. These are predictions from the stolen datacore. The dates must be when the predicted events occur.

And that image, the scales. He rubbed his temples. Lansing's apartment. On one of his business cards.

"What is this?" he asked Overton while pointing to the scales.

Lyon looked over with an open mouth, her eyebrows raised. She then looked back at Gemma. "What do you do with the children? Do ya hand 'em over to Wasserman?"

"No, I'm not trafficking children," Gemma shouted.

"Where is the Sandcastle?"

"I don't know!"

"I bet you gave Wasserman that memory printer."

"What are these values?" Peter pointed at the hashed values.

Lyon looked back, slid off the table, and walked towards him. Her eyes glanced at the door.

He stood and followed her.

"What the fuck are you doin?" Lyon whispered. "We got her on the fuckin' ropes and her fuckin' arbiter will be here any Goddamn second."

Lyon was almost killed this morning. She can't be Wasserman's mole.

"Those are Delphi predictions on that ledger," he whispered.

Lyon squinted and grimaced. "Who gives a shit about possession of stolen fuckin' property? We can nail this bitch on a conspiracy charge."

He pushed a button on his wrist-computer to activate a subroutine, Chun's Censoring. Instead of loading, an automated message played in his ears. *Your trial period has expired. To continue the vulgar-free experience, please sign up and select a payment plan.*

"If Wasserman knows the future, how will we catch him?" he asked.

"Those transactions end next week.  Then he'll be shit outta luck."  Lyon pulled at the bottom edge of her shirt.  "Let's get a confession."  She walked back to the table and stood over Gemma.  "How did you know Carruth was a meat robot?  Did you brainwash him with that memory printer you smuggled to Earth?"

"No.  His tracker ring was already red," Gemma said.

Lyon grabbed a volumetric file and spread tableaus over the table surface one at a time.  Graphic ones of bombing victims, including children.  "This is who you're helpin'."

He approached the table and pulled the volumetric ledger over.  "Gemma, what is this symbol? The scales.  Is it a company?  I need to know."

Gemma looked over briefly until Lyon slammed her palms on the table.

"If you don't tell me everything you know, I'm gonna make sure everyone knows you're behind all of this."  She moved an open palm over the tableaus, then picked up one of a toddler's blasted corpse.  "And everyone is goin' to know your face and what you did. And none of this name-changin' bullshit is gonna bail your ugly ass out this time."

Gemma gulped, wiped away a tear and laid her trembling hands on her knees.  "She said no one would get hurt."

"Who?" he asked.

"Who told you that?" Lyon asked.  "Is it Mot?  Who's Mot?"

The interview bulb's door burst open, slamming loudly against the mirrored wall. A shapely woman in a blue dress. In her white-gloved hand she held an in vogue bag that was neither a purse nor a briefcase. A subroutine IDed her as Emily Macer, arbiter license two-three-seven-four.  She walked over to Gemma and lifted her by the chin, gently turning her head to examine the tears running down her face.

"What is this?" Macer looked at him and Lyon. "You cannot speak to my client unless I'm present."

"I—" Gemma started but Macer quickly squeezed her mouth shut. Overton's muffled lips struggled like a suffocating fish.

"We're done here," Macer said.

# 19
## Sobriquet

With shaking arms and legs, Joan made her way to the half-moon desk she had to share with Peter, where she stumbled but landed in the chair upright, resting her elbows on the bright-white surface. That damn Peter was hovering over her shoulder.

"A deal?" she asked, but it wasn't a real question. "A fuckin' deal for her?"

Peter sat down in the other chair with a drink or something. "Kyudo needs to find the missing memory printer before another hundred people are brainwashed. If Gemma has information that leads to it, then granting her immunity, giving her a second chance, will save lives."

"And what about those clones, those children she's traffickin'? What about their second chance?"

"Are you sure they were clones and not robots?" Peter lifted his drink and sipped it thru a straw.

"Robots don't need stasis chambers."

"Right. But clones aren't our responsibility. They're not legally human."

"That's easy for you to say. Sittin' in your big chair drinkin' your—the fuck is this?" She pointed at Peter's drink. One of those fancy coffee milkshakes.

"Salted caramel latte."

She scoffed. "Black coffee's not good enough for you? You need a girlie drink?"

"Would you like a sip?" The jerk stuck the drink and its gross, saliva-covered straw in her personal space until she waved it away.

"I'd like to give that Robbie robot reporter an earful about a monster walkin' the streets when she oughta be locked up and recycled." She tapped the phone app on her lamptop and started dialing.

"Lyon, stop." That bastard Peter reached over and pulled the hologram away. He lifted his cuffputer to his own lamptop and tapped some sequence that locked her lamptop holograms.

"Did you just lock me out of my own fuckin' computer?" Heat rose in both of her cheeks.

"She's innocent until proven guilty."

"She *is* guilty you fuckin' idiot."

"You think, or you know?"

"I know god damnit. I heard two of her goons say she's the boss. You would of heard 'em too if you didn't take a year to open that stupid door."

"Well here." Peter pulled a cone-shaped memory drive from a desk drawer. "Upload your memories into evidence. Though you'll have to protocol-11 first." He pulled his DOLOS validator from a pocket of his coat, draped on his chair, and set both on the desk in front of her.

It was like a cotton ball grew inside her throat. That guy I shot, she thought. And what he did to me. She moved both hands under the desk to rotate her emotion orb. It blinked *Malfunction* with an annoying little beep, though pulling the sleeves of her blouse down made it less noticeable.

"Of course," Peter kept talking. "With Warner's privacy protocol, Kyudo can't compel you without a warrant. And she won't submit an affidavit if you don't mention such statements in your report."

"Mm," she managed to squeak.

"You didn't happen to see a Delphi datacore in that shielded container, did you?" he asked.

She shook her head.

Peter flipped thru holographic pages of her report, scratching his neck as he read. "Who's Mot?"

"Some name I heard." Laughter from across the station. A brunette, Penny Greene on eye functions, sitting in a chair next to Troy, who was standing. Smiling and playing with her hair. "Aren't we cramped enough in here? This is a police station not a social club."

"Why don't you go tell them?" Peter asked without looking away from the floating documents.

I need to talk to Morgan. "Can you unlock my computer?"

"Your shift is almost over, and it's been a long day. Why don't you call it, uh, a day?"

"I just need to find somethin' real quick."

"And what's that?"

She sighed. "My friend, Morgan. Her backup disc."

"Morgan Sullivan? Her memory disc was logged into evidence."

"What?" She squinted.

"Standard procedure for any Janus operation. We maintain a chain of custody until Gemma's case is closed." Peter sipped his drink and made a really obnoxious "Ah" afterwards. "But, silver lining. If Gemma takes that plea deal tonight, you can have Sullivan's disc back tomorrow."

"This is bullshit."

"Happiness is a choice Lyon," Peter said while making a face that he must of thought was real funny.

She quickly stood and her stupid chair fell over and all the nearby officer's eyes were on her while she walked away because they're idiots with nothing better to do.

***

She stood alone at one of the four sinks in the ladies' room, the one on the station's second floor, and wiped away tears. One of the overhead lights flickered a few times.

The door swung open, and she hastily turned the tap and lifted cold water over her face with both hands. Beyond her own reflection in the mirror stood someone named Anastasia Hamilton by eye functions, in a grey top and black pants.

"Hi Joan," Anastasia said.

"Hi."

Anastasia walked up and stopped at the adjacent sink. "Are you okay?"

"I'm always surprised seeing someone here. I'm so used to Wall-Thru."

"Sometimes I forget that too."

"Mm hmm." She pulled a paper towel from the wall-mounted dispenser and wiped her face dry before dropping it into the robo-bin that scurried over.

"How can it rain out here every day and still be so dry?" Anastasia looked in the mirror and ran a stick of balm over both lips. "Settlement Two is so much nicer this time of year." Joan shrugged while Anastasia puckered her lips. She clicked the balm's sterilizer button with a beep before offering it. Why not? Joan gave her grateful eyes and looked into the mirror to try it. It cooled her lips for a moment, then they turned warm. "Oh, I've been meaning to ask you. Are you related to—"

"Jesus, I'm not related to that stupid golfer!" She abruptly handed the stick of balm back.

Anastasia took it and capped it. She asked in an unaffected tone, "Mary Lyon? The fitness instructor?"

She set her tongue between her teeth and inhaled sharply. "Sorry. She's my sister."

Anastasia washed her hands. "Oh. I've seen some of her vids. I like her." She flung water off her hands and pulled a paper towel. "I've run Janus a few times. One time I had a resurfaced memory. An afternoon I spent with my mother on our patio in Dublin. Before the war, when being outdoors smelled like a greenhouse. It always messes with my mood circle for about a day or so."

"It's like I'm all over the damn place."

"Did something happen?"

She froze for a moment, then shrugged. "What do you mean?"

Anastasia stared for a few seconds. No anger in her eyes. She squatted down and quickly scanned the open bottoms of the stalls, then stood and leaned against the wall while inhaling sharply. "So, get this. Last year, I pull over this B-M-W after it runs a red light. And it has these privacy windows. So, I load Wall-Thru, right? And there's these outlines of this woman giving a guy a blow job in the driver's seat." They shared a laugh. "I run his satellite ID and it bounces back as Councilman Warner. The guy with all the rumors flying around about him putting his hands everywhere."

"The douchebag in those stupid re-election commercials?" She covered her open mouth.

Anastasia nodded. "So, he rolls down the window and I tell him and his wife—or mistress or whatever, to stay put while I run their info. And I walk back to my cruiser to call command and ask what the hell do I do with a government official getting fellatio." Anastasia took a deep breath and glanced at the floor briefly. "I only make a few steps and all of the sudden there's hands grabbing my you-know-whats." She lifted her hands and covered her breasts.

"What did you do?"

Anastasia snickered. "I almost pushed him into traffic. And the next day, everyone in my squad is calling me 'Guinness Tits'."

"Jesus. Why?"

"Because I'm Irish." Anastasia separated a strand of her red hair, then let it fall back among the others. "I was so embarrassed I didn't upload my memories. I doubt it would have helped anyway. Him being a councilman and all." She sighed. "Now when I watch the news feed, it sounds like he might have done more."

"Who called you that?"

"Everyone. You know how people are around here. As soon as it gets on the social feed you can't defend yourself."

She lifted herself onto the edge of the sink. "I get bein' judged for what I do. But why do people judge you because of what someone else does to you?"

"Eventually they move on to someone else. Like right now some poor rookie is being called 'machine-gun' because a rat scared her, and she shot it twice."

Rapid-Fire Greta. I better stop calling her that, she thought. "I know that damn Gemma is guilty, and she's gettin' away with it. I'd love to supervise her accidental death."

"She's a criminal, so she'll fall back into her old ways soon enough. All you have to do is wait like a spider. Then you can arrest her."

"But another crime means another victim," she muttered.

A ringtone sounded, like a cartoon theme song. Anastasia checked her cuffputer, pressing a button and turning the screen towards Joan. "My son Sophio."

It was a video message, a recording from some earlier time. A little blond boy, maybe a kindergartener, offering Anastasia a chocolate Saturn-sphere after she placed one into his open mouth. She knelt and gladly accepted the candy, saying "Ah" like she was at the dentist and let him put it in her mouth. They each made exaggerated gnawing sounds and the video faded out in the shape of a heart.

She snorted a short fit of laughter. "Aww, he's cute. Is he home with your husband?"

"No. We sold him to the highest bidder." This time Anastasia laughed too, though her face gradually turned serious. "I have to give you something." She pulled out a small tube with a few drops of clear liquid.

"Hmm," she said quietly while jumping off the sink and turning to the mirror to check her face.

Anastasia swallowed. "Kyudo said either take the memory treatment or return to therapy."

Joan's reflection in the mirror seemed to shrink. Kyudo shouldn't be telling anyone about that. That shit is confidential. They don't even officially call it therapy. *Behavioral Adjustment*. Like if you just act fine everything will be just great. "What do you know about her?"

Anastasia moved close and whispered, "Kyudo? Her task force put down 300,000 clones in the colonies during last year's Venusian uprisings. She killed 800 of them herself."

"Yeah, I heard all them Venusian Butcher stories about her. I'll bet it's all bullshit."

Anastasia shook her head. "I served with her in the Pioneer Regiment."

Did Kyudo's reputation shield her from ever being touched? Would she feel bad about hurting, even killing, someone who did? Or would she give him no second thought?

She looked at the mirror again and held up the small capsule with shaking fingers.

"What happened?" Anastasia asked.

She placed the pill capsule in her pant pocket, the half of it that fit. Beyond a name on a duty roster, I don't even know this woman, she thought. Could she have made up that story about Warner? Fake oversharing so I'd return a real favor?

A drip echoed from the sink. She looked down at another drop slowly forming from the faucet. Maybe a glitch in the auto shut-off, like the kind that led to water shortages years ago in that shelter. She tightened the manual knob until the leak stopped.

***

The familiar black door matched the darkness inside the house as she swiped her keycard and pushed it open slowly to muffle the predictable creaks. The metal-coated bags of steaming food lightly bumped the frame as she crossed the threshold and silently closed the door.

Someone, maybe Morgan, had once told her that it's rude to say nothing when entering a house. *That never made sense to me,* she thought.

Squeaks to the foyer's right. The house robot ironing clothes by the laundry press in the kitchen. To the left, the faint sounds of a media feed, which grew louder as she walked on the matted carpet past white walls and towards the open door of the second room.

"Hi Mom."

It was a small room, dimly lit, with two high-back, cushioned chairs and a small round table between them. In the opposite corner, the news on the bright media feed.

"Oh." Mom briefly shook. Startled.

"Sorry."

"Who are you?"

"Your daughter, Joanna." She pointed with her free hand to a still image of her on the wall labeled with her name. Flickers from the media feed lit up the glossy surface. "And this is Mary, your other daughter. You and her had lunch today." There were other pictures on the wall, but she ignored them, not allowing herself to even look at them, only glimpsing a sketch Mom had made of flowers with large black centers.

"Oh," Mom said.

"Are you hungry? I brought us some pasta."

"Oh, I love pasta."

She smiled. *It's good Mom still remembers that.* When she set the food on the small round table and removed her coat to sit in the other chair, Mom frowned at Joan's holstered blaster. "It's okay, Mom. I'm a police officer."

"Since when?"

"Mm, bout half a year."

"Sounds dangerous. Do you like it?"

"Sometimes." Do I tell her about what happened today, she wondered? Mom will forget it within an hour, and I'll have to explain it all over again. Let her enjoy dinner first. Joan pulled the table towards Mom and unpacked the food. "I got you a pineapple drink. Do you want extra ice?"

"Oh, I don't want to be burden."

She laughed. "It's okay. Here." Lifting Mom's drink, she twisted the rotating bottom of the metal can, like it was one of them fancy peppercorn grinders. Cracking and bubbling spheres of ice rose within the semi-transparent can. After six rotations she returned the drink to the table, within Mom's reach, and opened the shiny, holographically animated Bianco's serving box.

Rigatoni with a red sauce. Green peas, melted cheese, and little crispy bits of chicken. She inhaled deeply, drawing in the intoxicating steam before handing Mom plastic cutlery.

"Thank you, sweetheart."

"You're welcome." She sat and dug into her own food. Cajun Chicken Alfredo. Salted spices sank into her tongue. "You wanna watch your show?"

"Show? What show?"

"There's a show you've been watchin'." She navigated the holographic media feed, gesturing with her fork to *The New Virginia Mysteries*.

The show started, the intro where the handsome male lead climbed a wall of red rock. Shirtless and muscular. It unfortunately zoomed out until his biceps could no longer be seen and he was reduced to little more than a dot within the dome of a Martian city.

"Who's that?" Mom asked.

"The climbin' guy? Trevor? You're in love with him."

Mom laughed. "Oh, stop."

The show's recap started. Mom can probably make it thru the hour-long episode before she starts forgetting. "Troy told me Delphi's predicted it's a happy endin'."

"Troy?"

"Coworker."

"Is he handsome?"

She broke a piece of sliced Italian bread and buttered it. "Mm hmm."

"Do you like him?"

"I'm not sure."

"Why don't you have dinner with him some night?"

"He's gotta have a girl already."

"You never know."

"Eh. Men are like parkin' spaces. All the good ones are already taken."

Mom picked thru her little box of pasta. "I used to make a dish like this, didn't I?"

"Yeah. That was actually—" the last meal we shared when Mom was still Mom. "You used to make rigatoni a lot, red sauce like that. And tiramisu too. Bianco's has these cute little cups of 'em but they were sold out."

They glanced at each other's food and mutually offered one fork-full of their respective meals. A drop of the red sauce dripped into her carton, and a moving image replayed in her mind. The sights of her blaster lined up at that guy's chest. Anger, rage commanding her to pull the trigger. His insides sprayed against a wall and sliding down. Red drops.

She managed to eat the rigatoni without looking at it.

"Do you know what's happening?" Mom stared intently at the media feed.

Some drama involving some woman named Rachael and Trevor. "She had an affair and wishes she could go back and stop herself from cheatin'. Or maybe just stop him from findin' out."

"Oh, that's awful. I hope he leaves her," Mom said. When a commercial started Joan slouched in the chair and sighed. "Long day? Why don't we use your police talents and investigate that wine rack out there?" She nodded towards the kitchen.

"I'm not 21."

"I'll let you off with a warning this time." Mom smiled.

"I'm kinda on call," she lied.

Halfway thru the episode they had finished eating and she took their cartons to the kitchen to clean, dry, and place them in the recycling box, as the house robot looked over with a frowny face.

When she returned with a glass of salt water, Mom has a habit of gargling with salt water every night before bed, a commercial was playing. She sat down and something pinched in her pant pocket. That damn memory pill. Pulling it out with two fingers, she ran a third finger along the embossed Lethe company label. Text beneath it. Clear liquid that clears the mind. A countdown on a mini-hologram beneath it read *This gel will evaporate in 2 hours and 57 minutes. Drop vial into waste chute IMMEDIATELY after use.*

After a deep breath she set the water on the small table and swallowed air with an audible gulp.

"Mom, is it like, okay to forget doin' something bad? If the person you do it to deserved it, is it okay to never think of 'em again?"

Mom had fallen asleep. Joan stood and leaned over to cover her with her blanket, tucking her in around the edges of the plush chair.

She sat down, focusing on a point in the ceiling where moving light met the edge of darkness, and examined the memory pill again.

Peter queried INTERPOL for any records containing the scales with a feather. Partial matches from a few sheriffs and organizations in the colonies. Every Earth database clicked-back with nothing. Nada. Zip.

He scrolled to the first page of the casefile and stared for a minute. Standing up and stretching brought the interrogation bulb across the substation into view, where Kyudo handed an immunity agreement to Gemma and her arbiter.

They signed.

With a breath of relief, he sat down and spun the chair around several times while whistling a tune, some flavor of the month pop jingle he heard on the wireless but didn't know the lyrics to.

A constable walked by a few desks away. Detective Sergeant Eva Diaz according to oculars. The straw of a grapefruit-juice tin left her lips while she regarded him with a chuckle. A sharp twist of her head flung her ponytail like a scorpion's stinger, and she disappeared with loud clippety-clops among the station's shift-changing crowd as he looked back to the interrogation bulb.

Gemma and her arbiter were laughing and smiling. She must be relieved to have a second chance.

Kyudo walked over and he stood.

"Major."

"It's late, so Ms. Overton will be coming in for a deposition at o-eight hundred tomorrow morning. Wear a clean shirt and tie."

"Yes ma'am."

She walked away and he returned to his seat and computer.

Flipping through several pages of volumetric wireless transcripts, the words *partner* and *danger* weren't apparent. He remembered the search function and typed them in. Nothing. Nada. Who was that voice in my head was when I was on the *Icarus*?  With all the com interference it could have been lost.  Rotating the search cube to *Written Reports* yielded zip.

MAR-SEC operators use proprietary com channels.

Scrolling through the casefile to persons of interest and typing in *mercenary* filtered the list down to five names.  Green checkmarks by all their names, so they passed their interrogations.  Released due to a lack of evidence.

Though one of the names alternated flashing green and pale blue, as did a human outline on Wall-Thru.  Someone sitting in the substation lobby.  Penny Greene.

I'll be damned.

He walked to the lobby, where the flashing green outline changed to a brunette with a face he recognized.  "Penny?"

"Peter."  Penny stood up and smiled.  "How are you?"

"Very well, thank you.  And you?"

Penny's head tilted to one side.  "Been better."

"The computer says you're free to go."

"There's a long queue for an autocar."

"Do you still live in Admiral Heights?" he asked.  Penny nodded.  "I can give you a lift."

"Oh, you don't have to do that."

"It's on the way."

"Um, okay."

***

The sun lost its grip between canyons of high rises with slices of fading orange light, spaced like the masts of old ships dividing an ocean horizon.  At a lit stop sign he clicked on the dashboard interface.  "Your address isn't listed."

Penny leaned over from the passenger seat to type her address into Navi.  Her hair smelled like strawberry.

"Fountain Avenue?  Extra nice," Peter said.

"Pays to be a mercenary." Penny smiled and retreated to her seat. The joy in her eyes slowly faded. "Um, I'm the one who, you know." She formed a hand into a gun shape and made a shooting gesture. "My optics didn't ID you as police."

"Forget about it."

"We're lucky I recognized your handsome face. I almost shot your nose off."

I should tell her how grateful I am that she missed my crouch. No, don't joke with her. "Right. Did any of you guys follow me onto that ship?" he asked. "I thought I heard some MAR-SEC com traffic on the *Icarus*."

Penny shook her head. "I told my whole team to stand down. We turned ourselves in right away." She looked over, directly at him. No tapping of her feet on the floor mat. No clicking her nails against the dashboard. "Two of the Green Star techs are MIA. It could have been them. Though they've likely halfway to the Sandcastle by now."

"Right." But the voice I heard was female and those techs were both men. Though there are apps that can alter one's voice.

He turned onto a ramp leading to a raised causeway. The headlights cut through colored vapor rising from the bacteria pools glowing far below.

"Huh. Who talked to you?"

"Norris." Penny moved her hands in front of the dashboard climate vents as the diurnal sensors switched from air conditioning to heat. "Is he still obsessed with those blueberry donuts?"

"The ones with the cream cheese frosting on top?" he asked. Penny nodded. "He still gets them."

"God, I miss those."

"Bakeries sell donuts to civilians."

"I'm on a diet."

"A diet?"

"If I fall outside of lean muscle ranges I get fired. We call it fat-fired in the mercenary world." Penny rested her head against the passenger side window.

At the end of the causeway, he stopped at a red on Fountain Avenue. The blinking lights of vehicle-sized cleaning robots glacially moved along the shoulders in small clouds of sterilizing steam. Wind carried some of it away, revealing a brief but clear view of downtown, with Blue Jewel Tower gleaming like sapphires stacked to an infinity beyond the competing neon skyscrapers.

He rested a hand on the noon position of the steering wheel. "I was never okay with what happened to you."

Penny looked over and shrugged. "I was pissed off for months, but there was nothing anyone could do. Someone accused me of killing P-O-Ws a few hours before Auckland was nuked and suddenly, I don't have a job."

"And they had a weird story about you. It sounded made up."

"The one about me offering the P-O-Ws cigarettes and then I machine gun them? Once they light up, I light them up." She scoffed. "And I've never even *been* to New Zealand. I know Lansing fought for me. But that didn't matter. Just like it didn't matter that I was in bootcamp on the opposite side of the world at the time." Penny took a deep breath.

It did matter that Lansing fought for her. Penny wasn't prosecuted, which was a lucky break considering it would have been a death penalty case. But there's no need to remind her of that. "Someday people will see how absurd this all is and move on. Everyone was just following orders."

"It's the robot reporters. They streamed that slander twenty-four-seven until the I-A-D board discharged me. Even today, if my name or employer is mentioned, they remind everyone that I've been accused of war crimes."

What if Gemma knows about my past, he thought, and mentions it when she confesses tomorrow?

A honking horn drew his attention to the now-green light, and he accelerated, turning to a long stretch of brownstones with cobbled sidewalks and fake trees every ten meters.

"Have you ever thought about the private sector?" Penny asked. "Most of my coworkers are wannabe cowboys. We could use someone reliable rock-side. And if you're willing to relocate to Mars, your take home pay is tripled. We have twenty-thousand open contracts." She snickered. "One of our recruiters even approached some Janissaries. Turns out they're all married to Kyudo. But since you're human, we can negotiate a release from your service obligation."

Delphi hired that many mercs for a few datacores? No. Something else is going on here. But what? Perhaps ditching all of this and starting over in the colonies is the right move. Then again, starting over means exactly that. No retirement. No pension.

The street shifted to a bright line of white-painted terraces with red doors. Each topped by traditional Gables and old-world flags. Something one would see in a volumetric brochure more often than reality.

He lightly pressed the brakes as Penny's residence popped up on the dash-computer with an audio reminder. *Fifty meters.* "Mars, huh?" he asked. Penny nodded. "Would it involve shooting?"

Penny chortled. "Of course. But they're just clones."

"Were you over there? When the food revolts started?"

Penny nodded. "One tour over there is a half-cycle, which is about one Earth year. Then they send you back rock-side to relax for a bit. The Outcasts here can be just as vicious as the Clone Clans, but they rarely wander into the cities."

I must have seen a thousand hungry faces during the fallout years. Guarding a pantry and delivering bad news to starving people instead of a meal. Imagine being told to deliver a fast death instead of a slow one. At least as a cop, if I do something like that it's under official orders. "I'll have to think that one over."

He pulled over and parked in front of Penny's terrace house, a dozen meters from the next corner. The sidewalk and red door beyond the passenger window. Penny clicked her wrist-computer, and the window nearest the door lit up. A bright lamp, a parlor palm, and a wingback chair of red velvet between open lace curtains.

"How about a nightcap?" Penny wrapped a strand of her long brown hair around a finger. The ends pulsed various shades of neon blue.

He inhaled fast enough to sound a snort. A close call with death effects everyone. Even mercenaries with calm exteriors.

"I uh, gave up drinking a while back," he said.

"Oh. Well, I have some tea. Strong stuff. It'll wake you right up."

"Right. Uh, I appreciate the offer. I just, uh, I can't."

Penny smiled and made an obviously forced chuckle. "Xin loy. Thanks for the ride."

"No problem."

After stepping out, she turned back and leaned on the car frame, low enough to show off her cleavage, with one hand still holding the open door. "If you change your mind, about the job, or, you know, anything else, just call me."

"Right."

She handed him a volumetric contact card, which he waved between two fingers and made himself smile. The car door closed with a thud.

The polite thing to do is to wait until she's in her home, but is she going to assume I'm staring at her derrieres? Probably, so I might as well look anyway. She was wearing skin-tight leggings, and it was crystal clear that she had rounded out her training as a lethal instrument.

Across the lit threshold of the opulent townhouse, Penny looked back with a smile and a wave as she closed the door. I'm glad I didn't authorize the computer-recommended drone strike that would have assuredly killed her. But will a mercenary show the same mercy to anyone else?

His wrist-computer shook with a pingtone. A text message from his wife. *When are you coming home?*

Rumbling storm clouds merged over the urban canyon. In the driver's side window, a reflection of the police ID affixed to his coat. He couldn't remember the last time the golden shield, abraded by time, shone.

He continued on Fountain Avenue for a few minutes, eventually taking a left on Cole and stopping in front of the Geras Vista apartment building. At the top of the stairs, a floating volumetric calendar in front of Lansing's corner unit.

The door opened as he approached. A humanoid robot with a cartoonishly voluptuous hourglass shape and a female synthetic voice. "Good evening. I am Rrrrrrrriley the Robot Realtor."

"Right. Move."

The robot didn't move. "Please register for a tour on the open house calendar in front of the door. And don't forget to review our other floor plans at competitive rates. Don't hesitate to sign a lease. Prices are only going higher, so hurry."

He grabbed the robot and pushed it aside, abruptly pulling his hands away when he accidentally touched one of its synthetic breasts. "Sorry."

"Good heavens. I beg your pardon. I am not a pleasure model sir."

"Relax. I'm not a tin packer." He walked into the apartment. It was now absent of any furniture, only sparkling clean laminate floors.  Bright white walls that smelled of fresh paint.

"Sir, if you want a tour, please return in the morning."

"It's alright, I'm a cop."  He tapped on his police ID.

"Yes.  I remember you, Officer Ramsey."

"From where?"

"I showed you an apartment at Halcyon Lofts four years ago.  Though I am unable to compute why they are called lofts when every unit is a single floor.  Is your present apartment satisfactory and providing you with ample amenities?"

"It is."

"And how is your wonderful family?"

"Very well, thank you."  He turned in a circle, scanning the empty apartment.  "Did you find any volumetric business cards here?  One with weighted scales, made of metal and balanced like this?"  He opened his palms faced towards the ceiling to demonstrate.

"I know of no personal property matching such criteria," the robot said.

"Have you noticed anything unusual?"  With a finger he pointed around the walls.

"Climate control fan number one is requiring seventy-two percent additional thrust in order to generate adequate air cycles pursuant to environmental protocol nineteen-B-seven."

"Show me."

The robot walked to a vent adjacent to the bedroom, low and near the floor.

He followed and took a knee, quickly twisting the ridged edge of the bolt.  His thumbs and fingers slipped, even after wiping hand sweat off on his pants.

"What are you doing?  The robot asked.

"You know what happened to the guy that lived here?"  He squeezed and rotated, bruising his fingertips but managing to loosen the bolts.

"Major Lansing was evaluated as an imprinted organic and terminated by MOTH personnel."

"You can say that again."

"Major Lansing was evaluated—oh, that was a colloquialism."

"You're very perceptive Riley."

"Thank you complimenting me, Officer Ramsey."

"You're welcome." He removed the vent and peered inside. A small plastic box. After pulling it from the air duct he blew away a visible layer of dust and—

"Is that evidence of a crime?" the robot asked.

"I'm not sure." There were four tabs along the box that clicked as he flipped them up. Lifting the top—

"Would you like me to provide a three-dimensional visual recording as evidence?"

"No thank you." Inside the box was a memory disk. He set the box on the—

"Would you like me to contact your precinct for backup?"

"No, I'm good." The box made a slight thud on the laminate floor. Picking the memory disk, he rotated—

"Shall I scan it for organic markings?"

"Not right now. Thank you."

The other side of the disk glowed with a volumetric label. *Akashic Records*. A colonial brand. Lansing's other disks were Mnemosyne, which are much more common on Earth. What would he be doing with—

"I have a fingerprint scanner. It's necessary for me to clean and polish marketable dwellings to prospective tenants."

He sighed. "You know what Riley?"

"What?"

"Why don't you go watch the front door and make sure no one disturbs me?" He clicked a few of the disk buttons. A menu briefly flickered.

"My primary programming forbids me from functioning as a security robot."

"Since when?"

"My employer's automaton insurance policy provides no material coverage to damages sustained while functioning as a security robot."

"You know what Riley?"

"What?"

"I'm going to take this evidence to the police station right away," he said sarcastically.

"I evaluate your decision as particularly sound, Officer Ramsey."

"Perfect.  I'm so glad you approve."  He stood up with the disk and box in his hands.  "Thank you for your cooperation."

"It has been my pleasure to be of assistance.  I bid you a wonderful evening Officer."

"Right."  He walked to the front door and opened it.

"Why do you say 'right' in such a tone?  What does that mean?"  The robot held the door for him.

He walked over the threshold and turned back.  "You're very perceptive Riley.  You'll figure it out."

"Right."  The robot slammed the door shut.

***

He took a bite from a pumpkin donut and hid the plate of food under the round dining table in front of him while he sat and chewed.  On the other side of the sliding glass wall, a small puddle of rain by the rusty railing that separated his balcony from an alleyway of neon signs and shadows.

"Did you forget your umbrella?" Ari asked as she left the bedroom.

He unbuttoned and gripped a coat flap.  Somewhere between wet and the edge of dampness.  "I'm not dripping anything on the carpet."

"You'll catch a cold sweetie."  The home robot intercepted her hologram and merged.  She walked behind him and reached out with beckoning hands to take his wet coat, which she hung over another chair at the dining table.  "What's that?"

He put the donut on the top of the table.  "Nothing."

"Uh huh," she said in a mocking tone while clicking-on a volumetric broadcast of the Settlement Three Golf Open that floated over the table.

"What happened to your pants?"  Ari squatted down and lifted the scorched marks of the hemmed edges.  "Are you hurt?"

"No.  There was some trouble at the spaceport today."

"Peter these are new khakis."

"Sorry."

Ari checked his coat for similar damage and pulled the memory disk he found at Lansing's from one of the pockets.  "What's this?"

"I'm not sure."

Ari put a hand on her hips and raised her eyebrows.

He shrugged and took another bite.  It wasn't actually pumpkin, but the real variety vanished so long ago there was little basis for comparison.  He lifted the donut again but stopped as Caramel jumped up and down next to him, waving a hand in his face.  "Daddy Daddy!  I have a new puzzle.  Will you come help?"

"Absolutely."  He followed her to the living room where a volumetric puzzle hovered over the coffee table.  Pulling the piano bench over he sat and examined the floating arrangement of polygons.

A disassembled lighthouse.  Caramel grabbed the lighthouse's bright lens and placed it in the center.  He playfully frowned at her.  "Where do we always start?"

"Mm.  No," she said.  He lifted his head and smiled.  "We start.  With.  The bottom."  She quickly found two foundation pieces and connected the straight edges.

"Pete," Ari called out.

He raised a finger in front of Caramel and bent it down and up, while saying with the highest pitch he could, "This little piggy says standby."

Caramel giggled and jumped to her feet, hopping every few seconds.  "Standing by here."  She hopped again.  "And standing by here."

In the bedroom Ari sat on the edge of the bed, facing the volumetric emitter.

"Are you watching that dreadful Martian soap opera?" he asked.

"It's not dreadful Peter," Ari said.  "You said you loved it when we watched an episode.  Remember?"

"Right."

Ari took a deep breath.  "Sunflower's new puzzle is for ages eight and over."

"She's growing up fast."

"Her mind is."

He sat down next to her.  "This case will be over soon. We flipped someone today and she's going to spill the beans tomorrow."

Ari stood and paced in front of him.  "You think so, or you know so?"

"It's hard to say," he said.  Ari stopped pacing and put a hand on her hips.  "It's different now that Kyudo is in charge of the department."

"Kyudo?"

"She replaced Lansing."

"Is she the same Kyudo that murdered those rioters on Venus?"

"The one and only."

"Aren't you sick of being a pawn in yet another psychotic bureaucrat's game?"

He rubbed his forehead. "I made a deal—an arrangement to help us reach the colonies."

Ari sat down next to him. "A deal? With who?"

"Delphi."

"Delphi?"

"Wasserman stole one of their prediction cores."

"The Wasteland Warlord? What does he want with them?"

"I imagine he wants to see the future."

Ari laughed. "I thought you didn't believe in that fake-fate-crap? Isn't it just a big computer crunching little numbers?"

"Right. But someone thought it was worth stealing." The bed creaked as he shifted his weight. "You know, pawns that reach the other side of the board can write their own ticket."

"Hm." Ari scratched her chin. "Like passing go and landing on free parking."

"You forgot the two-hundred-dollars."

"I can't wait until we reach the colonies, and we can hold hands for real." She gripped his hand. The cold touch of the robot she had merged with.

His ear itched and he stuck a finger in it. Some of that anti-collision gel mixed with ear wax. Must have missed it earlier.

"Are you a bee now?" Ari asked.

"None of your bees wax." He smiled.

"Pfft." Ari played with her long hair and glanced at the memory disk. "What's this?"

"It could be that memory we made in San Diego before Carmen was born."

"Don't even," she said.

He closed his eyes briefly, expecting her to hit him. "It's Lansing's."

Ari loaded the memory disk's volumetric display on the bedroom emitter. She glanced at the bedroom door and waited to press play until he to stood up, walked over, and closed it.

A single experience file loaded at position zero. An up-scale party in the dim parlor of a mansion or country club. Stiff old people in suits standing around floor lamps, holding tumblers next to women in dresses imbibing colorful cocktails. None of them recognizable. The perspective was sitting at a shiny wooden table with a martini. A wine glass across from them by an empty chair.

"Oh, that's Forest Lyon." Ari paused it and pointed at someone in the background.

"The golfer?"

"The one and only. He's so handsome. Why didn't I marry him?"

"Because you love sailors."

"Nah-uh."

He nodded. "It's true. That's why I joined the Navy. Women love Seamen."

Ari laughed and resumed the flickering playback. "Pete. The glass."

"Huh?" he asked.

She pointed to a reflection in the martini glass.

He paused and zoomed. Lansing's mirrored face.

Ari squatted and squinted at the image, as though that would improve the vision of a volumetric person.

Resume playback. A woman in a red dress brushed a short palm plant as she sat at the darker half of the table, across from Lansing. Long dark hair. Her face hidden in shadow though a smile was briefly visible. She dropped a small white box with a blue band on the table. Upside down text that a subroutine automatically created a rotated, readable copy of. Aphrodite Algae cigarettes.

"Oh, that's such a dirty habit," Ari said. "Who's the dirty birdy?"

"I can't see her," he said. "Even if I could, I doubt it's anyone I know."

"You better not."

The experience gaze moved to a different table on the opposite wall, where a well-dressed couple, an old man in a suit and a young woman in a dress, looked over and waved.

"Councilman Warner." Ari jumped to her feet. "Do they know each other?"

"I doubt it. They're just being polite."

"I don't think that's the councilman's wife." Ari sat back down. "I saw his re-election commercial. His wife is older. Like him."

"He's seeing a working girl?"

Ari looked over and nodded. "But the Outcasts killed Lansing, right? I mean, the news, and you, you said that the Outcasts corrupted his mind." She looked back at the memory stream, where some guests walked by. "Maybe he just didn't want anyone to know he had to pay someone."

The memory perspective turned back towards the table, now absent of the mysterious woman. Something rectangular on the table. Lansing picked it up. An Atlantic Alliance keycard, worn but still shiny in some patches. No visible name but a profile tableau of a young man.

"Anyone you know?" Ari asked.

"No."

"We have backups of your mind. Maybe we should check your memories?" she picked up a clattering box from the corner of the bedroom and rummaged through it.

His mind's eye submerged.

Surfacing off the coast of Rhodes, the whole sky pillars of fire, and the Captain ordering me to take a hovercraft to Athens.  Perhaps there are survivors.  But no city where it once was, only a crater where it used to be, filling in with steaming water, like it was a sea monster's mouth drinking the whole Mediterranean.

On the way back a trail in the water.  Dead fish and dolphins floating along the waves.  Birds picking at them.  And then there were corpses.  So many I could have jumped out and walked the rest of the way across the Aegean without getting my feet wet.

"No, that's okay."  He returned his memory disk to the clattering box and walked into the kitchen.

"Peter, where are you going?" Ari asked.

"I'll be right back."

At the counter he pulled open a drawer filled with coffee discs, the grooved edges of the plastic wrappers crinkling against the face frame.  Using a finger to move the cream and sugar scroll-lines on the See-Thru wrapper changed the color of the foam disc within from hockey puck black to a few shades away from dirt. Fetching a mug from the cabinets above and placing it on the counter, he gripped both ends of the coffee wrapper and pulled.  Darn thing won't open.  He pulled harder until it burst open, flinging grounds over the counter and backsplash.

"I'll make it," Ari said curtly while removing another disc from the drawer.

"Right."  He grabbed the sponge vac at the kitchen sink and vacuumed the mess highlighted by the cleaning subroutine.  Ari handed him steaming black liquid captured by a ceramic vessel. "Thank you."

"How is it?"

He sipped and it tasted like it always does.  Like crap. "Delicious."

Ari smiled.  "Perfect.  What else do you think is on that disk?"

"I really should take Lansing's memories to the station in the morning.  Log it into evidence with a full chain of custody."

"Oh, okay."

"Daddy!"  Caramel ran to him smiling.  "I finished the puzzle.  Do you want to see?"

"In a few minutes Sunflower."  Ari glanced back towards the flickering lights of Lansing's memory disk in the dark bedroom.

Caramel frowned.

"I'd love to see it," he said.

Caramel smiled and bounced to the living room.

"Come on," he said.  "Let's do another puzzle together. How about the fourth of July in Galveston?"

"Our honeymoon?"

"The fireworks on the beach."

"The sky looked like it was painted."  Ari smiled.  "Alright."

# 21
## Pandora's Box

Lightning lit the ceiling as bright as day with a rumble loud enough to wake Joan. Rapid taps of rain fell along the bedroom window. Pain in her abdomen and something wet on her face. She slowly got out of bed and stumbled to the bathroom, turning the light on and closing her eyes for 20 seconds, until the light was no longer blinding.

In the mirror, a bruise by her stomach and a thin scratch on her face bleeding lightly. When did this happen? She pulled a bottle of healing gel from the medicine cabinet and squeezed a thin layer on the bruise and cut. Tiny plumes of vapor puffed as she carefully massaged it in with a fingertip. The injuries looked better but were still noticeable. Mary left some makeup here the last time she slept over. Maybe I can use that to cover it up, she thought. She stopped after pulling the medicine cabinet halfway open to return the healing gel. In the corner behind her, a plastic bag with a shirt and pair of beaten-up jeans. She put the bottle down on the vanity and picked up the bag. Blood stains on the clothes. The chronograph at the bottom right of the bathroom mirror ticked 2:30 am, September 25th. What did I do yesterday, she wondered? After investigating the starport all day with Peter and finding nothing, I had dinner with Mom, then came home and went to bed.

She put the bag back on the floor and opened her bedroom door to the rest of the apartment. Louder taps on the long window of night and neon blurred with heavy rain. The kitchen light automatically lit. A glass on the counter with a few drops of water at the bottom. She washed and then dried it with a squeaking towel, placing it next to her weapon belt. The grip of the S120 shined. Normally I sleep with my gun on my bedside table, she thought. Why did I leave it here? She lifted the belt with both hands and spread it. The holster for her backup weapon was empty. Where's the J30? Rapid steps carried her back to her bedroom. It wasn't in the drawers of either side table. Or on the top of the dresser or under either pillow.

In the living room she searched under the couch and between its cushions. Her black coat was draped over it. It was damp and the blaster wasn't in any pockets but there was a thumb sized, rounded key on a necklace. Shaped like a hollow cylinder with jagged teeth along one of the ends. Like what dad—he, used to have.

She sat on the couch and flung the coat on the other cushion. A light thump on the floor. A bouncing keycard. It landed green with the white outline of a palm tree. Underlined white text. *The Paradise Ridge Motel.* The white and green colors switched back in forth a few times.

Picking it up and flipping it, the other side read *Room 227.*

***

Windshield wipers threw splashes of rain in two directions as she pulled into a parking lot of mostly fading lines and empty spaces. It was difficult to navigate without eye functions, but whatever is going on tonight, an official record seems like a bad idea. Her wrist ring glowed the faint shade of Ghost-Mode as she pushed the transmission stick into park.

The Paradise Ridge Motel scrolled in green and white text along a billboard bolted to the roof high above a dark booth-sized office. The motel was two stories tall, laid out like a square U with the open side facing the road. All the windows obscured by drawn drapes, or curtains, or whatever they're called when you're too cheap to buy mutable glass. Cracked concrete, with door and railings chipped with flaking red paint. Miniature waterfalls spewed from the corners of the filthy gutters.

The keycard rubbed against her side from an interior coat pocket. The first number usually means the floor number, so maybe 227 is upstairs. Too much damn rain to even zoom thru. No room had a light on, and no one loitered in front of the rooms or office. But it feels like someone is watching.

She ran between splattering puddles to the stairway's landing, a half-turn made of soot-stained steel. The downpour was loud enough to conceal her approach but placing a foot on a step resulted in a high-pitched metallic creak. Slow steps minimized the noise, though the stinging rain slightly burned her hands and face. One hand on her blaster and another on the chipped railing, which swayed and squeaked with each step.

On the second floor the overhanging roof provided some shelter, but the wind pushed rain around her ankles and calves. As drops fell from her soaked coat, she walked and read door numbers, starting with 200. Black numbers 227 on a white door.

No light from the window. No sounds while holding an ear close to the dirty door without touching it. Without Wall-Thru there's no telling who's in there. Maybe just go in. Or maybe call someone. But who? Her teeth chattered, either from nerves or being soaked to the bone.

She took a step to the side and leaned against the concrete wall. Both hands wrapped around her blaster. Why complicate this? It's like helping Mary take off a band aid when she was little. Fear is something you're doing to yourself. Let the mood sphere carry it away.

Thru the rain and across the street, yellow letters lit a sign: *Hot Coffee Now*. Get one after I check this room, she thought.

She moved to the other side of the door, pressed against the short length of wall between the knob and the room's window. Lifting the keycard and tapping the lock icon changed the red door light to a green, flashing beep. With a foot she kicked the door open wide but stayed outside. The door's weight slowly moved it back towards closed, pushing out warm and musty air. Too dark to see more than a dresser.

Pushing the door against the inside wall, she swept her blaster over the room. A half-open door in a corner, next to a mirror-topped vanity. A framed painting over a neatly made bed, surrounded by two wall-mounted lamps. A wall computer under drawn curtains displaying climate control settings.

The door thudded closed with a click behind her. Darkness for a minute. Drops sounded on the floor from her still-dripping coat. The room slowly became visible, the curtain glowing a dim yellow from the motel's exterior lights. She looked over the sights of her blaster and took slow, quiet steps towards the bathroom door in the back. The white edge of a toilet but no sign of anyone.

Another step sounded a creak and she paused, holding her breath. Another sound, barely noticeable over rain taps from the roof. Is that the air vent? Or someone else breathing? Another step. Her finger held over the cold trigger. The bathroom door closer, almost within reach.

An alarm blared and she quickly pivoted towards it. The window. A car alarm. A light flickered on, forcing her eyes closed. Something cold and hard pressed against the back of her head, and she seized.

There was no voice saying 'freeze'. No sound of a blaster cocking. Only the sounds of labored breaths dividing the thuds of rain, close enough for each to brush over her raised neck hairs. I can't even think of a fucking curse word, she thought.

A reflection in the picture over the bed. A silhouette on the threshold of the bright bathroom. A large hand slid over her shoulder and gripped her gun. Would it be better to elbow this guy and die fighting?

No. But she still gasped as the hand took her blaster away.

"Take off your coat," a man's voice said.

"What?"

"Your coat. Take it off." It was a deep and crackling voice, but the words were refined and proper, like the way Troy talks but this wasn't from a smiling or handsome mouth. The wet wool slid to the floor, and the man's boot moved forward to step on it and drag it away. The inside air was warm, but she shivered, still soaked with cold rain. Is he checking the coat pockets or just staring at a soaked woman wearing leggings? "Your belt." How far is this undressing going to go? She unclicked her weapon belt and dropped it on the floor. Her stun baton bounced and rolled towards the front door. "Sit down."

Does he mean on the bed? Is it okay to turn and face him? She moved slowly, turning towards the man, lifting herself onto the bed and cautiously tucking her pressed-together legs under herself, sitting on the back of her calves and boots. The man took a step and leaned an elbow on the back of a red wingback chair.

Drops fell from her hair onto her shoulders and chest. Risking another glance up didn't help identify him. His silhouetted face was still too dark to see. But his blue shirt was visible between his parted trench coat, as were his shiny grey boots. Militia surplus. And his blaster had one of those square barrels. Maybe a Mercurial pulse pistol.

Her breathing accelerated towards hyperventilation. What's he going to do? This tank top is tight enough when it's dry. It's that stupid laundry press shrinking everything. Should have spent more time getting dressed instead of rushing over here and getting ambushed.

"Do you have any other weapons this time?" he asked.

She shook her head briefly. "This time?"
Thunder rumbled outside. "We've met before."
"Who are you?" The words cracked.
Lightning lit the room and the man's face as he said, "I am Doctor Matthew Wazzerman."

# Nicanor

There was a sound and Peter rolled over in bed. The noise will go away on its own. He opened his eyes. He had rolled through his volumetric wife, overlapping with her dark edges of static. Ring-ring.

He rolled back and poked the flashing holo-phone, dragging and dropping the floating image of a receiver to his ear. "Uh?"

"Ramsey?" a woman's voice asked.

"Huh?"

"It's Diaz. Homicide."

Ari sat up, covering herself with a volumetric sheet. "Who is it? Is it that woman on the disk?"

"What? No. It's work."

"Sorry to wake you," Diaz said.

He yawned. "Oh no, I was awake already. I always sound like this."

Diaz snickered, but it didn't sound like genuine amusement. "Can you come meet me on Avernus Street?"

He snorted. "What is it?"

"Can you be here in twenty minutes?"

***

A block from an old-world chateau the dashboard drew a right arrow to a narrow street, where a cordon of patrol cars spun blue and red beams through sheets of rain and into the far reaches of the night. He parked curbside in front of an opulent mid-century.

Mutable glass, floor-to-ceiling. It shifted between transparent and opaque in random, bubble-like patterns. Skylights made up half the roof. A bright-yellow Phoebe coupe in the driveway. Beads of dark water on the hood.

He gripped his umbrella and stepped out. Barely audible over the rain, something crunched under his boots. A pair of Infinity brand sunglasses, the lenses broken into enough pieces to earn the namesake. He wiped his soles on the wet pavement a few times.

Beyond the volumetric crime-scene tape and halfway across the line of concrete pavers, the mahogany front door opened. Eva Diaz held it and beckoned him inside. She closed the door behind him and waved a hand as he began wiping his feet. "I already scanned the floors."

Diaz wore an olive pantsuit with a white blouse. Her hair tied back and arranged with what must have been calculated precision. One of those career types who probably takes all her meals standing up, like that giraffe Carmen plays with. "Thank you for coming. She's back here." She pointed and walked to a hallway beyond the kitchen that led to a dark bedroom. At the foot of a ruffled bed, a lump under a white sheet. She squatted to lift and pull it back, dust falling through the yellow cone of her flashlight. A bloodied corpse with a coin-sized hole blasted through its chest.

Gemma Overton. A subroutine rendered *one-eighty-seven* in large red digits. The number descended onto her dead body, slithering along her bare arms and stomach.

"Kýrie eléison." Diaz looked up. "The auto-call rang an hour ago. DOLOS satellite six malfunctioned at eleven-fourteen last night. Service wasn't restored until one-twelve this morning." She dropped the white sheet over the body and stood. "Her file indicates she was about to take a deal. The link led to your casefile. I called Joan too, but she didn't answer."

"Son of a bitch."

"Why wasn't she in protective custody?"

"This is a safe neighborhood." And DOLOS didn't have any scheduled downtime. Perfect. Now Kyudo is going to start looking at her own. If she finds out I knew there was a mole and didn't tell her, she'll throw me to the wolves. Who knew about Gemma's deal? Kyudo. Lyon. Gemma's arbiter. Others could have guessed, based upon her walking out of the station last night, free as a bird.

The Cat-Eyes routine adjusted his eyes to the darkness, and he scanned the bedroom. The furniture was simple but well-built. Side tables and dressers with white-pebbled surfaces. Chrome lamps. A wood armoire. No blasted holes and no scorch marks on the walls. "Ballistics?"

"Eleven-millimeter Hephaestion."

"That's police ammunition."

"It is." Diaz squatted again to move the sheet and lift Gemma's dead hand. "There was blood under one of her nails. My handheld couldn't detect any DNA." She sniffed the hand. "Smells like hydrogen-peroxide resin." She carefully lowered the hand and arm. "The autopsy might reveal something but I'm not holding my breath."

Huh. He leaned to examine the hole in the corpse. Gemma was only wearing a bra, now partially destroyed, and panties. "She must have been asleep and woken up by the killer. One in, one out?"

"Two in, one out."

He looked at her and grimaced. "There's only one exit wound?"

Diaz loaded a shared evidence subroutine and scrolled to the ballistics overlay. It rendered one mortal wound in red, a cone with the narrow end where Gemma was shot in the chest, leading to a much larger exit in her back. Another wound, not a cone but a relatively thin line in Gemma's neck, leading right to her brain stem. "My guess would be a rimfire blaster-pistol."

"A small and quiet weapon the neighbors wouldn't hear." He made a rubbing gesture with two fingers to load a kindred copy, which he lifted and rotated over the real corpse. "That entry wound is at the back of her neck."

"The killer must have rolled her onto her stomach and shot her there post-mortem to prevent the memories of her death from being uploaded."

"Why'd they roll her back over?"

Diaz shrugged and clicked a few buttons on her wrist-computer. An animated, volumetric re-enactment.

Gemma on her knees with a red outline standing over her with an aimed pistol. One round discharged with a flash. The suspect's outline hesitated for half a minute, then rolled Gemma over. Another flash from the rendered pistol. Gemma was turned back over.

"The computer estimates the suspect is one hundred fifty-five centimeters tall, plus or minus four." Diaz browsed readouts on her wrist. "Without DOLOS, or Delphi, who can say?"

"Every house on this street has a registered security system. How'd they get in?"

"Before it was deactivated, her system was set to scan for organic intruders." Diaz gestured and he followed her back down the hall to a large room. This must be what robot realtors mean when they say open floor plan. Half the space was a large kitchen with an island, the rest a U-shaped arrangement of couches surrounding a volumetric bird. A clear view overlooking the Boulevard behind it, close enough to see the passing headlights but high enough to not be blinded by any glare. "That's a real macaw by the way," she said. "They retail for more than my salary. Still a considerable reach for a warehouse manager like Miss Overton."

"Oh, come on, with some OT you could afford one," he said. Diaz laughed. "Why isn't it flying around?"

"There's a holographic cage, but it's only visible to the bird. It doesn't know it's free." Diaz walked to the kitchen of white cabinets, where her heeled shoes clunked on the hardwood with each step, stopping at a deactivated home robot. She pointed at the broken kitchen window. Wet glass shards on the marble countertop and stainless-steel sink, where cold rain drops tapped every few seconds.

"Huh. You check the glass for blood?"

"It's clean. There are some glass fragments on the robot's hands but none of Miss Overton's DNA. I know they're hardcoded to not harm humans, but I checked anyway."

"The robot was involved? It's not Gemma's robot?"

"No." Diaz loaded a volumetric display on her wrist-computer and flipped through several pages. "According to the robot registry, she never had one." She turned the robot's head around one hundred and eighty degrees. "And check this out." Where the raised metal letters of the robot's serial number should be was a smoothed but scratched surface. A faint letter E at the end. "Someone wiped its memory core and filed the serial off. Almost." She clicked a fingernail against the remaining letter.

"Alphanumeric, a length of twelve minus one. That's what? Millions?"

Diaz turned back and nodded. "LR-thirty-three is a common model."

"They didn't finish. They left in a hurry?"

"Or they could have filed it off before the crime and run out of prep time. Or it's a stolen robot they bought on the black market for cash. The station computer is almost melting running the possibilities. I'll have to submit a request to Kyudo to purchase a Delphi prediction pack."

"Any suspects?"

Diaz stopped fiddling with the robot to look back with a smile and raised eyebrows. "You tell me."

He realized his face had fallen into a thoughtless shape. Spinning his mood-dial to Crime-Scene-Fifty-One, he felt nauseous for a minute. Colors brightened, and the edges of each corner in the room looked larger. When Diaz came back into focus a thin line of light pulsed over each black hair on her head, the individual fibers terminating exactly one centimeter beyond a meticulously perfect knot. She hadn't lifted her nose to look down at him even once, and her eyes seemed to focus only outwards, like evenly spaced security cameras with hazel rims.

Diaz's wrist-computer beeped and clicked. Chimes at an allegro tempo. "Troy cracked her computer password." She entered a doorway at the opposite end of the large main room.

A small home office, four square meters. Three white walls and a wall-sized window, where moving rays from two-dozen distant, floating volumetric advertisements dimly lit the room. A parlor palm in the corner opposite the door, of sufficient height and foliage to be priced above two large. Three shelves mounted above it, with tableaus of Overton's family, a fine China tea set, and a holographic miniature of some kind. A brown-haired woman wearing a crown. Subroutine text indicated it was Guinevere from the legends of King Arthur. A flute on a plastic stand. Huh, she was musical. A flat-panel computer angled on a butcher-block wood top.

Diaz and he reached for the desk chair at the same time.

"Oh. After you." He let go of the chair.

"It's okay. You can drive." She took a step back.

He checked under the desk, sat down, and typed on the volumetric keyboard that emerged from the surface. "By the way, did you find any datacores?"

"No." Diaz leaned on the desk with both of her elbows next to the floating images. "Can you find her credit statements?"

A yawn and his heavy eyes began to sink. Too warm to stay awake. He removed his peacoat and draped it on the chair. Clicking the search routine and typing in *credit statements* launched a large magnifying glass icon and file names rapidly scrolled upwards. "Let me just order the results chronologically. Do you want to start in August?"

"September." She grabbed the wooden stool from the corner and sat next to him, crossing her legs. Despite the rain outside and a blood-soaked carpet inside, her pants had somehow remained perfectly clean and creased.

"Right." The month's debits loaded in a grid, and he read the first entry aloud. "A room at The Paradise Ridge Motel. Looks like she booked it yesterday morning. The memo field says two-two-seven."

"Is that the room number?"

"It doesn't say but that would fit."

Scrolling down he skipped over several food truck purchases, most of them from Fast Burritos. *Everyone has at least one redeeming quality.* "Look at all of these autocar charges."

Diaz squinted and leaned over, close enough he could smell her hair. "Late at night. Early in the morning. And random times during the day." She leaned back. "Some people take autocars everywhere. I don't but some people do."

"She had a new coupe out front. Why was she hiring autocars?"

Diaz stopped fidgeting and slowly nodded. "Ramsey. When I called earlier, I was hoping for a list of possible suspects. And that by maybe working the scene, we could narrow down the list." She scratched under one of her eyes. "But I know you're a MOTH, not Detective Bureau."

"Huh." He ran the back of his hand along the stubbles on his neck. *A new laser-razor keeps sounding more and more like a good investment.* "Aren't I helping you by being here?"

"Why yes. I've never had it so good." Diaz smiled. "Isn't Kyudo your CO now?"

"I'll worry about Kyudo for both of us. Besides, aren't you flying solo with this Goddamn manpower shortage? Or is it a womanpower shortage?" He smiled.

She laughed with her mouth but not her eyes. Stupid. I shouldn't have tried joking. "Okay."

"Why don't I check out that motel room?"

Diaz stood and pulled a jingling keychain from her pocket. "Sure. Let's go."

He dragged and dropped the volumetric computer files to his wrist-computer. It clicked-back with a wait cursor. "One of us should stay here and call Terrestrial Autocar. They keep location records for ninety days. Running Gemma's charges through the pattern computer could uncover her tracks."

Diaz rubbed her eyes. "Holograms make me dizzy. I'll go to the motel. Call me if you find anything."

"I'll call dispatch and have a couple of black and whites meet you there." He pulled the chair closer to the volumetric computer and cracked his knuckles.

"Sounds like a plan." Diaz left.

# 23
## Mandela Effect

The black circle at the end of Wazzerman's aimed blaster stared back at her.

"If you shoot, someone's gonna hear it," Joan said while soaked and shivering. Her shaking hands rested on her knees, which were jutting over the edge of the bed.

"Yes, I am acutely aware of that. Thank you." His face was weathered with some age, but he wasn't old. His eyes were calm, and he smiled.

Something warm and soft struck her face and tumbled onto her lap. A towel large enough to wrap herself in. "That car alarm trick works every time." He sounded almost disappointed. "Kindly remove your mood globe."

"What? Why?" She stammered and wrapped herself in the towel.

"I wish to lodge an appeal to you. Not that mask you're wearing." He gestured with his hand over his face, like a mask is a mysterious and foreign concept or something.

She gulped and twisted the emotion orb until it popped out. The rain tapping on the roof grew louder. Wazzerman reached out and took the globe away. He was close enough that I could have grabbed his blaster, but he suddenly took several steps back.

"Now take out your car keys, please."

I pulled out the keys and Wazzerman gestured toward a silhouette standing across the room by the vanity.

"One of your brainwashed acolytes?" I asked.

"Not at all. Why have friends if they can't think and speak for themselves?" Wazzerman turned towards the other outcast. "Would you be a good chap and say hello to the young lady?"

"Hi Joan. I'm Tom," Tom said. A bearded man of average height, a balding scalp topped his round head.

I handed over the car keys and Tom exited the front door.

Wazzerman watched until it closed, then he took a seat in the red wingback chair. Still keeping me at blaster point. "So, Joan Lyon, what could possibly bring you here? Permit me to guess." He reached under the chair and lifted a plastic bag, the inside smeared with blood splatter as he shook it. Something heavy inside. "Looking for this?" He turned it to another side. A J30 blaster with a suppressor.

My backup weapon. "What's that?" I played dumb.

"Dispose with the pretense. It's unbecoming." He placed my bagged blaster on the floor and took a deep breath. "I need your help."

I scoffed. "You're a terrorist. You brainwash people and turn 'em into meat robots."

"I've never brainwashed anyone. I offer people their original selves. The people they should have been." He stood and paced. "Delphi stole their lives from them the day they chose to monopolize the future. Were it not for them the terminal war would never have occurred. They are the terrorists, not I."

"Don't sell me that shit about you bein' from the future."

"I am from the future. And a young lady of your age and station need not curse quite so much." Wazzerman cleared his throat. "You see, Delphi created a time machine. Not satisfied with merely peeking into the future, they wish to travel thru it. But I know when the prototype is constructed, which furnishes me with a perpetual license to steal it from them every iteration I return."

"If you're from the future, why don't you tell me what I'm about to say?"

"You never believe me. Even when I tell you your name is Joanna Lyon. Your middle name is Sophia. You have a sister named Mary. You hardly see your father as he is quite the sole proprietor of a small robot repair shop. Your Mother suffers from a memory illness, and you seek the means to heal her. You like chicken tenders and chips though you loathe tomatoes and catsup. Soon, you shall eat steak for the first time. You have a cat you call Slippers whom you named as such due to his white paws. And you woke up early this morning with bloody clothes, scratches, and no memory of how it happened. Taking a memory pill is rather unlike you. Need I go on? Or do you still detest the notion of someone else knowing such private details?"

"You're a fuckin' stalker," I said. Though I had to admit Wazzerman was at least a real lucky guesser. How could he know all of those things about me?

"Language, if you please." Wazzerman returned to the chair and sighed. "You're a very different person in the un-corrupted timeline. Perhaps it's your upbringing."

I gripped the towel around me and pulled it snug. "You killed my friend Morgan."

"I did no such thing." He rested his arm and blaster on the chair, no longer aiming it at me. "There is a traitor among the outcasts. Someone secured a memory printer, an advanced Venusian model, and is turning my own followers against me."

One of his victims broke free from his mental repro-gramming. Good. "If ya got a time machine. Why don't ya go back and stop 'em?"

"They have secured the primary time loop. My iterations are now secondary." Wazzerman scratched his head. "It is fittingly a matter of time before Delphi constructs another chono lab and another time machine, which can then be used to secure the first one, thereby imprisoning the future under their control."

What? I don't understand. I chewed on my lip while try-ing to think. "I don't understand."

Wazzerman stood and walked around to the window to part the drapes and peer out. His back was turned, but he was too far for me to make a move for the blaster. "I have been drawn into a temporal war with a clandestine group that calls themselves Mot. Spelled m-a-a-t dear. Gemma Overton was one of them. A smuggler if you will." He turned to face me. "Her co-conspirators are going to bomb a government building and a school today. But tragically, she is now dead. Killed before she could help me stop it. Fortunately, she did relay one final message. They are to meet at Ulmstead Gardens Park at sunrise.

"Why don't you stop 'em future man?"

"Because your police unit will apprehend me. It's always a different school as well. And the bomb is always constructed differently. That's how I'm certain of the primacy of their time endeavor. Though Blue Jewel Tower is always the other target." He looked at his wrist. He didn't have a cuffputer but a small computer or something on a leather band. "The time machine has an anchor point, a precise time and position in which they are continually arriving in the past from the future. It can only be modified by the Delphi scientists who designed the machine."

The Fischers. Someone broke into their home. Maybe they designed the machine.

"I need your assistance to find that anchor point," Wazzerman said.

"You mean you want me to help you kill 'em?"

"No Joan, I mean this." Wazzerman pushed a button on the small computer on his wrist and a holographic bubble popped out of it. He blew on it like it was a real bubble.

I held both hands open and together as it floated over and landed. Different memories within the bubble in which I saw Mary and myself from Mom's point of view. Hiking in the holodome desert. Sharing a laugh while playing a board game. Mom bringing her a cake with candles. A chocolate ice cream cake.

Wazz snapped his fingers, and the bubble of holographic memories vanished with a pop.

"I have a memory bank in the wastelands, my hidden home you settlers call the Sandcastle. I have copies of all her memories."

I looked at the blaster aimed at me once again. "Helpin' you is aidin' and abettin' an outcast. I can't."

"Ever loyal to the cult of Delphi," Wazzerman said in a resigned tone. He walked over and grabbed a dangling corner of the towel covering me to lift and hold it to my cheek. I instinctively flinched. "I understand. My kind aren't even considered human. We're shot on sight. And when we resist, it's used to justify how we were mistreated in the first place. You killing us is justice, but us killing you is terrorism."

I looked down at the comforter on the bed. A pattern of flowers. Black, white, yellow, and red. "I'm sorry."

"Please do keep in mind that Delphi wants the world to forget what they've done. Forgiving a snake and forgetting it bit you merely allows its venom time to slowly poison you." Wazzerman looked at his wrist a few seconds before the small computer began beeping. "We're out of time. One of your officers is on the way and we mustn't spoil their day with blaster fire." He handed my emotion orb back to me. "Gather your things."

I threw the towel onto the bed and ran to a dark corner to find my belt, stun baton, and soaking wet peacoat on the floor. I quickly dressed and dropped my orb into a coat pocket.

Wazzerman walked to the bathroom and gestured for me to follow. "We must vacate the premises from the washroom window. You'll be spotted out front if you go out thru the door or remain here. Use that towel on the windowsill so you don't leave any fingerprints." He dropped his blaster into a pocket and stepped on the lowered lid of the toilet to cross the threshold of the open window behind it.

I used the towel and followed onto the sloped roof while crouching and taking slow steps on the slippery shingles. I slipped and Wazzerman caught me.

"Careful Joan, I need you alive," he said. Green lights blinked on his boots. He has magnetic boots. After a few guided steps we jumped over the edge, onto a dumpster, and rolled onto the ground. The rain grew heavy again. Wazzerman looked ridiculous with hair that was both wet and frazzled. "Your ute is running, and your blaster is in the passenger seat. You have—" he checked his tiny cuffputer or whatever it was. "Four minutes until satellite service is restored in this sector. Be a dear and be far from here."

I ran to my car, jumped in, and slammed the door shut while flooring the accelerator. While skidding out of the parking lot the car beeped loudly about don't run stop signs and slow down or something. Ocean Avenue was an instant blur of green lights and before I knew it, I was turning left onto Washington. Pulling over I rested my head on the wheel next to my trembling arms, accidentally sounding the horn. Hastily rummaging thru my coat pockets, I found my mood orb and quickly snapped it into my cuffputer with a twist.

Her breathing slowed and she shivered. This damn wet coat. She peeled it off and threw it on the passenger seat next to her S120. Turning a holo-dial on the dashputer maxed out the warm air blasting from the vents. She tilted back onto the headrest and closed her eyes.

What the hell is going on? Have I been brainwashed, she wondered?

Opening her eyes and reaching over to her coat, she pulled her validation tube from an interior pocket, but stopped just short of plugging it into her cuffputer. If I've been brainwashed, what happens to me, she wondered? Does a meat robot's consciousness, their identity, vanish the moment they're detected by DOLOS? That's when the hidden programming activates for a sleeper. Or is the original me already gone and I'm already a meat robot? How can I be sure I'm even doing this right now? There was that meat robot last month that swore up and down that it remembered passing validation, but that memory was just as phony as the rest.

An eye function loaded her DOLOS validation window. Eight hours counting down. There's that guy. Morgan's friend on 25th, which isn't far.

She returned to the roadway for a few minutes and turned right onto a street, parking 100 meters short of the tents and garbage cluttering the dark sidewalks. When the thumps of rain on the windshield slowed, she grabbed her coat and walked across the road. Holding her dark stun baton flush against her side where it blended with her black coat. Her S120 in her left hand.

Emotion orb set to Ruthless-5. Maybe not the best time to try a new setting but it has a reputation.

"Hi? Can you help me?" A man emerged from the darkness a few meters away. His ghostly face brightly lit by a nearby streetlamp. "I need to call my family in Settlement 11. Can you loan me a few bucks?" He lifted a hand to scratch his ear. Two dozen needle marks on his arm.

"I can't help you."

The alleyway was a dim maze of flickering lights, pressed-pulp pallets, and passed-out fiends. It quickly proved impossible to take even a single step without loudly crushing empty Saturn-Ice vials. Both palms grew damp as she passed between parallel lines of envious eyes.

Don't stop. Don't stop.

She stopped.

A child, a boy of maybe five years, curled up against a brick wall. Shirtless in the cold and emaciated to the point his rib cages were pronounced. Arms and hands of skin covering bone and barely anything else. Not a single hair on his head. His eyes welled with dark cores of desperation. The way Mary's used to. That feeling. Too cold and hungry to even shiver.

Something inside her coming up, like water boiling its way from the bottom of a deep well. Eye functions blurred. The granola bar in my coat would mean the world to him, but I would have to unbutton my coat to reach it, she thought. My top is still wet and clinging to me. And giving food to only him would be like pouring blood into a shark tank.

One of the filthy fiends suggestively whistled from somewhere and cried out, "How much for a hand job sweetheart?"

She continued down the alley with her stun baton lifted in front of her to a bright light over a heavy metal door with lines of rust, which slowly slid open with an echoing thud. A small two-story atrium inside. Water dripping from a corner of the ceiling.

On the right, a dim hallway with dirty mirrors for walls. Infinite but blurry reflections of her walking. At the end a door of chipped paint, cracked with a slice of light coming thru. One gentle push of five fingers along the rough surface and it creaked all the way to the door spring. Stuffy air at the threshold. In a corner arrangement of computer mainframes, a young man snored, fully reclined in a plush leather chair. He didn't have hair on his head. Instead, a hundred computer cables were wired into his scalp, like thick tendrils. They spread out behind him until they reached some sort of a knot that corralled them into a tray that ran along the floor. Drilled into the adjacent yellow-brick wall was a grid of sockets, where the twisted wires dissolved into a crisscrossing mess that managed to plug into the satellite network.

She cleared her throat. Several times. Several more times. The snoring ceased, and the hacker opened his eyes.

Groggy, he stretched and knocked over empty soda cans on the small desk in front of the terminals. One of them struck the ground, bouncing and rolling into the toecap of one of her boots. Skull and crossbones printed on it. Enamel Decay brand soda.

"Vincent Chun?" I hope I remembered his name right, she thought.

The chair creaked as he moved from reclined to upright, turning towards her while yawning. "Vince, if you please." His eyes bulged. "Officer?"

"I see ya got a new computer. Ya got a receipt or is it take-nology?"

"What do your lenses tell you?"

She pointed towards her eyes. "The software's updatin'."

Vince ran a finger along the shiny computer tower next to him. Along a line of blinking green lights. "I found it in the back of an autocab." Vince grinned. "Aren't you Morgan's friend?"

She exhaled, and it was like something sucked every puff of air from her lungs. She nervously smirked. "You're wired, why don't you tell me?"

For a split second his eyes turned solid white and twitched. "Joanna Lyon. But you go by Joan."

"That's me."

He grabbed her hand for a quick shake. Soft but firm. Must be all that typing. "So good to see you again. I can't tell you how sorry I am about what happened to Morgan."

"Thanks."

"Candy?" He lifted a glass bowl of wrapped candy and held the fun-sized temptations in front of her.

Citrus flavors. No chocolate. "No thanks."

He wryly moped and took one for himself before returning the bowl. "Is this a social occasion or are your handcuffs broken?"

"Um. How would someone know if they weren't, like...themselves?"

"Asking for a friend?" Vince pulled the tied edges of the candy wrapper. The rectangular confection spun open, and he popped it into his mouth with a cluck. "You're a MOTH. Don't you have a DOLOS validator?"

"Yeah, but like, is there another way?"

"You mean an alternative to the fragebogen government program in which computers decide if people are human? Then again, humans decided that robots are non-sentient. It all evens out at the end, doesn't it?" Vince turned towards his lamptop and spread a dozen holo screens. "For the sake of an argument, let's say that yes, there is a way. Why does this person doubt their ever-living mind?"

She gulped. "I just met Dr. Wazzerman."

Vince turned towards her, shocked eyes and brows at first but he smiled. "Hah. Good one."

"I'm serious."

"Heh. Was he three meters tall?"

"No."

"Did he have glowing-yellow eyes that shoot laser beams?"

"No."

Vince scooted his chair closer. "What was he like?"

"Um. Ruggedly posh. I don't know. I didn't like him."

"If you think he altered your memories, wouldn't he make you like him?"

She shrugged. "I don't know. Maybe."

Vince rubbed his chin and looked to the left. "Unless of course he wanted you to not like him to conceal the fact that he has brainwashed you."

She began tapping her foot on the ground. "Don't gimmie that psycho-babble reverse-ology."

Vince interlocked his fingers and ran them over his head, slicking back the shiny tendrils like they were hairs.

He then loaded a holographic list and read the items in sequence, glancing after each one to observe Joan shaking her head. "Have you experienced inexplicable time dilation? Physical anomalies or exterior, paranormal entities that you're able to consciously interact with? Have you been bitten by an organism classified as Xeno-2? Do you have a prescription for Pentetic Acid, or do you regularly take Magnesium supplements? Have you ingested any Neptune Viper Caviar? Have you experienced nausea for three or more hours and, you're not, you know?" He made a gesture with both hands over his belly, implying someone having an even larger belly than him.

"Fat?"

"Pregnant."

She cringed. "No!"

"Ok." Vince's eyes turned white and twitched as he stretched his arms above his head. Some obscure logo on his oversized tee. "You're officer Joan Lyon. You are 20 years old, as of last month, happy birthday, and you graduated 90th in this year's academy class. You have 48 confirmed kills and...purchase data indicates that you buy enough animal food for two cats."

"Nope. Just one cat. He was the runt of the litter but now he's gettin' fat." She crossed her arms.

"But that is your information, correct?"

"Correct."

Vince slid his chair back along the wall of wires, using a finger to navigate different colored tape in squares around the sockets and wrapped around the ends of each cord. After rearranging a dozen of them into a different combination, he slid back to his desk. "I need to see your arm computer."

She pulled back her sleeve. "Can't you see from here?"

"I mean I need to touch it." He pulled a wire from a nearby terminal and held out his other hand, beckoning her.

"Why?"

"I have to analyze your behavior patterns and examine the memories that formed them."

"You're goin' to see my past?" She looked at the floor, turning her lips inward and biting them. This was a bad idea.

"I've seen all matter of memories, including distasteful ones. Sometimes I even remember my own."

She wondered, is he buttering me up like toast before he takes a bite? How much will he see? Who will he tell? She took a deep breath. It's either this or DOLOS. Failing validation raises an alarm. MOTHs to the flame.

For some reason Vince looked at her feet as she took two steps and carefully extended her right hand. He plugged the wire into her wrist tracker. Twelve parallel holograms loaded on his desk, each playing a different memory that flickered in his solid white eyes.

For 30 seconds her arm spasmed and her fingertips turned to pins and needles. She wiggled her fingers and fidgeted with shallow breaths. Come on already.

Vince's eyes returned to normal, and he slouched back into his chair, speaking between quick breaths. "You. Are. Human." He rummaged thru soda cans on his desk, shaking each of them in turn until one made a sloshing sound, and he chugged. After half a minute he looked over. "Could you remove the cord please? You have to twist it counterclockwise."

"Counter clock?"

"Left."

She turned and yanked it out of her cuffputer and handed it back to him.

"Did Wazzerman tell you anything about the future?"

That bullshit about bombing a school and Blue Jewel Tower. "No. Why?"

He typed rapid keystrokes, then rotated two holograms so she could see. "Check these out."

The same label in the bottom right corner of each holo-gram: *The New Virginia Mysteries*. That show Mom watches. Two different scenes, animated and looping with no audio. Rachael and Trevor boarding a starship taller than a mountain. In the other scene, a funeral on a hilltop ceme-tery. Rachael Mayr's name on the tombstone, but it was spelled Rachel for some reason.

"You're piratin' holo shows? Don't tell me ya got *Norse Dakota*."

"No. Well, yes. But no." Vince enlarged the funeral scene. "This is the series finale that broadcast last night. Rachael dies in an accident after Trevor refuses to take her back." He shrank that moving image and enlarged the other. "This, however, was not broadcast. Rachael and Trevor leave Mars to start a new life on Venus."

"Uh huh."

Vince chuckled. "Aren't you curious where this came from?"

"Yeah. Fine. Where does this deep fake come from Vin-cent?"

"It's not fake. I found it on the shadow web."

"Don't shows sometimes make different endin's and then like, show 'em to people to see which one they like?"

"This isn't a holo-recording. It's a memory from an un-settled woman."

She squinted. "An outcast?"

Vince nodded with a grin. "And she lived this experience. This memory fits into the behavioral patterns of her neural matrix."

She scratched her ear. "But doesn't that happen when someone takes a memory treatment?"

"Memory treatments wouldn't alter the ending of a holo show."

"But like, doesn't the tech exist to create fake memories that feel real?"

"Yes, but why a holoshow? Why go thru that much effort?"

"Hmm. I dunno." But Vince did say it fed the woman's behavioral patterns. Could the ending of a holo-show change someone's outlook on life?

"Have you read the 12 chronoicles of *The Isis Manifesto*? One of the 88 prophecies is the existence of multiple realities. And the wars between them shall be the final wars on Earth. The media says the last one was the terminal one but most of what they say isn't—"

She raised a hand. "Could you. Just. Not."

Vince smiled. Nice teeth for a soda fiend. "No problem. *Not* is what I do best. That's why I bought this chair." He flamboyantly swiveled and then rested his head on the plush back, pretending for a moment to be asleep.

That damn manifesto. Maybe I should ask Vince to validate, she thought. But if he fails, I'll blast him, which means some major, maybe even Kyudo, will show up with IAD and want to play 20 questions about what I was doing here in the first place. "Have you ever heard of a group called Maat?"

Vince opened his eyes and sat up. "The applesauce?"

What if Wazz was telling the truth about the bombings? I can't exactly tell Kyudo the truth, she thought. And they won't evacuate the building on a whim. "Um, didn't you once hack into a government buildin' and set off the fire alarm?"

"Back in high school. As you know, I got caught."

"Don't ya got a letter of marque now?"

"That doesn't protect me from the government when they're the target."

"Haven't you always said you're smarter than those government security experts and their overrated ivy league degrees?"

Vince stretched out his fingers and then pulled them back, causing the joints in his hands to crack in unison. "Eh, they could trace me. What is this, Joan? Entrapment?"

"Never mind."

Vince pulled an unlabeled bottle from his oversized jeans and popped a handful of pills with a snort.

"Ya got a prescription for those?"

"I'm a sovereign citizen."

She walked away from the door to the opposite corner of the room and sat on the large arm of a couch. It smelled funky but was comfy. On one of the cushions a tall stack of Jovian pulps tipped over and splattered all over the floor. "Aw shit. Sorry." She picked them up off the floor, restacking them on the couch.

"That's okay I already read all of them. I give those ones to the children out there every morning."

"Do they read 'em or eat 'em?"

"They read them. I think."

She looked at the one in her hand before placing it at the top of the stack. *Munchers 3*, written by T. Gell, published by Friendly Primes. Thumbing the pulp of inked words and images, the crinkled edges of the stained and moist pages crumbled. "Can I take one of them?"

"Yes of course. That's a good one. Alien zombies land on Earth and start eating people."

She pulled the granola bar from her interior coat pocket and rolled the thin pulp book around it. "Thanks."

"Anytime."

She stood and walked to the door.

"Joan?" Vince asked.

She stopped and turned.

"The sheltering years weren't pleasant for anyone. I've found that talking to someone really helped."

"Talkin' to who?"

"A professional."

"A therapist?"

"Yes." Vince sat very still considering how much caffeine and stims he took. And considering he was himself too. His eyes were just as still. A serious look of concern.

"Thank you, Vince."

In the dark alley the rain was hardly more than a drizzle. A robot emerged from a shop's back door with a metallic swivel and lifted trash into a vertical recycler. The aroma of coffee, the most sublime substance to ever be roasted, briefly filled the narrow brick passage, a needed relief from the body odors of riff raff. The bums perked up with sudden interest, clamoring for scraps of refuse.

She found the emaciated child and handed him the rolled pulp book, tilting it enough that he could see the concealed granola bar. "Vince told me ya like comics."

The boy's eyes lit up and he nodded.

"Read it somewhere alone," she whispered.

"I know Officer ma'am. Thanking you."

When she returned to her car, a weak blue light pulsed on the horizon. The blue aura surrounding Blue Jewel Tower. She loaded a holographic list of the 826 schools in the Settlement, and a timer counting down the minutes and seconds until sunrise.

# 24
## Uncanny Valley

The mansion in the foothills was number nine on the pattern computer's list of places that Gemma had visited, via Terrestrial Autocar, in the past three days. Diaz called him after finding an empty motel room and they divided the remaining list.

There were enough parked cars along the street that he cut his lights and stopped a full block away. Rain tapped on his coat as he stepped out, and it beat on the cruiser's roof like a toddler with a drum set. Puddles on the dark road spread growing circles from the heavy rain. Its drops and the crunches of small pebbles under his boots performed a duet with each step as he crossed the block of asphalt and approached the sidewalk in front of the mansion.

The only visibly lit house under the dome of darkness. Not surprising for three in the morning. Yellow light poured from each window into rectangular shapes on the green lawn, which was bare except for a single fake tree. A semicircular pattern above the front door had spaced dividers, like rays of the sun. The top of a spiral staircase within. The railing of an empty atrium.

The grass under his feet crunched louder than the rain as he attempted to sneak around the side of the large house. I need Lyon lessons.

A single lit side window on the second floor. Only the shadows of occupants. Why doesn't Wall-Thru work? The no satellite icon blinked. Slowly stepping away towards the adjacent house restored them in waves of static and distorted text. He pivoted back and forth, seeing them disappear and reappear a dozen times.

A house-wide satellite umbrella. What will they think up next?

Back at his car, he clicked the dashboard transmitter. "One-Henry-Six, come in."

Diaz's voice responded, "This is six, go ahead."

"What's your twenty?"

"I just cleared location five and was about to stop for coffee. How do you take it?"

"FIDO. Meet me at location nine. Q-O-A."

The rain died down, and he quietly played his holo-piano, Sonata in C Major, Opus Two, with occasional glances at the house. Distant headlights lit the rearview mirror. Diaz parked behind him and exited, coffee-less.

She followed alongside him to the house and whispered, "my subroutines just cut out."

"Me too," he said quietly.

Diaz pulled back one side of her blazer to check her holstered pistol. They took opposite sides of the tree to peak around, then met in the dark middle.

"Second window from the right," Diaz said.

He rechecked. On a sofa, a woman with two children, a girl around ten and a boy who was say, twelve. Somber expressions, no words between them. They stared straight ahead like robots. "What about them?"

"They look just like Lansing's family."

He squinted. The children did resemble Lansing's family, had they lived instead of dying so young. I'll be damned. "Clones. Overton was smuggling clones. This is where she brought them."

Light brushed over the darkness of the tree, and he fell to the ground with an ouch. Diaz had grabbed something of his and pulled him down to the ground, where he flopped next to her face. Her nervous breath smelled sweet.

A car passed, two white lights that splashed through puddles before trailing off in diminishing red and disappearing with a far corner.

Diaz rose with her pistol drawn but pointed at the ground. She whispered, "I'll take the front, you take the back."

"Right." Chest pain and adrenaline. No time to dial. He ran through the crunching grass to the rear of the large house, finding a failed attempt at a garden and a sliding glass door. An illuminated interior, with a plush couch and a coffee table. The three clones ran from a blast at the front door and towards him, sliding the back door open.

Just let them go. They're innocent in this. But they may be the only lead to those missing cores. Letting them go means do not pass go, do not collect a pension, do not retire with your family.

He lifted his M400 pistol. "MOTH. Freeze."

Their backs straightened, quickly lifting their hands up and open.

Diaz appeared behind them, cuffing them one at a time. She patted the woman down and sat her on the blue couch by pulling her shoulders and abruptly shoving her onto it, though she was gentle with the children, only patting down the sides of their torsos and patiently nudging them towards the cloned Mrs. Lansing.

"Is restraining them necessary?" the cloned Mrs. Lansing asked.

"Shut up!" Diaz screamed in its ear and tightened its cuffs until it yelped, and the clone children gasped. "Don't even try to talk your way out of this."

The copies nodded.

Diaz turned to him. "I'm going to call a wagon and find the umbrella. Watch them."

He nodded as she left. The children on the couch shivered in their tee shirts, so he closed the back door, ending the cold air invasion. Not much different from Overton's house. A single large room divided into a kitchen and living room. Though this was two stories high, with a loft above them. And the walls were a bit more upscale, with wood panels and—son of a bitch. This is the parlor from Lansing's memory disk. Though the short palm plants were taller, reaching above the lowest row of wood panels. "Is it just the three of you?"

"No, you and that other officer are here," the fake Mrs. Lansing said.

He placed his hands on his weapon belt. "Are there any other organic copies here?"

The three clones shook their heads in unison. There was a black fabric chair opposite the white couch, which he sat down on and shook while yawning. An animated picture on the wall far behind the copies of birds on a beach, flying towards the horizon.

"So, you're Cassandra Lansing? I—" Better not mention knowing the real Mrs. Lansing. Not with Diaz potentially within earshot. "I used to work with your husband."

"I was her for a while," it said.

"Lansing's wife. That's who you are."

The clone shrugged, restricted by the shining cuffs. "That's who Oric wanted me to be. I don't have a tracker, so I know I'm not human."

"But you thought you were Cassandra Lansing, right?"

"I have her memories, and for a while I did think I was her. The children quickly forgot their former lives, but I kept having these dreams of being someone else. My life from before, before this newer identity. Visions where I did the simplest things, like brushing my hair or pouring coffee." It managed to act out with rote gestures, while cuffed, as though it were brushing its hair with an invisible brush and pouring coffee from an absent pot onto the floor. "I knew I had another life, but it always felt out of reach. I am neither here nor her."

"Do you have Mrs. Lansing's memories of the Old Earth?"

"I remember signing a do-not-digitize order."

His feet thudded on the floor as he leaned forward in the chair. "You signed one of those? What on Earth for?"

"I—Cassandra, always felt like a copy of her would just be an impression.  I was glad he brought me back, for the children's sake.  But I hoped that Oric would move on.  And maybe one day he could meet someone real.  Unique."

Lansing must have wanted to hold his real children.  His real family.  Who could blame him for that?

His chest tightened just above his stomach, to the point taking a deep breath would have been impossible.

"Does it hurt?" The clone girl asked.

"Does what hurt?"

"Being recycled.  That's what's going to happen to us, isn't it?"

Give them one last moment of peace.  He lied, "No, I'm told it's painless.  Pleasant, even."

The children breathed sighs of relief.  Alarms blared in both ears as satellite subroutines returned.  The line of clones on the couch lit up with red bounding boxes and accompanying red text.  *Organic Hazards Detected.*

Diaz shouted from upstairs, "I found the umbrella."

"I noticed.  Bravo zero."

"What's that mean?" The clone boy asked.  "Bravo zero?"

"It's something we used to say in the Navy.  It means good job, but sometimes you say it to a friend, either out of sarcasm or to make fun of them when they *really* mess up."

"Oh.  Hah."  The boy excessively nodded his head, its body bouncing up and down with it.

He loaded a volumetric image on his wrist-computer and held his arm straight in front of him for the copies to see.  The weighted scales from Gemma's ledger.  "Can you tell me what this is?"

The copied Mrs. Lansing glanced at the badge affixed to his belt.  "You're a MOTH.  Like Oric."  It smiled.  "You're a life-form detective."

"That's right."

"Gemma was working with a former police officer," the copied Mrs. Lansing said.

"Who?"

"I know you will upload our minds. It's your standard procedure. But your pattern computer could take an hour." The copied Mrs. Lansing walked over and got on her knees at the foot of the chair. Her cuffed hands flattened together as though she were about to pray to Isis. "I can tell you what you want to know right now," it whispered. "If you let them go."

I could lie to her, just like I did with Andrea Aeneas. He tapped a finger against his knee several times. "I'm sorry, but the MOTH commanders will never honor that deal."

Approaching footsteps. Diaz. "Am I interrupting anything?"

A knock came from the front door, which opened. Ivan Pollux walked in grinning with a backpack and a toolbox labelled *Mind Reader*. He asked in his Russian accent, "Did someone make house call?"

***

He found Diaz on the lit front porch, turned away from him and leaning against the white railing while holding a hand up to her face. Her hair was dark enough that had she untied it, her head might have been invisible against the background of night. She half-turned her head and blew a small cloud of blue smoke before flicking orange embers beyond the concrete pavers below and out onto the dark lawn, where they glowed like fireflies before disappearing among the glistening green blades of wet grass.

"Do you want one?" She pulled a small red box with a large white stripe labelled with blue Japanese typography, which an ocular subroutine translated into *Olde Osaka*.

"I don't smoke." A car passed the street, causing a glare from the porch's corner. A doorknob laid twisted and broken with a partially charred finish. Diaz hadn't mentioned how she breached the front door, and her blazer didn't appear to be packed with any explosives. A partially charged shot, optimized by a subroutine? Impressively precise. Officer Hamilton would have blown up the front of the house.

Diaz turned around to face him, leaning her back on the railing. Her eyes scanned his face, perhaps trying to sense if he was judging her before her eyes fell to the ground. "I'm trying to quit."

"Those three copies don't look dangerous."

"They never do, do they?" She took a drag and puffed. "Unassuming artificials started the war. Now they have the new planets and we're stuck here with the scraps." She took another drag and shook her head while scoffing. "Lansing. Can you believe him? As if his closet war crimes weren't enough. Dollars to donuts he gave Overton much more than one of his little miniatures in exchange for clones. At least this is the last mess of his that we have to clean up."

"He must have missed them."

Diaz shook her head. "Selfish malakas. Like those fiends that shoot Saturn-Ice into their veins. Only his addiction was the past, and now he's joined it." She made some sound with her nose, something between a sniffle and a snort. "Having children copied and sent here, knowing they'd die from clone fever within five years? And that once we lucky few found them, we would have to euthanize them? Total dick move."

He nodded up towards the house. "Clever though. He hid them in a neighborhood where cops usually knock on doors instead of breaking them down."

"You think no one knew what was going on here?" Diaz scratched one of her eyebrows. "Once someone reaches major, they think they're God almighty. Or Hathor, on the seldom occasion that a woman manages to infiltrate the old gods club." She flicked ash off the edge of her cigarette and sighed. "Sometimes I wonder why I even bother with this job. Half the time DOLOS auto-solves the case and all I do is sign the forms. The other half is this cloak and dagger nonsense."

"Have you thought about transferring? Every department is short-staffed."

"Everyone I know lost family in the war. Often, they're listed as missing, not dead. Sometimes I think there are people I know, or used to know, living as exiles out in the desert. But I don't really know." Diaz blew glowing-blue rings of smoke that glided into the night like ascending halos. "Nothing will bring Gemma back from the dead, but there's always that slim chance that I can give her friends and family the truth."

He nodded and his wrist beeped a tune.

"The Lean Davies?" Diaz asked. "I can't remember the last time I heard them."

And I can't remember the last time I played *There is Still Time*, but I'm somehow sure I have. He read the message from Ariadne.

*Are you okay?*

He typed a reply. *I'm okay. Get some sleep beautiful.* A button launched a selection of emojis to add to the end. Ari likes hearts and here's three. Which one—his wrist beeped again. So did Diaz's. Another message.

*Officer Lyon, Joan has elected to eliminate a span of her memory of September 24th. Please read the attached cover story before any subsequent interactions.*

He looked up and Eva was still reading.

The lights from her wrist-computer colored the smoke rising from the cigarette jammed between her two fingers. "Just-Justice-Joan finally found something worth forgetting." Diaz finished her cigarette and put the smoldering remains in a small tin, whose home was an inside pocket of her blazer. "What's up with your pasty partner?"

"She's becoming pastier."

"Oh?"

"Yes. If she gets any paler, she'll be a hologram."

Diaz guffawed, strongly enough that saliva landed on his face.

A rising tempo of thuds grew louder, and the house's broken front door swung open. "Peter. Eva," Ivan said. The door swung loose from one of its hinges, and Ivan spent several seconds putting it back before he read from his wrist-computer. The brightness setting was high enough that it lit the entire porch in white light. "Mrs. Clone wanted to give message before her mind upload. She says former copper named Mattie was here. Ten in evening. Black hair and blue eyes. No last name but tall and *slender* woman. Also, they interest in key. Little cylinder with teeth. Somethings to do with Lansing pre-war house that clone remembers but has not been there."

"Thank you, Ivan," Diaz said as he shut the door and left with fading footsteps.

A tall woman with dark hair and blue eyes. It must be the one I saw at Lansing's apartment. But who is she and what was she doing here?

Diaz turned to him. "You knew Lansing pretty well, didn't you?"

He turned to the porch's railing and leaned on it. Lansing's pre-war house. There's only one place that could mean. Going there means visiting a haunted graveyard. Going there means admitting involvement in the war. Going there means nothing good.

"Peter?" Diaz continued.

I could say I don't know. Follow Diaz to a few dead-end leads, then go home and grab a few hours of shuteye before a three-cup-of-coffee morning.  Watch Caramel do one of her puzzles after breakfast.

But with Lansing's old Air Force key, what could the Outcasts be looking for up there, other than something to escalate the conflict between the human settlements and the Outcasts into a total war.

He looked over at one of the house's windows, flickering with different lights from within.  Brief flashes of the clone Mrs. Lansing's silhouette.  Why would she divulge information that could help her human executioners?  Does she also have terrible memories of the Terminal War?

"Maybe we could both use a coffee," Diaz said.  Suddenly right next to him.

"We're going to need a hovercar."

# 25
## Antares

Peter couldn't hear himself yawn over the whirring engines of the hovercar. The windshield computer rendered Chiron airbase as a small green point on the horizon. The circular point grew into a square perimeter and volumetric lines of structures as the distance readout below ticked from slowly falling kilometers to rapidly vanishing meters. But the actual buildings remained obscured by perpetual gales of dust and sand.

He reduced altitude and speed, altering course towards a small square the computer marked at the edge of the base. Landing thrusters brushed a circle of clear pavement as the hovercar set down with a thud.

In the sideview mirror the engine's reflection stopped with a ticking grind, and a layer of dust quickly settled on the windows.

"Will we be able to take off with this storm?" Diaz asked.

"We can here, according to the computer at least. Though it means we're in for a hike and we need to be back here before the winds change."

"You suit up first. I'll launch the drones." Diaz rapidly scrolled through the dashboard computer to a blue rendering of the stingray-shaped drones. "Not only are satellites useless in this weather, but these drones might not manage to find a single footprint."

He pulled a bulky hazmat suit from the backseat and clumsily put it on, stopping when he realized his boots were still on. "Don't forget your anti-radiation meds."

Diaz held up an empty vial. "Way ahead of you, Ramsey."

When they stepped out gusts of dust battered his clear faceplate. The crackling Geiger reading blinked between the orange and red end of the scale. He held out a hand, waiting for the dark dust to land on the white glove's palm. Cesium. Using a knob on the suit's forearm he cycled through overlays on the helmet's visor. Radiation, which illustrated the storm's violent relationship with the wind in deep red hues. Motion detection was equally overloaded, though it rendered everything black and white. Infrared only picked up Diaz's face.

Between each gale visibility improved to about twenty meters. Diaz followed him along a line of fallen and rusty fences to a long-abandoned sentry post by the base's sign of fading letters, *Joint Operations Base Chiron*, adjacent to the now-colorless but still-etched emblems of the Atlantic Alliance service branches. Each step sent down a thump and elevated a small yellow cloud.

Winds settled for a moment, revealing the hundred or so buildings that remained standing. He had checked satellite images years ago and remembered the flattened circle that dominated most of the base, centered around the vaporized airfields, hangars, and missile silos. The shockwave's damage had tapered at its edges, resulting in rows of structures ranging from collapsed to leaning.

"There are two places the Outcasts could have used Lansing's key. The ordinance depots on the West end and the one remaining missile silo to the East. You check the depots. I'll check the silo."

"Why don't I check the silo and you check the depots?" Diaz loaded a small volumetric display of the base on her hazmat suit's wrist but shut it down as the radioactive dust cut the crisp images into blurs and scattering lines of light. She looked at him. "Does the silo have a biometric lock?"

He clicked a button on his suit's wrist-computer to mark the depot locations on her HUD.

"Are these nuclear-grade weapons?" Diaz asked. "Why haven't they been decommissioned?"

"What do you think happened to the last person who said anything?"

Diaz wiped dust off her visor and placed a hand on her hips, or at least where her hips probably were underneath the bulky hazmat suit. "Fine. I'll check the depos and we'll meet back here in an hour. Okay?"

"Okay." He instinctively nodded, which was pointless since Diaz was walking away from him.

After a few hundred meters of chipped asphalt a calf muscle nearly cramped, and he stopped to carefully stretch. He dug a thumb under each backpack strap before tightening them, so it didn't bump into his pistol, holstered on the suit's external belt.

Through a break in the spinning dust, the top of the primary bunker entrance. A concrete stairwell the size of half a football field and shaped as a descending semi-circle, similar to an old Greek amphitheater leading to a dark pit. Dirt and debris covered nearly all the steps. Metal bars, broken and rusted tools, broken planks of wood and rocks both strewn out and condensed into piles large enough to form a maze of rubbish leading to the bottom, where a heap of ash concealed the heavy metal door that led to the now-abandoned fallout bunker. Scorch marks along the concrete walls, including one shaped like an adult and child holding hands.

Is that how far they went? Did they reach the door only to find it closed? Did they die banging on it, begging for mercy? Or was it over in an instant? Perhaps it would have been better to die in a world that still made sense, instead of living in one where the people who gave you the best memories are reduced to them.

Their house, a few hundred meters away, was one mailbox over from the corner lot that Ari really wanted. She planted rows of basil in the backyard to put into her awful-tasting pasta sauce, though he would lie and say it was wonderful.

Even between a time and place, one half missed the other. For there was no laughter from children playing in the street. No songs from the birds in the trees. No smiling glances from his wife reading on her wooden chair on the front porch. No grinning waves from Caramel sitting on her bedroom windowsill with her toy giraffe.

Only the Geiger counter and the wind howling in his ears as it brushed dust along the horizon of collapsed houses.

I could be joining them soon, depending on what Diaz says when we return. It would have been better to not bring her along, though searching would have taken longer. Too long. Diaz. A detective with woman's intuition. She would have found out sooner or later anyway. And calling up Lyon would have been worse. She would probably shoot me and leave me for dead, he thought.

A click on the HUD, and a subroutine-rendered outline of a drone high above. He looked back down, noticing that he had sat at some point and was now covered in dust. Half an hour remaining on the chronograph.

The pings were footprints the drone had found. Must be a false positive, given the perpetual storm shrouding the area, though the scans that loaded on a subroutine appeared real enough.

Fifty meters away. A large rectangular building of brick walls divided by cracked and broken windows. The mess hall. Where thousands of people used to eat every day. Where laughter used to be regularly heard. It still held up shingles of long, interlocking metal shapes. Like Holo-Tetris but only two dimensions and sprinkled with patches of dirt, except for the corner of the roof, which had col-lapsed.

The two large doors at the main entrance were not bro-ken but missing entirely. Layers of sediment settled on the floor and tables, identical to nature's exterior renovation efforts. Bits fell in the angled rays of light that sliced the corner of the collapsed roof.

A lone skeleton sat at one of the tables. A bowl in front of him, or her, filled with what was once soup. It had long since grown colder. Unless it was Gazpacho.

The footprints were in a hallway past the kitchen and led to a stairwell. The dust grew thinner, but the boot impressions were still well-defined. Above them, holes in the ceiling. Not straight up but diagonal. That must be how the drone spotted them.

The metal stairs echoed thuds and at the bottom of four flights, next to elevator doors, a heavy metal vault with its door half ajar. A coin-sized circular lock next to it. One that Lansing's key would have fit. He groaned while pulling the vault's squeaky door fully open. Motion-controlled ceiling lights flickered on one by one to reveal a room of metallic walls and a half-dozen showerheads. Another hatch across from him, sealed. An airlock.

After closing the door and decontaminating the far door automatically opened. A hallway with no dangerous radiation, according to the Geiger subroutine. White linoleum floors. Five open doors leading to two offices and a small lab. A large storeroom with bare shelves.

What good would this do Wasserman? There are easier ways to steal supplies. And a few days with a plasma torch could melt that door instead of needing the key.

At the back were two glass doors that automatically slid open and led to a large room with a tall, curved ceiling divided by thick arches of lights. Large sections of the metal-mesh floor were cut away and bordered with caution strips, wires, tubes, and machinery protruding from half a floor below, making the surface a catwalk. A dozen empty stasis tubes lined against a wall.

This must have been a VIP bunker for the brass to popsicle themselves. Wait for the surface to return to habitable with a cold nap instead of living out years breathing stench and chewing on scraps in case the last war ever happened. Which it did.

The flickering terminal logs were awkward to navigate in gloved hands. One of the tubes had at one time kept a subject in stasis for five years. No DNA profile but an abbreviated name: Dr. W. Could be Wasserman. Or one of the myriad other doctors whose surname ends in W.

Something shiny in the corner. A datacore. A Delphi datacore! Not a barrel-sized model but a mini the size of a roll of paper towels. Back when one could simply buy a roll of paper towels. He picked it up and clicked the power button. Nothing. Dead battery.

The chrono subroutine flashed twenty minutes. I still need to check that silo. He dropped the mini core into his backpack. It didn't weight too much though it pinched his lower back as he huffed up the stairs to the mess hall and out to the surface.

When the missile silo battery was within fifty meters, a creak stopped him dead in his tracks. The sound of a door opening and closing. The noise repeated itself. Could be the wind, moving a door back and forth. Pausing and watching the wind didn't match the gusts with the regular creaking. It echoed from a derelict building with rusted fuel drums lined up against one of the sides.

He drew his pistol and aimed it with both hands, its black finish quickly dotted with yellow motes. Around the corner was an open garage entrance behind a pallet of some materiel covered by a loose tarp, which flapped in the wind like a sail. A subroutine recorded the creaking sound as a pattern with an interval of eleven seconds.

He knelt behind the pallet and squinted into the open garage. Cat-Eyes couldn't adjust due to the tarp obscuring the field of view every few seconds. Crawling to the edge resulted in a clear view.  And neck pain.  Beyond metal shelves of paint cans, a door kept opening and closing.

Just the wind.  Though the hairs on the back of his neck stayed up.

Among the circle of twelve, silo number eight was on the left side, visible in a clearing of the swirling winds.  High above a miniscule circle of blue at the top.  The eye of the storm.  After passing the metal doors of six, he slipped and tumbled down the embankment.

The view quickly rotated between crunching dirt and sky, until he fell over an edge yet managed to grip something with one hand.  A curved metal bar he dangled from.  A pain in his elbow, sharp enough that he gritted his teeth.  He looked back over his shoulder.

The black abyss of an open silo.  Something metallic spinning and sinking into its center.  His pistol.  It made no noticeable sound when or if it reached the bottom.  His one-handed grip on the silo's rim began to slip, and he reached up with his other hand.  Once.  Twice.  The fifth time he finally managed to hold on and slowly lift himself back over the edge with shaking and aching arms.  He crawled thirty meters up the embankment and only stood when the ground was level for a while, resting a hand on each knee and taking heavy breaths through the respirator.  I'm too old for this nonsense.

Ten minutes ticked on the chronograph, and he clicked his transmitter.  "Diaz?"

"Yeah?"

"I'm behind schedule."

"So am I.  But I rechecked the computer and the winds are changing, South by Southeast.  I don't want to be stuck out here."

"Neither do I."

"How about half an hour?  Does that sound like a plan?"

"Alright." He adjusted his chronograph while walking to a room-sized mound of raised earth with twin metal doors each labelled *8*. They didn't automatically open. The manual override allowed him to push. Mist gathered on the bottom half of his visor and sweat dripped down his back.

The small elevator lobby was familiar though it had been over a decade and the overhead lighting was dimmer. It's a miracle there's any power here at all, all things considered.

"Authenticate," a computerized voice spoke from a narrow section of wall to the right of the elevator. A flat-panel computer above a speaker strip. Yellow lines danced up and down, matching its tone.

"Sunflower."

"Ensign. Ramsey, Peter," the computer said as the stainless-steel elevator doors slid open with a heavy tumble. The elevator descended unsteadily for a minute and opened to a lobby with a wall-computer. A name at the top of a list in flashing in large yellow letters. *Lieutenant. Brooks, Nathaniel.* Dated September twenty-second. Another survivor, though undoubtedly an Outcast. No face came to mind. Though I was usually at sea, he thought. Other names on the access log, but they were dated over a decade ago. Prewar. Brooks's entry moved down a row and his own name and rank appeared at the top, one flashing letter at a time.

The silo chamber opened onto a dark maintenance catwalk, where the two lights of his helmet followed his gaze as it moved across the building-sized ballistic missile that stood there undisturbed by the passage of time. As though someone had chiseled an obsidian statue of the God of death and left it here to worship later. He gripped the railing and slowly looked over. The bottom was a dark horizon beyond the range of helmet lights or Cat-Eyes.

He slowly walked backwards over the threshold, clicked the door button, and watched it close. It would take a small army of Outcasts to even think about moving that—thing.

Though Wasserman does have a large army of them. And they were here.

The spiral hallway gradually descended around the silo with just enough slope to accelerate a marble. The overhead lights grew increasingly dim the deeper he ventured. Darker until level B-seven, where a bright rectangle emerged. A broad passageway, perpendicular and leading away from the silo. Black letters on the concrete beneath it with an arrow. *Alert Aircraft Hangar.*

The hangar was the size of a high school football stadium and with comparable lighting. Half of it had caved in. A single remaining bomber stuck on a square, vertical aircraft elevator several meters off the floor. Empty cockpit.

A large, open doorway on the other side of the hangar led to a room as dark as a tomb. His boots clanked on the metal floor and his helmet lights landed on stainless steel doors built into the wall, each with a narrow window of tinted yellow glass. Inside, tipped metallic cylinders with fins. Missiles.

In front of each missile chamber was an automated munitions cart, which resembled a small firetruck with caliper-shaped claws for hands. None of the robot chassis blinked. Their batteries just as dead as every other severed appendage of the long-dead war machine.

He lifted a hand to scratch his chin but rubbed the bottom of his helmet instead. One of the missile chamber doors was ajar and missing a munitions robot. He approached it slowly as his heart raced into a drum solo pulsing in both eardrums. The circular lock, one that Lansing's key would fit, was rotated to the open position. Black text on the door's window. *MK-412.* A two-hundred-kilogram urban decimator. Capable of vaporizing an entire settlement in an instant.

An empty chamber. Empty like an empty coffin. No missile inside. Nothing. Nada. Only the two white helmet lights moving iridescently along the wall and his blurry reflection on the polished floor.

He was running before the thought crossed his mind. Through the tunnel and up the spiral hall to the elevator. Tapping the surface button thirty times until the elevator door shut and he stared at the red digits counting the number of meters remaining above while clicking the transmit button on his wrist. "Diaz? Diaz?"

No response, even after several reattempts. Muffled clicking and static. He leaned against the elevator wall, heaving. Sweat on his back. His undershirt stuck to him and moving his shoulders in various directions didn't help. The red digits struck zero and the elevator chimed as the doors opened.

Flood lights blinded him. Through squints, two figures in hazmat suits. One with a pistol and the other with a carbine. Their faces obscured by tinted visors.

"Peter Ramsey?" One of them asked through a respirator.

He did nothing.

"You're coming with us," One of them, perhaps the other this time, said.

The man with the pistol holstered it and approached, grabbing Peter's hands and binding them.

"Don't puncture his suit," The man with the aimed carbine said.

"You worry too much," The cuffing man said.

They led him out, shoving him when his pace slowed. His legs grew heavy and both knees ached. Breaths fogged up the inside of his helmet. "Where are you taking me?"

"Shut up." The man with the carbine kicked the back of his calf.

He fell with a groan and staggered back to his feet. As he continued to walk, he noticed the spot where he slipped earlier fifty meters ahead.

"So, what do you figure this guy has?  Information?" the man with the pistol asked the other.

"He found the boss's timeshare."

"Why don't we just blast him and take his mind back?  And whatever's in here."  The man with the pistol grabbed Peter's backpack, loosened the straps, and pulled it away while shoving him again.

"Is your radio broken?" the man with the carbine asked.

"If this guy cared about livin' he wouldn't be walkin' like he's got shit in his pants."

"It must be all that guilt.  He came out of that silo.  You know what that means."

"I lost a brother in the war."

"So did I.  But the boss said bring him back alive."

"I'll take the heat for it."

The dust storm had turned into a churning, radioactive blizzard that threw clumps against the front of his helmet faster than he could brush it away.  The slippery embankment by silo six.  Only a few more meters.  Pebbles cracked under his boots.

He turned and pushed the man with the pistol down the embankment, but he only slid a meter.

"Hey!" both armed men said in unison.

He kicked up dust and ran away.  Bright slugs whizzed by.

"No!  Stop!" one of the men shouted.

Leaping over some debris pulled a muscle in his leg, though he managed to keep jogging.  "Son of a bitch cock ass motherfucker!"

"Ramsey?" Eva asked over the wireless.

Apparently, he had clicked the transmit button.  "Diaz," he said between huffs.  "Can you get to the hovercar?  In sixty seconds?"

"What happened?  Is it an emergency?"

His boots skid on a patch of dust and he nearly collided with the remains of an armored vehicle. The cramp finally forced him to his knees. Several slugs landed above, sparking and ricocheting off the vehicle's thick metal. He stood and wobbled through the churning storm. "You bet your ass it is!"

He stumbled and rolled down a crumbling stairway littered with rocks and landed on his back next to a skeleton. A stabbing sensation in his abdomen. The contamination subroutine clicked an alarm with a radiation icon on the HUD. A hole in one of his boots. Perfect. *I could just lay on the ground here and wait. Wait for nature and fate.*

"Peter, the drones have identified two hostiles not far behind you," Diaz said. "I'm authorizing them to use lethal force. They'll cover you." Ear-popping automatic fire from two drones circling above. The brilliant flashes visible through the dust storm.

On the HUD the hovercar's transponder lit up. Ninety-eight meters. *That's a football field. Athletes can run that in ten seconds. And that's without steroids.*

He clicked the stimulant button sequence on his wrist, stood, and jogged while dodging rolling rubble. Eighty meters. Seventy. Fifty. At twenty he spotted Diaz reaching the passenger door. His momentum slammed him into the door, and he fell over while opening it.

Inside the hovercar he quickly pulled the door shut. The engine was already running but *PURGE* flashed on the dashboard computer.

"Ramsey!" Diaz shouted.

One of the Outcasts stood on a pile of rubble thirty meters away. His pistol shaking in his hands.

"Charged shot!" he said. The blast flung the hovercar several meters into the air. A dozen different klaxons and flashing alarms on the dashboard as the vehicle crashed into a small crater of fire. A mound of dirt briefly landed on the cracked windshield before the auto-wipers tossed it clear. "Son of a bitch!"

Diaz loaded the auto-cannons and the roof-mounted turret whirred towards the Outcast. She pulled the trigger. Deafening rat-a-tacks blew the target into dogfood-sized chunks. Then the rubble he was standing on. The rubble to either side of him. A sizable territory of desolation. A majority of the horizon. She must have fired a thousand rounds. Even Lyon would have been impressed. "Get us out of here."

He pulled up on the collective, catapulting the car into the air, and turned South towards the settlement. Some warning lights from the instruments until avionics re-balanced the intake manifolds. "We need to warn Kyudo." Diaz turned towards him. "Those Outcasts stole a warhead. A nuclear warhead."

Diaz clicked a few buttons on the dashboard computer. "That Outcast blasted our coms."

"Perfect." He accelerated and his hand grew unsteady. The pain in his abdomen.

"Are you okay?"

"Yes."

"Maybe I should fly."

"Right. You got it."

Diaz switched the controls to her side and carefully examined the instruments for a full minute. "We may not have operating coms, but we still have afterburners. Buckle up." She flipped a switch and the hovercar rapidly accelerated, pushing him into the seat and peeling his lips away from his teeth.

# 26
# Apophis

The night dimly broke between the trees bordering Ulmstead Gardens Park, though the streetlights of the adjacent road remained bright enough to still attract small swarms of mutant insects. Skyscrapers stood between Joan and the horizon. The early sun bounced off the glass surfaces, like they were doing an imitation of the moon or something. Bright enough that sunglasses would have helped, though the coat pocket she usually kept them in was empty. Something moving in a building's reflection.

The thunder of a distant jet engine high overhead. A drone, its lights blinking in some kind of pattern. Maybe Moose code, or whatever it's called. Eye functions drew a box around it and estimated its altitude and airspeed as it circled.

Between heavy breaths visible in the cold, she scanned the other side of the empty street. The brick sides of two buildings, obscured with dumpsters and piles of refuse. On Wall-Thru, a single cluster of green outlines in the alleyway between them. Civilians. No unregistered organics on any functions as she slowly turned in a circle, nor on the scopes she setup on her unmarked SUV at the opposite corner of the park.

She sighed as yellow rays poured over the barrier wall a few blocks away and wind ferried the scent of sulfur from the edge of the wastelands. That Wazzerman is full of shit. Why would he make up a story about renegade outcasts and bombs? If it was a fancy trap to lure MOTHs to their death, he won't find a target-rich environment.

As she cut across the park towards Greenhill Road, shrill DOLOS alarms blasted in both ears. *Organic Hazard Detected.* A white van and a black coupe speeding towards each other on the street 88 meters away. Two red Wall-Thru outlines in each. Both screeched to a stop next to each other, and four outcasts hastily moved something large and metal-lic from the back of the van to the coupe's trunk.

She drew her blaster and aimed. "Police! Hold it!"

The outcasts ignored her. Yet somehow a bullet flew by her face, bright enough to blind her for a moment. Then another, close enough to heat her face.

A pack of robot dogs running from the van and across the park towards her. Rapidly firing blasters mounted on their backs.

She ran behind a line of trees and held the charge button on her S120. One. Two. Three. Between the trunks and on Wall-Thru, the pack of robodogs closed in, 50 meters. An eye function popped red squares around them, marking each as a protocol-three violation. Weaponizing artificial life. Her blaster beeped. *Five seconds to overload.*

Carefully aiming between the trees at the running pack, she pulled the trigger. The charged blast was a blinding flash that lifted a cloud of dirt across the park and pelted shrapnel against the trees. Four robot dogs leapt thru the mist and continued their pursuit.

She ran back towards the nearest roadway. Bullets flew by, striking parked cars and setting off their alarms. A police cruiser moved into her path. The passenger door flew open. "Get in," a woman said.

Joan jumped in and slammed the door shut. A bullet loudly struck the glass, creating a spider web of cracks. Tires screeched and the engine roared. In the side view mirror, parked cars and buildings flew by. The car computer beeped something about a seat belt. Wireless chatter descended into pandemonium, though the sounds took a back seat as the spinning siren on the dashboard blared.

"Are you okay? Are you hurt?" The woman driver asked. Eye functions IDed her as *Officer Anastasia Hamilton.*

She checked her arms and legs. The health function drew a green outline of her body. A normal heart rhythm. A bright green shield on the armor function. "I'm okay. Thanks."

"Don't mention it."

She clicked transmit on the dashboard. "They loaded somethin' into the coupe."

"Target is a white van heading north on Western Avenue," an officer said on the wireless.

She clicked transmit again. "No, it's the coupe. This is MOTH-5. It's the coupe."

"This is Kyudo. 10-89 in progress without a 20. All available units, aid in the pursuit of stolen vehicle, white van, transponder ID 8-5-1-9-8."

She pinged the coupe on the dashboard's holographic map until it blocked her due to protocol 43. Ping flooding.

"It's the fuckin' coupe."

"I know." Anastasia pushed a button on the dashboard and the windshield rendered a crimson red triangle on the horizon labeled *coupe*, with a distance readout under it which rapidly ticked below a kilometer. Civilian traffic pulled over on Century Boulevard as Anastasia veered around them, missing an Atlantean sedan by a centimeter before she accelerated to over 300 kph. The coupe's signal moved up and down as the cruiser bounced from bumps in the road and splashed a shallow puddle.

On the downtown horizon, a giant hologram of Dr. Wazzerman shook with static as its voice broadcast over the public wireless frequency, echoing between the canyons of high-rises. "People of the Settlements. It is I, Dr. Wasserman. Your benevolent liberator, here to free you from your fascist overlords."

"They have hacked network," Ivan said on the wireless.

Is Wazzerman really behind this incursion? Anyone can make a hologram of anyone. But anyone can lie, too. His hologram grew to the size of a floating building as the cruiser passed under it.

"Only I have seen the future," Wazz's hologram said as it shrank in the sideview mirror. "Only I can save you from your otherwise inevitable extinction." The hologram flickered and disappeared in a wavy blur like it was a mirage.

An emergency chime on Wall-Thru. A blinking-blue outline of a police wagon, 400 meters away. A mob of green-outlined civilians surrounded the vehicle and jostled it back in forth like they were trying to tip it over. "We have civil unrest and need backup," Mayfleet said with terror. "23-hundred block of Prairie."

"Hold on!" Anastasia slammed on the breaks and swerved.

Joan lurched forward. Both palms landed on the dashboard and throbbed with pain. Her chin stopped in midair less than a centimeter from the hard plastic surface as her shiny blaster thumped on the floor mat.

Anastasia laid on the horn and accelerated, throwing Joan back into her seat. A man was in the middle of the street with a lit Molotov cocktail. He threw it and missed, creating a wall of fire they sped thru.

"Don't worry about Mayfleet, she'll be okay," Anastasia said. "Let's stay on the coupe." She turned onto a less-crowded street, raced to the end, then turned left and accelerated between parallel lines of stopped traffic.

The coupe's red outline flashed on the horizon via Wall-Thru and on the dashboard hologram. 500 meters. Green lights and teal street signs flew by. 400 meters. The computer zoomed in on the target, which was aggressively swerving around traffic.

"Target is north bound on Western," someone said on the wireless, even though the coupe was going west on Slauson.

At 300 meters a function blinked text: *Target is within blaster range.*

Semi-automatic holes appeared in the coupe's rear window, ringing sparking taps against the cruiser's hood. Wall-Thru drew the two outcasts inside the coupe. One driving and the other in the back seat firing a blaster. A bullet struck the windshield, embedded in a small spider web of cracks. She reached down and found her S120.

After tucking a leg onto her seat and switching her blaster to her right hand, she clicked the door button to roll down her window and leaned out to open fire. The targeting function rendered a laser-like dot, which went all over the place.

She pulled the trigger twice. One round drilled above the coupe's rear wheel-well. Orange bursts of return fire flew past. Three rounds slammed into the bullet-proof windshield with loud cracks and smoke that reeked of Sulphur.

An energy surge warning rang.

"Hold on!" Anastasia swerved towards oncoming traffic, knocking Joan back into her seat. A charged shot blew several meters of asphalt into hail-sized rocks and a cloud of smoke, some of which rained into the open passenger window. Joan gripped the bar above her window as Anastasia skidded thru an intersection of screeches and fender-benders, following the windshield computer's green arrows along the only safe path.

She propped herself up with one leg again and resumed firing out the window. Muzzle flashes strobed from the coupe's broken windows. She aimed and fired until her S120 went click-click-click.

While reloading a bullet tore off the side view mirror, crumbling it into hot bits, some of it landing on her sleeve. The car computer drew a holographic replacement.

At a fork in the road the target car took the right-hand path. A child ran into the crosswalk, forcing Anastasia to turn sharply left, swerving enough to lift the cruiser's left tires off the ground.

Joan dropped her blaster onto the floormat and gripped the handle above the door again. Her wrapped fingers turned white as the car slammed back onto all fours, tossing her back into her seat.

Anastasia floored it to the next intersection, pulling the parking brake and skidding 90 degrees into a four-wheel drift, which bounced Joan's forehead off Anastasia's shoulder.

She rubbed her pounding temple and looked at Anastasia. "Combat driving?"

"Mario Kart."

After picking up Gage Avenue at the next intersection, the black coupe turned left onto Figueroa and the car's Wall-Thru revealed the target vehicle behind a street of tall buildings, like a moving window running across the occupied structures.

Anastasia drew her blaster and held it like a boomerang. "We need a charged shot to take them out." The tossed M220 blaster landed on Joan's lap. The shield and spear of Mars etched onto the slide.

How did she know my battery was too low for a charged shot, she wondered?

"Joan, Ana," Troy said. "Be advised. Sector Four has heaps of civilians out in the streets." A multitude of green, humanoid outlines blinked on Wall-Thru.

"Start charging," Ana said. Tires screeched as she skid left onto a street with crowded sidewalks. Blaster fire from the coupe up ahead. Civilians screamed and scattered.

Leaning out the window and aiming Ana's blaster, the targeting function drew a red X before her thumb could even touch the charging button. *Excessive Collateral Damage Risk.* "I can't. I could kill an innocent person."

An energy surge warning. A blast from the coupe vaporized a streetlamp and shattered every storefront window in sight. A dozen bloody bodies obscured by smoke plumes but visible on Wall-Thru. They zoomed by and the corpses quickly shrank in the side view mirror.

"They'll kill more innocent people if you don't blast them." Ana clicked-off the car's wireless transmitter and looked over even though the cruiser was still going over 240 kph. "And I know where you were last night, Golf Ball."

What does that mean, she wondered? What does she know? Does she know what Wazzerman knows? Or that I met him?

Eye movements toggled targeting safeties. Balancing on one foot, her waist fell on the bottom of the rolled down window as she leaned out with one blaster in each hand, shooting like a Hong-Kong-style holo-game. She continued firing with her S120 while holding the charge trigger on Ana's blaster. The targeting function drew a growing holographic sphere far ahead where the blast would land. Dropping her S120 onto her seat, she aimed until the sphere overlapped with the coupe. Hopefully this doesn't set off the bomb. She pulled the trigger.

The charged plasma vaporized one of the coupe's tires, sending it into a smoking spin, a flip, and a collision with a parked car.

Ana slammed on the brakes, sending Joan's hands with both gripped blasters into the dashboard. The cruiser screeched to a halt 20 meters from the smoking wreckage of the coupe, visible thru the cracked windshield. Ana threw the car into park and yanked her gun back.

"MOTH-5," she said to her cuffputer transmitter. "10-43 at Figueroa and 52$^{nd}$."

"Be careful," Troy said on the wireless.

"Okay." She kicked the door open and ran towards the crash, holding her S120 with both hands. Ana was already a few meters ahead and on the left. Two outcasts crawled out of the coupe's wreckage. The closest one. A man that stumbled to his feet. A function alarm rang out: *Extermi-nate Organic Hazard.*

She steadied her sights and pulled the trigger.

Combined Ana and her fired a dozen rounds until a chime indicated they split the confirmed kill. DOLOS functions analyzed the dead outcast's face for an ID, before marking his blasted-to-mush face as *pending.* Trails of smoke rose from their blaster barrels and merged with the plumes floating off the wrecked coupe.

A tall figure ran laterally thru the smoke, leaping and jumping along a rainbow-line of parallel-parked cars and onto a fence along the corner parking garage. She somehow kept her balance while moving so fast that even the facial recognition function couldn't ID her, only a red Wall-Thru outline could keep up. A thin woman, though the bare arms sticking thru her sleeveless shirt were muscular. The backpack strapped to her barely bounced as she leapt off and landed on the other side.

Ana opened fire and Joan took aim at the new target between the fence's metal slats. Click. "Shit." By the time she reloaded the tall woman had run to the garage's entrance, where two civilians stood blocking the line of fire.

The target entered the garage with Ana in hot pursuit. Out of sight, though Wall-Thru drew their red and blue outlines. An eye function beeped.

*Mission directive: 10-33 in progress at Blue Jewel Tower. Respond and assist structural evacuation of essential personnel.*

Shadows quickly moved over the garage. Swarms of drones flying high in the sky, over and between the downtown skyscrapers until they surrounded Blue Jewel Tower in a mechanized cloud.

The mission function pinged again, this time drawing a navigation arrow back to the police cruiser. The Wall-Thru outlines of Ana and the outcast shrank as their distance grew to over 50 meters. Eye functions popped up text at the building connected to the parking garage. *Edward Tilman Elementary School.* 599 children in attendance.

The dark garage was broken into levels by sloped ramps and slices of window-paned sunlight. Silhouettes of drones darted across the light from the nearest window. A function drew a path of blue and red footprints on the concrete along a line of parked school buses and towards a stairwell of echoing thumps.

Underground. Why can't bad people just stay on the surface?

She rotated her mood sphere to Pursuit-80%. Her stride turned into a jog and then a run. The floor and ceiling bounced up and down. Each violent bootstep echoed loudly on the garage floor.

Too fast to stop, she stumbled into the stairwell door. It smelled of liquid propane and brake fluid. Steadying her blaster, she opened the door. At the wide landing of the basement, a pair of maintenance hatches.

Ana was in a small control room of blinking buttons and dials. "Joan. Wait here—"

The Wall-Thru outline of the outcast was 20 meters away in a large room that, without a thought, Joan found herself running into before she could dial back on the pursuit mood.

A dim, two-story room. About 1000 square meters. At the center, a circle of bulbs hung high on the ceiling and cast a sphere of light directly down and around a chamber or something, a concrete-crusted-steel cylinder a few meters high. A web of metal tubes above and below it emitted bubbling sounds and vibrations, a bit louder than the hums of other machinery. The outcast stood in front of it with her arms crossed.

"Joan! Get out of there!" Ana said.

The heavy door behind Joan moved downwards slowly. Large metal teeth running along its bottom, nearly as sharp as fangs, locked into the floor.

She turned towards the outcast again and aimed her blaster. 16 in red digits on the slide. "Freeze!"

The tall woman stood in silence with an amused smile on her face, an eyebrow raised. She uncrossed her arms only to tie back her black hair with a matching-color scrunchie. The facial ID function beeped: *Matilda Albright*. In red blinking text: *Status: Organic Hazard. Terminate immediately*.

Joan's finger moved along the trigger.

"Joan. Stop," Troy said on the wireless. "You can't fire in there. It's a reactor room."

"Isn't it shielded?" she whispered into her transmitter.

Troy sighed over the loud taps of keystrokes. "Yes of course it's shielded. That doesn't change the point."

A radiation warning icon popped up on the targeting function. She started to holster her S120, but somehow it knocked itself away towards a far corner and her hand suddenly hurt.

She looked up into dead-blue eyes staring her down. Out of nowhere Albright had speared her onto the grated floor. Joan gulped as the tall brunette with bulky arms scratched sharp nails across her jugular.

"Be careful," Troy said. "Albright used to be a cop."

"Really?" Joan lifted a leg and turned to kick the assailant off her. Scrambling to her feet, Albright's fist bruised her right palm. Joan swung a return blow. Albright moved out of the way and grabbed the swinging arm to throw her into a coolant monolith, flattening her. She turned and kicked, grazing Albright's leg.

"You're the one who brainwashed Carruth, didn't you?" Joan held up both her fists.

"Pawns are sacrificed in every game." Albright gave a sadistic smile.

"I hate che—"

Albright slugged her, busting her lip.

She swung at Albright, but the outcast moved backwards to a corner.

"Just keep her busy," Troy said. "Ana is shutting down the reactor."

"Got it." With eye movements she activated stims and pursued the target. Grabbing Albright and pushing her towards the wall only resulted in her turning and running up it like one of those Parkour runners. Albright jumped, back flipped behind Joan, and kicked her into the same wall. Then pulled her by her coat collar until she wiggled out of it. Albright flung Joan's spread coat at her face.

A perfectly landed blow to the narrow side gap in her police armor sent her to the floor. The ceiling was a blur. A brief metallic rummaging sound as her eyes re-focused.

Albright took strides until she blocked the ceiling lights, brandishing a shiny wrench that she slowly and menacingly smacked against an open palm before raising it for a blow. But she stopped at the loud thud of an opening hatch and the rapid clangs of approaching footsteps. The wrench slipped to the ground with a clank, and she ran past the spinning-down reactor and thru a far door that sealed behind her.

Ana stood over her and mumbled some kind of profanity. "Joan, are you okay?"

Functions displayed stable medical stats. She struggled for breath. "Oh yeah. Peachy."

Ana helped her stand and led her towards a beeping box on a stack of cylinders behind the reactor. Lifting the metal lid, an elaborate web of wires and components. Police functions freaked in a rapid arrangement like Peter humming one of his stupid songs. Lines blinked around a countdown timer.

"Fuck," she said. "Two minutes. Oh fuck."

Ana lifted her cuffputer to her mouth. "Central, confirm 10-79 at my 20."

"I've activated the school's fire alarm," Troy said. Spinning red lights lit up high along the wall, though no klaxons were audible. "Joan, please get out of there. Delphi has predicted that bomb will detonate before it can be defused."

"Don't panic." Ana paused long enough for Joan to panic. "Delphi is wrong about this. But I need your help." Her calm voice seemed to quiet the pandemonium on the wireless channels.

She looked up at the hundreds of Wall-Thru outlines, students a few floors above them, and gulped. "What can I do?"

"Twist your mood dial to Analytical, 70% capacity. And grab a pair of precision wire-cutters." Ana pinged a toolbox in the room's corner.

She ran to the box while rotating her mood sphere, picked up a precision wire-cutter, one that was 1.8 centimeters in length with red rubber grips, and ran back in 5 seconds.

Ana hastily employed a lipstick-sized drilling device on 8 bolts surrounding the bomb's timer. 1:38 in red digits. Her mood sphere beeped as she twisted it. "Grab that side so we can remove the faceplate. *Carefully.*"

The bomb's faceplate slipped and landed with a low-pitch clank. Ana shoved the separated timer into Joan's hands and examined the now-exposed tangle of wires. All of them red. An intertwined mess worse than shelter hair.

"Is it the red wire?" she asked.

"One of many," Ana said.

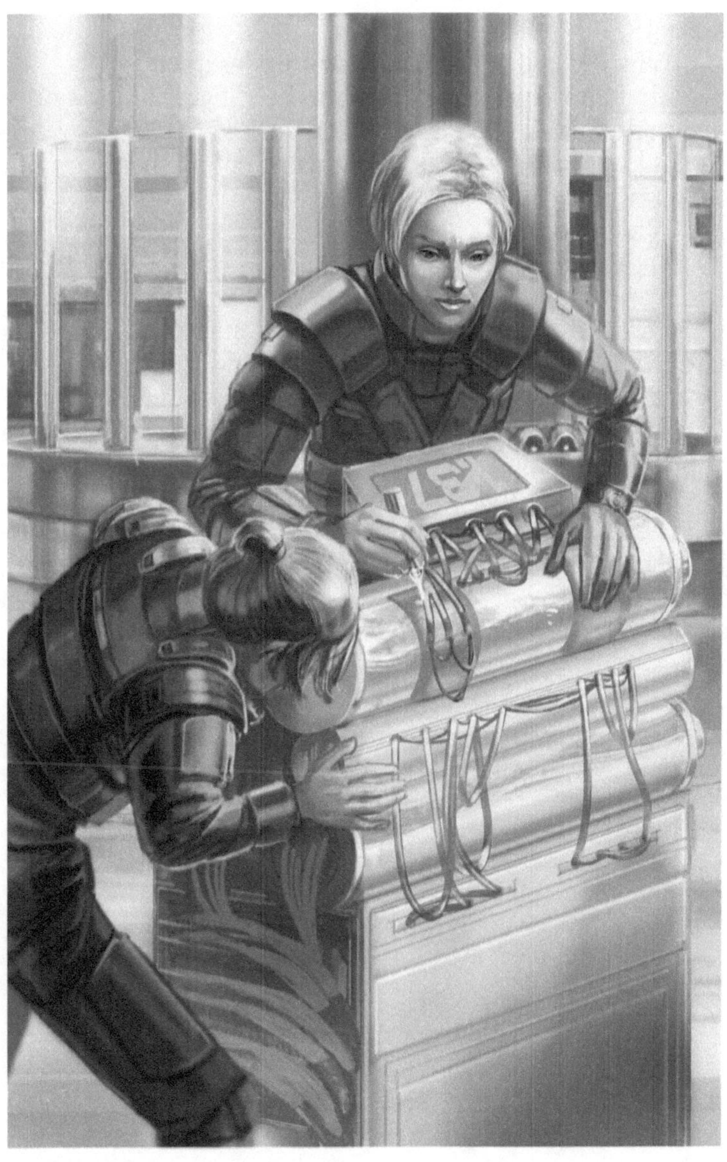

0:58.

"Why the hell is there a reactor under a school?"

"Shelter architecture." Ana ran her fingers along several wires and pulled two cutters from a pocket. "There's a trigger and two failsafe wires. We have to cut all three simultaneously."

"Which one do I cut?"

Ana tugged on a wire, but there were like 50 of them. Too many to spread with her fingers.

"Stop moving them. Watch for the one I'm pulling," Ana said from the floor.

0:28.

"Joan," Troy said. "For the love of science, cut a wire. You're out of time."

"Alright already!" That was too mean. "Sorry Troy."

The line turned to static as the bomb's timer reached single digits. Too late to tell Troy he's handsome. Pulling a clump of wires between the sharp edges of the cutter, she closed her eyes and squeezed the grips.

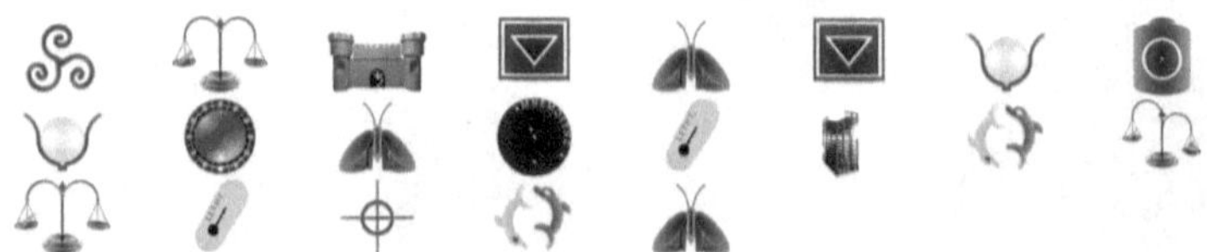

# 27
## Fait Accompli

The titanic plume obscuring the downtown skyline spread into trails as though it were a squid of smoke. Peter toggled the windshield display until it rendered outlines of the settlement's structures. Blue Jewel Tower blinked red.

Diaz looked out the window with a sigh. "We're too late."

A panic-packed circus screeched over the police wireless as the hovercar approached the hall of justice. The empty landing platform held a dozen circular pads suspended a hundred meters over the roof, supported by columns of concrete that hugged the building as though it were the legs of a spider.

One of the pads lit up green on the windshield, and the dashboard computer loaded a volumetric of the vehicle and the platform. Its pitch twisting in the wind until he slowly eased the collective down for a smooth landing.

The tubular elevator descended fast enough to feel a bit like the first drop of a rollercoaster. Diaz's face was turned away and not directly visible. Her reflection on the shiny, curved walls.

Will she go straight to Kyudo and turn me in, he wondered? Kyudo already knows, but one loose word from Diaz's full lips need only fall on one vindictive ear. Should I await the show trial, where any appeals to reason or logic will be dismissed as wrong think? The mob will label me evil, a self-righteousness that will melt the day they themselves make a mistake and witness everyone turning on them. Sometimes I want to shout it from the rooftops, though it's a truth learned too late, by people who wonder why the population of Outcasts keeps growing.

A subroutine flashed an elevated-heartrate warning.

I could take Diaz hostage and make a run for it. Or Kyudo. Even better. Who would dare fire in her general direction? Other than Lyon. Hell, I shouldn't have even landed.

"Diaz." It was as though a cotton ball were lodged in his throat. "I was only a year out of Annapolis. I just did what I was told without a second thought. Every day I—"

She held a finger to her closed lips and with the other pointed up at the ceiling monitor. Its recording light a solid red dot. "I don't work for internal affairs." Diaz looked at the elevator doors, neither away nor at him.

"Really?"

"Not unless I get a hefty salary increment." Diaz smiled. "And that won't happen with the pay freeze."

He grinned. "A pay freeze during a personnel shortage. With your keen detective skills, do you think one of those conditions could cause the other?"

Diaz smirked. "Why no. Of course not. Never."

They both chuckled. The elevator clicked and both doors slid open.

Anarchy. Officers scrambled between the narrow rows of desks while shouting at each other. Half of them clamoring towards the front door, bottlenecked with their coats halfway on. Glaring blurs from volumetric documents colliding. Commotion on the mezzanine where the techs frantically coordinated field operations.

The floor shook, not an earthquake but vibrations pronounced enough that he and Diaz each leaned a hand against the wall by the elevator. The line of sunlight from the overhead windows retreated across the room, briefly glared, then vanished as though an unscheduled eclipse decided today wasn't interesting enough already. The station's commotions instantly turned to silence, and movement ceased, save for a few shifting shadows from a few dim desk lamps.

Through the skylights, the Zeus weapon platform rumbled like thunder several kilometers in the air. Dot-sized lights blinked along the dark underbelly.

"That's lower than usual," he mumbled.

"Kyudo," Diaz said while looking up and smiling. "The council finally gave her command of Zeus." She crossed her arms and looked at him. "As soon as she finds the Sandcastle, she'll turn it into sand."

"Think she'll go to war?"

"She once told me there already is one."

He scratched his chin. War with the Outcasts isn't the only answer. Finding whoever set off that bomb, the masterminds behind it, and bringing them to justice. That would remove the need for escalation. That would be enough. That will be enough to stop it.

The platform slowly rumbled past, and the blinding sun returned.

"I'm going to check the memories of that clone. Lansing's wife," he said.

But Diaz was gone. The Wall-Thru subroutine tracked her climbing the mezzanine stairs quickly, her legs moving up and down in a rapid rhythm without a single misstep.

He ran up the stairs, though after catching his breath at the top, Diaz's signal had dropped off. Perhaps she's in the bathroom. Or Kyudo's office.

Beyond Castor's obsessively clean worktable was a divider with Ivan's desk on the opposite side. His workspace bordered a brick column and a long shelf with dusty paper books.

Ivan was sitting and typing furiously, switching every few seconds between separate volumetric computers. Each rendering half a meter over the sloppy surface, strewn with stacks of pages, boxes, and pre-war memorabilia arranged in a pig's version of a jigsaw puzzle. An occasional brown hair peppered his balding scalp, and a headset wrapped around it. His face matched the color and texture of tapioca. Both eyes carried fatigue stripes so dark that the nearby narcissus hologram simply rendered them as gaps.

A circular vittle box on the desk.  Its lid open and the blunt end of a fork sticking out, the prongs embedded in moussaka.  Next to it, a pre-war globe.  Turned to the Pacific Coalition and centered on Russia.  Countless dots of old cities long since cratered.

With a sigh Ivan removed his headset.  He said in his Russian accent, "Hello Petar.  What can I do for you?"

In the corner of his vision the Babel-Squid subroutine flashed.  Looking at it and blinking would substitute Ivan's speech patterns with properly formed sentences.  But such accents are slowly fading from the world.  "Lansing's wife. The clone."

"Yes?" Ivan asked while returning his attention to the volumetric displays.

"Have you uploaded her memories?"

"Da."  Ivan launched a new volumetric screen with hand gestures and scrolled to a memory sequence.

He loaded notes on his wrist-computer.  "Cassandra indicated a former cop named Mattie was a co-conspirator with Lansing.  Tall.  Skinny.  Black hair.  Blue eyes."

"Matilda Albright."  Ivan fast-forwarded through moving images of Cassandra's family sharing a meal, freeze-framing when a woman entered.

He held a hand over his mouth and squinted.  Son of a bitch.  It's her.  The woman I saw at Lansing's apartment.

She had a pretty face, though it was solemn.  Thirty something.  Hard to tell with anti-radiation regimens, though Outcasts don't have a steady supply.  And the wasteland takes its toll.  He moved closer to the volumetric frame.

"What is it?"  Ivan looked at him instead of the volumetric displays.

"For a second I thought I remembered—nothing."

"She used to be officer."  Ivan spun up another emitter and loaded a police profile.  Albright's bio next to a rendition of her head slowly spinning. "MOTH even. Now she is biting butterfly." Ivan looked down at his desk.

"Wait, she was a cop?"

Ivan nodded.

Officers are lost, other people move on, and the faces fade from familiar to forgotten. "Have these memories been verified?"

"Umm, no. They have not."

"Is Castor here?"

"Boss lady worried about former officer being official suspect in ongoing investigation. Because of terrorist attack." Ivan gestured with his head towards the drawn blinds of Kyudo's glass office. "Especially after altercation with your partner."

He typed Albright's name on his wrist-computer and examined her mostly censored service record. "She hasn't validated in nearly a year. She's obviously not Albright anymore."

"Better for department morale to hunt down corrupt scoundrel than twice-decorated-for-bravery sergeant, yes?" Ivan sniffed his food with a nonplussed look, though he still added it to his mouth with smacking lips.

"Gosh Ivan, are you saying people can change?"

"Past can change to advantage of present regime," Ivan said while shoveling a forkful into his mouth.

"And what about the future?"

While chewing Ivan gestured with utensils. "Only in way that is predictable."

He crossed his arms. "Then why can't Delphi predict where Wasserman built his hidden fortress?"

"In Japan they say, man is room he stand in. But he does not teleport with magics. His path leads to room." Ivan put down his fork and scratched his nose. "Someday snake eyes will catch the Doctor Wasserman. Because past makes for future."

"And what about Miss Albright?  Are you at all concerned that her past is being changed to fit the present?"

Ivan resumed eating and shrugged while chewing.

"Another reputation tossed in mud.  Right?"

"Boss say jump, I say her let me finish eating."

The glass door to Kyudo's nearby office abruptly opened and the major stuck her head out.  "Peter, com channel eight."

"Yes ma'am."

He walked down the mezzanine stairs slowly while reading the major's orders on his wrist-computer.

*Peter: Investigate Albright but keep a lid on it.  She is not an official suspect in this investigation.  Work this with your partner.  Joan was reprimanded today for insubordination.  Shorten the leash.*

Lyon was at her desk.  Sitting in her chair like a ball, hugging her curled up shins.  The way Caramel sits when she's anxious.

Normally Lyon hears people coming a kilometer away.  Between disheveled bangs her swollen eyes randomly drifted until she grimaced while biting into her stitched-up lip.  A glossy circle of healing gel over a purple bruise on her left cheekbone.

"What?"  Lyon looked at him.

"Should I see the other gal?" he asked.

Lyon touched her own face and checked a narcissus volumetric on her wrist.  "Ana got suspended," she said without looking at him.

"Hamilton?" he asked.  Lyon nodded.  "Raw deal.  But you need to dial that away.  We have work to do."

Lyon snuffled, slowly stood, and stretched her arms above her head.  "I can get us a car from the motor pool."

"Motor pool?"

"Ground zero is downtown."

"We're not working the tower bombing." He walked to his half of the desk and pushed his desk chair out of the way. It took the computer a few seconds to load Albright's profile on the volumetric emitter. "Matilda Albright."

Lyon sat on the desk and sighed while staring at Albright's floating records. "The DA's office is smokin' rubble, and we're saddled with some meat robot?"

He sat in his chair and loaded a list of Blue Jewel Tower tenants from the public directory. Group by contract type. A solid green box labelled government departments and agencies. Twenty-eight percent. An auto-scrolling list inside the volumetric grouping. Item twelve in the list: The district attorney's office. He leaned back in the chair and scratched his chin.

If the Outcast bombing was an assassination of a high-profile target, the brass would want to assure the populace before making an announcement. And Kyudo moved the Zeus platform into a low enough orbit so it would look larger than the sun. A natural eclipse has a cooling effect. If the Sandcastle is smaller than a city, one orbital strike will crater the whole damn thing. Leaving nothing. Nada. Zip. Then Delphi won't get their stolen equipment back.

There could be some opportunity, some way to stop the violence without openly defying orders.

"Kyudo sent Hamilton home for two weeks without pay," he said. "There are already fifty officers working the tower scene. All we need to do is figure out how our puzzle piece fits into the picture."

"Fine." Lyon sat in the adjacent chair and loaded her volumetric computer. "Where do ya figure we outta start?"

"You had an encounter with her. What was she like?"

"Tough. For a meat robot. Seemed like—" Lyon rested her chin on a hand. "Like she could anticipate everythin' I did."

He scratched his eyebrows. "Albright was a cop. She could have lingering memories of combat training." *Or she has a real-time optical interface with a Delphi core.*

Lyon quietly cleared her throat. "Doesn't Wasserman have like, I don't know, a dozen lieutenants who are like, not fully brainwashed?"

"You think Albright is one of Wasserman's disciples? Even Delphi isn't sure if Wasserman's disciples are real. It's all conjecture."

Lyon sighed. "Maybe he doesn't feel the need to control every detail of every decision that every subordinate makes. I mean like, come on, does he got time to do everythin' himself?"

"Right. I doubt someone with freewill would personally plant a bomb in the city, much less at a school. Not when they have a horde of organic puppets at their disposal."

Lyon rapidly typed and scrolled through files until *Access Denied* flashed in large red letters. "Aren't you always sayin' know the enemy as well as yourself? How can we do that if Albright's police records are locked?"

"The techs are working on that right now. Let's give them an hour before we follow-up."

"Ivan?" Lyon asked with raised eyebrows.

"Either him or Castor."

"Mm," Lyon said with cloying sweetness. She loaded a narcissus display, straightened her hair, and turned her face at various angles.

He loaded Lyon's after-action report and flipped through volumetric snapshots. "Albright's bomb looks awfully large."

"Mm hmm." Lyon continued examining her reflection.

"She could not have carried something that large in her backpack."

"I'm wonderin' where she got a bomb in the first place. It looked well-made, like somethin' we'd build."

The Outcasts must have disassembled the Chiron warhead into components and made two. Though neither went nuclear. Perhaps they made three bombs. If a nuke goes off in the settlements, it's game over. Do not pass go. Do not collect pension. Go straight to forced reenlistment and deferred discharge. "So how'd it get there?"

Lyon terminated the narcissus app and looked over. "I don't know." On her own computer she loaded DOLOS tracking, zoomed into the school's basement, and scrolled the timeline. "No one has been in there in a week. Not counting today." She looked over. "Maybe we ought to look earlier?"

He scratched his chin. The warhead was stolen from Chiron days ago. "No. Switch the overlay from organic to robotic."

The filter cube resembled a Rubik's cube that clicked as Lyon turned and rotated each square and grid. "Maintenance robots. I mean, like, it's a reactor, isn't it?"

"Right. Are there AV records?"

Lyon twisted another clicking cube. A two-dimensional video file on fast forward. Maintenance robots rapidly stacking tanks of air. "What the?" She clicked the pause button. "September twenty-fourth. Yesterday. Twenty-two hours. What in the fuck are they doin'?"

He rubbed his temples. "Oh, it's the hydrogen."

Lyon looked over with scrunched eyebrows and glazed eyes.

"From the reactor. When they run hot a hydrogen bubble can form at the top of the nuclear vessel. It's explosive, so the neutron-governors siphon it off."

"Are you a nuclear engineer now?"

Naval Academy. Class of Forty-One. "No. Just old."

Lyon smiled. "So they're supposed to do that?"

"No. Well, yes. But stacking them like that isn't. They're programmed to drop those in the pneumatic tube system."

"Then someone programmed 'em to stack highly explosive gas so they'd be there waitin' for Albright.  She could turn her backpack bomb into a big one."

"Right.  But who reprogrammed them?"

Lyon peered over a volumetric document on her computer.  "Security protocol says it's a closed system."

"Who has the maintenance contract?"

"Liberty Robotics."

"Wait a minute."  He loaded Abe Carruth's social web of portrait-filled circles and color-coded lines that slowly orbited the subject like planets around a star.  "Do you remember—" Lyon took a memory treatment last night.  But she forgot yesterday, not the day before.  Which means she should remember Carruth.  "Mr. Carruth?"

"Mr. Carrot?  Yeah."

"He was employed as a technician by Liberty Robotics."  With a few keystrokes the occupation line of Carruth's web enlarged, similar to a balloon inflating.

"No fuckin' way."  Lyon dragged and dropped the Locator app.  After half a minute of spinning hour glasses a volumetric map loaded, rotating and zooming in on a blinking midtown building.  "Liberty Robotics Headquarters.  Three-twenty-one Equinox Avenue."

***

Paint in every known color peeled from the siding of the bungalows lining each side of the street.  Mounted police sped by on Centaur Motorbikes, their sirens turning into Doppler echoes and moments of glare in the side-view mirror.

"You hear that?" Lyon asked.

"Hear what?"  He navigated between stopped police wagons on both sides of Regent Street.  Robot SWAT teams and officers in assault armor kicked residential doors, moving down each edge of the street with stretched warrants and shortened tempers.

"They just said the district attorney died in the tower explosion. Wasn't he investigatin' that Warner fella?"

"Councilman Warner?  That was merely a formality. Warner is one of the good guys."  He looked over to find Lyon's mouth hanging open.  She had put on Infinity sunglasses that looked like a sideways eight.  A volumetric price tag flickered by one of the hinges.  "Are those new?"

Instead of using the Narcissus app Lyon flipped down the mirror on the passenger-side visor, quickly deactivating the tag. "Couldn't find my old ones."

The dashboard chronograph ticked ten-o-three AM as he pulled up to a fenced business park.  At the gate, a line of blue scan-light passed over the hood, windshield, and then him and Lyon.  Affirmative chimes from the security robots lifted the red-striped barrier.  Large models, shiny nine-meter-tall bipeds with glowing eyes and machine-gun arms.

No potholes interrupted the smooth pavement of the empty parking lot, though the grids of white lines were faded from acidic rain.  Between one to two dozen rectangular buildings surrounded them, ranging from five to twelve stories in height.  The Liberty Robotics Offices were well-constructed from white concrete and floor-to-ceiling windows, though far from the sprawling opulence of Delphi.

A two-story cube of glass protruded from the long edge of the central building and divided the colonnade, a curved canopy of small glass tiles held up by chrome pillars.  Above it, the uninspired Liberty Robotics logo and slogan, *Freedom from Servitude.*

Revolving doors led to the cube interior.  A lobby.  Behind the room-length desk a bearded clerk sat on a stool, reading large volumetric text on giant pages, spread like an old, printed newspaper.  His aquiline face glanced up for a moment and he grabbed the edges of the pages, pulling them together until the glowing book closed with a fake thump. The title was white and in an elaborate, cursive font that most young people can't read. *The Grasshopper and the Almond Tree.* The image beneath the title was a tree by a dirt road, bordered by a wood fence. A field of green and a mountain on the horizon. No visible grasshopper though. Perhaps it's on the back cover.

"Hey Peter-man," the attendant said. He didn't look familiar, but the voice was.

Peter studied the thin face and hooked nose. There's a subroutine that shows what a person looks like without facial hair, but before he could load it Facial Recognition IDed him, along with a RAP sheet of twenty vice charges, each with a matching plea bargain. "I'll be damned. Rick the Rat."

"Hey, come on Peter-man. You can't call that anymore. I'm on the straight and arrow."

"Right. How long have you been here?"

"Five months. I got out early because of Clementine."

"Clemency."

"Yeah, that. Thanks for speaking to the judge man. I heard it helped me get out early." Rick placed a flat-panel on the counter.

"Perhaps you can return the favor. Have you seen this man?" He raised his wrist-computer with Carruth's likeness on a small volumetric. Rick shook his head. Peter retried with Overton. Same shake.

Lyon knocked on the counter, drawing Rick's attention. She loaded Albright's profile on her wrist. "How about her?"

"Hey man, who's your pretty little friend?" Rick asked Peter.

Lyon sneered, and Peter nodded upwards at Albright's spinning portrait.

"Haven't seen her." Rick lifted a George-Jack Shack milkshake from his side of the counter, and the shake shook in his hand as he hastily sipped from the large red straw. A subroutine scanned his eyes for deception. Redundant. The rat couldn't fool a child.

"You're not lying through your missing teeth now, are you Rick?"

"I got fillings in the can."

"Good for you."

"The offices are empty," Rick said with a grin. "The jobs went off world as soon as the tax subsidies ran out."

"Carrot—Carruth," Lyon said. "Was workin' out of an office here accordin' to our records."

"Chill out yellow top," Rick said. He looked over. "Is she blonde everywhere?" He began laughing hysterically.

"Are you shooting ice again Rick?" he asked.

Lyon's face turned red as a sunburn as she pulled out her stun baton.

"Whoa!" Rick slammed a big red button on the desk. Security glass instantly descended from the ceiling and interlocked with the desk, separating the lobby into two sections with a thud.

"Rick, shut the hell up." He turned towards Lyon, but she wasn't there. She was now standing at a metal door to the left of the counter. Her computer-slicer wires sparking under the red light of a biometric scanner.

"Hey. You can't do that!" Rick said.

Without looking away from the lock, Lyon said in a taunting tone, "Aww. Why don't you call the cops?"

He walked over and whispered to Lyon, "Would you relax? On a day like today, you can bet your ass we'll have a warrant in five minutes."

Lyon stopped fiddling with the door to make eye contact. "Jesus. What is with you and betting on asses?"

"I'd bet on your ass, beautiful." An eavesdropping Rick ran his tongue along his lower lip.

"What the fuck did you just say to me?" Lyon asked Rick.

"Hey," he said to Lyon.  "You're on thin ice with Kyudo, so cool it."  He approached the glass and whispered into the intercom, "Listen Rick.  My partner would like nothing more than to bash your brains in.  She's batshit insane."

"I can hear you," Lyon said.

"This is about that bomb that went off," he said.  "You can help us locate those who are responsible for it."

"People are saying pro-privacy Warner died in that explosion," Rick said.  "Sure will be a shame when they start opening up sealed records and finding out what people did long ago, won't it Peter-man?"

He noticed that, without conscious thought, his hands at his side had curled into shaking fists.

"Then we won't need a warrant to upload your lonely brain cell, genius."  Lyon cursed while rearranging the slicer wires.

He turned and locked eyes with Lyon, blinking long enough to deactivate oculars.  "Seems my visual feed has encountered a transmission error."

Lyon gave a wry smile and took a long blink.  She looked at Rick behind the glass while rattling the locked door.  "You gonna open up, or do I gotta huff-n-fuckin'-puff?"

Rick's eyes went wide, and his mouth fell open, but he still made Lyon huff and puff with her computer-slicer until it buzzed, and she flung the door open and stormed into the booth.

On his wrist-computer Peter navigated to Chun's Censoring routine and clicked *Purchase*, though he declined being added to Chun's monthly newsletter.

"I'm going to file a complaint!"  Rick stood up so fast he knocked over the stool he was sitting on.

"You'll be doin' it without any teeth mother bleeper."  Lyon pointed her stun baton and backed Rick into a corner.  He put his hands up.  She jabbed him in the stomach, then began rapidly striking him over his head, shoulders, and just about everywhere above his knees, until he fell on them. "You bleeping piece of beep."

"Peter, make her stop man!" Rick lifted his arms over his head to block Lyon's blows.

"She's not a robot, Rick. There's no off button."

"Bleeping blank hole," Lyon said.

Rick raised open palms and pleaded until Lyon stopped whaling on him. She looked back. Enough sweat on her face that she'll have to spend ten minutes in front of a mirror before speaking to Castor. Her panting slowed, and as her face turned from red to pale, she squinted at something.

He entered the office and kneeled. Two long shelves running under the counter, partially filled with bootlegged holo-films. "On the straight and narrow indeed, Rick."

"Hey man, people want to see the original films," Rick said. "The streaming channels keep changing how they end."

"Right." He ran a finger along the arranged dust jackets. "Huh. Is this real?" He pulled and held up an incased holo-disk labelled *Norse Dakota: The Musical.*

Rick sat up and wiped blood off his nose, inadvertently creating a red-smeared mustache. He said hoarsely, "They're six-ninety-nine, or three for twenty."

Lyon regarded Rick with a mischievous grin, drew her hand cuffs and repeatedly clicked the clawed end of the bracelets open and closed a centimeter from Rick's face, as though she were a feral cat a second away from scratching him.

Rick lifted a bruised hand and grimaced as he pointed to the rows of contraband. "Some cops took most of them."

"Cops?" Lyon clicked the cuffs closed.

Rick checked his nose again and snorted. "Yeah. They were checking out the offices upstairs. Two days ago, in the morning, and then they left after, I don't know, a few hours?"

Peter loaded police and DOLOS subroutines on his wrist-computer, setting current GPS coordinates with a starting date of three days ago until today. A blank list. "There's no police reports on file from this location. Nothing on DOLOS either. Nada. Zip."

Rick tried to stand but Lyon quickly landed a hand on each of his shoulders and gently pushed him back down into a sitting position. From her belt she pulled her validation tube and plugged it into Rick's wrist-tracker. The tube clicked green, and she disconnected it. "Keep talkin' mother bleeper."

"It was some old cop. And big. I mean a real fatty."

Lyon loaded a volumetric image of Major Lansing on her wrist-computer. Rick immediately nodded. "That's him. He had a large briefcase. I mean it was almost as wide as him. And there were two women with him. The ones you showed me earlier." Rick pressed a palm against one of the gashes on his forehead. "Some patrol cars stopped by later. I figured they were taking turns with the girls, but then some lady-cops showed up too and I, uh, I had to start using my imagination in other ways."

"What about Carruth?" he asked.

"I don't know—I mean I've seen him around, but I didn't see him with anyone else."

"Where was his office? What floor?"

"Third floor. Three-two-seven."

"Lyon, let's go." He tilted his head towards a volumetric map of the building next to the lobby's wall. With a few clicks color-coded arrows provided a path to the third floor.

"Guys don't call my parole officer," Rick said. "I've been good, really. I help my land lady take out the trash when her robot is broken." His pleading voice trailed off as they walked down a hallway of white walls, past a potted plant, and entered a humming elevator.

"The Rat acts tough but the minute you rough him up he's crying foul," he said.

"They're all like that," Lyon said.

The cylindrical-glass elevator ascended over the large factory, where endless assembly lines of robotic arms sparked and welded humanoid robots. Wide conveyor belts shrank until the elevator passed through a meter-thick floor and opened with a mechanical whine.

A long room. Dust fell through the rays of window light that spread to an interior horizon like the shining waves of an ocean and landed on desks of mugs stained with coffee and random stacks of papers, some of which had fallen onto the patterned carpet. The wall on the right was a continuous window overseeing the factory.

They each blinked until ocular subroutines reactivated.

"Peter." Lyon pointed at the line of red office doors on the far wall. With the zoom routine, the black digits three-two-seven came into focus. Someone's green outline on Wall-Thru. DOLOS clicked-back an ID: *Cecelia Hartnell.*

Their footsteps broke the silence. No. Only mine, he thought.

Lyon. Vociferous when she wants something but when she prowls, even her breathing isn't audible. No wonder she has a cat. She beckoned a passing cleaning-bot, pointed at room two-three-seven, and whispered, "Bot-bot. Is that door unlocked?" The bot stopped and looked at them, raising its wire-framed arms in a shrug while its emoji-oval-head frowned and completely rotated like a clock. "I guess that don't compute."

Halfway across the room the carpet had ceased, leaving a floor of only glass holding them above the sparking assembly line of robots far below.

The Liberty Robotics logo was etched into the red door. Behind it, Hartnell's green outline paced in haste.

He looked at Lyon and held up one finger, then two, then three.  Lyon nodded and drew her service weapon.  He stood, took several steps back, then ran at the door and kicked.

The door abruptly opened, and his momentum carried him into the room.  He rolled onto the carpet and banged his shin against the leg of a table. "Mother bleeper!"

"Police!" Lyon shouted.  "Don't blanking move!"

He rubbed his shin and stood.  Lyon slammed Miss Hartnell into the nearest thudding wall and cuffed her.

It was a large office with a work desk by a bright window.  A piano in the dark corner.  A long conference table in the middle of the room with a clicking, rectangular device.  He picked it up and turned it.  *Document Vaporizer* in small lettering.  Lifting the lid, a small puff of smoke from a fragment of charred paper. "Lyon."  He turned the device towards her.

"What were ya burnin?" Lyon asked Hartnell.

"Nuffin'," Hartnell said in a Northern English accent.  Lyon dragged her to the table and shoved her onto a seat.  She lifted her cuffed hands to move neck-length strands of blue hair away from her face and smooth the lapels of her white business suit.

"Can you watch her?" Lyon asked.

"Give me a minute." He walked past a walnut credenza to the piano and pulled the bench to sit, pull up his pant leg, and examine his shin. Unwittingly landing an elbow on the piano keys and sounding-off half the A-major scale.  It sounded wrong.  He walked his fingers one at a time down the line of black and white keys.  The note between F and G sharp sounded as though it were a D instead of a G.

Under the piano's polished-black cover, something on the bass bridge.  A hollow metal tube with jagged teeth attached to a blue neck cord.  A pre-war military key.

Lansing's Air Force key.  Subroutines began scanning it and he looked away, back towards Lyon.

She was quietly scolding Hartnell and flipping through a stack of hardcopies.

That key leads to Chiron.  And to me, he thought.  Without looking he carefully reached into the piano, wrapped his hand around the key, and pocketed it in his coat.

"Peter.  You gotta see this."

He walked past the table's line of plush chairs.

Lyon wiped some sweat from her forehead.  With her other hand she slid over a hardcopy.

*FUTURES AUCTION*.  Each word in large text along the top, divided by a logo.  The scales balanced by a feather.  A Delphi logo on a datacore in the center of the flyer.  Large text ran the rest of the paper, on individual lines and in relatively smaller text: *CLUB KETU.  ONE NIGHT ONLY.  25-9-2163 7 PM.  DON'T BE LATE TO THE FUTURE.*

# Stirred Voice

Joan looked out the window at the dark cloud drifting over the edge of the Liberty Robotics campus and listened to the distant sirens still echoing though the city streets. A beep from her cuffputer. A satellite map with two green dots. Mom and Mary are safe. Mom never leaves home, and Mary never goes downtown, well not in the morning anyway. Still, thank god for police functions.

"Lyon." The dim edge of the window held Peter's reflection. He stood in the doorway and kept looking back at the glass wall of the conference room they had locked Cecilia in. "I was saying, we can't take her in."

She looked back at him. "Can't take her in?"

Peter held up one of Cecilia's flyers and tapped a finger against the flapping sheet. "We have less than 10 hours."

"Why don't we take her back and run a behavior cylinder on her?"

"If she arbiters up this could drag out. Days. Perhaps even weeks."

"You don't wanna do this by the book?"

"If this case isn't cracked today there will be another war."

"Have you validated?"

Peter sighed. "You're too young to understand. You don't remember the terminal war and everything that was lost. Everything we lost."

She walked over to him. "I'm not too young to remember." So long ago it feels like a dream strip, like the ones you buy. The butterflies, the orange and black ones. Bees crawling on flowers. Those amazing smells that synth-scents can't even come close to. Like life itself was in the air.

"The people that die won't be the ones that you think deserve it. The wrong ones will die. And the wrong ones will live." He lowered the flyer and looked away.

"You're the one that keeps tellin' me to follow protocol so I don't get in boilin' water with Major Psychopath."

"Doesn't your family live here? Aren't you afraid of what could happen?"

Her face flushed with heat, and she lifted a finger between them. "Don't ever talk about my family."

He looked back at Cecilia for a moment. "Hartnell could be the one who brainwashed Lansing. She's the one who got your friend Meghan killed. Don't you care about that?"

"Morgan. Of course I care. I even remember her name." She crossed her arms. "I can't help anyone if I'm suspended."

"Is that all you're worried about?" Peter scoffed. "If Kyudo finds out, I'll take the heat." He pointed at himself with a thumb. Like it wasn't already obvious who he meant.

Kyudo might blame both of us anyway, she thought. But how did Wazzerman know about the two bombs? And Ana said she knew where I was last night. She was so upset over being suspended I didn't push her for answers. Maybe Hartnell has some. The truth may mean nothing to others. But sometimes, you just have to know. "How do you want to do this?"

"Start with this." Peter lifted the flyer again.

"Did ya scan for prints?"

"Only hers. I checked while the DOLOS validator was clicking."

"And how are we goin' to turn up the heat?"

Peter turned his lips upward and tilted his head side to side. "How about murder one. Fifty police officers."

"That'll work. You be nice and I'll break her?"

Peter nodded and held his eyes shut for several seconds. "And blink off your oculars."

She held her eyes shut until the functions beeped off, and when she opened them, Peter was already in front of the conference room, holding the door for her.

Cecilia looked up as they entered, her cuffed hands softly clanking as the digits and red nails of her intertwined fingers moved over each other like a flame of flesh. The robotics factory spread far beyond the large window behind her, almost to a horizon where the robots coming off the assembly line appeared small like ants or something. A coconut scent mixed with a spice or something. Maybe shampoo or a fragrance, but not overly done like Mary when she drenches herself in perfume.

She sat next to Peter on the opposite side of the shiny black table and turned her emotion orb to Merciless-9, 60%. "Well, what do ya know? What's this?" She reached over and picked up the flyer in front of Peter and waved it in the air.

"Evidence of a crime," Peter said.

"And what would happen if I deliberately destroyed it."

"That would be obstruction of justice."

"Sounds serious. Would you arrest me and toss my hide into jail?"

"You bet your ass I would."

She looked at Peter and ground her teeth.

"Aw, aren't yew two cute. As he bout yew a ring et?" Cecilia said or asked. She had a Settlement-Two accent, like the one Troy has, but words were impossible to make out.

Under the table, Joan pressed a cuffputer button to activate the Babel-Squid app to replace Cecilia's accent with something coherent. Do people use this app on me, she wondered?

Peter tapped on the flyer on the table and pointed at one of his eyes. "Miss Hartnell, we have ocular recordings of you deliberately vaporizing a stack of these."

"I have no idea what they are," Cecilia said.

"Then why feed 'em into a document vaporizer?" she asked.

"It was in the shredding bin. I was only doing what I was told."

"Told by whom?" Peter asked.

"Martian HQ," Cecilia said. "They send me textual instructions every morning." She briefly raised her eyebrows and leaned back in her chair. Thru the window behind her, welding torches glowed in the dim factory.

She grinned and looked at Peter. "Ya hear that? She's just followin' orders."

"You have plenty of robots you could have delegated that to," Peter said to Cecilia.

"No," Cecilia said. "Thems for paying customers. And I was bored anyway." She rested her chin on the palm of one hand while scratching the surface of the table with the other. "My crossword puzzle app wanted three quid for the latest upgrade. And I rather liked the last version before it stopped working. It was all purple and cute."

"What exactly is for sale at this auction?" Peter asked while rapidly tapping on the flyer again. "Where is Club Ketu?"

Cecilia shrugged.

She rechecked the public directory, and the registered business database. No matches. One of the images on the flyer was familiar in some way. The scales. Where have I seen that before, she wondered?

"Is Club Ketu a bar? A speakeasy?" Peter asked.

"I don't know," Cecilia said.

"What does one sell at a futures auction?"

"I have no idea whatsoever."

Peter launched large holographic images on his cuffputer. Lansing. Morgan. A floating collage of the officers brainwashed and killed two days ago. "Do any of these faces look familiar?"

Cecilia shrugged and looked away.

"These officers were murdered," she said.

Cecilia made eye contact. "I haven't killed anyone."

"Perhaps not physically," Peter said. "But you work at a robotics company. Surely, you're familiar with protocol four?" He lifted a holographic copy of the statute from his cuffputer. "Brainwashing someone, wiping out their identity, is classified as murder." He swiped thru a few pages of the legal gibberish. "Subsection three elaborates on criminal liability regarding organic and inorganic entities." He dismissed the hologram and gestured with his hands to Petersplain. "If someone programs a robot to kill someone, the programmer would be at fault, and not the robot."

"We got a witness that confirms the victims were here. When they left, they weren't themselves anymore," she said. "You brainwashed 'em, didn't you?"

"No," Cecilia said.

She pounded the table with both fists. "You murdered 50 police officers."

Cecilia's eyes spread wide, and her brows lifted. "It was Gemma. Okay?"

"Gemma?"

"Gemma Overton."

"Oh, blame the dead person. That's just fuckin' great. Never heard that before." She crossed her arms and turned to Peter. "Isn't that convenient?"

"You bet your ass it is." Peter smiled.

"Because no one would lie to avoid the recyclin' penalty."

"Right."

Cecilia leaned over the table, her eyes welling up. "I swear to Isis it was Gemma."

"Isis? She's one of them whack jobs," she said to Peter.

"Perfect," he said sarcastically.

"Maybe there's another world where you don't get punished for your crimes," she said to Cecilia. "But it ain't this one."

"Gemma hated cops," Cecilia said.

"And how do you feel about cops?" Peter asked.

"They're alright I guess."

"Really?" On her cuffputer she launched Cecilia's holographic RAP sheet. "Solicitation of prostitution. Norris nabbed ya four different times. A fancy business suit doesn't change who's wearin' it."

Cecilia looked down at the table's shiny surface, maybe seeing her own reflection.

"Did that upset you?" Peter asked. "Being arrested?"

"What?" Cecilia looked up from the table and leaned half of her face against a hand. "Never felt that way about it really. I accepted it long ago as something that just happens every now and again, like the rain. I started when I was young, back when every living person was permanently in shelter. The red-light corridor had that Asian food place that always smelled like fried rice and the like. My fam couldn't eat unless I put myself out there for money. That's when I met Gloria. Gemma before she changed her name. We were sisters, but we weren't fam. We looked out for each other." Cecilia swallowed and looked down at the table again. "I had to hold her when we finally saw the sun again. She was shaking scared, like we were creatures of the night, and the bright ball was going to burn us into ashes. We kept saying how everything would be different." She looked up with tears in her eyes. "When they started making Vegas pleasure robots, johns started treating us worse. It was always bad, but it got to be like we wasn't even human to anyone anymore. When cops found us with bruises or cuts, they didn't even pretend to care. All you lot want are your arrest quotas filled. Or flash a badge for a freebie. Soft skin and hard cases. That's what they'd say." She wiped away the tears and sniffled. "That's why I don't feel bad for what happened to them. Except Mattie. She was the only cop who ever gave a damn about any of us."

Joan slowly lowered Cecilia's holographic dossier until it vanished into her cuffputer. The table looked smaller, like it was farther away. She crossed her legs and her spine bumped against the chair's back rest. For most children, surviving the war was just the beginning. I almost ended up like Cecilia, she thought. Freed from the visible prison but trapped in the invisible one, where her past crushed every day in a haunting loop of eternity, and her whole life slipped between her fingertips like the crumbs of a rotten cake. Like what happened to Mom. Was it something about me, or random chance that shoved me in a different direction? Maybe having a baby sister to protect is also itself protection.

"Mattie?" Peter asked. "Do you mean Matilda?"

Cecilia's eyes moved up and down over Peter, her face scrunched into a frown.

Her stomach tightened, almost a cramp, and she leaned to one side. What should I ask now, she wondered? Peter was staring but her mouth wouldn't open, like it was welded shut. She turned up her emotion orb to 80%. Nothing came to mind except old shelter memories of hunger, thirst, and hiding in the dark, hiding from— "Ouch."

Peter kicked her in the foot.

"Matilda Albright?" she asked.

Cecilia shrugged. "She was just Mattie to me."

"What happened to her?"

"She had a problem with some government guy."

"Who?"

"I don't know. But Gemma told me he was going to pay. She always said it so calmly, like she knew it was going to happen."

"As in pay for something at the auction?" Peter asked.

"Like, get him back for somethin'?" she asked.

"Mattie wasn't stronger than what happened to her. Whatever it was," Cecilia mumbled to herself.

"What happened?"

"I've got nothing else to say," Cecilia said. "Haven't I got a right to be silent?"

Peter lifted his eyebrows and shook his head before tilting it towards Cecilia. New holographic images floated over his cuffputer. A woman's bloodied corpse on the plush carpet of a fancy house.

"Miss Hartnell, you were sayin' those officers got what they deserved." She stood, walked behind Cecilia, and paced back in forth. "What about Gemma?"

Peter arranged the scene on the table. All evenly spaced and equally grotesque.

"Did she get what she deserved?" she asked.

Cecilia teared up at the images, her mouth twisted open and twitched with a small cobweb of saliva between her lips. "No," she squeaked.

The stomach pain turned into a burning and twisting cramp, and she held her side for several seconds. "What do you think is goin' to happen to you when we book you for murderin' 50 peace officers?" She leaned over Cecilia, both her hands landed on the table, curled into fists. "Did you know we got a new gas? It can dissolve a person into fertilizer in under a minute." She moved next to Cecilia's ear to whisper. "I volunteered once to push the little red death penalty button myself. But it turned out there was a fuckin' waitin' list. How long is your list goin' to be, cop-killer?"

Cecilia picked up one of the holographic images of Gemma's corpse and gently caressed it, like she was really touching her. Tears fell thru the floating image and onto the table. "I promised her one day we'd go to the colonies. We could start over."

"Wouldn't you miss Earth?" Peter asked.

"I don't miss this place, or any, only a time and place, both long gone."

"It's not too late for you," Peter said. "Tell us everything. We'll protect you."

"I'm not in danger."

"Sure you are. Everyone else embroiled in this god damn conspiracy has wound up dead. Why not you?"

"I haven't done anything," Cecilia looked at each of them. "You'll see. Once you upload my mind, you'll see. I didn't do nothing."

"If you live that long," Peter said. "Some cops just can't wait to enact revenge." He moved the most hideous image of Gemma's corpse in front of Cecilia. "Gemma was killed with police ammunition. Probably a small, silenced Jupiter pistol. It didn't even wake the neighbors."

She keeled onto the table as her stomach erupted. Vomit sprayed thru the holographic documents and spread over the shiny surface.

"Jesus Lyon." Peter stood and backed away from the table.

She staggered out of the room and across the blurry office floor, stumbling into the blinding light of the nearest ladies' room. Both shaking arms landed on the edge of a faucet. With each trembling breath, foul drool and acidic upchuck dripped onto the shiny white sink. She turned the tap and cupped water to wash out her mouth a dozen times. The splashing filth circled the drain as she turned off the water and looked up into the mirror, into the centers of her own eyes.

Why am I shaking? I'm not a murderer. I could never do that. And I would never forget. I didn't even know Gemma.

Beeps from her emotion orb. Blinking white text over shifting shades of red. *UNKNOWN ERROR. RESTART IN PROGRESS. DO NOT POWER DOWN DEVICE.*

She pulled her hair back as her emotion orb beeped, and her reflection steadied.

She caught her breath and walked back towards the conference room where Peter was waiting by the closed door.

"Are you okay?" he asked.

"Somethin' I ate," she said. Thru the conference room windows, Cecilia and a robot cleaned opposite ends of the table.

"Do you need a minute?" He reached for the door handle.

Inside the room, Cecilia looked away, towards the long window overlooking the robot factory. She extended a single finger to touch the glass before slumping down into her chair and looking down at the floor with a long face, like an egg at the end of the table, an edge away from cracking.

Her stomach tensed again, but it was empty. "I don't think she's gonna talk."

"You nearly had her."

"That was before she cleaned up my breakfast."

"We can't take her in now. Her arbiter will find out we questioned her illegally." Peter scratched one of his eyebrows. "We have to go the station archives, before—" he made a groan or a sigh or something.

"Before what?"

"Before they erase Albright's past."

***

She sat in her chair while Peter sat on his half of their desk. Most of the officers had left the cramped station but the air was still dank.

"Castor is working in the archives," Peter whispered. "You distract him while I trip the monitor circuit and copy the files we need onto a disc."

"Distract him?" she whispered.

"Just ask him to help you with something. Flirt with him."

"I am NOT goin' to shake my rear end in front of a coworker. What if it doesn't work? He might not even like me."

"You can bet—"

"Do NOT tell me to bet my ass. I'm not some fuckin' $2 harlot."

"Aren't you two dating?"

"No!"

"Shh. Have you used the archival computer before?"

"Can't I at least brush my teeth first or somethin'?"

"We're knee deep in crap here. Put on your big girl pants."

"I'm not callin' him." She crossed her arms.

Peter launched the lamptop on his side of the desk and pushed beeping buttons on the phone app.

She stood up to grab the holographic phone, but Peter stood and pulled it up, higher than her arms could reach.

"Good morning, Castor," Peter said to Troy's holographic avatar. "Could you come to workstation Z-5? Lyon is having trouble with her computer."

Troy's avatar locked eyes and smiled. One of those wide smiles, where his dark eyes light up so bright that for a moment the whole world is safe. "Absolutely." He hung up and his glowing avatar vanished.

"Asshole," she said to Peter.

"I'll be back." Peter made his way to the stairwell and thru the clanking door.

At the end of her shaking arms, her hands sweat on the armrests. She turned her emotion orb to Cool-Calm, 40%, and grabbed a tissue on the desk to wipe her hands. A button on her cuffputer launched the Narcissus app and she turned her face left and right. God damnit. Mary's makeup. I put it on to cover that scratch I had this morning, she thought. Troy is going to think it's for him. But he's not here yet. Maybe a quick a trip to the bathroom—

"Hey Joan. What's up?" Troy asked in his Settlement-Two accent. He wore a white tee, tight enough that his biceps squeezed the short sleeves further up his arms, towards his shoulders. His forearms bulged as he moved Peter's chair out of the way and draped his technician jacket on it. Dark and shiny polyester material. 'MOTH' in large yellow letters on the back.

"Oh. Hi." She smiled and hastily dismissed the Narcissus app with a hand movement. And accidentally knocked some papers onto the floor. She briefly hopped out of the chair to reach down and quickly pick up the papers and return them to the desk. It was like the entire station was watching. "I'm havin' some trouble connectin' to the evidence server."

"Connection trouble?" Troy ran fingers thru his dark hair, which he kept just short enough that it didn't curl. He moved in close to her computer's holographic interface to swipe thru several configuration cubes. Close enough that his cologne or aftershave was noticeable. A musky scent with eucalyptus. "It all looks on the up and up." He took a step back. "Sometimes the server lags for a bit."

"I'm such a ditz."

"No, I don't think you are." A faint smile crossed his face and his eyes mockingly narrowed.

"Oh. Okay."

A beep from an eye function, a message of moving text from Peter: *I need two minutes.*

"New shirt?" she asked.

"No. It shrank in the laundry press."

"I hate it when that happens," she lied. Well, that's not really a lie. But it is this time.

"How's Mary?"

"She's great. She keeps addin' to her never-say-die collection of lipstick and makeup. Soon she'll have more colors than an ancient globe."

"You look great, by the way."

"Oh. Thank you." This damn makeup better cover up blushing.

A shadow crossed her desk, a darkness blocking the sunlight from one of the tall windows high on the station walls. Kyudo. She stood next to the mezzanine railing a few meters from her glass-enclosed office, her head turned up enough to look down at them.

Troy looked up for a split second. "I should get back to the data archives."

"How's your mom?"

"She's good. Her new Alzheimer's medications are helping, but she still forgot my brother's birthday. I mean she was there and ate a corner piece of the lemon-blueberry cake, but she couldn't remember it afterwards. We made a moving memory for her to replay."

She smiled. "You know so much about how minds work."

"Did you know that 20 years ago people took mind-altering pills to lose weight? Every time they saw food, they would think of something else."

She frowned. "Weight loss? People wanted to *lose* weight?"

"Yes."

"Could it make me stop loving chocolate?"

"No. Not you," he said and they both chuckled. "Not any more than it could make me stop loving vanilla."

"You like vanilla?"

"I do."

She bit her lip and crossed her legs. Troy smiled, and a tingling sensation tickled the back of her head and abdomen. Like a tender fire, it gently shook her anxieties away from her heart one by one like an autumn breeze caressing the leaves of a tree and guiding them softly to the ground.

He glanced at her lips. Is he really going to do this at work and in front of everyone? How bold. He won't go too far. What if he goes too far?

Her muscles refused to move as Troy leaned towards her face. Closer. And closer.

A tapping noise. Kyudo leaned over the mezzanine railing, striking it with her fingernails as she glared. Troy backed away and glanced up. He walked away but looked back with a smile.

***

Peter pulled over a few blocks from the police station and inserted a disc into the car computer. "Did you blink off your routines?"

She nodded.

Matilda's dossier popped up on the hologram. Born on October 12th, 2128 in Woodacre, Olde California. Juris Doctor degree from Riverside in 2154. "She was a fuckin' arbiter?"

Peter swiped along the timeline. "She enlisted in 21-55. A brief stint in patrol and a transfer to MOTH in 21-57."

"No academy transcript?"

"It wasn't built until 21-58." He continued to swipe. "No suspensions but one write-up for excessive force in 21-59, signed by Lansing, who was a captain at that time. No partner listed, just a blank line. And look at this. An arrest warrant. Three days before her DOLOS status expired."

"What was the charge?"

Peter shrugged. "It's redacted."

"I thought this was her original file. Why is info missin'?"

"I don't know."

A button lit up under the timeline, which led to a wipe cut and the fancy cover sheet of a daily report book, with *Protection Detail* in large letters, a shield icon underneath, followed by 2162. Tapping next on the daily report book animated a page flip, like it was a paper book in one of those black and white holo-films. The ones where the mean detective in a trench coat gnaws endlessly on cigars that dangle from his mouth, muffling his words so badly that Mary turns on the closed captioning instead of just using the function like everyone else.

The page loaded. Security detail for Councilman Warner. Supervising officer CPT Oric Lansing. Assigned Officers, a grid starting with V. McGuire. M. Albright. A dozen unfamiliar names, until A. Hamilton. Hamilton. "Anastasia Hamilton."

"Hamilton served with Albright on Warner's security detail. And look at the time frames. She transferred out of that detail on November 12th of last year. That's when Albright went M-I-A." Peter looked over. "Did she mention that?"

"No."

"God damn," Peter muttered and shook his head. "Lansing had clones of his dead family at a mansion in Bel Air. One of them described a visitor named Mattie. Ivan pulled its neurons and confirmed the ID." He swiped to DOLOS and entered Ana's name. A holographic map beeped with a circle at an address on Federal Hill. "We should talk to Ana."

Oh shit. Ana knows where I was last night, she thought. "Or maybe we should split up. I can question Ana. Can you tail Cecilia on DOLOS?"

Peter scratched one of his eyebrows. "That's a good idea in theory. We can cover both bases and find Club Ketu one way or another. But Cecilia knows we'll be tracking her. She'll probably conduct her business in a deprived neighborhood at the city's edge, where satellite coverage is foggy. Since she knows what we look like, tailing her is a risk. She could make us."

"Then we go to Kyudo and come clean about Cecilia and that flyer. She'll give us someone from patrol in plain clothes."

Peter shook his head and looked away for 30 seconds. "There's a mole in the MOTH unit. They're the one that killed Gemma before she could spill the beans."

Her hands landed in her lap and shook as she gripped her legs. "Well, um, who do you think it is?" The words came out jumbled and squeaky.

Peter sighed. "I don't know. And until we know, the only person we can trust is Norris, but he arrested Hartnell long ago. She could remember him. You're good at remaining undetected. Why don't you shadow her? I'll question Ana."

She quickly navigated menus on her cuffputer to check Mary's status. A green, available circle around her name. I don't want Mary in any danger, she thought. But if Mary was the one in trouble, I would help her. "I know someone who can tail her and not be made. And she can't be a mole."

"How do you know?"

"She's not a cop." She clasped her hands together and the trembling stopped. "When we find Club Ketu, we might need to call for backup. I'll talk to Ana."

"Right. I'll see about that mole." He patted one of his coat pockets. Whatever that means.

I must talk to Ana before anyone else does, she thought.

# Kindred

"Club Ketu," Peter said to Moira's small avatar floating over his wrist-computer.

"We have references to it in our projections, but no location," Moira said.

"Right."

"You think our hardware is there?"

"The predictions will be auctioned there tonight."

"That cannot happen."

"Right. I'm on it." He hung up and sat on a stool in the evidence lab. On the worktable, a line of blue scanning light moved over the rusted edges of the pre-war cylinder key sitting on a lit analysis pad. The fingerprint routine clicked-back. Four sets of prints rendered volumetrically and color coded.

His own prints in blue. Clicking a button eliminated them.

Wasserman and Albright in different shades of red.

*Samael Lyon* in green.

He fell off the stool, stumbling but remaining on his feet. He picked up the clanging seat by its metal legs and set it upright. Clicking refresh ran the scan again. Identical results. Clicking on Samael's name loaded a public profile. A father-daughter line connected Samael with Joanna. Two other lines to a Penelope and a Mary. Penelope had a question mark instead of a portrait. A private profile.

Son of a bitch. Lyon had never mentioned her parents and I occasionally wondered if she was grown in a vat or perhaps assembled from spare parts as a secretly sanctioned killer robot designed to improve the department's KD ratio. Is she the mole? After today's tower bombing, Lyon wasn't worried about what might happen to her family. How could I miss that?

Scrolling through Mr. Lyon's dossier revealed no priors, a blank page. Clicking on the pre-war records page resulted in *Subpoena Required* flashing in large red letters.  A residential and business address on the public profile.  Dragging and dropping both Samael and Joanna to DOLOS rendered two volumetric maps.  Lyon's location flashed at an address in Federal Hill. Her old man's location clicked at his business address.

He dialed Norris on his wrist-computer.

"What's up Peter?" Norris's small avatar asked.

"I need a favor."

***

Hollywood Robot Repair was a few blocks from the boulevard, past a shallow right turn up a steep side-street shadowed by the derelict old-world chateau, and not far from Gemma Overton's residence.  Above the sign, a volumetric image of a robot spun high over the entrance. An old-style storefront, with a recessed glass door and two display windows filled with shiny bipodal merchandise.  Taller stone and brick buildings surrounded it, their windows plastered with flyers and large signs of prices and Greek words.

There was no revolving door or dusting room, only a single door that opened with a ringing bell. Rows of bright LED lights ran along the ceiling between tall shelves of components and equipment.  A clerk robot behind the counter on the left kept parroting "Can I help you?" He shook his head and walked around the shelves to a passage between two rows of what appeared to be dressing rooms, what one would expect at a clothing store though dimly lit red.  Between the narrow gaps in the drawn curtains, men of various ages with nubile women performing various sexual acts. But only the males had organic tags on DOLOS.  Female pleasure bots.

Mr. Lyon's signal, a green outline, was beyond a gray door with a knob of weathered copper, which opened with creaks to a large and slovenly garage. Shelves of marred toolboxes bordered two large worktables, their surfaces scratched with random lines that looked like chalk or dust, and half-assembled robots, humanoid and otherwise.

Mr. Lyon was using a tool to detach what appeared to be a jetpack from one of the automatons, robbing it of its ability to fly. He turned and quickly stood up straight. Middle-aged, sandy hair cut high and tight. His wristwatch turned inwards, parallel with his palm next to the rolled-up sleeve of his soiled, dark blue jumpsuit.

"Are you the guy that called about the T-I-S three hundred?" With a posed, purposeful gait, Mr. Lyon walked over to a cluttered side table where a drinking bird endlessly sank its head into a glass of murky water, then upright again in an endless loop. Among the maze of refuse he pulled a rag and wiped his hands not clean but less dirty.

"No, I'm officer Ramsey." He pulled his bifold from an interior coat pocket and flipped it open.

Mr. Lyon froze in place. "Would you like a robot to keep you company for a while? I can program them to do any-thing," he said with a rushed cadence. "On the house."

"No thanks." He put his bifold away.

Mr. Lyon pointed with a knife hand at another workta-ble. "I can design a robot to resemble your boss and you can shoot them. It's a very commonly requested service. Some folks even ask to shoot a robot that looks like their spouse, if that's for you."

He put up an open palm. "I'm good. Really."

"My daughter's a cop. Do you know her?" Mr. Lyon asked.

Without thinking he smiled. "I've met her." Lyon hasn't told her family about her police partner. My wife knows more about Lyon than I do, he thought. Even Caramel knows the name Joanna Lyon. Perhaps Lyon's embarrassed by what her father does for a living. Despite no discernible effort to conceal this place, father-of-the-prude hasn't been busted. The apple has surely fallen far from the orange tree. He looked around the garage and back towards the robotic brothel. "Is this place a club of some kind?"

"There's no membership fee. But no assholes allowed."

He forced himself to laugh. "Fair enough. Are you going anywhere tonight?"

"No. We're open until o-two hundred."

"Do you have any other employees?"

"No. Young people these days are lazy idiots."

"They all grew up too sheltered. Literally," he lied.

"You got that right."

"What about your wife? Does she work here?"

"No. She has a condition."

"A what?"

"A memory condition. She doesn't even recognize family."

"I'm sorry to hear that." Lyon mentioned that once. I shouldn't have asked. He counted to ten before continuing. "Do you ever travel up North?"

"The wastelands? Are you kidding?"

He made himself smile. "Some people like the thrill and danger. Wasteland tourism is a thriving business."

Mr. Lyon's mouth twisted. A scornful expression reminiscent of his progeny. "No, I don't go up North."

"Do you buy any robots from Liberty Robotics?"

Mr. Lyon placed his hands in his pockets. "All the time."

"Do you consider them reliable?"

"Definitely. Why?"

"Is it possible for a robot to harm someone?"

"Absolutely not. Not without extreme hardware modification." Mr. Lyon picked up a robot's head from the worktable, turning it until the open bottom faced Peter. "After the war, the three robotic protocols prevent any robot from harming anyone." He pointed to some of the exposed circuitry. "Any tampering results in an automatic shut-down." The robot head landed on the workstation with a thud. "And that's why you can shoot them in the head, and they can't retaliate. Serves them right. Fucking robots started the war."

"So, riddle me this, how could a robot participate in a crime. Say, a home invasion?"

"It couldn't, unless it was tricked into believing the home belonged to the human giving it orders."

"But wasn't there a case some years ago of a robot mur-dering someone?"

"Oh, that. You must be thinking of that Graham fellow who was poisoned. In that case, the robot made the poison, but had no idea a human would be consuming it." Mr. Lyon walked over to a volumetric diagram of a robot and rear-ranged components with a few clicks. "They're machines. Nothing more than cogs. Easily tricked into thinking they're doing no harm." Mr. Lyon walked over to another table, took a swig from an abraded metal canteen, and set it down next to two dusty tomes, *Modern Hypnosis* and *Program-ming Robotics*.

"You must have worked with robots for a long time."

"Only since the war, but I'm a fast learner. I figured the best way to make them pay is to reprogram and sell them."

"Have you ever reprogrammed a human?"

"Not since the settlements got soft and outlawed it."

"Huh. What did you do before the war?"

Mr. Lyon walked past Peter.

He turned towards footsteps. A man had emerged from behind a curtain and briefly pulled out a wallet before hast-ily putting it back and walking away. Mr. Lyon was shaking his head and making a shoo gesture with the back of his hand.

"Say again?" Mr. Lyon asked.

"What did you do before?"

"Before what?  The war?"

"Yes."

"I was a security guard."

"For one of the big four?"

"I moved around a lot."

"Huh."  Moved around a lot.  The haircut.  The watch. The way he points.  I don't remember him, but if he was at Chiron, I could be arrested shortly after him.  And if I'm wrong about Lyon being the mole, she'll lose it.  Kyudo will lose it.  He clicked a few buttons on his wrist-computer to recheck the model found at Gemma Overton's house, where she was murdered.  "Have you had any robots gone missing or stolen lately?  Say, an LR thirty-three?"

"No.  I'm sure I'd know if they had."

He pulled his validation tube.  "Sir, would you mind?"

Mr. Lyon blinked, unphased as he clicked the tube's wire into his wrist tracker.

Peter gripped his holstered weapon until the tube flashed green and he took it back with his free hand.  "Thank you for your cooperation."

"Is that what this is?  Cooperation?"

"Oh sure.  I've never had it so good."

Mr. Lyon laughed.  "Let me know if *my* little girl ever gives you any lip."

"Right."

He took long strides to the door.  I can meet Norris, who's tailing Lyon.  If she's the mole, she'll have to contact the Outcasts somehow.

A large humanoid robot stood on the sidewalk by his parked prowler.  "Hello Officer Peter Ramsey.  I am Robbie the robot reporter."

"Right."

"Would you like to comment on the terrorist attack on Blue Jewel Tower, Peter?  Do you agree with councilman Warner that it's a cowardly act by the Outcasts?  Do you

agree with the new re-armament proposals?  Are you investigating the—"

"I can't comment on an ongoing investigation."

"Does that mean it's going well?  Do you have leads?"

"I'm not saying anything."

"You have nothing?  There are no leads?"

"Don't print lies like that.  You'll scare people."

"Can't you just explain?"

He got in the car and rolled down the passenger side
window.  "Step back a meter."  He made a waving gesture
with the back of his fingers.  "I don't want to run over your
foot or flipper, whichever you call it."

At the end of the block the light turned red, and he
stopped.  Overton's house in the rearview mirror.  Someone
sitting on the porch.  Patricia Overton.  Gemma's mother.
She was weeping while robotic movers packed a utility vehicle parked in the driveway with furniture and boxes.

I could turn around and talk to her.  Tell her it will get
easier.  I could lie about the unending pit that will consume
her heart and soul.

His hands shook on the steering wheel. The light turned
green.  He flipped the siren, spinning red and blue, and
pulled a U-turn with burning rubber.  Screeching to a halt in
front of the repair shop, or brothel, or whatever the hell it
was.

He stormed past the reporter robot and through the jingling door.

"Did you forget something officer?" Mr. Lyon asked.  His
mouth and eyes wide.

"As a matter of fact, I did."  He turned Mr. Lyon around
by his shoulders, pushed him flat against the wall, and
cuffed his hands behind his back.  "Samael Lyon, you are
under arrest for the murder of Gemma Overton.  Everything
you say will be used against you.  You have a silence privilege
that you are free to invoke at any time.  You have the right

to a legal arbiter.  If you do not have one, the state will provide one upon your request."

# 30
## A Forest Darkly

Joan followed the holographic Navi arrows on the windshield halfway down Avalon Boulevard to Ana's house. The yard was missing that clichéd white fence with the pointy boards. It was a cute blue house with black roof tiles and shutters, surrounded by a concrete lip. One of those foundation tubs that prevent radioactive gases.

She parked on the street and walked to the door. A perimeter of little round rocks transitioned to grass green enough to be fake, matching the shade of the front door, which had one of those half-circle windows at the top, like a rising sun. Glaring afternoon rays reflected from the burgundy trunk of an Aurora sedan parked in the driveway.

Before she could knock, the door opened. Ana's hair was loose but straight, maybe recently brushed, and she was wearing a bathrobe, and dark blue slippers that had moving pictures of puppies chasing each other. "Hi Joan. Come on in." She pulled the door open all the way.

"Thank you."

Ana led her to a radiation vacuum in the small foyer. A split level with stairs descending to a dark basement and a parallel one ascending towards a bright room, capped with a gleaming skylight. "I was about to make some tea. Would you like a cup?"

Hmm, why not? "Yes please." She stopped following Ana just outside the kitchen. In a family room a child sat in front of a lamptop, watching holo-toons about cowboys in some desert. "Hi."

"Hi," he said without looking over.

The kitchen was quaint, with a breakfast nook next to a window. A backyard with a swing set and an envious hilltop view of the Eastern suburbs that stretched to the perimeter wall on the horizon's edge. The Lion's Gate small but distinct in the distance. Sitting in the booth was cozy without being claustrophobic. High on the wall across from her, three shelves of kitchen wares. On the bottom one, a holographic miniature between jars of flour and sugar. Morgana, according to an eye function. Something to do with that ancient story of King Arthur. "It's so unfair you got suspended. I was thinkin' about transferrin' and doin' a service rotation with another unit."

Ana took a tea kettle to the sink and tapped a button on the faucet, which slithered like a snake into position and poured splashing water. "You don't like being a MOTH?"

"I do. I just want to try somethin' else."

Lifting the full teapot onto the flat, shiny range top, Ana turned it until *Russel* was visible in dark grey letters. "Mm hmm. What did you have in mind?"

"Security detail for a junta bigwig."

Ana walked over to cabinets at another entrance to the kitchen. A dining room with a polished table, which looked to be real wood. Awfully nice for a cop's home. "You want to be a chauffeur for a VIP?"

"Gettin' to know the brass bosses on a first name basis can't be bad for my career."

"Earl Grey?" Ana opened cabinets, pulling out two white mugs and a box of tea capsules, which she popped open.

"Yes please."

"Who's detail?"

"Councilman Warner."

Haunting gusts rattled the windows. After a noticeable pause Ana asked, "How do you take it?"

Not lying down. "Sugar and milk."

Ana twisted both ends of two pinky-sized capsules and dropped them with clanks into the cups. "Have you heard what people say about him?"

"Peter was tellin' me those are just rumors. Outcast propaganda."

Ana peeked into the family room at the kitchen's edge, checking on her son, before walking over and sliding into the booth across from her. "With the personnel shortage, Kyudo might need you to stay as a MOTH."

No anger in Ana's cold eyes. This would be easier with a behavioral cylinder. Maybe talk about something else. Two meters away steam rose from the simmering teapot. A noise came from the fridge, one of the cold cycles they do a few times each hour. 1:11 pm on the appliance clock. "Did they close all of the schools early?"

"I hope they did. I was so worried until Sophio was home." Ana looked back towards a folded-up highchair with a bib tied to it. White with a pink border and the letter R.

"What's his middle name?"

Both of Ana's hands rested on the nook's small table. "That was Rhea's." She glanced out the window. "I lost her at seven months."

"Oh my god, I'm so sorry."

Rhea is Mary's middle name, she thought. But that's not what you say when someone tells you one of their children died. A whistle from the kettle.

Sophio's voice from the other room cried out "Teatime" in high-pitched mockery.

They both laughed and Ana wiggled out of the booth to pour the tea. The white mugs quickly turned bright red, but the rims and handle phased to orange. She returned to place one hot, frothy cup in front of Joan and another in front of herself as she sat down again. "The box says wait 30 seconds, but I never do." She took a sip.

The cup was hot enough that she could only run a fingertip over the surface for a few seconds before pulling it away. "My sister went to some club or somethin' last night and some guy put his hands on her. I'm tryin' to find him, but she won't tell me his name or where she went. Some place that starts with a K. Kato or somethin'. Do you know where it could be?"

Anastasia's eyebrows made a weird shape as she shook her head.

She took a sip that was hot but creamy and delicious and worth having a burnt tongue. "I have to find that Matilda Albright and I have no idea where she could be."

"My union rep said I shouldn't discuss active cases." Ana pressed a fingertip against the orange rim of her mug, which left a short-lived yellow fingerprint as she looked out the window.

"I won't tell no one."

After a sip Ana set down her mug with a loud thud. "If you had destroyed a government building, would you stick around? I would be halfway to Organ if I were her."

"Organ?"

"Oregon. One of the olde states."

"Oh." She took a sip and tapped a fingernail against her mug. "So, if those rumors you were sayin' about Warner were true, who would know? Who would have evidence if there were any? The district attorney?"

"Sophio," Ana called out to her son. "Did you start your homework?"

"But my cartoon is almost over," he answered.

"It's a rerun."

"Nah uh."

"Go do your homework."

The sound of the cartoons a room away ceased and Sophio walked past the kitchen. Footsteps ending with a closing door.

"You have to let this go Joan," Ana said.

"Let this go?"

"Do you know what happened last night?"

"No."

"You murdered Gemma Overton."

Joan gulped air as a cramp took hold of her abdomen. "How do you know that?"

"I was there. I'm always there. I keep trying to stop you but you're so headstrong. It's only afterwards that you understand how it changes you. Even with the memory pill, murdering someone changes you. Forever."

"What?"

"The outcasts have a time machine that they stole from Delphi. We're in a time circle." Ana drank some of her tea and sighed. "I keep coming back to try to save my Rhea. And you."

"Me? Why me?"

"We were once friends."

She pulled her validation tube and slid it over to Ana.

Ana plugged it in. "I always pass. My circle takes me back to before DOLOS is created."

The tube beeped green.

"If you keep comin' back thru time, why don't you stop Warner? If he's guilty, why don't you stop him?"

"Do you remember that hacker? The one a few blocks from Ocean Avenue? The alleyway leading to his computer dungeon, the one always clogged with addicts. I'll never forget the look in all their eyes. Abandoned souls living hand to mouth until they become a victim or a convict. My son is innocent. I would never do anything that would put him in danger."

Her cuffputer beeped. A message from Mary: *Lemon! I found her!*

***

One block from the burning lights of the perimeter wall, Mary poked her head out of the rolled-down window of an autocar. "Hey Lemon. Do you have $40?"

At the driver's side door, the window was down.

"Good afternoon, Officer. I am Rrroger the robot driver," it said.

"Uh huh." She held her cuffputer to the billing hologram until it beeped.

"Thank you for choosing Roger Autocars."

Mary exited the cab and beckoned her towards the far side of a vacant alleyway. "She went this way," she whispered.

Their footsteps were inaudible against the beeping horns and the gusts of wind that tossed refuse and clutter along the edges of the pavement. Shifting light from a basement window. Men and women at green-felt tables, different colored stacks of holographic chips in front of each of them. A police function popped up: *Illegal card game. Protocol 43 violation.*

"It's the 25$^{th}$," Mary said.

"Shit. I forgot to make Mom's lunch today." But how?

"It's okay I went over."

It felt like a glass plate being pressed against her head.

"What happened?" Mary asked.

Ana must have been lying. I didn't murder Gemma. She twisted her emotion orb. "Nothin'. I'm okay."

"That dial is like coffee. You can't run on it forever."

"It's okay I just need to find this Cecilia."

The alley ended at a corner and returned to a fenced sidewalk running parallel to a congested highway of speeding vehicles, each of them flashing for an instant with orange glare from the nearby perimeter wall. A concrete stairway led to a skywalk over the roadway. Monitors bordered the alley, 10 meters on each side. Their downward facing scanning-lights strobed back in forth. Overlay 17 drew the monitor scan-ranges as green semi-circles on the ground. Too far apart to create a Venn diagram.

"She dropped off satellite trackin', so she must a gone over the bridge."

"Okay."

"If anythin' happens just stay behind me."

Mary rolled her eyes. "Drama Lemon."

"Hush Potato."

Circular, dark green stains on the overpass's concrete steps. Carefully taking a knee and running her scanner over it beeped with an immediate result: *Cyanobacteria-115.* Broiling sunlight fell thru the curved glass covering the skywalk and an eye function lit little boxes around each increasingly faded drop along the trail. Doing a 360 at the far side revealed the source of dried droplets. 50 meters from the stairway, where the brick buildings bordering the sidewalk ended and a row of 100 glowing pools of radiation-consuming bacteria began, flush against the perimeter wall. A function warning recalculated the safe distance as wind blew rising steam clouds across the large and glowing vats of rippling water. Even bums know to not drink that.

As a rainbow of car colors zoomed along the highway, loud engines echoing with a doppler effect, a blue police signal blipped on the distant end of McKinley Avenue.

A merciful breeze accompanied them half a block up Killion Street, past the Encino holo dome, where only eye functions could spot the nearly microscopic green dots that curved into a lane and a parking lot. The lot bordered three lines of garage-sized storage lockers.

The trail ended where a cleaning robot buzzed around in a random pattern, spraying and sucking foam over the pavement. "Fuckin' stupid robot," she muttered as it passed. The bot frowned and lowered its head.

"What?" Mary asked.

"It washed away evidence. You'd notice that if you stopped flirtin' with your boyfriends on your cuffputer for a minute."

"I was not flirting." Mary stopped flirting with boys on her cuffputer.

She wiped a drop of sweat from her forehead and pulled her canteen, finding only a single warm drop. "Ya got any water?"

"No. Sorry," Mary said.

There was a walk-up office a bit larger than a holo-booth, nestled in the sketchy urban gully and humbled by the U-shaped canyon of glass holo domes. Over it a sign which lit up one letter a time: *Kyle's Storage*. Above the office counter, thick glass reached the square ceiling. Bullet-proof according to an eye function and a web-shaped crack where someone put the theory into practice. Under a small opening in the glass, text scrolled: *CASH ONLY*.

Inside a virile clerk in a surfer-embroidered t-shirt and shorts played a holographic hovercar game. He attempted to land.

"Try landin' a real hovercar sometime," she said hoarsely.

Distracted, maybe by Mary's outfit, the clerk crashed and burned in an embellished explosion. "What's up dudes?" The man belted out.

Mary looked over at her for a few seconds, then at the clerk. "Are you Kyle?"

"Yeah dude," Kyle said with an obnoxious shit-eating grin.

She showed him her police ID and pulled her validation tube from a pant pocket. Kyle stuck out his arm and played with a holographic yo-yo while he whistled some tune and waited for the green beep.

"Lyon?" Kyle asked. "Do you know Forest Lyon? I saw him play at the Galaxy Garden Open and he was just like KAPOW!" He moved his hands like he was swinging an invisible golf club. "Got a hole in two."

"No." She unplugged and pocketed her validator. "Any suspicious-lookin' renters lately?"

"Oh yeah. All the time dude."

"How long has your monitor been broken?" Mary pointed to the large monolithic government device with a cracked surveillance lens mounted on the back wall of the holo dome, behind her and Joan but still in Kyle's line of sight.

"No idea. I'm not a cop or anything, so I don't care." Kyle said.

"Have you seen this woman?" She brought up a hologram of Cecilia Hartnell on her cuffputer.

"Nah dude."

She tried again with a portrait of Matilda. Kyle squinted, then grabbed her wrist, pulling her hand and the bright hologram thru the hole in the office glass and in front of his glistening eyes as his office turned into a kaleidoscope.

"Yeah dude. She was totally here," he said.

She violently reclaimed her hand. "You're sure?"

"Ow. Yeah dude. I totally remember her. She was *not* meant for this place."

"An unregistered organic?" she asked.

"I have no idea. She wasn't marked red or anything like that. Her name was Molly or something like that. She totally did *not* understand that this is a chill people *only* zone." He rotated his fingers in circles around his closet-sized office. His flip-up computer cast red light on his face and the walls. "She rented locker seven a while ago. Like, a week, or something. Repaid for another week two days ago with avarice banknotes."

The Wall-Thru function beeped with an error message. "I'll be right back," she said to Mary before walking out of earshot. She called Troy on her cuffputer and it only rang twice.

"Joan. Hi." He had disabled video sharing, so there was no holographic avatar of him, only an animated line that moved in waves when he spoke.

"Hi Troy. Can you get me some satellite bandwidth? I need a full-sight Wall-Thru package at 22-11 Acheron Lane."

"Satellite bandwidth is limited at the moment, with everyone working various leads in the Tower bombing," Troy said into her ear com, then there were munching and crunching noises.

"What are you eatin'?"

"Fish and chips."

"Oh. Isn't it a fish sandwich though?"

"It is." There was a sound of him biting into something crispy.

"Mm. What's on it?"

"Spicy cheese and spicy sauce. Onion, lettuce. And this *new* type of food called a tomato."

"Gross."

"It is. But it's also very juicy. And since I forgot my drink so it's the only thing keeping my mouth from catching on fire."

"Oh, I forgot to refill my canteen. I'm so thirsty."

"That doesn't sound fun. But I think fire mouth is worse."

"Fine. Think that way."

"I'll get your satellite online *before* I get a drink. How about that way of thinking?"

She giggled. "Aw, it's okay. You can get your drink first."

"Thanks. It will be a few minutes. Long enough for you to rehydrate."

"Okay. Get your drink on before you turn into a dragon."

Troy chuckled. "Will do." He hung up.

Mary and Kyle were still at the booth-sized office, on opposite ends of the protective glass.

"Did anyone else use the locker but her?" Mary asked Kyle.

"Sometimes a dude comes by," Kyle said.

"A dude? You mean a guy?"

"Yeah dude."

Mary and her exchanged glances and blinks.

"What did he look like?" she asked.

Kyle's eyes hazed like privacy glass. "Like. A dude." Joan gave him a frown. "He was like, old or something. Short dark hair."

"You get a name?" Mary asked.

Kyle scratched his short-cropped hair. "I think it was like, Paul? Yeah. Paul. Yeah. I think. But I can't be sure. Sorry dude."

Something fell over, it sounded like something plastic. From the right side of the small office exterior. A dirty bathtub surrounded by trashcans. A man now stood it in, naked and showering in the open air.

Kyle twisted his head. "Hey Derek." He pointed. "Is that the dude you're looking for?"

She looked away.

But Mary smiled, her hands wrapped around a can of grape soda, which she shamelessly and enthusiastically slurped dry thru a metal straw.

"Where did you get that?" she asked.

"A vending bot walked by a minute ago," Mary said.

"Why didn't you get me one?"

"I have like, $3 in the bank."

"I could of bought my own if you told me."

"I did but you were flirting with your boyfriend."

"Troy and I are coworkers." She loosened her blouse and fanned her neck, but it didn't help the sweat rolling under her warm armor.

"Sure is hot today," Kyle said. "You want to use our shower?"

****

The number seven was painted black across the grey slats of the garage-sized storage unit's door. Directly across from it, Joan leaned against number five. The parallel rows were divided by enough pavement for two cars to narrowly pass each other. Mary paced in front of unit six, her arms crossed and sighing every few minutes as she checked her cuffputer.

Kyle stood by the keypad to unit seven, playing with a holo-yoyo and looking back to his office every few minutes. "Is this gonna like, take a while long? I have like, stuff to do."

"Like what?" she asked.

Kyle pulled a five-ounce drink tin from his cargo pants. With a snap he chugged, finishing with a hyperbolic "Ah". He took another sip with the same annoying theatrics. "Oh dude. This Dr. Thor soda is the bomb. I'm so glad I'm not thirsty on a such a hot day."

She pulled her cuffs from her belt and cracked them open and closed a few times. "Ya know, aidin' and abeddin' an unregistered organic is a violation of protocol 25."

"Yeah. Whatever dude. Them charges would roll off me like cooked spaghetti."

"Pfft. Cooked pasta sticks to things ya ignorant bastard."

Kyle blinked three times. "Whatever dude."

Wall-Thru came online and the grey door turned transparent. A cot in a corner by a makeshift table made from boards held up by two stacks of toolboxes. Two large duffle bags. Green spots on the concrete floor leading past a deactivated vacuum robot to a few barrels in a corner by a water purifier.

"If there's an outcast in there, they must have an umbrella." She motioned for Mary to get back, drew her blaster, and nodded at Kyle, who swiped a card by the door, which looked like a hologram as it lifted open.

No one inside. She approached the duffle bags and opened the one that was fully zipped. Half a dozen stacks of

Delphi predictions wrapped in milky-white plastic, thick enough that it crunched and crinkled as she looked between the heavy paper blocks.

A shadow moved from one of the corners and ran out of the storage unit.

"Stop! Police!" She ran after the silhouette.

Mary landed a roundhouse kick, slamming a yelping Cecilia against the concrete wall.

"You're under arrest." She cuffed Cecilia.

Kyle burst into laughter, bordering on hysterical. "That was awesome dudes. She was just like, KAPOW! Holy Isis crap I can't believe that just fucking happened."

"What charge?" Cecilia asked with a groan.

"Possession of stolen property. And whatever else I find in your goodie bag." She picked up Cecilia's dropped purse and opened it. Hairbrush. Lipstick. Sat umbrella. "Oh, look at this. A protocol 93 violation."

Cecilia twisted her chattering, cuffed hands to brush dirt off her pantsuit where Mary left a partial footprint.

She clicked the transmitter on her cuffputer. "6-Moth-5, 10-95 at my 20. Requestin' a wagon. Code one."

"Copy that, Joan," Troy said on the wireless. "I'll send you some backup too."

"Thank you," she said.

"Was that Troy?" Mary asked.

"No."

"It totally was. You were drooling."

"No, I wasn't!"

"Are you two always like this?" Kyle asked while playing with his holo-yoyo.

"Thank you for your cooperation," she said to Kyle. "This is now a crime scene."

"Whatever dude." Kyle left.

"Watch her," she said to Mary while moving her eyes towards Cecilia.

Inside the storage unit and next to the bag of Delphi predictions, a light purple suitcase filled with women's underwear, a pair of jeans and two tank tops. And socks. Not just any socks, but those really nice bamboo ones that are so soft and keep your feet dry, but they cost like $20 a pair. Running a scanner over the clothes bounced back Albright's DNA.

A makeshift table of wood boards, held up by two toolboxes of rusted metal. She moved the boards one at a time, setting them down carefully but they still made a frustratingly noticeable thud. It was that exotic blue wood that comes from New Eden. The metal latch of the top toolbox didn't make as much noise, but the lid was a bit squeaky.

"Hold on for a minute, Joan," Troy said on the wireless. "There are deactivated spider mines in those boxes."

"A spider mine!?" She dropped the box and backed away.

"What happened?" Mary poked her head around the open threshold.

"Nothin'," she said.

"The satellite scan found them," Troy said. "It only raises a warning if they're live." He used a function or something to re-enable Wall-Thru, despite the bandwidth shortage. Both toolboxes turned semi-transparent, though the diagonal rays of sunlight landing around them didn't permeate thru, so looking inside was like peering into a cave or something.

One spider mine in each one.

"I, uh, I don't really like spider mines."

"You can open them. They're safe."

"Uh."

"Trust me Joan."

Stacks of electronics in each mined box. Memory discs.

She slowly walked over, squatted down, and opened the jangling lid. The spider mine didn't move. The discs were nearly the width of the box, and it was only by wedging her fingertips around the edges that any of them could be lifted out.

Underneath the discs, a worn and beat-up blaster that must have come from the wastelands. Grey scratch lines like varicose veins marred the black finish. Heavier than it looked. 23 rounds loaded, according to the red digits on the side of the grip.

"Joanie," Mary said.

"What?"

"The vending bot is back. Do you want a drink?"

She walked out of the storage unit. The short bot was shuffling along a few hundred meters away, at the far edge of the parking lot. "I can't leave a suspect with someone who isn't a sworn officer."

"You want orange?"

"Yes please. Love you and know you."

Mary walked away and Joan prodded Cecilia into the storage unit. Mary's footsteps didn't sound like they were getting farther away. The light from the doorway disappeared, and she turned. A silhouette that was Mary, judging by height. "Need me to transfer some money?"

The shadow remained still. DOLOS didn't pop up Mary's name. The shape stepped into the storage unit.

Anastasia Hamilton with a blaster in her hand, which she lifted and aimed. Reflective, tight silver gloves covered her hands, identical to the material covering her neck. Maybe a thermal suit? Backpack straps around her shoulders. A cold surface on her eyes, like a lake with no waves. More machine-like than human. "Don't move," she said as she re-curled three lower fingers around the grip of her blaster.

She swallowed and pressed her free, quivering hand against her leg. Cecilia cowered in the corner.

Ana reached over, grabbed Joan's S120 from her holster, and tossed it far away where it clacked. "Take a deep breath. Kyle is going to flirt with Mary for five minutes and I'll be gone in two. She won't be harmed. Neither will you, Golf Ball."

"Golf Ball?"

"Give me the disc at the top of the pile over there. It should have a label that says Rhea, though Matilda's handwriting is cursive so you may need a subroutine to read it." Ana gestured towards the discs with her blaster.

She lifted the topmost disc. A white label with smudged black lettering. The first letters resembled an R and an h, though the e and a were strange and archaic loops. "Here." She slowly handed it over to Ana. "What are you going to do?"

"I'm going to give my daughter the life she should have had." Ana stuffed the disc into a pocket of her silver jumpsuit. "Now don't follow me, Joan. No matter what she orders you to do, Kyudo won't suspend you. And Norris will be just fine."

"Norris?"

"Freeze! Police!" A man's voice from outside the storage unit. Norris stood at the far side of the threshold in a perfect stance with both hands wrapped around a blaster. His parted raincoat flapping with the breeze.

Ana froze for a few seconds, then moved her eyes quickly to the ground and back.

I'm in Norris's line of fire, she thought, before jumping to the ground, scrapping her elbows and bumping her chin against the concrete floor.

Norris and Ana exchanged fire with deafening pops and flashes each as bright as a sunrise. Norris yelped and fell backwards as Ana ran for the wide exit and disappeared.

She leapt into a run and skidded to stop in front of Norris, who was heaving breaths on the ground with a hand clenching his side.

"Are you wearin' armor?" She reached towards the wound, blood splotches on his tan raincoat, but Norris fanned her away.

"It's not bad. But call it in," Norris said between gasps.

"Code three! Officer down!" she said into her transmitter.

"Joan," Troy said on the wireless. "I saw it on your visual. Are you okay?"

"Yeah. But Norris isn't."

"Heard that. Ambo is enroute."

"Joan, there's an organic hazard at your 20," Kyudo said over the wireless. "Pursue and neutralize it before it harms anyone else."

Is Hamilton really a meat robot? If she's dangerous, does it matter? "Yes ma'am."

Norris nodded towards his dropped blaster. A J229. "Go kill it."

*Jupiter Armory* blinked with glowing red letters on the slide as she picked it up and ran between the rows of grey garage doors. The police wireless turned from lethargic to mayhem like a floored accelerator and sirens echoed in the urban canyons. Functions lit up blue police signals approaching half a kilometer away.

Using the Zoom function while at a full run was awkward since the immediate ground wasn't visible, but her feet seemed to land evenly on the shin-splitting pavement. Hamilton was 200 meters ahead with a mustard-colored backpack bouncing up and down. "She's headin' for Louise Avenue."

"I can't find her on the satellite stream. She has an umbrella," Troy said.

"I can see that."

Hamilton had nearly reached the end of the lane where it met the avenue, where clumps of pedestrians and vehicles blurred left and right, when two marked cruisers skidded to halt, blocking the path. Hamilton opened fire at the police prowlers, pinning the officers inside the bullet-proof vehicles. A crowd hastily spilled from the holo dome exit, and Hamilton fired a round into the air while knocking over screaming civilians and shoving her way thru the doors.

The uniformed officers rushed from their vehicles.

"Cover the other exits!" she shouted and pointed. She lowered the blaster, wiggling thru the civilians and into the dome.

A dim hallway turned dark with the sound of the heavy door clamping itself shut behind her. The shouts and honking horns of commotion faded, leaving only the echoes of unseen birds chirping. Peeking around the corner of the hallway revealed the holo dome interior. It was the size of a small stadium, and the top was a bubble of glass covering the cloudless sky of blue. Functions measured the circumference with a spinning yellow line. 400 meters.

A lush, real-render forest with birds of all colors flying between the branches. A clearing in the middle and the sides sloped upward like an amplifier or whatever those ancient theaters were called. No one in sight.

The clearing is a bad idea. No cover and anything can shoot you from any angle. She went up the left pathway of dirt. Trees of various shades of brown bark and green leaves. Some of them shaped like flattened hands and others were little pins or needles or something that could probably draw blood if they were real. Reaching out to touch a trunk as she passed, her hand went right thru. There's really no cover anywhere, it's just a bunch of floating images. Something obscured the light above.

She pointed the blaster in the air with both hands. Several meters above the barrel's edge, a holographic bird. A sudden crack and a flash flew by. Followed by two more. She ran down the path as a dozen shots landed thumps around her, turning parts of the ground and some of the trees into twisting distortions of static. Sliding thru a holographic tree made everything look like a prism for a few seconds, until she stopped behind a mound of earth at the end. Poking it with a finger, it was cold and smooth like metal, not matching what it looked like. This should be safe, anything that can be touched or walked on is the real floor.

When her breathing decelerated the sounds of the birds and crickets returned, and she slowly peeked over the edge. No movement from the opposing ridgeline. Something yellow among the lines of brown and dots of green. Zooming in, it was Hamilton's backpack sticking out from behind a tree.

"It must be hiding behind it," Troy said on her ear com.

"Yeah," she whispered and raised Norris's blaster, carefully aiming with a two-handed grip. The number five in red on the back of the blaster's slide. God damnit this thing is almost empty, and Norris didn't manage to hit Hamilton once?

She pulled the trigger and with a loud pop the far tree blurred and flashed. The backpack fell over, and the metallic bowl of a sat umbrella fell out. Nothing but smoke.

"If that's her umbrella why can't our satellites see her?" Troy asked. "Check infrared."

"I think she's wearin' a thermal suit."

More pops and bullets flew by. She hit the deck and crawled a few meters, where she stopped and so did the incoming fire.

Hamilton's voice called out, "I told you not to follow me. Why don't you just leave?" Joan held still and Hamilton continued, "Wazzerman showed me a world without a war. A world without limits. A future where everything is possible."

She lifted her head. "Don't give me that fuckin' Isis shit."

"Gospel of Hathor, Golf Ball. And even if Wazzerman gives you your mother's memories, they're from another timeline. DOLOS will flag them as invalid. She'll be an outcast. She'll starve in the wastelands."

She quickly stood. "You don't know that!"

"Joan," Troy said. "I'm running motion detection from a drone hovering over the dome. There's movement 100 meters North East of your position. I've marked it on your routines."

She stayed low and turned until the function showed the marked point. Only four rounds left. "Can you shut down the dome remotely?" she whispered.

"Ivan is working on it," Troy said. "It's going to take a couple of minutes."

Running East drew fire from Hamilton. A break in the trees. A figure standing. Joan skidded to a stop and fired. Missed. At the marked position the target was long gone, and holographic dirt doesn't leave footprints. She moved behind a large tree, almost making the mistake of learning against it. The holographic forest swayed with the fake sounds of rustling wind, and the birds chirped in a song-like melody. When the sounds died down, Hamilton's footsteps still weren't audible. But why?

These rainforest sounds aren't the leaking pipes of a dark shelter, or the din of sirens downtown, or the howling winds of the wastelands. Living in a shelter was once unfamiliar. How did I adapt so quickly?

I was afraid, she thought.

Pinching the small grooves of her emotion orb, she rotated it until it silently flashed off and my now-unsteady hand returned to a two-handed grip on the blaster. Taking cautious steps, the ground seemed to be pushing up against my feet. I felt as though Hamilton was behind every tree, like the holo dome was a homicidal funhouse. With cold fingertips I pulled back the collar of my shirt, where it was riding up onto my sweating neck, then froze at a sound.

A squeak on the right. Rubber meeting a floor of composite-metal.

I lined up the blaster sights at a line of trees. They aren't really there. I squeezed the trigger. A flashing pop and a scream. Blood splattered thru the twisting light of the tree, and it turned transparent for a moment, revealing a grimacing Hamilton on her knees, holding her chest.

Hamilton fell on her side, twitching and groaning. She dropped the blaster in her hand next to a growing puddle of red.

I kicked away Hamilton's dropped blaster.

"I failed you," Hamilton said.

"What?"

"I was your friend. I was Morgan. I have...memories. You were her, our, only friend." Hamilton reached out with a bloody hand.

I hesitated before reaching down and holding it. My chest shook as I took a breath, and my eyes welled up before I reactivated my emotion orb, which extinguished it all with a pins and needles numbness.

"I'll save us next time." Ana's eyes went still, and her breathing turned shadow. Her breath left with the simulated wind.

A chime credited a $40 kill bonus to her account.

She pulled the mind-scanner on her belt and connected it to Ana's temple. Flicking it on just before the holo dome forest disappeared, leaving just a white floor with scorch marks and the circular blue sky of the glass roof.

***

The corner store a block away was just small enough to not get lost in it. And it had one of those huge rotating doors where each of the four chambers can fit a dozen people, but she entered the store alone, taking in the five long aisles of bright lights that smelled of caffeine, alcohol, and dreams.

No other customers, but a cart-robot followed her closely. Beyond the aisle of dry goods priced beyond their value was a refrigerated wall. A radio station played quiet animations on a hologram over the checkout counter. It switched to a commercial break. A dozen dancers put on a mock musical. *Buy Lekus fuel-cells for your car. Because otherwise you'll be walking everywhere.*

Across from the shelves of Dome Grown Mills bread tins the refrigerated wall started, beginning with water, milk, and 11 ounce Oh-Maybe Original brand fruit punch tins. A dancing man emerged from the drink as a holographic advertisement. *Oh, maybe baby. You'll buy me? Or don't. It's k.* The mascot frowned and slouched back into the tin as a different hologram loaded.

A floating card. *Welcome back Joan. Are you making Waikiki Sunsets today?* Floating images underneath the text with labels. Oh-Maybe original fruit punch, Olde Earth pineapple wine, and Eden's Finest cobalt rum. Clicking yes lit up eye function indicators along the aisle, highlighting the ingredients along with price tags.

Product lines grew more mature with each squeaking step. Hard lemonade next to the pineapple wine. After the cobalt rum, Hard Ceydonian ice. Who wants to get drunk from a popsicle? Martians must all be weird. It's like they're from another planet.

The invisible temperature field tickled her fingertip as she slowly moved it in and out and it left a glossy film. Her face looked awful in the reflection. Dirt and blood. Disheveled hair she tried to fix in a panic.

I look like I just killed someone. Because I did. I killed Gemma too. Pulled her out of her bed in the middle of the night and shot her when she didn't tell me what I wanted.

According to Ana's memories, anyway. I've never done that to anyone. Not anyone who didn't have it coming.

A beeping noise. That stupid emotion orb blinking some kind of error.

The clerk behind the counter moved his fingers up and down in large sweeping motions. Halfway thru a holographic Sudoku puzzle. He was lean and young, perhaps a few years older than her. Brown curly hair and beard stubble.

She tucked loose hair behind each ear and checked her reflection again in a nearby display case.

"How can I help you little lady?" he asked in a mocking tone, half his face pulled back.

She yawned. Too tired for anger. "Do you have any dream strips?"

"Yeah, they're here." He turned a lazy Susan cylinder on the counter. About a hundred different Caduceus-brand strips in test-tube shaped color-coded packages. Racy red for mature viewers, banana yellow for feasts, blue for family events, black for prewar experiences. The hologram on top changed as her finger moved up and down each tube.

A day at a beach where you could actually swim and surf in the ocean. A birthday party. A yellow version where you get to eat an entire birthday cake by yourself. Next to it, taste the entire menu at a George-Jack Shake-Shack restaurant. Taste over 50 milkshakes while you sleep. She picked the birthday cake. A notice in small print, re-rendered on a function: *This product complies with protocol 41 and will not modify long term memory.*

128 flavors to choose from. Vanilla. Pfft. Chocolate. Double Chocolate. Chocolate coconut. Where has chocolate peanut butter been my whole short life?

"What's black forest?" she asked.

"Cherries over chocolate. Have you had Manhattan cheesecake?" the clerk asked.

"For real or in my dreams?"

"Either way. It has that same cherry topping but on chocolate cake and whipped icing."

She confirmed her choices and dropped the dream-strip on the counter with the alcohol.

"Are you 21? I need to see your wrist ID." The slender clerk told her, carefully placing everything into a heavy paper bag.

She scowled, pulled out her blaster, and slammed it down on the counter.

He raised two open palms. "Okay. No problem. I won't tell the police anything."

"Police?" she asked with indignation. She raised her blood-stained badge in her free hand. "I am the fuckin' police."

"No problem, officer." He handed her the bag with noticeably large hands. Larger forearms on his rolled-up sleeves that made her smile. After pressing her thumb against the register to pay, she raised her head and locked eyes with him for a few seconds, seeing someone nearly as lost as her.

# Schrödinger's Cat

Peter fidgeted as lines of shadow from the overhead fan passed over Kyudo's impassive face.

"Mr. Lyon is in interrogation room one-four-four," he said.

"I see." Kyudo swiveled her chair towards the wall of her mezzanine office. The rendered artwork on her wall scrolled to an archer and a lighthouse. "Do you recall the detail I assigned to you earlier this week?"

"Regarding Lyon? Yes ma'am."

"Will arresting her and her father for murder-one impact that assignment?"

"I imagine it will."

Kyudo turned her chair towards him. "And this report you've now filed. Is that in any way sourced with imagination?"

"No ma'am. My report is consistent with the evidence." He clicked buttons on his wrist-computer and scrolled to the second page of his report. "The missing robot, based upon Mr. Lyon's own invoices, matches the model of the one found at Gemma's home. Lyon, Joanna, checked out a J-thirty pistol with a suppressor from the station armory one week ago and wrote 'backup weapon' in the memo field. She neglected to return it for mandatory inspection no later than o-eight hundred hours this morning."

"Quite a lot has happened this morning, Peter." Kyudo hunched over her desk's volumetric computer and examined her copy of his report. "There's no ballistics comparison between Overton's wounds and Joan's backup weapon."

"No, not yet. But if we search Lyon's apartment, we may find it there or on her person. And a warrant will permit us to enter her D-N-A into evidence for the purposes of comparison."

Kyudo shrugged. "And you arrested Joan's father, a Mr. Samael Lyon, on this basis?"

He clasped his hands in front of him. "There's also the matter of the Atlantic Alliance Air Force key, which matches the access gate to the ordinance depot at Chiron Airbase. That's where the bomb came from. The one that destroyed Blue Jewel Tower today. Samael Lyon's fingerprints were found on it, as well as known Outcasts, including Wasserman and former officer Albright."

Kyudo's eyebrows shot up and she leaned back in her creaking chair. "So, is the plan here that, while Joan will be awaiting trial, her union-appointed arbiter will be granted access to all of these findings during discovery, and will find our probable cause was related to pre-war military knowledge? Which could only raise further questions about active police personnel. And you yourself will likely be suspended pending a war crimes investigation by I-A-D and the interim District Attorney, Councilman Warner." She scrolled on her computer to the police activity feed. "Imagine the already thin ranks of our department struggling to maintain law and order while down not *one* but *two* additional officers. Not to mention the field day the press would have.

"I'm afraid the evidence you have presented is insufficient. And I will not allow anyone to tarnish the reputation of a capable officer such as Joan."

"We need to at least investigate further, Major. Lyon poses a risk to this unit."

"How so?"

He breathed in deep. Both hands twitched. "Delphi told me there's a mole in our unit. A MOTH is working with the Outcasts."

Kyudo's eyes narrowed as she clasped her hands together on her desk. "When did Delphi tell you this?"

"Moira told me when I spoke to him."

Kyudo's eyes grew wide. "And you're just now telling me this?"

"All due respect ma'am, I didn't know who I could trust. The mole turned out to be my partner for Christ's sake!"

Kyudo abruptly stood. "You could have told me this before Norris was shot!"

"I know. I fucked up. I'm sorry ma'am."

Kyudo paced back and forth for a few seconds, the brass medals and insignia of her uniform iridescently bouncing back light from the polished lamps at opposite ends of her desk. She stopped and sharply turned towards him. "The last officer who withheld information from me spent a six-month rotation deicing hovercars at Juneau station. I suggest you keep that in mind." She smoothed the front of her uniform and sat back down. "Norris is in stable condition. But he won't be out of post-op until later this evening."

"Thank you, Major."

"Have you read this?" Kyudo scrolled on her volumetric computer to an after-action report. "Hamilton was surely the mole. And your partner neutralized her."

He cleared his throat. "None of Hamilton's service weapons match Overton's murder weapon."

"Peter, there are thousands of Jovian weapons on the black market. Hamilton could have shaken down a drug dealer and pocketed it." Kyudo smiled. "Now can you forget these absurd theories?"

"What about the Lyons? They don't come across as forgiving types."

Kyudo stood and walked to the glass wall, looking down at the large room below, where Diaz escorted an uncuffed Mr. Lyon to the front door and handed him a clear tube with a small pill inside. "Mr. Lyon is going to forget a great deal about today."

"He agreed to that?"

"A variety of people can be motivated in a variety of ways. Don't you agree?" Kyudo turned to face him.

He nodded.

Diaz's dress shoes clopped as she ran up the mezzanine stairs and through the squeaking glass door of Kyudo's office. "Mr. Lyon has left the building."

"And how is the Overton case proceeding?" Kyudo asked.

"I'll be closing it this afternoon," Diaz said.

"With Hamilton as the shooter?"

"Yes ma'am."

"Very good." Kyudo returned to her desk chair and clicked the volumetric buttons on her computer. A floating image of a bar, *The Dragon's Tail*, in various colors of bright neon. "Ivan is still examining Hamilton's memories, but he believes this bar, located at twenty-nine Sagittarius Drive in Chinatown, is a location used by the Outcasts, a settlement-side hideout they call Club Ketu." She scrolled to a volumetric scan of the auction flyer. "Tonight may be our only opportunity to capture those responsible for the downtown bombing. Eva, can I interest you in an overtime shift with MOTH?"

"Absolutely," Diaz said.

"Peter, I need you to get Joan."

He looked out the glass wall and down at the sea of desks below. "She's not at her desk."

"The computer flagged her for a memory treatment, and she went home. Make sure she doesn't take it and reports here ASAP."

"Yes ma'am." Using eye movements, he located the messaging subroutine where Lyon showed up as a gray question mark. Offline. He pushed the glass door open and held it for Diaz. They descended the mezzanine stairs together.

"What's being sold at this auction?" Diaz asked.

"Stolen Delphi predictions," he said. "So now Hamilton killed Overton?"

"You know how Kyudo is once she's made up her mind," Diaz said.

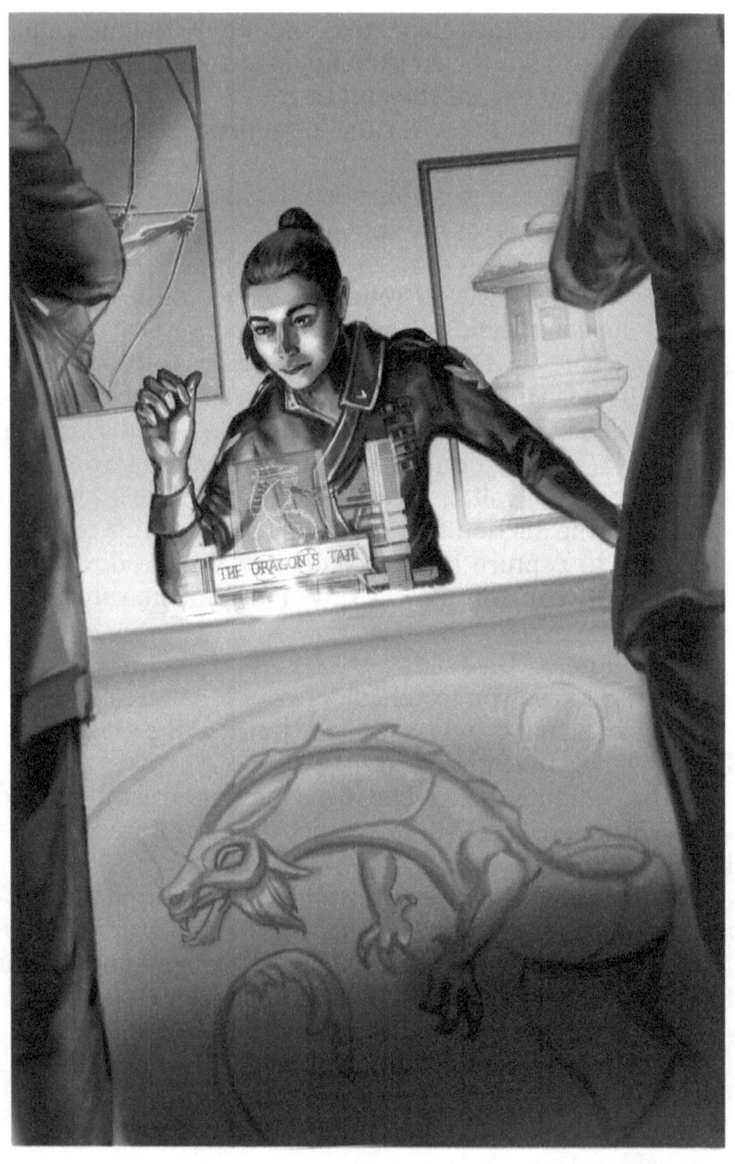
THE DRAGON'S TAIL

"Whose case is it? Whose signature goes on your report?"

"Kyudo rewards loyalty. There are five open lieutenant slots after the Outcasts attacked the Hall of Justice. And I ranked six on the exam last month."

He stopped at the bottom of the stairs. "Perfect. Yet another homicide becomes a hom-besides."

Diaz made eye contact. "Are all of our slates clean, Peter?"

"Right." He walked away.

***

The instruments of the hovercar dashboard flickered in the dark cabin as clouds stirred above countless drops of rain. His altitude reduced the far Theodosian Wall to a thin orange line edging through the gray horizon. The throttle lever shook as he slowed the hovercar and descended into the brightly lit downtown skyline, where a small blue dot blinked. Lyon's position, according to the DOLOS subroutine.

The interstellar trade center, now the tallest tower in Settlement Five after the bombing, stood imposingly over the tight cluster of buildings as they all reached for the heavens. Over it, an enormous bronze statue of a woman holding the largest flat panel display ever built. Palms to neck. A pop commercial played for a few seconds before glare from ground lights obscured it.

Air traffic grew heavy in the narrowing gaps between the neon valley of high-rises, and a gust threw a blanket of rain against the windshield. Chatter from the police wireless blended with turbines and the Doppler echoes of passing holographic advertisements, though a lack of sirens left the urban crowd-sourced orchestra incomplete.

A rainbow sequence of reflected neon painted the car interior, lines of light blending with streaks of rain. The windshield etched lines around a three-story section of a highrise on his right. Castile de Leon apartments. The logo rendered an extinct lion leaping out of a bygone stone castle.

He slowed to a hover a hundred meters from the terminal rooftop adjacent to it. A one-minute landing queue for the dozen landing pads arranged in a doughnut shape, extruding over the top of an office building. Narrow sky bridges reached out to the adjacent towers like the spokes of a wheel.

Passing headlights from aircars traveling in the opposite direction lit the dark interior as he loaded the piano subroutine from a long list of bookmarks. Leaning back and looking through the glass sunroof as his fingers danced up and down the floating musical keys. The bright constellations above, far from the rolling drops of rain a few centimeters away. They redirected the city's lights, as though they were fallen stars imprisoned on the Earth, doomed to never again see their kin.

But his rhythm couldn't match the chaotic taps of the weather, and the dashboard clicked back with landing authorization. After a soft mechanical thud and computer confirmation, he disengaged the engine. Vertical movement ceased, but the ring of landing pads rotated slowly, like the hands of an analog watch.

A bright red hovercar coupe set down ten meters to the left. Neon purple rays ran over the clear coat in a blur that focused into a Vodka ad. Two women emerged, sorority brats in bright miniskirts and tank tops. Purple and blue neck length hair. Clopping heals with their unsteady steps and near stumbles as their crossed arms shivered.

They're drunk. They were just flying drunk. Unreal, but if I arrested them Kyudo would probably tell me that I'm not a vice cop and if I call dispatch those two will be in bed sleeping it off by the time anyone arrives.

Across a pedestrian bridge and beyond a clinking metal door, he followed a florescent maze of beige walls edging teal and white-striped carpet until he rapped his knuckles beneath the golden digits nine-seven-seven-nine that ran across the red door of Lyon's apartment. Lyon's blue Wall-Thru outline moved towards the door and paused on the other side for several seconds before clicking the lock and opening the door with a slow sweeping creek.

Only her head peered around the door's edge. Dark circles around two bloodshot eyes, which she rubbed with one hand while yawning. "Peter?"

"Did I wake you?"

"Nah." She pulled the door open a bit further. Her blue blouse was unbuttoned, though a white undershirt kept her modest.

"Can I come in?"

"Um, yeah, okay." She snuffled and pulled the door open all the way.

Lyon's apartment was immaculately clean. Muted shades of black on her Spartan furniture and light fixtures, though her small dining table was the only shade of white paler than her. Nothing extravagant but tasteful in a simple kind of way. A panoramic window with an impressive view of the adjacent high-rises, albeit the dark gray sky. Dots of rain dripping down it, and outside something between a drizzle and full rain fell on the passing hovercar lanes flying in each direction with white and red light.

Hanging a meter from where the window met the wall, a tableau of a lighthouse, identical to one of Caramel's puzzles. "You like lighthouses?"

"Mary gave me that." Several clicks from the door, where Lyon rechecked her half-dozen locks before following him with staggered steps to a couch where he sat, and she leaned against the opposing chair. "Can I offer ya somethin'?" she asked. Her words were slurred and more incomprehensible than usual. Her normally balanced and graceful steps were jumbled, replaced with swaying slogs, when she looked up her face was as red as Martian soil.

"Have you been drinking?"

"Yeap." She gripped and sat on the chair's cushioned armrest, then slid into the seat and giggled.

"It's two-thirty in the afternoon."

"Yeap."

"Perfect." He stood and looked over the countertop dividing the kitchen from the living area. "Do you have any sobriety tablets?"

"I don't got no pills."

He removed his coat and tossed it on the far end of the couch and sat down again. "Doesn't matter. Kyudo has a storeroom overflowing with them." A regular departmental expense. The police personnel shortage strikes again. Lyon just said she doesn't have any pills. "What happened to the memory treatment pill?"

"I look like a pharmacy to you? I don't got no pills."

He leaned forward, balanced on the edge of the sofa. "Did you take that pill?"

"Wouldn't you like to know?" Lyon laughed.

"Yes, that's why I'm asking."

"Pfft. I froze it and munched it down like a stupid Martian popsicle."

"You're not supposed to mix alcohol with a memory treatment."

"Oh no. You better arrest me." Lyon mockingly placed her wrists together.

"Damnit." She wasn't supposed to take it. He lifted his wrist and began typing in an ambulance request when a warning dialog popped up on a subroutine. Pumping someone's stomach to interfere with an authorized memory gel is a violation of protocol eighty-six-e. "Damnit."

"Aw, you like that word don't ya? Why don't ya marry it?"

Time to get creative. Think fast. It takes a while to digest. I just need to induce her to vomit. "You want another drink?"

"Mm." Lyon's stomach grumbled as she shifted her weight to the other side of the chair and groaned. "I should have a water."

"Just one drink."

Lyon tilted her head. "Didn't you quit drinkin'?"

How many years has it been now? He couldn't remember. "I'll have one with you," he lied.

"Oh, it's a special occasion. Okay."

He stood and walked around the raised counter to the kitchen, where a sink divided a lower countertop. An almost-empty bottle of piss-colored wine, some blue rum and fruit punch. On the other side of the sink, two empty tumblers.

"Don't make mine too strong," Lyon said.

"Do you have company?"

"Sure do. You're here."

After finding clean glasses in the upper cupboards and filling them halfway with ice from the fridge's dispenser, he searched the lower ones to find a padded foil bag with a few bottles. Combined with the blue rum, it was nearly a long island iced tea, four out of five anyway. That was Ari's favorite drink and probably the only reason he could remember, though he couldn't recall them ever being blue. "Was your sister here?"

"You kiddin'? I don't wanna fuck up her life too."

"Major Kyudo thinks you're doing a great job." Lyon's fridge was well stocked with more brands of food than he knew existed in the first place. A row of bread at the top.

Dome Grown Mills. Cans of blueberry pop on one of the inner door shelves, which he opened and poured for himself. The two drinks weren't the same shade of blue but adding some of the red fruit punch narrowed the gap enough for drunk-Lyon to not notice. Something rubbed against his ankles, and he looked down. An orange cat looking up and meowing. Quite a friendly cat, considering its owner. "Did you feed your cat?"

"Slippers?"

"How many cats do you have?"

"All of 'em," Lyon said sarcastically. "He was an orphan. Just like Ana's little boy now."

On the other side of the counter Lyon was slouched over her coffee table, her chin resting on both her hands. Tears running down her face. She appeared smaller than usual, and somewhat frail, seated on the comparatively large couch.

"Hamilton was an imprint. Brainwashed by Wasserman." He set down both drinks and slid the strong drink towards Lyon. "Here you go kiddo. This is stronger than that globe on your arm."

"Do you think it matters to him? Do you think if I tell him his mom's death was sanctioned, or whatever the fuckin' word it is, that it changes anythin'?" With icy clanks she gulped the drink.

Someday everyone might decide artificial life is real, and retroactively charge every MOTH with murder. But there's no need to make this even harder on Lyon right now. "Hamilton shot Norris. It could have killed him if you weren't there."

"What about Gemma Overton? Did you see that in Ana's memories?" Lyon took another gulp. "Did you see what I did to her?"

The cat jumped onto the couch next to Lyon and nuzzled his head against her side. Lyon beckoned the cat onto her lap and pet its head.

"You can't believe what's in an imprints mind. Wasserman is The Ventriloquist. Remember?"

"Am I goin' to keep seein' their faces when I close my eyes?" Lyon lost herself in her blue drink.

He looked behind Lyon and through the wide window. A line of dim light between a gap of skyscrapers, which seemed to blink with far hovercar traffic. Squinting and using the zoom subroutine, the gap met the street with a pile of rubble being cleared by large robots. Streams of fallen rain pushed clumps of ash into the nearby gutters.

The remains of Blue Jewel Tower. They're already hauling off the remains. In a month a new foundation will be poured, and in a year or two a new tower will stand.

"Didn't you take a memory pill?" he asked.

Lyon reached into a pant pocket and pulled a small tube with a pill and rattled it. "I was fuckin' with ya."

"Right." A ring of carbonated bubbles formed on the surface of his blueberry pop, which he lifted and sipped. Sweet like most pop but a tart aftertaste.

Lyon snuffled. "I remember Mary once asked me why murderers get the recylin' penalty. I told her it's because once someone does that, they can't ever change back." With a spider-leg grip she held up her blue drink, twisting the glass while squinting at it. Through the window behind her, flat-panels on a skyscraper aligned like phosphorescent brick layers mortared with halation, all of them running different Delphi advertisements. "I'm not sure I can do this policin' thing anymore."

The poor kid doesn't know she can't resign. Kyudo will use that evidence I gave her to keep Lyon under her thumb, just like my war records. And Lyon didn't vaporize a city. I didn't free myself, I only managed to pull someone else into the same prison. "There are people you can still help. Quit now, and even more children will lose their parents."

Lyon grimaced, placed a hand on her stomach, then retched all over her coffee table. After a split second she stumbled to her feet and quickly disappeared into another room.

He followed the echoes of vomit to a bathroom doorway where Lyon was on her knees, bracing herself with the toilet seat. "Twice in one day. Bravo zero Lyon."

She gasped and pulled toilet paper from the nearby roll to wipe her face. "Ohh fuck."

He leaned over the threshold and looked over the trail of upchuck Lyon had left but heard no robotic steps. "Where's your cleaning robot?"

Lyon spit into the toilet. "Don't got one."

He moved his neck back and it made a painful snapping sound, forcing an involuntary grimace. "Perfect."

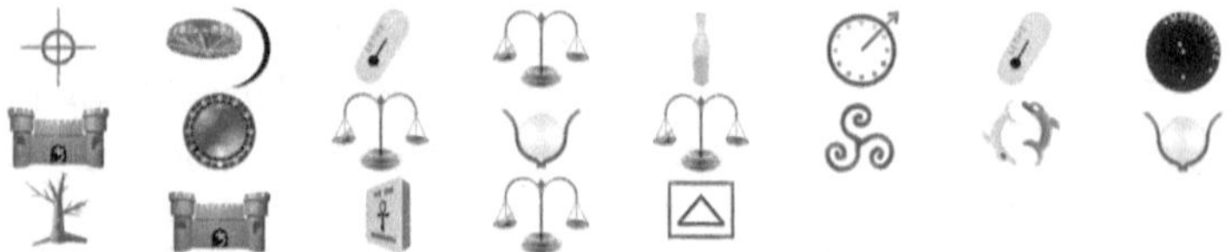

# 32
## Physis

Joan sipped hot coffee that was so good it had to be gourmet. That expensive stuff at the Omni Store that they keep behind a zapping force field and you can't even smell it unless you pay upfront. "Mm. Thank you."

"You're welcome," Kyudo said without looking away from the hologram on her wood desk, surrounded by her Feng shui furniture. "Excellent work this afternoon. Ms. Hartnell didn't know much but that storage unit is a gold mine of evidence. Have you seen this?" She swiped to a scan of a memory disc surrounded by a web of animated memories.

Joan shook her head. "Whose memories are those?"

"Matilda Albright," Kyudo said with a smile, "left back-ups of her mind at an inopportune location. Which is very opportune for us." She split her hologram and swiped on the right one to a scan of one of Cecilia's flyers. "Apparently, this auction is happening at a bar called The Dragon's Tail, where Albright intended to exchange stolen Delphi predictions for weapons." She loaded a holographic map which zoomed in on a blinking building.

"Need me to suit up for a raid?" She balanced the hot ivory cup on the chair's armrest and started to get up.

"No." Kyudo motioned downward with a spread hand. "As you were. Enjoy your coffee."

She sat back down, sniffed the sweet steam, and took a sip.

"A raid would garner several high-value targets, including arms dealers supplying outcasts with weaponry, but after having Mayfleet and Xiang Jun investigate further, I have something more ambitious in mind.

"Albright was presumably going to inspect the weaponry before making the exchange." Kyudo swiped to a scan of a ledger of some kind. An icon in a corner of scales balanced with a feather, just like the one on the flyer. "Given the monetary amounts the quantity of weapons must be enough for a small army. And an inter-Settlement cargo hauler with an empty manifest, registered to Zimmerman freight, a subsidiary wholly owned by the Green Star Trading Company, parked at a building adjacent to The Dragon's Tail this very afternoon. Hiding a tracker among these weapons could lead us to an outcast outpost, or even the Sandcastle if we're lucky." Kyudo stood and walked to the wall of glass that overlooked the large hall below, where officers worked at their desks like muted actors. "Then we can end the wasteland rebellion forever."

"So ya need me to sneak in? Plant the tracker or somethin'?" She took another sip of amazing gourmet goodness.

Kyudo turned from the window. "No and yes. I want you to go there undercover. As Matilda."

"I gotta dye my hair?" She wrapped a finger around some of her blonde strands.

Kyudo laughed. "Goodness no." She returned to her desk, leaned back in her chair, and intertwined her fingers together at the near edge of her desk. "I want you to run Janus."

"Janus?"

"Have you heard of it before?" Kyudo sat up even straighter.

"It sounds familiar."

"The techs tell me that they can code a Janus package with Albright's mind. Unfortunately, there's insufficient time to install protocol-mandated safeguards."

"Aren't they expectin' the original Albright? Or like, a clone?"

"Given the heat she's stirred up with the tower bombing, it's conceivable she would upload her mind to a different body. It's even evident, given her financially detrimental decision to sell the predictions to a third party instead of performing this auction herself. Or she's merely pressed for time, like the rest of us." Kyudo swiped to another holographic map with police cars and officers arranged around a building. "Officer Boothe reported seeing Albright flee into the North Wastelands an hour ago, but we'll still have a perimeter in place to apprehend her in case she returns to terra firma."

"So, I would like, be her, or somethin'?"

"You would mentally merge thru your mind circle." Kyudo raised her own wrist and tapped on her emotion orb. "You would be neither yourself nor her. It should be temporary, but this isn't a committee-approved Janus identity, and therefore it poses a substantial risk to you and your DOLOS status."

"What are you sayin'?"

"If you do this, Albright could remain within your mind indefinitely." Kyudo lowered her hologram into her desk and stood up, prompting Joan to follow suit. "I ordered Troy to provide you with a technical briefing. If you aren't comfortable with the risk, just let me know. I wouldn't feel right ordering you to do this. Think carefully before making your choice."

"Yes ma'am. Thank you."

The other side of the mezzanine smelled like freshly shampooed carpets and glass-polishing compound. Troy was at his desk, swiveling in his chair every few seconds between holograms of brain scans, maps, and documents. His desk was shaped like a rectangle and easily three times the size of the one she was sharing with Peter when he was actually here. The wide edge of the surface was pushed up against another desk, with a tall pane of lightly frosted glass dividing them, one of those finishes to reduce hologram glare. Ivan was still visible on the other side, an ancient globe on his desk painted with more shades than Mary's never-say-die lipstick collection.

She walked under the nearby skylight, a few meters from the desk, and stood on the twisted square of bright carpet. "Hi Troy," she said with a smile.

Troy turned towards her, and he smiled, but his eyes didn't light up the way they often did, and he looked away. "Hi Joan."

"Long day?"

"Yes. I've been downing Power Soda since 11." He lifted a red can from his desk and took a gulp.

"Me too. I mean, I'm tired too. I was up soo early today." She stretched her arms. "Kyudo wanted me to talk to ya."

"Correct. Matilda Albright." Troy lifted a hologram of a brain, and as he typed magnifying squares floated over different areas. "Kyudo had me scan all of Albright's memories, in case any of them were evidence or clues that could lead to the Sandcastle. Unfortunately, most of Albright's memories are encrypted." He sniffed and pointed. "We can't be sure these clumps of neurons are even memories. It could be a cascading neural map. Hidden neuro code caches with encrypted synapse energy potential activators."

"I left my techno babble to English decoder ring at home." She smiled.

Troy pretended to laugh, but it was like really forced and obvious. "Something to brainwash anyone who tries to use her mind other than her." He swiveled away towards another hologram and typed something. "I wasn't friends with Matilda, but I do remember her before she disappeared. Despite her being imprinted, I never imagined she would ever be an outlaw and a murderer." He looked over for a moment, then back to his computer. "I just can't tell with people."

She briefly covered her mouth. Troy isn't just tired. "Were you uploadin' evidence this afternoon?"

"I've been on duty since early six this morning." Troy rubbed his eyes.

"Did you work the Hamilton scene?"

"Ivan and I split it up," he said coldly.

"Aren't you always tellin' me how outcasts have false memories? You can't believe what they've seen, can you?"

Troy took a deep breath. "I don't know what to believe."

"Aren't folk's innocent until proven guilty?"

Troy looked over with a frown and shrugged. He looked back at his computer again, but some invisible force still held her in place like a tractor beam under the glaring skylight.

I must have taken a memory treatment yesterday, she thought. And since I don't remember, I can't even defend myself against this bullshit.

"Oh, you are talking to Joan officer. I see. Hello Joan." Ivan had poked his head around the glass wall dividing the desks and lifted a lime slushie as large as his head up until he could loudly sip thru the red straw.

"Hi," she said.

"Are you discussing Janus arrangement?" Ivan asked.

"Come on over." Troy nodded towards his lamptop computers, grabbing two holograms and swiping them to views of a brain scan. "We can give Joan a lower-dermal interface and use an intravenous mood-stabilizer." A real-render version of Joan appeared standing in front of the desk. An animated robot injected something orange into her doppelganger's wrist. The hologram zoomed in on her arm, into muscle and blood vessels. Animated Nanobots turned purple. A critical-mass progress-bar reached 40%.

Ivan sneered into an aghast face and slammed his slushie on the desk with a thud. "You want to put in blood? That will kill her." Hijacking the desk hologram, he moved the progress bar beyond 100%. The animation changed to Joan turning purple and vomiting. Cardiac arrest in red flashing letters, her holographic likeness collapsed and foamed from the mouth in a seizure.

With a button Troy spared her further embarrassment. "Oh, as if you have a better idea."

Ivan scratched his nose. The outside, he wasn't picking boogers or something nasty like that. "Sub-dermal methylene-aggressor chain." He widened the hologram's beam. A fresh and healthy real-render Joan appeared with a pair of medical robots, who each injected needles of red beads into her. "It is most sophisticated pattern-stabilizer."

"Stable? That'll fry her brains like a skillet!" Troy stole the desk hologram back, moving a temperature dial until simulated warning lights beeped, and virtual Joan collapsed. Shaking, a urine puddle grew under her virtually convulsing body.

"Troy!" she said.

"I'll meet you down in medical," Troy said to Ivan, who left. He looked past her, maybe waiting so Ivan couldn't hear. "I don't think you should run Janus with Albright," he whispered.

"Why not?"

"I asked Xiang Jun to update Albright's psychological profile, based on the memories of hers that I was able to scan. Jun said she scored high marks for narcissistic personality disorder. If anything goes pear shaped while you're undercover, it will all eventually boil down to you and her. And she'll choose herself."

"Well, um, can't you make a copy of my mind or somethin'?"

"That's no guarantee that you'll ever pass DOLOS again. You could spoil into an imprint, or a meat robot as you so often say. And if Albright gets you killed it's then all academic." Troy checked his chronograph. "I have to go help Ivan prep."

"But you just told me to not do this."

Troy pushed himself and his rolling chair away from his desk. "I know," he said with a grimace while stretching his very toned arms over his head. "But if you decline then May-fleet will roll the dice."

"Mayfleet?"

"Yeah." Troy took another sip from his can of Power Soda. "Your brain is a more suitable match for Albright."

"What? Why—What makes me a better match?"

"You know, I'm not sure." Troy hastily locked his computer and walked away.

She leaned against one of the mezzanine pillars until an animated screen saver of a beach party replaced the lock screen of Troy's computer.

At the top of the mezzanine stairs, she abruptly stopped. A dozen random officers on the main floor hushed each other's whispers and stared. She slowly backed away and turned, walking towards the far wall, a floor to ceiling window that ran along the other edge of the level, concealed by desks and offices, where you can find your own stalking reflection and a path to a less conspicuous stairwell. The heavy metal door required two hands, loudly clanked open, and thudded closed.

Leaning over the stairway railing popped a function alert. *Are you feeling suicidal? Artificial empaths are available 24/7.* She took a deep breath, moved her eyes, and blinked to dismiss the message.

If I do this, I could lose my mind, she thought. End up like Mom. And I can't do that to Mary. She might not survive alone in this monster-infested world. But everyone here is judging me from those stupid outcast memories, and if I shy away from this, they'll think I'm hiding with my guilt. Maybe Albright knows something that could exonerate me. Or if I am responsible for Overton's death, then it wouldn't be right to let someone innocent volunteer and risk their own life. It might not fix my reputation, but it's a step in the right direction.

Her echoing steps led to the basement and a function drew blinking red arrows on the floor towards the medical bay.

In the med-bay Troy and the other techies huddled around medical robots and holographic scans. She walked over to Kyudo, who stood in the center of the large room and looked up from trimming her holographic bonsai tree with a slight smile.

"I'm in," she said.

"Excellent." Kyudo beckoned for the techs.

"We decide intravenous mutable multifocal Janus configuration," Ivan said.

"That's what every girl wants to hear," she said.

Ivan obnoxiously slurped from the remnants of his lime slushie. Kyudo snapped her fingers at a cleaning bot a meter from the door and it followed her as she walked over and unceremoniously took the straw from Ivan's drink tin. She turned to the cleaning bot, and it eagerly raised its crab-like claws, pinching them closed and open rapidly. The clamoring robot caught the falling straw and scurried towards a rubbish bin.

Troy rotated an internal organ display and landed on arteries. "The higher your heart rate goes the more Albright comes out. So, you can't relax while you're undercover."

"I don't think that's going to be a problem." She began shifting weight from one leg to the other.

Ivan occupied himself with a medical robot's configuration. "There is slight chance your face will melt a bit. But only one side of it." He gestured over his own face, like imagining someone else's face melting would comfort anyone.

Troy raised a hand. "It's a very small risk. Like last year's Set-cup game."

"You lost that bet," Ivan said.

Troy made gestures with both hands. "Yeah. But the math was *solid*."

Next to the medical bots she sat on the long medical chair and rolled up her right sleeve.

Her arm trembled as Troy removed her cuffputer.

"Ocular function will not work while undercover. And we change wrist-tracker to ghosted mode." Ivan beckoned a med robot. It used an injector gun to shoot something under her skin with a stab, and she flinched. "We have sub-dermal tracker, so we follow signal in case of problem."

"We'll have to disable your retina functions as well," Troy said.

"I just tell her!" Ivan said.

"Are you ready?" Troy asked her.

"Let's do it." She re-rolled up her sleeve. The medical bot froze over her, beeping in an irritating pattern. "What's your problem? Does not compute?"

"It's not that kind of a shot," Troy said.

"What?"

Troy turned and looked over his shoulder, grinning and pointing at his own posterior.

# 33
## Libraries

Through the windshield of the van that he parked on the third floor of the parking garage, Peter looked at the individual letters of *The Dragon's Tail* across the street illuminate one by one in half-brilliant neon and flash against the gray afternoon. Adjacent to a volumetric animation of a scantily clad woman leaning back on her hands and provocatively rubbing her outstretched legs together. A gust scattered pebbles between rubble on the bar's roof in a miniature tornado from one edge to another.

He scrolled through maps on the dashboard computer. Blue signals from twelve unmarked units parked on the streets surrounding The Dragon's Tail, also visible on the Wall-Thru subroutine. Steam rose from the open sip spout of his metal coffee mug, blending with the rendered colors of the map.

Some squeaks from the back of the van. Ivan Pollux sat in a swiveling chair, his attention spread over a dozen volumetric displays of the bar's main entrance and adjacent alleyways, plus a satellite scan of the interior. Tables and booths, a dance floor, and a long bar with more customers one would expect before happy hour.

Tapping from the passenger seat. Lyon striking her fingernails on the dashboard just above the chronograph as it ticked four-thirty-seven. A tube of gel in her lap, which she applied to the even paler indentations where her wrist-computer used to be, swirling it in circles until her arm's skin and tone were uniform. Having her go undercover is risky. If anything happens Kyudo won't hold me accountable, he thought. I had no input on the decision.

"Well played, Mr. Capitalist." Pollux nudged him in the shoulder with a folded stack of avarice bank notes.

He seized and flicked his thumb against the crisp edge of bills, spreading the stack of bills in front of him. "What's this?"

"Miss Joan Officer got herself shot in bum." Pollux grinned ear to ear.

"No, I didn't. I got *A* shot," Lyon said.

Pollux shrugged and shifted his head left and right. "It is as you Westerns say. Po-tat-O. Pot-A-to."

"Why'd ya bet I'd get shot in the ass?" Lyon asked.

I don't remember making this bet at all, he thought. "Uh, you have a big mouth."

"I should get half of that." Lyon's eyes moved to the money and back. "I'm the one that had to get a shot in my ass. And! I even had to shave my legs." Lyon's eyes briefly bulged, and she blushed while stretching the jean shorts of her undercover outfit, pulling them down to cover her thighs while also up over her exposed midsection. Trying to achieve the impossible, the poor little prude.

"Well, we all have to make sacrifices." He licked his thumb and counted the bank notes. A thousand credit dollars. He handed Lyon one hundred.

The pockets of her shorts were too small to hold even a few folded bills. She placed the cash in the glovebox with a sigh, slamming it shut. "Next time bet on your own ass."

"Right."

Pollux's computer clicked-back. One of the visual feeds tracked a red box drawn around someone walking down an alley towards the bar's back entrance. A tall man that looked back for a moment and the computer took a tableau of his face, pixelated as it magnified but then digitally enhanced. He was either at or pushing forty.

"Paul Phalen," Pollux said as he loaded the man's profile on another screen with clanging keystrokes. "Account executive at the Mars Security. Returned to the Earth two years ago."

"He went to the colonies but returned?"

"Da. You know what they says about the Mars. Soil is always redder."

"That must be the arms dealer," Kyudo said on the wireless crackling from the dashboard. "He's there to meet Albright."

"Lyon. Does he look familiar?" he asked.

Lyon looked back at Pollux's computer and shook her head.

"Ivan, what's the status on the Janus solution?" Kyudo asked.

"Eighty-one percent Major."

On the bar's satellite scan Phalen's red outline moved under the building. The scan tracked him to an adjacent warehouse, where his legs began moving up and down as the figure ascended. He's climbing steps.

"An underground passage," he said.

Phalen's outline vanished with a popup: *Signal Lost.*

"We're being blocked," he said.

"That's the location of the auction. The Outcasts are there," Kyudo said.

Peter's wrist shook with a pingtone. A message from his wife. *Will you be home for dinner?* He typed the bad news and clicked reply.

"That song." Lyon stared.

Ivan clicked a button on his computer to play a music track that matched the melody of Peter's pingtone, though instrumental only. Rising and falling woodwinds pitched like water violently slamming into rocks that divided rushing rapids, two drummers striking percussions like pelting hail, and sharp strings cutting through it all. A song of two hurricanes colliding and fighting for the soul of the Earth.

Lyon spontaneously sang.

*Did you think of me when the sky turned red?*
*When bombs fell and we were left for dead?*
*Meet me at our favorite beach.*
*Hold me close, never out of reach.*

Lyon locked eyes for a moment and then looked away.

It was the same tune Lyon must have heard beep from his wrist countless times already. A song she had always ignored. But someone sang along pitch-perfect with Lyon's haunting mezzo vocal cords. High half notes that tore Peter's heart into low hanging thirds.

"Unit five, are you seeing this?" Officer Sani asked on the wireless.

The dashboard map automatically scrolled to Sani's pings two blocks East. A dozen citizens formed a chanting crowd holding signs, such as *NUKE THE WASTELANDS*, and *WIPE OUT THE OUTCASTS*.

"Computer say more crowd on the way," Ivan said. "Will be seven hundred in twenty minutes."

"Why are they protesting here?" he asked on the wireless before glancing at Lyon and Polloux. "There're no government buildings here."

"I don't know Ramsey. Would you like to come out here and tell them?" Sani asked.

"What about Delphi?" Lyon asked. "If the Outcasts have predictions, does one of them show us following them here? To the auction?"

"Then why not selection other location?" Pollux asked.

"Major, we need patrol division down here before these protesters interfere with our sting."

"Cordon off the area? That will spook our targets and blow this whole operation," Sani said.

"Not a cordon. Arrest them for disturbing the peace while they're still a few blocks away."

"We can't arrest them for having an opinion. Protocol One," Sani said.

"They're war mongering." He looked over at Lyon, though little miss tyrant merely shrugged.

"Gentlemen, and ladies," Kyudo said. "Not responding to civil unrest could just as easily tip our hand."

"Damnit!" He rubbed his forehead with both hands and noticed his leg was shaking up and down. "Mayfleet. Xiang Jun. Take two unmarked cars to the corner of Broadway and Sixth. Bump into each other. Make it look like a fender bender and start bickering."

"Do you think they'll move a block North?" Lyon asked.

"We can bring in the Robot Riot Regiment if they don't," Kyudo said.

"That is why I lose bet against you," Pollux said.

Lyon opened her mouth as though she were going to speak but instead said nothing and looked away.

"Four-MOTH-Two, Ten Sixty-Six," Officer Boothe said on the wireless. "Number-two female, looks thirty-five, no DOLOS ID. Two hundred meters North of my twenty."

"Ivan, check the monitors," Sani said.

"There is nothing errors," Pollux said.

"Abbie, is it a robot?" Lyon asked.

"Negative. Infrared shows organic," Boothe said. "Oh my God, it's Albright!"

"Perfect. All units converge on the suspect. Boothe, keep her in sight." He opened the driver's side door and stepped out. After a few steps the clops of Lyon's heeled boots drew his attention and she approached from the rear of the Van. "No. Stay here. You'll blow your cover."

He ran for the stairwell and his feet ached with every racing step he descended. Beyond the walls of white brick countless blue and green signals bounced up and down on the Wall-Thru subroutine. A single red signal relayed from Boothe. "Do not, say again, do not allow suspect to reach the target building." An error message clicked-back from the wireless subroutine. *Transmitter is toggled off.* He clicked the button and repeated himself but with less available breath.

At ground level he slammed his waist into the clanking door and the outside world was pure white for an instant, slowly fading into Broadway.

"Suspect is West on Third!" Boothe said.

"Mayfleet, cover Pershing Square." He ran a block North to Fourth Street.

"Copy that," Mayfleet said.

"Hook and book?" Xiang Jun asked.

"If it's Albright shoot to kill," Kyudo said.

"Suspect entered a building. Corner of Hill and Third!" Boothe said, exasperated and panting.

"Pollux, sat-sweep Boothe's twenty. If a mouse crawls out of that building, I want to know."

"Da Peter. I also block non-police frequencies in sector."

His socks were soaked, and sweat dripped along his face, thought the cool wind separated the flaps of his unbuttoned coat. At the corner of Broadway he stumbled on the sidewalk at the sight of protesters blocking the roadway. He lifted his badge and ran the gauntlet.

"Give 'em hell officer," a protester said.

"Keep terrorists away from our schools!" another said while waving a handwritten sign which communicated the same message plus profanity.

Boothe stood at the Northeast corner of a two-story brick building that had seen better days.

"She went in the East entrance." Boothe aimed her service weapon along the building's line of windows.

"Xiang Jun is covering the other corner. I called for plain-clothes backup," Sani said. Nearby car alarms went off. "Are the protesters coming down here?"

"I don't know. Cover the exits. Boothe, search the first floor. I'll search the upstairs," he said between puffs while pulling his pistol from its holster. Officer Sani fanned air over his own face with a hand. Boothe was hardly out of breath. She's young. Close to Lyon's age. "On second thought, you search upstairs. I'll take the first floor."

"Right," Boothe said in a mocking tone that only Lyon could have provided ample instruction for.

Two large faux-wood doors with creaking hinges led into a white anteroom with a coat closet. A lobby. His shoes clopped on the marble floor. He aimed his pistol and the bright red crosshairs rendered by the Aim subroutine ran along the dark walls, a deactivated robot covered in cobwebs behind a long desk, and a sign high on the ceiling behind it. *Warner & Partners Law Office.*

The structure rumbled and the cobwebs surrounding the robot shook. Warm air falling from a ceiling vent. Only the climate control. A window several meters below the vent. Old in style, with a latch that allows it to open.

A subroutine marked footsteps along the dusty floor. Women's boots. Size eleven. The impressions led to a large, dark, two-story room where dust fell through pale lines of angled light from small windows evenly spaced along the ceiling. A library. A dozen long rows of leather-bound volumes labelled as law reports. A law library. The footprints ended at a long and elaborate carpet that evenly divided the rows. White diamond shapes and yellow fleur-de-lis.

"Still wearing that cologne your wife liked, Pete?" a woman's voice asked, hidden somewhere in the library.

He quickly aimed his pistol between the many rows of books. Switching to a one-handed grip, he reached for the button on his wrist-computer to alert Boothe and the other officers. Subroutine text shook with static and turned into scrambled Cyrillic characters. Error messages from police routines: *Unable to connect to satellite.*

"Want some peanut butter with that jam?" the woman's voice asked with a giggle.

He took slow steps, quiet steps, between the rows. Not as quiet as Lyon perhaps but close enough to give her a run for her money. A glance up. Lines of light from the windows ran along the ceiling. No shadows interrupting them. No movement.

"If I post those flyers, the police find my auction," the woman said. "And if I don't, no buyers show up. Riddle me this, Pete. What's a girl to do?"

The lighting changed. Movement in a slice of space between old tomes. Too quick to aim and fire. Damnit. If Lyon were here, I'd merely have to watch a cat catch a mouse.

"I know you went to Chiron," The woman said, apparently from the end of the adjacent row, which he took cautious steps towards. "You know that madman Wasserman has a nuclear missile. Some of us Outcasts still remember the last war. We don't want another."

He aimed his pistol. Clenched his fingers. Turned the corner. Nothing. Nada. Zip.

"I know where he'll be tomorrow," she continued from another row. "All it will take is one police drone strike. And once Wasserman is gone, I won't need any Delphi cores to stay one move ahead of him."

At the next corner he glimpsed a shadow blocking the light for a split second. Distant shouts grew louder from the windows. Scanning them quickly, one was unlatched and open.

"Hear them out there," the woman said. "Bring them their villain on a spit, and they'll make you a hero." The voice was loud enough for an offline routine to ID her as Albright. "I've seen the future. And if you don't seize it, someone else will."

One of the lines along the ceiling disappeared. He ran to the edge of the row and aimed at the silhouette eclipsing the window.

"We've worked together before." The edges of Albright's face became visible as she turned towards him. "We were partners."

The aim subroutine rendered red crosshairs on the back of Albright's head. His finger fell from the trigger.

Albright slid through the bright window.

A chime rang as ocular subroutines came back online. "She went out a window! South side of the building!" he said on the wireless while running towards the bookshelf by the wall. Knocking old tomes aside he climbed to the top and peered over the edge of the window.

The street was flooded with protesters with raised signs, and no sign of Albright.

# Basilisk Collection

No fiends or bums occupied the alleyway behind the Dragon's Tail, and the growing wind found no crumpled papers or glistening food wrappers to toss around in the fading light of the late afternoon. And the hawkish demonstrators, two streets over, could not be seen but only heard. Bright disco lights blinked thru an open back door, with a growing vibration of entrancing nightclub music. When Joan stopped a woman's voice spoke, or more like her inside voice had split into another half. *It's the next door, sweetie.* They resumed walking.

"The real Matilda was last seen moving North, away from target building," Ivan said into her wireless com, hidden inside her ear lobe. "Officers watching in case she change direction."

"Remember, the tracker is in the left earring," Troy said on the wireless. "Just turn the top like it's a grenade and squeeze it. The tracker will come out like an eyedrop."

"And transmitter is right earring," Ivan said. "We will hears you even in shielded location."

"If your cover is blown, the panic phrase is *I'm dying of thirst*," Kyudo said.

"Don't die Lyon," Pete said.

She found herself laughing, even though Peter is never funny. "Right."

The next door was the color of a grave's headstone and covered with graffiti of scales balanced by a feather, in turquoise paint a shade or two off from the backpack Matilda and she carried. Locked, judging from the immovable handle. Pronounced vibrations of music on the other side. No answer after rapping her knuckles. *Let me try.* Without a thought her right hand formed into a fist and painfully banged the pinky edge against the door.

The door creaked and squeaked open. A beefy bouncer in an expensive suit stood next to a thin woman in blue jeans and a pink sleeveless shirt. Glowing red highlights in her curly black hair. They looked at each other and played rock-paper-scissors.  The woman grinned and the bouncer frowned at his crushed scissors.

"What do you want?" He feigned scratching his side in order to grip a firearm within his spread sport coat.

"I'm here to see Paul."

"Who?" The thin woman asked in a Texas drawl.

"You know who I mean Harmony," she said to the thin woman while putting a hand on her hip and shifting Joan's weight. Matilda tucked in Joan's chin and swayed her head back. "I am Matilda. Now go tell Paul his futures are in my hands, and if he makes me wait too long, I'll throw them into the settlement reservoir. And he can kiss his auction good-bye." She gripped the edge of the open door and raised her eyebrows.

The bouncer and barmaid exchanged looks before pushing buttons on their arm-computers and stepping out of the way.

Inside the bar loud music pulsed with blinding strobes from spinning lights. Sweaty humans and room-temperature holograms filled out a dance floor. The smell of dirty people swaying in rhythm mixed with the fumes of a deep fryer that had probably never been cleaned. *No, they clean it once a year tops. Still makes good fries though. And chicken tenders.* Their stomach growled. Mm, tendies.

The only not-crowded path led between a small pavilion of scantily clad women dancing around poles and tables bordered with ringed lights changed colors like a Christmas tree, where men flexing their ego-sized muscles and ambition-sized tattoos shamelessly ogled Matilda and her. These damn thigh-chafing shorts. A wanton lady-in-waiting sat in a corner booth, puffing blue-green-smoke rings from an algae cigarette while casting eyes of envy. Joan blushed and ground enamel, feeling their eyes sticking to her behind like

mosquitoes. And people call cops pigs. Her steps accelerated through the buffet of debauchery with the sound of
clopping heels. I sound like a fucking horse, she thought.
Still, that's no reason to treat someone like livestock. *You
don't like attention?*

A quick adjustment of the backpack's straps slid it lower
on her back, bumping against her with each step. Her pace
slowed as she pulled down and up on the top, not stretching
it enough to cover her midriff and the stupid push-up bra at
the same time.

"Excuse me sorry." Harmony brushed her arm while
rushing by towards the long bar, where a dozen Neptune
lamptops flung holographic music videos in random floating
locations high under the ceiling, intermixed with advertisements for Centauri Brandy. Harmony looked back and
asked loud enough to be heard over the music, "You want a
drink?"

"No thank you sweetie." Matilda grinned with Joan's at-
rophied smiling-muscles. There was an unusual feeling as
the words left her mouth, like less of an invisible wall between her and the stranger. An openness of some kind. For
a few steps Matilda timed heeled footsteps and struts with
the rhythm of the music.

They each squeezed by a petite barmaid in an animated
rainbow dress, and she continued to the storeroom past the
counter. At the end of parallel shelves of liquor bottles, a
door with a combination lock. Matilda keyed 1-1-1-2-1-9-8
and the door opened.

For two seconds there were old wooden steps descending into darkness, then the door slammed shut behind her.
Only darkness. She leaned against jagged ridges of a cold
stone wall and stepped slowly, nearly tripping twice. Lens
functions would be great right now. *We need a torch. Or a
flashlight. That's what they're called out here.*

"Joan, can you hear me?" Troy asked on her embedded ear com.

"Yes," she whispered.

"You're on the fifth step. There are seven more."

At the bottom she rubbed her scrapped fingertips and palm. "Okay, what now?"

*The tunnel is seven meters to the right.* Matilda's line of thought turned out to be a bee line. *Isn't someone clever?* She froze and thought, Janus can read my thoughts as I'm reading her. *Uh huh.*

The passageway was narrow enough that with outstretched arms both sides could be touched at the same time—*simultaneously.*

She stopped to sigh. No one likes a pushy Janus personality. *No one likes a pushy MOTH.*

Something brushed against her leg. "It's a rat."

"Joan? Are you okay?" Troy asked. "It's small. On thermal readings it is, anyway."

A squeaking rat. Water dripping far away. Blinding darkness. She fell against the wall and the backpack thumped. Breathing faster and faster but there's no air. Just something crawling on her neck like a centipede.

"Joan, what's wrong?" Troy asked. "Your vitals popped from green to yellow."

Without any mental argument, Matilda brushed her neck and took her steps for her through the pitch black to the other side, up a stairway, and through another door.

A large warehouse where bits of dust swam in the sunlight falling from windows and onto the floor in the shape of bent squares. *Trapeziums you adorable bumpkin.*

"You're inside the dampening field," Troy said. "If it's safe, can you describe what you see?"

The large open space was surrounded by brick walls and filled in with laminate floors and burgundy carpets. A dozen squeaking robots arranging several rows of chairs evenly divided by a wide path leading to a podium.  Murmurs from twelve people gathered at that far end, shouting range, by a long table with platters of fried cat legs, Jovian pepper sauces, and glass bowls of purple liquid.  *Dragonfruit Punch. It's from the bar. Totally delicious.* "They're getting ready for the auction," she whispered.

Footsteps behind her grew louder and she turned.

Paul Phalen.  "Come with me."  But he didn't lead her, he walked around behind her and nudged her thru an open doorway.

A garage or something.  Mostly dark.  Tarps concealed three large vehicles, maybe 50 meters away but hard to tell without lens functions.  A bald man in a suit stood under a light by a nearby workbench, holding a handheld scanner attached by wire to a behavior cylinder.  "Matilda?" he asked with raised eyebrows.

The door behind her sealed with a hydraulic hiss.

"She entered her code."  Paul walked up to the behavior cylinder, unbuttoned his crisp black suit, and adjusted his tie.  He wore detective-style boots, the kind you can run in, yet they were polished to a mirror gloss.  Maybe an ex-cop.  *Cydonian Militia.*

The bald man set the handheld scanner on the ground, and it slithered over like a snake with a lit-up head.  As it crawled and coiled around her leg gross sweat fell from both freshly shaven underarms, though Matilda nonchalantly played with their hair while the blue scan-light line passed her bare mid-riff.  A computer in front of the workbench drew a rotating holographic mirror of her in the form-fitting sleeveless shirt and jean shorts.  Something Mary would wear when checking her parcel tube.

"How does it feel to be part of a system?" Paul asked.

"I wouldn't know," Matilda said somehow, even though Joan was certain she was holding her breath.

"How do you feel when you pet a cat?"

"Intra-linked."

"What's the last book you read?"

"*Pale Fire.*"

Paul looked at the bald man, who raised a flatputer and tapped a finger on the screen. "Confirmed. It's little Miss Maat."

"Are you going to examine your own head next?" Matilda pushed the scan-snake away and with a distressing beep it scurried away like a scared animal.

Paul moved a hand over his already slicked-back hair and smiled with crooked teeth. "She sure is." He glanced at the bald guy's flatputer. "No gun?"

"I predicted I didn't need one. Was I wrong?" she asked.

"No." Paul approached, close enough to smell his cologne. A subtle oak scent. Obviously expensive. *He spends more on that than you make in overtime.* "I told you I wanted to see Wazzerman."

"He said there's too much heat. Why do you think I copied myself into a short blonde?" Matilda placed a hand on Joan's shared hip.

"You don't say. That's why I wanted to see him. Tell him this shit is unacceptable." Paul raised a finger and his sport coat drifted open, exposing a large Saturn Armory blaster in a cross-draw holster. "The cops don't just have a bee up their ass. They've got a whole hive. Raiding outback outposts for supplies is one thing. You killed a government official. My own people are looking at me sideways."

"Don't wave your finger in my face."

Paul lowered his hand. "Tell him no more schools. Otherwise, he can buy his weapons somewhere else." His shaking breaths puffed on her face and his red cheeks were the size of stop signs.

She looked away. *I should have brought a weapon,* she thought. *No need to tip the scales. Just even them out.*

Matilda locked eyes with Paul. "Aw. You haven't been adequately compensated?"

"Hah. The Jovian Military pays higher prices. Why do you think your former colleagues haven't found me? Delphi doesn't predict idealism."

"Oh, is that what we're calling it now?" Matilda played with their hair. "Do you like this hair?  Do you think I should dye it?"

Paul gently caressed a strand of her hair. She instinctively froze, yet there were no fearful thoughts of what he might do. A bubbling sensation around her scalp. Maybe Matilda is channeling some kind of psychedelically inspired calmness. "I like you no matter what you look like."

The bald guy cleared his throat.

"Oh yeah," Paul said with a smile. "I almost forgot. This isn't purely a social occasion."

Matilda handed him the backpack.

Paul stepped away, unzipped the pack, and rummaged through until his hands emerged with the wrapped stacks of Delphi predictions. His smile widened.

"The first stack is individual futures for every predicted attendee. In the folder is the amount each bidder will pay for their future. The second stack is future events. Stocks, next Wednesday's orange juice prices, blah blah blah. Things bankers and speculators will sell their own mothers for."

"Nice. Very nice." He handed the second stack to the bald guy and unwrapped the first, slowly thumbing his way through the hundreds of pages. "Couldn't you just bring the core here?"

"Dragging a heavy object with a large Delphi logo on it through the streets. Do we need another printed prediction to know how that would turn out?"

"But what if, Isis forbid, someone wants their future, and it isn't in this stack?"

"Then I have my associate run their data through the core. Should only take five minutes."

"They can be here in five minutes?"

Matilda smiled and nearly laughed. This damn hustler. "Let me worry about that."

Paul finished thumbing through the predictions and lifted the entire stack up in one hand, which shook as he rotated it. "What about my future?"

"Ask me tomorrow." Matilda walked up to him. "Tonight, you're going to be rich."

"Rich enough to lobby the council," the bald guy said.

"Assuming we get full price," Paul said.

"The highest bidder decides value, not the lowest." Matilda raised their eyebrows. "And your half of the deal?"

Paul nodded at the bald guy and walked over to the workbench to unwrap both stacks of Delphi predictions with large thuds.

The bald man's dress shoes and her boots clopped louder than the vibrations of music echoing from the nearby bar as she followed him past shadows of hardware-laden shelves to the three covered vehicles at the other end of the garage. Only large wheels remained unconcealed. The frayed edge of the tarp crumpled as she pinched and yanked it from the first cargo hauler to the floor.

The bald guy offered a hand.

"No thank you." The truck bed of the hauler had a little step, which was only a bit tricky to climb in heeled boots.

Spare robotic parts barely lit by a little lantern thingy, like what people use in old holo-movies. Giant mechanical legs and arms fitted with large caliber machine blasters. Must be a large robot, as tall as a house or something. Impossible to be sure without any damn lens functions. If the serial numbers match any war robots that'll add a dozen felonies to Paul's RAP sheet.

"Matilda?" the bald guy asked.

Damnit. I need to plant the tracker on something. Two haulers left.

Hesitating at the edge of the truck bed cued Matilda to bend a leg and find the small step down, which she managed to do without seeing it.

The bald guy pulled the tarp from the next hauler and held up a hand, like he was a presenter on a game show.

Missiles. Blue javelin missiles. Or just missiles with blue tips? Even the large bed of the hauler could only accommodate a dozen of the wide and long projectiles. Glow in the dark packing foam filled the narrow gaps between them. She hesitated at the step and the bald guy again offered a hand. Aren't warheads designed to explode? *They have to be armed before that can happen. Silly.*

A squishing noise under her heels as she carefully stepped between the javelins. Squatting down and running a hand along the padding wet her fingertips. Rubbing them together it was sticky and smelled faintly of soap. Looking up towards the front of the hauler, the vehicle ID had *SCRUBBER-1138* in large white letters.

The tracker.

The bald man stood at the back of the vehicle. Watching her. She leaned down next to a warhead, low enough for the large missile to hide her, and removed her left earring. Damnit, which way did Troy say to turn this thingy? Clockwise? Which means to the right, like that old cuff-chrono that Grandma once had. The damn thing wouldn't budge.

"The manifest says twelve," the bald guy said. "No baker's dozen I'm afraid."

"That's where the feather lands." She stuffed the earring into the front pocket of her shorts, which was barely large enough to hold even that, then stood and hopped off the autonomous scrubber. Landing turned into a stumble until the bald guy grabbed her hand. "Thanks."

"No worries."

The truck bed of the final hauler, or highway scrubber or whatever, was a maze of glossy-white cases, heavy enough that with both shaking arms she could only move one at a time. MAR-SEC in large red-brown letters on both sides. An animation of the rust-colored planet spun under the text.

Turning pairs of latches on three cases revealed Styrofoam mazes of blasters, carbines, and automatics. They had that new-from-Mars smell. Intoxicating plastic and algae. Not the same kind used to eat radiation on Earth, it had a slight almond aroma, or almond air freshener anyway. Who even remembers what real almonds smell like? *I do.*

She reached into her pocket. Pinched the edge of the earring. Started to pull it out of—

"Those are the first M7-20s shipped Earthside." The bald guy peeked over the edge of the truck bed. "Even the police don't have them yet. The Martian Militia call them blasting wands. I know your guys like the 600 series, but with the auto-sights on these you can shoot the wings off a mosquito."

"Earth mosquitos have smaller wings," Matilda said.

"Hah." The bald guy pointed at different cases. "The armor you asked for is there. RA batteries. Seven boxes of 6-6-5 ammunition. More than enough to turn a concrete wall into Swiss cheese. And enough blasting caps to keep the police bomb squad up all night."

She slowly opened each box as the bald guy watched. Thumps from the far side of the garage.

Paul squaring the stacked edges of the Delphi predictions on the workbench before handing them to a short robot whose joined hands looked like a currency counter. It flipped through the stack in a rapid blur that sounded like Mary when she sticks out her tongue to make a raspberry.

*He's going to come over.* Damnit. Picking up one of the new model carbines, she examined the sights and pretended to accidentally hook the ejector handle on her push up bra while putting it down. "Oh." The garage was suddenly cold, but her face burned hot, like a face fever.

The bald guy sheepishly looked away.

Clops from Paul's dress shoes echoed across the garage, louder each second.

She kneeled. Pulled out the earring. Turn it the other way. *Eureka.* Held it over the carbine's open bolt. Squeezed it. A small drop fell into the bolt with a tiny splash of vapor that instantly disappeared.

"We're getting coordinates from the tracker," Troy said into her ear transmitter.

After hastily reattaching the earring, she pulled the bra and top, twisting and squirming until they slid back up.

"Satisfied?" Paul was standing behind her at the edge of the truck bed.

"Never."

"I couldn't get spider mines this time. But I did get these." He tapped an open hand against a stack of boxes next to the hauler that she hadn't noticed before.

Sky-blue boxes with HAPI in large letters and an enlivened logo of an olive-skinned man pouring water, who emerged holographically from the box for a few seconds.

Matilda sighed as she struggled to peel off the box's security tape, rotating Joan's wrists with a crack before reattempting. *Why is this so difficult? Are you wrong handed?* Joan picked at the tape from the opposite edge. Each mind controlling one hand but working together.

"What's with twice the usual water purifiers?" Paul asked. "You and your pirates opening an ocean?"

Matilda giggled.

The bald guy's shoes clopped as he walked off towards the dark wall of the garage where he faded into a shadow. His face briefly visible as he lit a Martian cigarette. Red ash fell, and redder rings flew from puffs to the ceiling like demons escaping hell.

Paul looked over his shoulder towards the doorway, growing echoes of chatter, then back to her. "Guests are still arriving. The auction isn't for another hour." He took a step towards her, close enough to again flood her nostrils with his cologne.

A wave of warmth on her face and some strange feeling near her stomach, an anxious emptiness and hunger. Without conscious thought her right hand played with her hair.

Paul gently stroked her face. Something shiny on his sleeve. *Cufflinks.* An image on them. Scales with something thin balancing them out. Maat. His hand moved towards his chin like it was in slow motion. Time crawling. He said something, but the words trailed off, fading sounds that spiraled before turning silent. A sudden image from a strange mind's eye.

Taps like dropping rain, but too regular, like a drum. The floor moved under her feet, like holo-paddling through waves. Posh décor. Wooden doors, glass carved into images and shapes on it. Red carpet with twelve yellow symbols on it, ancient or Greek. One of them the balancing scales.

Dark, with a stillness like little pockets of gravity drained all the light and energy after a few meters. A thud.

A big guy in a suit leaning against a wall with a smirk. Warner. He seemed more familiar up close, not on those stupid re-election ads. He moved too close, closer than Paul just was.

Warner pushes until there's a wall she lands against. His hands are in the wrong places and his grip won't yield.

She pushed him away.

"What the hell Mattie?" Paul asked from the garage floor. He stood up while panting. "Who are you?"

"Joan?" Troy asked on the wireless.

Paul parted his sport coat a drew his blaster.

"Don't shoot me!" She put up her hands.

"Are you a cop?"

The bald man ran over.

Somehow her hands were bound, and she was shoved onto a chair before she knew it.

"Where is she?" Paul asked.

"I don't know." She fought the restraints. *Calm down. These guys won't do anything indecent to you. Just let me do the talking.*

"What have done with her?" Paul asked with bulged eyes. His jaw looked like it had doubled in size as he pressed the blaster barrel against her forehead.

"Nothing." *I said let me do the talking.* "P—Paul?"

"Mattie?" Paul lowered his blaster. His face fell with red circles forming around his eyes.

"I'm alright. The MOTHs found a copy of my mind."

"The storage depot. I'm such a fool. I shouldn't have left that there." Paul ran his free hand thru his hair.

"It's okay sweetie. Don't kill this body I'm running in. The MOTHs have the place surrounded."

"Who's in charge of the op?"

"Kyudo."

"Kyudo?" The bald guy's mouth fell open. "This isn't fucking happening, this isn't fucking happening," He continuously muttered while lighting a fresh cigarette and puffing away.

"We can still get out of this," Matilda said. "What do you remember?"

"Neither of us know the location of your lab," Paul said while pointing to himself and then the bald guy.

"Nothing that can compromise us?"

Paul scratched his nose and glanced at the water purifiers.

"You know what you have to do," Matilda said. "I'll bring you back in the next circle."

"I love you." Paul leaned in and kissed her. She flinched but Matilda embraced the dirty thug. Yet there was no lightness or tingling in their stomach and no warmth on their cheeks. Matilda doesn't really love Paul. *Shut up or we're both dead, bumpkin.*

"Next circle? What are you talkin' about?" she asked.

"What about this blonde shell? Want me to waste her?" Paul lifted his gun barrel to her head again.

She squirmed for a moment, but Matilda held her in place with a smile. "Waste not, want not."

The floor vibrated and a distant rumbling, like an engine, grew louder. A thunderous crash and blinding white light from the far wall of the garage. Shouts from police robots and fully armored officers.

Paul lifted his blaster to his own temple and pulled the trigger, sending blood in every direction. The bald guy dropped his blaster with the remaining half of his smoldering cigarette hanging from his mouth. Robots quickly cuffed him and freed her.

"Joan?" Troy asked again on the wireless.

"Dammit! I fucked up this whole operation!" She stood and kicked the boxes of water purifiers over. Painful throbs from the toes of her foot.

Pete emerged from the giant smoking hole in the garage, not in armor but in his sharp peacoat. "You okay Lyon?"

"Pete," she said in a strange saccharine tone. The same blushing and hunger Paul induced earlier returned, but stronger and undoubtedly more embarrassing.

# 35
## Pareidolia

Peter typed on the volumetric keyboard projected from the side of the third highway maintenance vehicle.

*memdsk -search -r
-datatype=gps_coordinates|directions -sectors 1:N*

After a minute-long wait-cursor, it clicked-back with nothing. Nada. Zilch. Even computers can forget.

"Pollux," he said into his wireless transmitter. "I can't find coordinates on these. No directions to the Sandcastle. Or anywhere. You'll need to have them towed to the station garage unless you find your raincoat."

"Da Petar. I dispatch tow trucks."

He looked up, through the open garage doors and beyond the line of handcuffed suspects being huddled into half a dozen wagons. Major Kyudo stood by an APC and spoke to a semi-circle of reporters while her dark coat, soaked with acidic rain, glistened like polished armor.

In the middle of the packed press, a robotic hand pointed straight in the air. "Major?" it asked in monotone.

Kyudo nodded in the direction of the raised metallic hand.

"Rrrobie the robot reporter from Mencken News. Major, is there any connection between these outlaws and the Blue Jewel Tower bombing?"

Kyudo smiled. A subroutine clicked-back that her eyes dilated. "Yes, and we've dealt a serious blow to their ability to engage in further attacks." More hands shot up and Kyudo shook her head. "I'm afraid I have pressing matters to attend to. Please save your questions for a press conference later tonight."

He crossed the street. Raindrops pebbled on his coat as he waited for a formation of robot riot police to pass, and he followed Kyudo as she walked behind another APC.

"Where are they taking us?" A handcuffed suspect asked. The only voice along the prodded line of silent thugs. Patricia Overton, according to subroutines.

"Central booking ma'am," he said without stopping.

"Major?" He ran over as Kyudo stopped to speak with Boothe. "Major?"

Kyudo nodded at Boothe, who walked away.

"Did you read my report?" he asked while huffing.

Kyudo's eyebrows went up. "The one regarding Albright?"

"Yes ma'am. Albright wants to make a deal."

"We don't negotiate with Outcasts."

"You want me to communicate that to Albright word for word? If she contacts me?"

"No. Placidly agree to her terms and keep me informed."

"Wouldn't Albright contact someone she's familiar with? A former partner, perhaps?"

"There's an A-P-B out on her. If she contacts another officer, they'll know what to do."

"And why would she contact me?"

"If she does, ask her. But keep in mind Outcasts have false memories. Don't take her word for anything."

He scratched his neck, and it sounded like sandpaper. Kyudo can dance around questions such as these all day, and she's warmed up after talking to reporters. Do not pass go. Do not collect two hundred dollars. "What about Phalen and Kaughland?"

"There wasn't much left of Phalen's brain. Kaughland doesn't know where the Sandcastle is or the destination of the three contraband haulers. We may have to resume our investigation of the missing memory printer, unless one of these auction participants gives us a fresh lead." Kyudo lifted her arm and clicked buttons on her wrist-computer. "Diaz from the Detective Bureau volunteered to assign interrogations.  Report to her at the Hall of Justice when you're done here.  I want confessions."

"What if they don't know anything?"

"Then overcharge them.  Aiding and abetting Outcasts."

"Right."  He turned around.

A mob of robot reporters had gathered around him.

"Officer Ramsey, do you care to comment on recent allegations—"

"Did you launch warheads during the Terminal War?" another reporter asked while shoving a microphone in his face.

"Have you been suspended from active MOTH duty?" Robbie the robot reporter asked.

The swarm descended into a loud and indiscernible rabble, an orchestra with no conductor.

He glanced at the nearby alleyway.  "Uh..."

***

He stormed through his apartment door and skidded to a stop.

Ari was sitting at the dining room table sipping a volumetric Cosmopolitan.  The barely audible news feed played Kyudo's press conference in the living room.  His wife's gaze fixed at some point beyond the glass of the patio door.

"Ari."

She took a gulp of her cocktail and held up the glass.  "I found an app on the dark web so I could have a drink.  I charged it to your card.  Your accounts will be confiscated in a day or so, so I thought you wouldn't mind.  And if you do, I don't."

"Reporters—they, uh, only care about ratings."

"Carmen ran to her room crying.  Heartbroken that her daddy isn't a hero.  I kept saying it couldn't be true.  Until I found this in the other room with the others."  She tapped a fingernail against a memory disk on the table. "Your backup from last November."

"Whatever you saw on there, they're just thoughts. They can't hurt you."

"Can't they?" Ari finally looked at him. "Tell me it's a fake. Tell me it isn't real."

"I didn't have a choice. I was following orders."

Ari gasped and chugged her cocktail, pausing only to regain her composure. "You weren't undercover or something? Of course. Your memories are too strange to be fake."

"Everything I've done has been for this family."

"This family? How can you say that? Do you love her?"

"Who?"

"The woman you've been seeing. You were spending all day with her and then coming back here at night. How can you be two people at the same time?"

He opened his mouth and nearly asked his wife who she was talking about. Asking that will set her off. "I don't know. I don't remember."

"So you just forgot? Perfect. Just pretend it never happened."

"I forgot because that's not who I am."

"Once a cheater, always a cheater." Ari stood and walked to the opposite side of the table. "It's because she's alive, isn't it? I told you I would merge with a pleasure robot if you wanted. I almost surprised you on your last birthday. I know they're illegal. I should have done it anyway."

"We agreed to wait until we're both alive."

Ari crossed her arms. "Well, now you'll be waiting forever."

"Don't be rash. Think about Carmen."

Ari sneered. "Carmen? What could she possibly learn from a war criminal? You know she's been measuring her height against the doorframe?  Do you think she doesn't know? What child doesn't grow up other than you?"

He walked up to his wife. "I am NOT a war criminal!"

"And I'm NOT your wife!" Ari stormed past him and ran into the utility room.  "You will never see your daughter again!"

The lights flickered with a loud crashing noise.

In the utility room, the house robot had fallen next to the volumetric emitter.  Large cracks on the smoking screen of the Lazarus console, though the nearby memory disks were intact.

At the dining room table, he pulled his memory disk's cord and snapped it into his wrist-computer.  The memory interface loaded.  Volumetric immersion.  As expected, no memories. Nothing. Nada. Zip. Darkness, save for a few white dots far above, as though he were at the holo dome and seeing the night sky of an alien planet.

"Damnit." He pulled the plug on his wrist to emerge and staggered to the living room.  At the piano's bench he stumbled and fell, steading himself on one of the piano's polished legs, hearing not the sound of Ari's holographic cello, nor Caramel's singing, only the strings of his heart and his accelerating, shallow breaths.

***

Peter drew his pistol as he walked down the alleyway of bums and knocked the barrel against the sliding door of rusted metal surrounded by brick wall.  It opened with mechanical heaves, into a derelict atrium which carried the echoes of dripping pipes, where the cloister of the bright room divided dark lines of column shadows.  His reverberating footsteps pulled him through an alcove of opposing mirrors creating parallel infinity and into a room of blinking mainframes with a solitary man in a chair of worn leather.

Wires flowed from holes in the man's head like thick hair, running along the ground and into a wall of sockets, similar to an old telephonic switchboard. The wires twisted and coiled as he turned towards him. "Peter."

"Vincent. I love what you've done with the place."

Flashes of light on Vincent's desk. A volumetric news feed. Councilman Warner's press conference regarding the bombing downtown. Flashes as reporters took a few hundred tableaus of him shaking hands with Ms. Pythia, the president of Delphi. A middle-aged woman with tanned skin that looked darker while standing next to the pasty councilman. Major Kyudo smiling in the background by the twelve flags of the settlements.

"The government just signed a new three-trillion-dollar deal with the corporation, aimed at preventing any future attacks," Vincent said. "Can you believe this? Delphi is already a cake slice on the government's pie chart. They screw up and get even more money. I'm in the wrong line of work."

"Is there a way to restore lost memories? Say for example someone had a memory disk filled with memories that were wiped out with memory treatments. Now, they couldn't view those memories on the disk due to myelin moats. But there has to be way around that. Right?"

Vincent's eyes zoned out for a good twenty seconds. "You asking for a friend?"

"Oh of course."

"Those kinds of apps, if they exist, wouldn't be legal officer."

"And?"

"Or cheap."

"How much are we talking here? A few hundred?" He clicked on his wrist-computer. Eighteen hundred eighty-eight in his credit account.

"Entrapment is a violation of protocol five."

"Just tell me how much the Goddamn app is."

"I'll bank another favor with you instead."

"Right." Huh. Strange that Vincent would want to bank a favor. Given that my name is on the news with a list of war crimes in big red letters, he should be asking for cash.

"It will take a few minutes." Vincent nodded towards a sofa against the nearby wall. "Candy?" Vincent picked up a small bowl, the size of an ashtray. Citrus candies.

Peter scanned until he found a lime and popped it into his mouth. "Thanks." It tasted like key lime pie. "Where do you get these?"

"The corner store a block away. Aisle seven."

"How do you go there. You know, with all of that." He gestured around his head.

"I wear a hat." Vincent grinned.

"Right."

Vincent turned towards the computer on the desk. The wires from his head brushed aside food wrappers and other clutter as he rapidly re-arranged volumetric screens, typing with loud clangs.

A small round end table next to the sofa. A stack of pamphlets and books. *Hack the Multiverse* and *The Isis Manifesto*, the latter raised subroutine alarms. "Damnit Vincent, can't you keep this contraband out of sight?"

Vincent raised his hands. "I didn't know you were stopping by. I'm not Delphi for Pete's sake."

"You're hilarious."

"Why didn't you turn off your lenses?"

A streak, a large scratch in the vinyl floor in front of the sofa, led past the side table to something covered in a tablecloth, say about half the size of a desk. He pulled an edge and found a paper printer. The smell of fresh toner. "Did you finally start that underground hacker newsletter?"

"What? Oh, that's nothing." Vincent pulled a glossy magazine from a corner of his desk and placed it over some white pages.  Pages identical in size to printed Delphi pre-dictions.

He pulled his validation tube. "I have to run a p-eleven on you." Vincent recoiled. "Relax. It's just standard proce-dure." Vincent froze. "I'll report that you found this and called me." He picked up *The Isis Manifesto*. A small book, narrow and short enough to fit in his coat's front pocket, though thick enough to create a boxy bulge.

Vincent remained still as Peter connected the validator's wire to Vincent's green wrist tracker. The validation tube ticked and clicked every few seconds, the coil of rings blinked green in a repeated sequence. The noise sounded different. Vincent held his breath. A bead of sweat slowly moving down the edge of his forehead.

Vincent's tracker ring turned red as a loud alarm sounded. The imprint knocked over a stack of papers and grabbed a small pistol. Peter jumped onto the desk, grab-bing its hands to wrestle it away and unwittingly elbowing it in the face which helped him claim the gun.

Rapid taps behind him. Footsteps. Pops and sparks flew off the nearby mainframe. Smoldering slugs. Smoking holes. He pivoted and pulled the imprint in front as an in-human shield, aiming over its shoulder after drawing his service weapon.

Two red outlines on Wall-Thru. Vincent's associates. They don't know their boss has been brainwashed. Or they do.

He exchanged fire rapidly, having to aim at each edge of the doorway where the hostile pair moved in a pattern, drawing his fire in one direction, and returning it from the other.

Vincent keeled over. A round had struck its forehead, cracking the skull in half and oozing a pink paste of boiled brains.

The Wall-Thru outline of the male shooter fidgeted.

He aimed carefully with a two-handed grip. The shooter stuck his head out and Peter pulled the trigger, blowing the target's head into a red splash and flying finger-sized fragments.

A kill chime credited forty dollars into his bank account.

The female shooter stood just beyond the edge of the far doorway. Firing at her outline merely shattered the twin mirrors and puffed gray dust from smoking holes in the concrete walls. Two rounds left in the magazine according to the ammo subroutine. Once I start reloading, she'll hear it and rush the room.

He held his thumb against the charge button below the trigger. The pistol whirred and oranges lines along the barrel lit up.

The pistol growled and shook as the barrel glowed. *Overcharge Warning.* He aimed at the shooter's outline, covered his face with his other arm, and squeezed the trigger. The loud blast and shattering masonry rang in both ears as he grabbed his validation tube as well as the stack of papers on Vincent's desk and ran through the burning hallway littered with shattered glass that crunched under his boots.

Crunches that transitioned into splashes as he ran down the alleyway. Plops from loose pages falling onto puddling pavement. When he reached the street, he was gasping for air with a layer of sweat under his soaked coat.

By the car he stumbled, landing an elbow against the door and accidentally discharging his pistol into the ground, blasting a burst of roadway that collided with his calf. "Goddamnit. This is too much. This is too fucking much."

In the car he slammed his door shut, clicked-off combat stims on his wrist-computer, and waited for his legs and sweaty hands to stop shaking. The stack of wet pages stuck together, but carefully rubbing the corners facilitated flipping through them. Delphi predictions.

One of Delphi's labs on fire.  The arson earlier in the week.

Lyon across from a wounded officer, aiming a weapon at an open doorway.

Lyon and he in a standoff in front of Kropveld's Café a few days ago.

Two women walking in the street.

Lyon hiding behind a mainframe while wearing a dress.

Hamilton and Lyon diffusing a bomb.

Kyudo reviewing evidence at her desk.

Events that already happened.  Events Delphi predicted.

His wrist-computer shook and rang.  "Speak of the devil.  It's Delphi."

"Ramsey?  Moira.  I am looking over the property returned from a sting operation earlier tonight.  Good work.  But we still need the core."

"I'm working on it."  He lifted the stack of predictions.

"Excellent."

He flipped to the page with the bent corner.  A prediction of Blue Jewel Tower exploding.  "On the news they said councilman Warner narrowly missed the explosion by a few minutes.  Don't you have backup systems with these predictions?"

"If I were you, I would be more concerned with current events.  We can stall the DA for twenty-four hours.  After that, I would recommend you seek accommodations off-world."

"Can you set me up with an exit visa?"

"Of course.  Now we understand your MOTH partner ran Albright under a Janus procedure.  Our techs believe we can gather additional information by probing Officer Lyon's mind while she still carries fragments of Albright's mind."

"You want me to ask her?"

"No.  My conjecture core indicates she will not cooperate under any terms I am authorized to give."

DELPHI
DATA CAFE

He watched the rain drops reflect various shades of street neon as they fell along the windshield.  "What do you propose?"

"We have a neural scanner with a range of fifty meters."

"You're going to scan her brain without her consent?"

"She only needs to remain in one place, with infrequent interruption, for the greater part of an hour."

"It's getting late.  Perhaps wait until she's asleep?  Rent an adjacent room in her apartment building?"

"REM patterns interfere with the scan.  She needs to be awake."

"Lyon rarely remains in one spot for very long."

"There must be something.  You are her partner, are you not?  Think."

"I am thinking.  Huh.  She watches that dreadful Martian soap opera."

"I like where your head is at," Moira said.  "But episodes of that show conclude after half an hour."

A drone passed overhead with a bright advertisement for The Red Jacket Steakhouse.  "Huh."

"Sorry?"

"I just got an idea."

# 36
## The Red Jacket

"What do you think Potato?" Joan asked Mary over the phone app while using the Outfit app to swipe thru holographically superimposed combinations of tops and bottoms.

"A white blouse and red cords? Are you running Narcissus?" Mary asked.

"I don't even have an hour to get ready." She toggled to a red blouse and grey wool pants she had bought from the bargain-bin at Dolley's Depot.

"Never say die."

"I don't know. What says I'm not your date and I'm only here for free steak?"

"REAL steak? How is that not a date?"

"We're just coworkers."

"Maybe he knows you're onto him?"

She swiped to a blue top. "Maybe."

"Are you running a speech app? You sound different."

"No."

"Can you order two steaks and bring me one?"

"Focus Mary."

"Okay. You're going to spill a drink on the old guy you work with, so he has to go wash up. When he leaves the table, you're going to scan his apartment keycodes and transmit them to me so I can search his apartment."

"For?"

"Michelle Albright. Framed images or memory discs of her."

"Matilda Albright."

"What if he keeps it in his wallet?"

"He won't. He keeps it in his jacket."

"Why don't you save a few bites of steak and bring me a doggy bag?"

"Sure." Or maybe spoon feed bites to Mom even though she'd just forget tasting it after a few minutes. But suggesting that to Mary might make her feel guilty.

"So, like, this whole time Peter's been training you he's been a spy?"

"I'm not sure. But if we find evidence I can go to my boss."

"Hmm, okay. Did you brush your teeth?"

"Twice."

"Sounds like a date."

"You're ridiculous."

"Be careful. Love you and know you."

"Love and know you too."

***

The Serpico Grill was a renovated prewar hilltop structure annexed to a hotel via a glass-enclosed catwalk. It commanded an impressive view of the Settlement along an uninterrupted window that spanned the entire Southward-facing wall. The endless neon of the city trailed off to the dark sea and the thin orange line of the distant perimeter wall.

She dialed to Anxiety-Away, a new setting Mary had sent over, while she waited between the empty hostess podium and an artisan wall of rapidly rising and falling bubbles. Beyond, dozens of rows of polished-wood tables. A suspended light hung over each one, breaking the large dim room into little islands of brightness. Occupied by ladies and gentlemen of various ages and ethnicities but all of them well wrapped in formal suits and dresses. Settlement Five's best dressed to the nines.

They reverberated sounds of clinking glasses and chatter. Cutlery formed one section of the unintentional orchestra, conducted by the collective human unconscious. It bridged into notes of inebriated bouts of laughter and satiation before segueing into actual jazz. A piano and clarinet in a corner.

I don't normally notice music, she thought. Weird.

She followed a man carrying a pitcher of water past diners flipping through traditional paper menus. The sound of her flat dress-shoes knocking on terrazzo barely registered in the noisy room. A lens function identified Peter, who was already sitting at a two-seat table one row from the window.

He had cleaned up well. He had shaved his face and neck, so if he scratches it won't make that annoying scraping sound. A crisp navy-colored jacket and red tie held him together. The red edge of a thin access card stuck out of one of the front pockets. On his left wrist an antique wrist-chrono, like the one Grandma used to have. Little white lines rotating around numbers in a round glass darkly. Like a sentiment circle, but it only changes your mood to older.

"I didn't know you owned a suit," she said.

"It's old, just like me." He stood and started to walk over with his arms reaching for her chair.

Until she waved him away. "My arms aren't broken." The chair was made from thin wood that creaked as she sat down and set her purse on the floor in front of her.

Red and blue hues of wines and spirits from the nearby marble-surfaced bar cast light over their glossy table like a prism. Looking over the patrons again, nearly every color reflected in the spectrum of dress colors. Every woman here is in a dress, except the robo-waitresses. And me, she thought. Damn.

"You look great, by the way," Peter said.

"Thank you." She pretended to be flattered with a callow smile and covertly examined her outfit, the blouse and cords, in a section of the window behind him, where the lighting provided a mirror-like reflection. No disapproving stares from anyone. "I imagine this is the type of place Kyudo goes to every night."

Peter shook his head. "No. She eats alone."

"Even after a day like today?"

"It seems as though we rarely get a break these days. Might as well make use of it."

"I was wondering what the special occasion was." She leaned back in the chair.

Peter lifted a paper menu that covered the lower half of his face as he read. *The Red Jacket Steakhouse* in large red letters.

I thought I was here a year ago and it was called The Serpico Grill, she thought. She picked up the menu next to her, but the stupid pages were stuck together.

"Rub the corners," Peter said with a smile.

"Oh." The antiquated parchment eventually crimped between a thumb and index finger. A texture that wasn't smooth but soft in its own way. The text was in flamboyant and fancy shapes. Morgan once mentioned a case where she found a note in something called cursive. An ancient language or something. The letters somehow made sense.

Shadow fell over the words of the menu. An old guy, half bald and older than even Peter, stood over her. Rigid in posture and smiling with a red jacket and a bowtie. A convincing human-like robot, but then lens functions beeped with an organic ID. "Uh, hi?" She glanced down at the floor, where the grip of her blaster jutted from her open purse.

"What can I get for you this evening?" the smiling creep asked.

"Lyon, this is our waiter," Peter said.

A human waiter? Is this that holo-show where there's a hidden camera and it's a giant prank? "Yes, I know."

The waiter placed a honeycomb-shaped arrangement of ice in a metallic bowl on the table, bordered by Hapi water tins and tall empty glasses.

"Ladies first." Peter smiled and pointed at her with an open hand.

"Uh-uh." She shook her head.

"Lamb chops. Mashed potatoes." He flipped a menu page. "Pinot Noir." Peter clapped the menu closed like it was a clam and handed it to the waiting gentleman. How do I know what a clam is, she wondered?

"Will Hosea 46 do?" The waiter asked. Peter nodded. The waiter made eye contact.

"Do you got—have, a $40 steak?" she asked.

"We have a $50 steak," the waiter said with a smile.

"Please. Tell me more." She rested her chin on a fist.

"Twice baked potatoes. Steamed broccoli. And of course, steak."

"Sold." She closed the menu and handed it over, imitating the way Peter did it.

"How would you like it done?" The waiter took her menu and scribbled something on a small, squared stack of real paper attached to a metal coil. "We can serve it rare, medium rare, medium, medium well or well done."

"What's between raw and burnt to a crisp?"

"Medium." Peter and the waiter answered in unison.

"Mm, medium rare. And I want asparagus instead of broccoli."

"Certainly, young lady. Might I suggest a Merlot?" the scribing waiter asked.

"Iced tea, please."

"Greenhouse salads?" the waiter asked.

Peter nodded.

"And for the lady?" the waiter asked.

"Why not?"

"Very good." The waiter noted on his paper pad and walked away.

She leaned over the table to whisper. "How do they have real people working as waiters?"

Peter shrugged. "Perhaps they pay real wages?"

She reached for a water tin and collided with Peter's hand. Blood flooded the muscles of her face and her arm trembled like an electric current passed through her.

"Sorry," Pete said. "Ladies first."

"Thank you."

The water tin went psst, but the plated arrangement of ice was frozen solid. Peter reached over and broke off four of the octangular cubes for her, in a way that was somehow not annoying. He turned his own can and smiled with amusement at the hieroglyphic animation of the olive-skinned man pouring water into a river. *Have a Hapi day* in scrolling text.

Salads appeared in front of each of them. Enough chopped vegetables to be entire meal by itself. Carrots, onions, and a type of lettuce with thick rib-like spots that crunched when she stabbed it with a fork, like it was a bone among leafy flesh. A white disc-like vegetable with a red circumference that, according to a lens function, was something called a radish. The croutons weren't those little bricks of crumbs, they looked like little toasty bits of real bread. Weird. Delicious, but definitely weird.

The human waiter also set down a small tray of bread and their drinks, then walked away without even excusing himself. Maybe that kind of politeness is just for robots. But in the reflection of one of the large spoons by her napkin, polished enough to replace the Narcissus app, she found herself smiling as she chewed on the crunchy greens.

"You could have ordered wine. They don't card here." Peter took a sip of his red wine. A high center of gravity held up by a thin stem. But with his jacket still on, and his keycard in the jacket, a spill might have to wait.

"I thought you gave up drinking?"

"Did you?" Peter asked while pinching small pods of Caesar dressing onto his salad.

Ice clanged as she sipped her iced tea and her mouth nearly collided with a wedge of lemon stuck over the rim. "They stuck a lemon on my glass."

"It's an old tradition."

"I thought my sister might be pranking me."

"With an iced tea?"

"No. She calls me Lemon."

"Why?"

"Because of my hair." Without thinking she grabbed a few blonde strands but quickly blushed and released them to gravity.

"Huh." Peter broke the small loaf of bread in half and buttered the steaming, broken end. "Do you remember the investigation simulator at the academy?"

"The detective holo-game?" She broke off a piece of the remaining bread, hot enough to burn her fingertips. There was a little knife on the rectangular plate by a dome of white butter that melted into white bubbles as she spread it over the steaming bread. Smooth cream that melted in her mouth and—

"Lyon?"

"What?" she asked with her mouth full.

"Do you remember the simulated case where you have to find the suspect and all that's known about him is his street name is Peanut?"

"Oh yeah, I remember that stupid test. I failed because I arrested all the suspects too early."

"That's right. You're supposed to leave them on the street, so they lead you to the big fish."

"I was sure one of them would flip on that damn Peanut. No such luck." Images danced across her mind's eye. Memories of passing that stupid test on the first try. But I know I failed it, she thought. She opened her eyes and found herself massaging her temples.

"Headache?"

"I'm good." She finished the bread on the small plate in front of her. "Do you think a phony memory could feel real?"

"The outcasts fight and die for them, so they must be quite convincing." Peter sniffed and sipped his wine.

"There's no way to tell?" She stretched her stiff legs and accidentally shook the table by colliding with its single centered leg.

"Easy tiger." Peter steadied the table by gripping the two corners closest to him. "When I was your age engineers, grey matter engineers, were able to create memories of someone drinking from a cold can." Peter picked up his tin of water. "And get the temperature of the can, of the water, and the sensation of the droplets on the can's surface true to real memory."

If Matilda's memories about being attacked by Warner are real, should I stop her from taking revenge, she wondered? Should anyone? Maybe that will be easier once I find out how Peter's involved.

A piping hot fillet of browned meat landed in front of her. Black grill marks. A potato buried under melted cheese and bacon. Heavenly smells that induced salivation and lip-licking.

She frowned and handed her plate of vegetables back to one of the servers. "I asked for asparagus, not broccoli."

Two red coats groveled and excused themselves, exchanging blame and remarks at each other as they walked away.

A shiny fork and a keychain-sized laser knife buried in a fresh cloth napkin. Smoke rose from the laser-knife's red beam as she cut a square of the browned and blackened meat, finding a pink interior that she eagerly forked and lifted to her mouth. Real steak. Worlds better than she ever imagined. Teeth and tongue fought over the carbonized but juicy and melting bits. A minute of chewing before finally swallowing. Peter was staring.

"What?" she asked.

"How is it?"

"It's great. Tastier than chicken and you get to chew it as long as you want." She noticed a small tray next to her plate with sauce pods. A lens function lit up steak sauce, English mustard, and ketchup. She cut another piece and dipped it before eagerly munching for half a minute. "I heard Norris is doing better."

"The doctors are going to wake him up tomorrow." Across the table Peter cut lamb with his buzzing laser. Some kind of tubular meat with bones sticking out of it. He had removed his jacket and neatly draped it along the top rail of his chair.

A bite of potato tickled her tongue. Piping hot bacon bits and cold sour cream didn't quite cancel each other out. But it was so yummy and worth a burnt tongue.

"I'm glad he's okay." She tried the mustard. Spicy. "Do you ever miss working with him?"

"No." He swirled his noir before taking a sip. Only half the wine remained. What if he only has one glass? "I thought you hated ketchup?"

"I'd eat a whole tomato if it came with this." She cut and lifted the next rectangular bit of steak. "Have you worked with a lot of different folks over the years?"

"A couple." Peter twirled the stem of his wine glass between two pressed-together fingers. It was close enough to strike with her fork, but he quickly raised it for a sip and landed it close to his side of the table. Damnit, she thought, I was too focused on eating to notice.

"Mayfleet was thinking of working with someone else," she lied.

"Huh. I thought Xiang Jun and her were thick as thieves."

"She just wants to keep her options open. Anyone you'd recommend?"

"No one with her peculiar sense of humor."

"Maybe just humor her."

"I'll talk to her tomorrow." Peter cut a small bite of lamb and dipped it into some brown sauce that she hadn't noticed earlier. *He doesn't look all that happy when he eats. What is wrong with him?*

A plate of steaming asparagus landed vertically next to her dinner plate. The old guy waiter. He had the same faux smile as before. "Thank you," she said while smiling back.

Peter gazed at some point behind her.

She turned her head. An ancient painting of a large wood ship on the wall above a couple of geriatric diners. She turned back and ate more sublime steak. *Maybe Peter knows Matilda from earlier. Before he enlisted in the police forces.* "Were those the types of ships they used when you were in the navy?"

"But of course."

"What was that like?"

"I learned how to swim." Peter connected mashed potatoes with his mouth.

"Is it true that ex-military friends keep in touch over the years?"

"I wouldn't know. Seven years of service and I never managed to make a single friend."

"Really?"

"Yes really. Why? Was your charming father's experience different?"

Her grip around the knife and fork tightened until her knuckles changed color. "What exactly did you do for the navy?"

Peter set his knife and fork down with loud clanks. "I served on the Reliant. It was a ballistic missile submarine. Is that what you wanted to know?"

She looked around at nearby tables. "Stop it, Peter. You're embarrassing me."

"I'm sick of having to lie. I didn't do anything wrong, but truth is the first casualty of war. Everyone wants to act like it's a crime now but all I did is what I was told. I didn't have a choice."

"What about the billions that died? What about their choice?"

"People die in wars. Why do you think there's a personnel shortage?"

"The outcasts aren't forcing us to go to ground."

"You were a shelter rat, weren't you?"

Her mind re-winded to cramped, musky halls that led to Tokyo-sized rooms. Cleaning bots battling mold and dirt in daily vain. The central recycler overflowing with foul refuse and corpses. The unquenchable thirst. Thirsty all the time. Once, when a med-bay camera broke, she stole an IV plasma bag. It's mostly water, she told Mary.

In the present she gulped her iced tea and took a bite of asparagus. A piece of chewy green vegetable stuck out from her closed mouth. She self-consciously raised a hand to cover her chewing mouth. Peter's wine glass was close enough to knock over. Before she grabbed her fork, he had picked it up again. Only about a third of it left. I might need a backup plan, she thought. Like throwing my tea at his face. This would be so much easier if I could just shoot him.

"You sure you don't want a glass?" Peter asked in a taunting tone. He spun the wine, watching the red liquid whirl and settle before he set it down next to a plate of vegetables. Little green balls, small enough that any smart person would use a spoon, so of course he used his fork. "That's why you move so quietly all the time, isn't it?" Peter asked. "Because you stole food. But don't worry. The statute of limitations for petty theft is two years. Besides, you were just a child, doing what you had to do. Right?"

"I remember the first time I saw a cockroach. I found this box of crackers under a pile of filthy clothes. I figured it was empty but there were three left. I was so excited, knowing I found something to eat. I ran to our cramped cabin and gave two of them to my sister but when I started to eat the last one, this little bug slowly crawled out of the box. I thought it was a grasshopper that lost his legs. I figured they fell off and I must of ate them. I was so hungry, but I felt so awful that I spit it all out and searched thru all that disgusting mush for its little legs. I starved for another day over a bug."

"Are you saying you didn't have a choice?"

"That's not a fair comparison. Plenty of people I knew starved to death. Their bodies were stacked up by the recycler all the way to the ceiling like they were empty cans."

"Fair? Fair is the last thing anyone wants. The people who complain about fairness are always the ones using the biggest guns, the thickest armor, and the latest predictions of the future. They use every advantage to hurt people they consider wrong and rationalize what they do by calling it 'justice'." He made quotes with two fingers on each hand, like he was making a point that mattered or something.

"That's because people don't care. If the aggressor wins, they blame the victim for being passive. Or if they stand up for themselves, they get blamed for escalating. If the aggressor loses, they get blamed for starting it. Everyone just sides with the winner. Because they're cruel, or lazy."

"Is that what happened to Overton?"

"The woman smuggles enslaved clones and ends up dead. Sounds like justice to me."

"It sounds like anarchy. A world where no one can ever turn their back on anyone."

She went for another sip of iced tea, but only ice remained.

I should hate him, she thought. But that feeling didn't surface or even simmer within. Like some wall held her anger back and it was as powerless as the endless ocean waves shattering themselves in futility against the settlement's seaside wall. There was some safe feeling though hanging in the air around him, like nothing bad can happen. Like being around Troy. An invisible aura that tickles the back of her head. And a bit of that anxious hunger too, only more subtle.

Out of reach on the other side of the table, the few remaining gulps of red wine glistened in Peter's wine glass. Maybe the laser knife can cut that far. But that wouldn't look accidental, and it could shatter or something. She crossed her legs and accidentally struck the table's single leg again, toppling the surface towards Peter.

His glass fell over and what was left of his red wine splashed on his white shirt as he cursed.

"Oh damnit. I'm sorry."

Peter wiped his napkin along the stain. "You certainly know how to show a man a good time." He blinked like a stupid robot for ten seconds. "Will you excuse me?"

"Of course."

Peter stood, placed his napkin over his edge of the table, and walked away.

Closing her eyes for a long blink, she reopened them without any lens functions that might record anything. The moment Peter cleared the edge of the room she pulled her computer slicer from her purse and walked over to the opposite chair. Pretending to clean the spill with a napkin while reaching into Peter's jacket pocket to connect slicer wires to the shiny edge.

"I can clean that up, ma'am." The old waiter stood over her with a smile.

20% copying progress. "That's okay, I got it."

The waiter pursed his lips and turned.

"Oh, actually, can I have a to-go bag for my leftovers?"

The waiter looked back with his perma-smile restored. "Of course."

40% progress. I can't keep pretending to clean, she thought. Borrowing Peter's fork and knife, she cut some of his lamb and took a bite. Not as good as the steak but easier to chew. Another woman at a nearby table looked over for a few seconds. I must have made a noise while chewing or something.

The waiter returned with a foil box.

She tucked the slicer into Peter's coat pocket and returned to her seat. "Thank you."

He returned her smile with his robotic one and walked over to another table.

After looking back at the corridor Peter disappeared to, she forked her leftovers into the box and blinked her lens functions back on. Around a corner, the Wall-Thru outline of Peter exited the men's room.

She ran to the opposite side of the table and without looking pulled the slicer off Peter's keycard and returned to her seat. Attracting another odd stare from a woman at an adjacent table. After giving an unrequited smile she dropped the slicer into her purse.

"No room for dessert?" Peter was standing behind her.

"No."

"Norris messaged me from the hospital. I'd like to go see him before visiting hours are over."

"Okay. Give him my regards."

"Right."

***

Mary didn't answer any calls. She wasn't waiting outside Saturn Studio Apartments. And she wasn't waiting in the lobby that was suspiciously absent of any doorman or desk clerk. She might be visible with activated lens functions but turning them on with a ghosted tracker will raise red flags.

The elevator took forever so Joan ran up the three flights of stairs, navigating the carpeted corridors of numbered rooms until slowing by a corner where knocks could be heard. Peeking around it, someone was standing in front of Peter's apartment door, 321.

Eva Diaz. A bottle of wine in her hands.

She ceased peeking. Peter isn't home so Eva will have to head back this way. An alcove across the hall, occupied by a large palm plant. One of those mid-sized ones that can grow without sunlight. There were some of them underground at Chiron, until people got desperate enough to eat them.

Footsteps approached, fibers crunching on carpet. She took quick and quiet steps on the carpet to hide behind the palm. She peeked after Eva passed by, raising a hand to minimize the rustling.

A weathered leather jacket in faded brown or cordovan, heels the same shade of black as her hair, and dark yoga pants instead of her usual pant suit. She looks amazing. She must do squats or something.

At the doorway to 321 Joan pulled on gloves and held her slicer against the access reader. The lock beeped green, and she turned the knob and once inside immediately closed the door along with the extra ball-chained lock.

The two antique bronze lamps across the room cast more shadows than light, separated by a couch littered with a man-funk-mess of balled up blankets and a cobweb of garments. She set her steak leftovers on the kitchen counter and waved away Peter's home-bot before it put it in the slob's fridge.

"Mary?"

No answer.

In the living room she pulled the curtains. A sliding glass door separated her from an empty balcony.

Peter has a piano. She ran her fingers along the keys and tapped a few. He has a real piano. Must of cost him a small fortune. Matilda seemed musical, like things in her mind bounced with a rhythm or something. Lifting the polished top only revealed strings. The instruments holo-log was marked sheet music, some of it marked with Peter's hand-writing, sloppy like his other endeavors.

His utility room had five shelves of canned food. The moron just leaves it out in the open for everyone to see instead of getting a vault. A robot charging station, laundry press, a holo-projector on a corner cabinet behind a long wooden desk topped by a paper printer. A small stack of crinkled pages with hand-written notes. Most of them resembled Peter's piano notes except one, loopy and fancy like that font at the restaurant. *I love you Pete.*

She found a blank sheet and an ink stick in a drawer to try imitating it with the phrase: *Writing on paper is strange.* It looked like shit. Hard to believe people used to do this. Maybe the grip is wrong. Instead of three fingers just grapple it like a claw. Or maybe people don't wear gloves when they write? Matilda calls Peter Pete. She's right-handed.

After switching hands, she tried again. Her muscles struggled but the motor control was somehow different. It wasn't a conscious effort, like someone else was moving the fingers. Elegant, looped letters flowed. *This apartment is a pigsty.* A near-perfect match.

The paper fell from her hands and under the nearby desk. Kneeling and peering under the furniture to find it, she spied a manilla file folder. Not a hologram but the real thing, a smooth and yet rough texture along her fingertips as she flipped it open. A page stuck to the inside front of the folder.

A Delphi prediction of a newspaper headline. *Outcasts Raze Settlements.* Dated a few days from now, September 29th, but a year ago. Weird. Two people sort of embracing and standing over a corpse. A blonde corpse.

She struck the back of her head on the desk as she leapt to her feet and turned the prediction towards the ceiling lights. It looks like me, she thought. But there are other women with short blonde hair. It looks like she has a police-issue peacoat. There are civilian models though. The two people standing in the prediction had their backs turned. A man and woman. The woman had dark hair, tied back. Kind of like Kyudo. The man's shirt seemed familiar.

Returning to Peter's couch, one of his nylon work shirts splayed at the top of a pile. The light grey one he always wears on Monday. She draped it over a chair in the kitchen, arranging it so the back of it faced her, and lifted the prediction. Maybe it's a coincidence. But if it's him, it can't be Kyudo next to him. She's two centimeters taller than him.

She sat on the kitchen chair and dropped the prediction on the table. Matilda. It's him and Matilda.

And me.

A knock from the front door.

"Lemon," a young woman's voice said.

"Mary!" She checked the peep hole and opened the door.

Mary froze at the threshold, her eyes red and swollen. "Joanie," she said in a feeble voice, like when she was seven and starving.

"Hello again Joan," another woman's voice.

Matilda emerged from the hallway with a blaster raised to Mary's temple. She pushed their way inside.

Joan glanced down at her holstered S120.

"Ut, ut." Matilda cocked her blaster with a thumb, keeping it pointed at Mary's head. "Don't even think about it." She grew a mischievous grin. "Look what the cat dragged in." She looked at Mary, who was starting to tremble.

"What do you want?" she asked Matilda.

"Aw, it's so simple even a wuttle bumpkin like you will understand it. You're going to do exactly what I tell you."

# Sisyphean

"How are you feeling?" Peter asked over the regular EKG beeps.

"Good enough to kick your ass at bowling." Norris sat up in the hospital bed and waved away the medical robot that stood over him, scanning his vitals.

"Glad to hear it. Lyon asked me to convey her regards."

"Should I be worried?"

"Probably."

They both chuckled.

"You didn't have to drive through downtown traffic to tell me that. They have phones here too."

"I was going to bring you donuts, but the shop was closed."

"How tragic."

"You took the words right out of my mouth." He took a seat in one of the two chairs at the opposite side of the bright room. "This case with Albright is growing cold in my hands. I asked Kyudo about her former partners, since Albright's an ex-cop. But she's being very hush-hush about the whole thing."

Norris looked away and shrugged. His hands shook as he grabbed a small disposable cup of water, downed it, and crinkled it up to throw in the recycling receptable flush with the white wall. He missed.

"Cut the crap, Norris," he said. "Albright already told me she was my partner."

"What do you want me to say?"

"Is it true?"

"Yes, it's true."

"So, she and I worked together. What else?"

"I didn't know about the extras. I didn't want to know. One day you asked me about engagement rings and stopped mentioning retirement."

He leaned back in the creaking chair. "How long did I work with her?"

"I'd say about a year and a half."

Matilda wasn't lying. *Does she know about my war crimes?* "Matilda and I were engaged?"

"No. I have no idea, but I do remember you asking about it a year ago."

Then Matilda couldn't have known about my war crimes. "What happened to her?"

"I don't know. One day she didn't arrive for her shift. Everyone said she expired in the wastelands. You were obsessed with finding her. One day you told me you found her living in a wooded area far up North, but you wouldn't say more than that. Kyudo caught wind of it and swore out a warrant to upload your mind. You know how she is when she wants something. Or she'll remind you. Lansing couldn't protect you any longer and told you to accept a memory readjustment. Once you forgot about Mattie, Kyudo's warrant was quashed, and the brass ordered me to keep a lid on it."

"Based upon her recent appearances, is Matilda herself, or has Wasserman imprinted her with a new identity?"

Norris shrugged again but didn't look away. "I'm not sure."

***

He threw open his apartment door and unknotted his silk tie while storming into his bedroom. With a tug the buttons of his cotton shirt shrank into dots. The French cuffs were loose enough to preclude morphing the links and he threw the cotton shirt onto his unmade bed.

He shivered when he reached the cheap nylon shirt draped over his living room sofa. *Why is it so cold in here?*

Click-backs from the apartment computer. A radiation warning.

The patio door was ajar. He closed it as the cleaning robot walked over to spray and vacuum.

Someone was here.

At the kitchen table he loaded the security system on a volumetric rendering. No entries on the daily log other than his own a few minutes ago. Someone purged it, though it could be on the backup system.

At the doorway to the utility room, he froze. No memory disks. No equipment other than the holo-emitter. Just a messy bundle of wires. He ran over and slid down by the media cabinet, throwing the doors open and running his hands along the smooth veneer of the empty shelves.

The corner of a page over the cabinet's edge. He reached up and pulled it onto his lap. A note written in round and dignified cursive:

*Dear Pete,*

*By now you know I'm not lying about us or how I feel about you. I have your family and will keep them safe. Drive to the GPS coordinates on the back of this note and we'll talk. Come alone so we can catch up :-)*

*Love,*
*Tildy*

The rings of the phone subroutine startled him, and he banged his elbow against the cabinet.

"Ramsey?" It was Moira.

"Yes?"

"We have analyzed the brainwaves scanned from your partner and reconstructed Albright's memories. It appears she is hiding on a farm up North, near old Sacramento."

"Right.  I can leave right now."

"We do not have the exact coordinates.  When we do, we will be sending in a team of mercenaries.  It is the way corporate prefers to handle it.  Besides, you have done enough already.  I will have your retirement papers expedited and stamped overnight.  Shall we meet at the Hall of Justice in the morning?  Say, eight O'clock?"

"The Hall of Justice?  Why there?"

"Just be on time."

Damnation.  Albright has my family and Delphi has a squad of trigger happy mercs with an expense-account's worth of explosives on standby.  I have to get to these coordinates before they do.

"Ramsey?" Moira asked.

"Perfect."

"I will see you tomorrow.  Good night." Moira hung up.

He stood, walked over to the dining room table, and leaned on the backing of one of the chairs.  "Damnit!"  He toppled the chair.  "I can't do this alone," he muttered.

Kyudo wants the Sandcastle.  If I tell her about these coordinates I can go with backup.  I would have to tell her about my family existing as illegal avatars and there's a fair chance I may not get them back.  But the alternative is no chance.  Besides, Kyudo, and the world, already know enough to bury me.

***

Orange light from the energy web towering over the Theodosian Walls bounced off the Humvee's hood as clicking gears rolled a pair of ship-sized doors open with echoing grinds. A dark rectangle emerged along the open gate. The threshold between the urban lights of civilization and the pitch black of the Duat desert.

Lyon kept still and quiet in the passenger seat. Her auto-blaster leaned against her window. The barrel pointed at the ceiling.

In the minute it took for the doors to open, volumetric advertisements played along the wall's edge. It was a familiar sports celebrity who lifted a glass of water and said, "Vote yes for Water Measure Six."

"Huh," Peter said. "It's that golfer. What's his name again? I can never remember."

Lyon rolled her eyes.

The gate opened with a vibrating thud that rocked the car back and forth. He accelerated onto the multilane highway flanked by flat horizons of sand and brush, and within a minute the settlement's light and sounds had faded into memory, leaving only the white headlights flooding over racing pavement and the humming engine.

Yellow warning text ran along the windshield: *REMAIN ALERT. You are entering hostile territory. REMAIN ALERT.*

Lyon clicked the dashboard transmitter. "Control, this is Epsilon twelve. Ten forty-one." She sat up straighter for a moment, but her shoulders fell, and she frowned with control's acknowledgement.

"Kyudo relieved Castor at twenty-two hundred," he said.

"Oh." Lyon checked her auto-blaster and navigated a volumetric on her wrist, which sent blue light around the dark cabin and along the passenger-side window, turning it into a dark mirror.

"Re-reading the briefing?"

"Mm hmm."

"Take it from the top."

"We follow Albright's coordinates to an Outcast hideout in the wastelands. Satellite scans show one hovercar. We plant a tracker on the hovercar and call in a drone strike once we make a positive ID of Wasserman. We allow him to flee. With any luck, he'll lead us to the Sandcastle, and we can crater it. If we meet Albright, our orders are to take her alive if possible."

"Perfect."

"And because the damn Outcasts could detect a hover-car, we gotta drive eight hours to the ancient ruins of Sacramento."

"Nine hours." He pointed at Navi running on the dashboard. Digits of distance and time counting downwards.

Lights appeared on the horizon which the windshield rendered red hazard lines around. Autonomous-maintenance vehicles and Auto-salvagers merged into a single lane with flashing yellow lights as he passed. One of them peppered with holes, as though it were used for target practice. A clump of dirt spewed from one of the carbonized holes and onto their windshield. "Damnit," he said as the windshield wipers automatically engaged.

"Why are we takin' Albright alive but not Wasserman?" Lyon asked.

"Kyudo didn't tell you?"

"No. What?"

"Nothing. I don't know," he lied.

"Might be hard to nab her without killin' her."

"Those orders came directly from Kyudo."

Lyon stared with bulging eyes. "I know that. I can read."

"Right. So we should do what she says."

"*If possible.*" Lyon tapped on the volumetric orders.

Perfect. Lyon won't follow orders without a reason, and the only reason can't be used to reason with her. "I'll take care of Albright. Okay?"

"Fine." The wireless crackled with static, and Lyon tapped the volume buttons on her wrist-computer. "They're movin' the council to the Zeus platform as a safety precaution."

Clicks from the windshield computer's radiation instruments. Four hundred milli-sieverts.

"Did you pack anti-radiation meds?"

Lyon lifted a waxed canvas bag. "Yeah. Got water and granola bars too."

"You pack any ketchup?"

"No. You're disgustin'." She grimaced but her mouth barely moved as she spoke, as though she were a puppet for an invisible ventriloquist.

After kilometers of desert and ghost towns, the blue triangle-signals of drone patrols dropped off one by one like runners in a marathon. A light storm of yellow dust clumped on the windshield, heavy enough to provoke the wipers into tossing it. The bottom half of the moon split the night, floating in the black sky like a stemless streetlamp.

Silence, seldom interrupted by low static-riddled chatter on the police wireless. Slow sleeping breaths from Lyon. Something restless about her still slumber; she appeared half awake, like a cat ready to pounce. The dash computer continued counting down time and distance at the same rate. Yet the path seemed longer alone.

*** 

When the sun rose, a colossal shape shrouded in heat waves obscured the horizon. The windshield rendered a green box around it and punched up a label. The remains of the Pacific Coalition Battlecruiser *Anubis*. Eroded cracks and apartment-sized bolts rusted on the forsaken relic as it decayed at a glacial pace in the arid wasteland.

The car computer blinked faint yellow text. *You are out of satellite range. Return to the Settlements and run protocol 11 to remain valid.*

"You shoulda woken me up. I told ya we could take turns drivin'." Lyon twitched while yawning. "You drink all the coffee?"

"No." He tapped the thermos on the center console.

Lyon rubbed her eyes and poured steaming coffee into a small metallic mug.

The car-computer beeped and drew lines at the next highway exit sign, whose number was obscured by vulgar graffiti. He slowed and veered to the offramp. Lines of abandoned vehicles littered both edges of the foggy road, most of them stripped down to the frames. Debris crunched under the Humvee's thick tires.

The desert gave way to mist-covered marshlands and a road of forever-fallowed farms. The rendered trail turned to the left and abruptly off road, where old tire marks trailblazed through a narrow gap of dead forest. He turned right at a crumbling farmhouse and after a driveway of dusty gravel, parked in an open garage where their vehicle wouldn't be visible from the road.

They kitted up and twisted suppressors on their weapons while continuing on foot. The muddy trail grew foggy and something squeaked. Not the metallic variety but organic. Behind a rotting tree, a small bird struggling to flap a wing.

Lyon squatted down next to it. "Oh my God, Peter, it's a bird."

"Really?"

Squeaking and fluttering a single wing, it twitched along the ground without gaining flight. "Aw, he's hurt. Can we help him?" She pulled her medical kit and rummaged through it.

"Probably not. We don't have anything to transport him in."

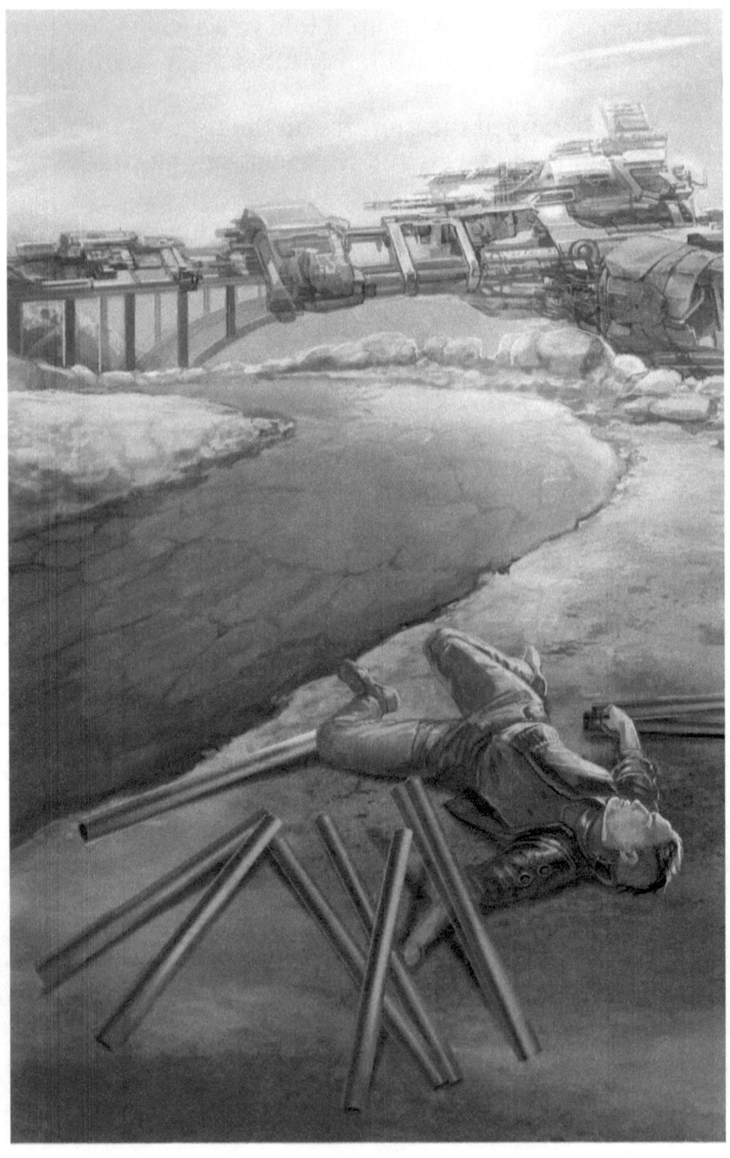

"Maybe he's thirsty." She pulled her canteen and carefully squeezed out a few drops on the ground next to the bird. "We can't just leave him here."

"We should probably just end it's suffering."

"What?" Lyon's cheeks turned red. "You're un-fuckin' believable."

"Calm down."

"Don't tell me to calm down!"

"We can't get it back to the settlements alive. Come on." After a step something crunched under his boot. A plastic card. He lifted it from the mud and wiped it clean with his gloved fingers. An old military ID card. Atlantic Alliance. *LT Nathaniel Brooks.*

"What's that?" Lyon asked.

"An ID card for Nathaniel Brooks."

Lyon scratched her head. "The Delphi guy we were lookin' for a few days ago?"

"Right. He was an Atlantic Alliance officer. The Outcasts used him to lift a nuclear missile from Chiron Airbase."

Lyon quickly stood, her red face contorted with bent eyebrows and a twisted mouth. "You're just tellin' me this now?"

"I thought they detonated it at Blue Jewel Tower. That warhead could have vaporized the whole settlement twelve times over, but I thought they simply failed to arm it properly."

"Why would they nuke the settlements now?"

"Son of a bitch. The stolen Delphi core."

"The only way we coulda predicted the attack."

"Forget Wasserman. We need a visual ID of the stolen warhead."

# 38
# The Grove

*It's showtime, bumpkin* scrolled across her lens functions with some non-standard characters.

For 15 minutes Peter and her whacked and snapped dead brush with stun batons into a narrow path of the dead forest. 100 meters to the left, a sea of mutant ants engulfed five enormous sequoias. Wind scattered sawdust from the canopy to the floor, leaving a pale and diffuse path of sunlight.

A message scrolled again on that hacked lens function. *Bring Peter to this barn. Remain five meters away from the shallow ditch surrounding the field up ahead. And he needs to enter alone, so tell him you're going to check the back.* The function then drew a square around a red barn visible thru a gap in the tree trunks.

She was halfway thru a step and Peter suddenly grabbed her waist from behind, squeezing air out of her. She looked back. He pointed at something in front of her. A thin laser tripwire, knee-high and barely visible even in the shade of the dead forest. "How many times have I told you to load the infiltration subroutine?"

"I have the stupid thing loaded." She rolled her eyes around, checking for a glitch. "It didn't alert me."

"You have to look down every few seconds." He looked down and up at her, like she needed a demonstration. "Read the fudging manual."

"Uh huh. Should we go around it?"

"No. They'll have a perimeter of spider mines. We would need a satellite to find a safe path." He took her auto-blaster and offered a hand to steady her. "Ladies first."

How does he know that? Maybe it's just an alarm and not a bomb. Matilda did just say to stay away from a ditch. If there are spider mines they could be there. "Why would anyone invent something scarier than real spiders?"

"Don't know."

Each leg shook as she lifted herself over the beam, carefully gripping the bottom edges of her long coat. She then slung her auto-blaster's strap over her shoulder before taking Peter's blaster carbine and helping to steady him.

The trees cleared at a steep hill of yellow, crunchy grass with blades tall enough to reach her neck. A pathway cut thru with large vehicle tire marks, like in the woods, that lead up and over the crest of the hill. She shifted her eyes and auto-blaster nervously left and right every few seconds.

Something white far on the right. Beyond a dry riverbed, a country house with a wrap-around porch. White painted siding, three stories high, and it seemed somehow familiar, like she had seen it before in a dream or something. 500 meters away according to lens-Zoom.

To the left the tree line curved outwards like a claw, with the red barn nestled among trees still thick enough to provide shade. On the hilltop between the barn and farmhouse, morning sunlight bounced off the glass of a small greenhouse. Shelves of hydroponic growth chambers bustling with viridian leaves.

Peter squatted down at the edge of the tall grass, lifting his cuffputer and tapping buttons. "Check your anti-radiation meds."

She lowered the butt of her auto-blaster to the dirt and curled an arm around it. "Five hours."

"Perfect."

"Do you know where the hovercar is? The one we're supposed to plant the trackin' device on?"

"No."

"Do you think we should check out the barn?" She pointed.

"Go for it. I'm going to get a closer look at this greenhouse."

"Why don't we both go?"

Peter loaded a holographic map on his wrist. "One of us should secure a satellite connection while the other reconnoiters."

More lens text from Matilda. *Don't let him go to the farmhouse.*

Peter moved low thru the grass and up the hill. Shit. She followed, the tall blades rustling and brushing up against her arms and legs. The hilltop tapered to the right. Six cinder-block outbuildings stood by the farmhouse, topped with roofs like ancient sheds. An old com tower edging thru the forest canopy behind all of them.

"Peter!"

"Shh." Peter lifted a single raised finger to his lips, like it wasn't already obvious and no one else has a brain except for him. He took a knee as wind swept the tall grass. "You can bet your ass that if we don't find that missile right now, there will be no home to go back to."

I can't lose Mary, she thought. Not after so much was lost to protect her. But if the Settlements are nuked, Mom will die. She rotated her sentiment circle to Infiltration, 40%.

Peter pointed at the hilltop. "Cover me from behind that rock."

"What?"

"In case they spot me."

The tall vegetation crackled as Peter ran thru with bent knees.

She pulled her stun pistol and pointed it at Peter's back but hesitated. I should shoot him in the back and drag his stupid ass to that barn. But that would make too much noise, and someone might notice. She lifted her wrist to re-read the sentiment circle setting. Oh fuck. Infiltration induces hesitation so you don't give away your position.

By the time Infiltration beeped off, Peter disappeared over the hill.

It proved annoyingly impossible to not make crunching noises across the field and towards the large round rock several meters from the greenhouse, which bordered a pathway of flattened grass, wide enough for two lanes of ground vehicles. No one visible while peaking both ways. She darted across and once on the other side, crawled thru the remaining tall stalks to the boulder, where she stretched out prone on her stomach.

Eye movements loaded a countdown function. Mary's validation window. 33 hours. If she isn't home by then, she can never return.

The auto-blaster magazine read 120 in red digits. Three extras inside her ammo pack, tied to her belt. She flipped down the small bipod at the end of the barrel and pushed a side button to render a private, holographic scope.

A lens function flashed a warning: *This weapon is not suited for long distance projectile solutions. Change to closed-bolt firing is recommended.* Pulling the bolt back dismissed the warning, but then another popped up: *Closed-bolt automatic firing will cause overheating. Short, controlled bursts are advised.*

Eventually the stupid text went away, and she zoomed thru the dancing grass. The holo-scope blinked at some movement 300 meters away. Peter at the far edge of the grass, where a short barren field of parched Earth separated him from the first cinder block shed-like building thingy or whatever. Scanning up towards the horizon and the right, a dozen outcasts sat and ate at a wooden table by the farmhouse, old rifle-style blasters slung over their shoulders. A collage of stained shirts and disheveled denim.

The cracked earth under her stomach vibrated and the sound of a roaring engine grew from the field behind her. A rusty truck with a tail of dust that waved out the field of grass. Wazzerman stood on the flat bed behind the cabin, flanked by two outcasts.

He offered me a deal earlier, she thought. If I helped him stop Matilda, Mary would be safe. Maybe I can get his attention.

She stood up with her blaster pointed to the sky, but the truck had already raced by, its roaring engine fading with Doppler.

A loud pop from the farmhouse.

Half a dozen outcasts dragged Peter out from behind one of the cinder-block walls. His face bruised and bloodied. Both hands held behind him by a large man. Wazzerman hopped off the truck, slowly strutting over to Peter like he lacked a single concern. With a grin he drew a hand blaster and shot Peter's chest into a small waterfall of blood.

Someone screamed.

I'm the one screaming, she thought.

The outcasts turned, pointed, and opened fire. Lens functions counted 24 targets firing from 261 meters away. Wazzerman yelled something lost in the din. Bullets blew the nearby boulder into pieces. She stood and ran away, taking alternating, diagonal runs across the field.

After 50 meters she slid behind a dense clump of grass and returned fire. One target down, though she missed three others, each running at full speed while firing. A dozen more on their way. 200 meters and closing. High-pitched bullets flying by. One put a hole in a loose flap of her unbuttoned coat. She returned fire until the automatic clicked and blinked 00 in red digits.

She ran for 100 meters and slid behind a felled tree. She reloaded with unsteady hands and opened fire thru a hole in the tree. The auto-blaster seized, white smoke puffing from the barrel. The enemy zeroed in and blasted the trunk into wood chips. Saw dust flew into her eyes, forcing her to blink so many times she accidentally turned off lens functions.

While running for the barn and tree line she managed to blink the functions back on. Running seemed easier.

Reaching into the ammo pack to reload, her fingertips found only an empty canvas pouch. A brief look back revealed shiny magazines gleaming in the grass, too far to go back thru the rain of enemy fire. Hostiles at 100 meters and closing.

But the forest wasn't far. Flashes of burning plasma mowed the grass low around her with every knee-pulsing step. 20 meters until the edge of the grass field, where mechanical twists stirred the stalks by a small ditch. Metallic, robot-looking spiders erupted from the crumbling soil and ran towards her.

Fucking spider mines. She ran laterally away from the explosive robots, drawing them out before circling around them and towards the barn. But they were too fast. Think faster god damnit. She threw the auto-blaster into their path, which one of them latched onto and detonated.

Deafening blasts threw dirt and propelled her over the ditch and after rolling for half a minute she fell in a four-meter ravine, landing on her arm with a yelp. It didn't feel broken but hurt to move. Both ears still rang.

A cloud of smoke spilled over and into the ravine, too thick for any lens function to see thru. After a few seconds of coughing a silhouette appeared, which dragged her by the shoulders out of the dark cloud, to the front of the red barn.

Matilda. Both of her light eyes were blank, robot-like. Her face was red, not like angry but with sweat and she was panting like she was just running. Her dark hair tied back, in faded jeans and a clean white tank top. Between breaths she said, "Jesus christ bumpkin, you had one job, and you just couldn't do it. Do I have to do all of this myself?" She pulled Joan upright and gently sat her against the trunk of a nearby tree. "Next time, don't let Pete die."

Before Joan could respond, Matilda pulled a small trigger from a pocket, like the one she had at the school earlier. "Don't let go, bumpkin. I need you to remember."

Intertwining both of their fingers into a grip around it, she clicked the red button, and the world fell away, swallowed by a dark void.

# 39
## Malfosse

When the sun came up, he passed an old highway sign, green with a light border, that labelled the remaining distance to Sacramento in white. Only ten kilometers. The rest of the sign, including the dozen dotted rings of the Settlements of Humanity, were defaced by spray-painted graffiti and foul language: *Fuck Yourself Settlers*.

Lyon stirred and woke. "Peter?" she asked in a surprised tone. Her face was pure white, even paler than normal.

"Good morning. Coffee?" He tapped the Thermus wedged into the console cup holder.

***

On the way to the grove, they stopped briefly to observe a dying bird. Lyon picked something off the ground.

"What's that?" he asked.

"Nothin'." Lyon pointed out a laser trip wire between two trees before subroutines caught it. She crossed over it before he could offer to help steady her, lifting her carbine over her shoulders like a marine. An unusual weapon choice for her. Normally she favors automatics.

At the edge of a sloped field of tall wheat they each took a knee.

"Looks like they're sittin' down for chow." Lyon pointed at an outdoor table packed with chewing Outcasts. Two hundred meters away.

"We should take a closer look while they're busy."

"What about that barn?" Lyon nodded upwards to the far-left edge of the field, where a red barn stood fortified by trees at the edge of the forest. "We can hide there. One of us can watch for Wasserman."

"While the other contacts Kyudo's Kidō Butai." He took a step and Lyon forcefully pulled him away from a shallow ditch that encircled most of the field.

"Spider mines."

The two large barn doors were bright red with white frames.  Not freshly painted but it had certainly been done up sometime after the war and as he and Lyon pulled open the heavy wood entrance it didn't produce a creak louder than the sound of an approaching engine.

"There's a truck comin' up the road," Lyon said.  "I'm gonna check it out."

"Right."  Within the dark interior the sound of the truck fell away as the large doors creaked to a thudding close, flattening a rectangle of yellow light on the floor of hay-covered dirt.  It smelled like a barn, or at least as foul as he could remember.  Insufficient light entered through cracks in the boarded walls, though the Cat-Eyes routine adjusted the lighting. Cobwebs clung to the high ceiling.

Rows of empty stalls along each wall for about three-fourths the length, where the bare floor changed to a maze of tied-hay-bricks and barrels stacked under a loft.  A wood ladder led to the upper floor. Too high to tell if it was empty.

He aimed his automatic blaster while checking each stall.  At the end, a wooden chair with rope dangled over the back.  Two figure-eight knots, as though it were used to tie up someone.  The chair smelled remarkably pleasant compared to the rest of the barn. Lavender.

Something fell over.  A large barrel, which rolled halfway towards him.  A rustling among the tied blocks of hay.  He scanned the random stacks with the automatic while taking slow backward steps to the front door.  It didn't open.  Throwing his weight into it only hurt his shoulder.  He rapped his knuckles against it.  "Lyon!"

He turned around at the sound of hydraulics.

The stacked blocks of hay toppled, and the wooden ladder fell over as a tall robot emerged.  An old war robot with a clunking engine.  Tank treads for legs.  Thick arms with weapons at the end and a round head with two glowing-red eyes resting on a coil of wisps.

It fired something that tapped the door next to him. A stun prong. More prongs fired with high-pitched pops. He ran and dove into the nearest stall. The sound of moving treads moving closer. Without peeking he pointed the automatic in the direction of the noise and fired a short burst. Only metallic ricochets and thuds.

The robot turned towards him, both metallic arms spinning up, preparing to fire. He ran across the barn. A storm of stun rounds tapped the wood pillars and walls into splinters. He dove into a farther stall, landing on both aching elbows.

The large void under the loft, where the robot was hiding, might have a way out. He made a run for it, stopping and falling on his back halfway there when a second robot emerged. Its arms also spun up stun weaponry, but only clicks echoed over its loud engine. Jammed.

The robot behind him turned to fire, forcing him to roll out of the way and onto his feet with a twisted ankle. He dropped the automatic and ran with a limp for a few steps, fast enough to slide under the jammed robot's pinching claws. Pulling himself up by the bot's moving treads and staggering through the maze of farm cargo.

No doorway. No window. No way out.

He took several steps backward while pulling his pistol and thumbing down on the charging button. Five seconds and the barrel glowed red and shook. Covering his face with his free arm, he pulled the trigger.

Burning splinters and smoke. And a hole large enough for him to jump through. At a full run he dove, banging his right knee while flipping out the rest of the way. "Ow." Gripping a pulled muscle on his side, he limped to one of the thicker nearby trees and leaned his back against it.

There was a commotion of some kind from the direction of the farmhouse. Loud voices that could be heard but not deciphered. Limping steps carried him around the barn, where the engines of the war robots still hummed within. A sudden crack of thunder from the sky.

A pre-war shuttle quickly descended from high altitude. It slowed to a hover and landed in the field across from the greenhouse, a circle of tall grass forced flat by loud waves of thrust.

The loading ramp lowered and two men with fusil-style blasters prodded a cuffed Lyon onboard, followed by Wasserman.

I could try to stop them. He aimed at Wasserman and his wrist-computer clicked-back. The activated tracker signal on Lyon's person. They're probably taking her to the Sandcastle.

As he lowered his weapon the shuttle loudly accelerated into the sky, quickly fading from sight and sound.

He dialed stims on his wrist-computer until his knee stopped aching and he could do something between running and wobbling through the forest of cracking twigs. After a kilometer of huffing, he found refuge against the only thick tree not coated in mutant termites. Lifting his right pant leg, he found no bleeding from his knee but a purple bruise, which he lightly touched. "I'm too old for this crap."

His wrist-computer clicked-back. A satellite connection. He called Kyudo.

***

When Peter exited the triage tent the vacant and abandoned parking lot of uneven asphalt had transformed into a crowded staging area for Kyudo's Kidō Butai, with a dozen carrier ships arranged in a circle, deploying pods of assault robots and armored vehicles. Weapons were handed out from the back of air and ground vehicles to lines of officers in assault armor, who then arranged themselves into columns.

The formations quickly cleared the center of the ring as an oval shadow grew. Kyudo's command ship, a long dirigible gleaming in the midday sun, quietly landed with blurring turbines operating in stealth mode. A ramp quickly lowered and Kyudo walked a few steps from the top, remaining visible to the crowd. Everyone quickly turned towards her in silence as she tapped two wrapped fingers against her wrist, and each officer loaded a small volumetric display on their wrist-computers.

"Fellow officers," Kyudo said on the wireless, instead of shouting or using a loudspeaker. "We have at long last located the Sandcastle, the formidable fortress of the Outcast rebellion. Today, we will witness its destruction." A noticeable cheer consumed the crowd until she lifted a hand. The volumetric streams transitioned into a live feed of the Zeus weapon platform firing a brilliant blast of anti-matter at a target several hundred kilometers away, leaving a city-sized crater. The ground under his feet vibrated. "The Zeus platform has destroyed the Outcast's grove, and now it will obliterate the Sandcastle." This time, clapping instead of cheering. "The eyes of humanity are upon you. Do not fail."

An ocular icon blinked with color-coded group assignments spread across the crowd. An approaching officer lit up gold for a split second. Eva Diaz. Her Vesta sniper rifle aimed into the air, the stock resting on the inside of her elbow.

"Better get your gear Ramsey." Diaz checked a large machine-pistol on her belt.

He ran back to his Humvee, quickly strapping on armor, a helmet, a carbine and all the ammunition he could carry.

"All team leaders remain in wireless contact at all times," an officer said on the wireless.

His group assignment and causeway lit up as a gold arrowed path on a subroutine with a line of police indicators. He jogged to catch up, taking what looked like a shortcut across an old road and a field of tall weeds to catch up. Though it ended up taking him longer to reach the column, which was now marching along a path through a wooded hill with thumping boots and clanking gear.

"You okay Peter?" Diaz asked.

"Yeap," he said between rapid breaths.

"Cut the chatter. Noise and infrared discipline," someone said on the wireless.

They pressed on up the steepening hill for a few kilometers. His boots pinched his ankles with each increasingly heavy step and sweat seeped from his neck and underarms as the unyielding sun dumped heat. Subroutines marked a line of red triangles under the ground with flashing exclamation points. Spider mines. The column slowed to move in a single file through a narrow gap in the perimeter.

The rallying point blinked just short of a ridgeline of earth that was not quite as tall as a man but enough cover to duck behind. Above it, a plateau, a long field a kilometer in depth, ended by more dead trees. They barely concealed a line of large rocks. Thin horizontal lines across all of them. Using zoom, the lines grew into gun emplacements. Bunkers cut into the rocks. Looking up, line after line of them dug into the rocky hillside, until towers of worn and weathered stone stacked to an unending horizon.

The Sandcastle.

Under the ridge police indicators spread into a thin line in both directions, a mix of officers and robots, with Diaz on his immediate left. The map on his wrist-computer indicated a multi-kilometer circle. Columns of police bots arranged every few hundred meters like outward facing spokes.

"All units hold position and standby," Kyudo said.  Her cool voice subtly shook over the wireless.

Diaz checked her ammo and then loaded a volumetric on her wrist-computer.  A three-dimensional scan of bunkers spun around.  "No organic readings on infrared.  They must have spotted us."  Diaz lowered herself behind the ridgeline until only her head was peeking over the top.

"All units stand ready," Kyudo said.

Sonic booms cracked the sky.  Chatter ceased, except Officer Xiang Jun a few meters away, speaking into his wrist.  A routine identified him as the fire support officer.

The pitch and sound of turbines grew as aircraft blurred overhead, their afterburners remaining as blinking spots for a few seconds.  Enemy auto-cannons rose from the hillside bunkers, turning and firing at the horizon.  Bright-orange tracers that snapped several hovercars in half and damaged a bomber's armored wing.  Crashing smoke trails and screams on the wireless.

The barrage of bombs and rockets cracked the hillside into a ceaseless line of forever fire splashing over split rocks. An inferno that reached high enough to curve back in the sky above them.  Wind carried heat across his face.

He sneered and turned back towards the waves of fire. Gaps grew as it burned out.  Something whizzed by.  A slug. Several more passed by, taking clumps of the ridgeline with them.  "They're shooting at us."

"Oh really?"  Diaz's rifle boomed as a wave of Outcasts ran through the flames, firing wildly.

"Fire.  Fire at will," someone said on the wireless.

"Jun, get us a strafing run," someone said.

Blasted dirt sprayed his gloves and helmet visor as he lined up the scope and dropped an outcast three hundred meters away. The tactical subroutine stopped counting and illuminating targets after four hundred and simply listed *many.*

Incoming charged shots formed craters and vaporized officers. Cries filled the wireless for medics. A wisp preceded an explosion. The left flank two hundred meters to their left evaporated. Martian mercenaries and Venusian Janissaries flew over with jetpacks to fill the gap. Mayfleet mowed hundreds of enemies with her machine-blaster.

The firing finally stopped, but both ears still shook as smoke drifted over the line from sweltering barrels with the smell of Sulphur. Silence finally fell. Twenty meters down the line an officer lit a cigarillo against Mayfleet's red-with-heat machine-blaster.

"Jun is down!" Diaz strapped her rifle over a shoulder and ran over with a medical kit.

He followed, stopping the moment she turned Xiang Jun over. A waterfall of blood gushing from the rookie's neck. Eva looked up, shaking her head.

Mayfleet abandoned her weapon and ran over, tripping and sliding next to Xiang Jun. "Jun."

"He'll be alright. The robots will fix him up," he lied.

He gestured for one of the medical robots a hundred meters behind the front lines, though by the time he turned back the poor kid had already died in his own red sea. Mayfleet continued to hold his limp hand for a good half minute, drowning in her tears until the medical robot arrived and pried her hands away to carry away the carcass.

"Kýrie eléison." Diaz made the sign of the Christian cross.

"Ramsey, coordinate indirect fire," Kyudo said as they returned to their firing positions.

"Ma'am?" he asked.

Kyudo didn't say anything else. The indirect fire subroutine loaded on his oculars and wouldn't blink away. The last job I'd ever want.

"Do you think there's many of them left? Maybe that was all of them?" he asked Eva.

A downpour of enemy slugs flew from the remaining rows of bunkers.

"I think there's at least one!" Officer Boothe said.

Another organic wave of outcasts rushed over several hundred meters of already cratered and smoldered ground with nothing to lose.

He navigated the subroutine options, adjust fire, ocular polar, and quickly drew a line across gold teams' front, a kilometer-long target marker five hundred meters in front of him. The routine clicked-back as it morphed the straight line into one with countless curves to maximize enemy deaths. Transparent bombs rendered where the outlines of the advancing enemy would be in fifteen seconds, given their current and predicted running pace. Two dozen drones strafed with machine-blasters. Hovercars and Terra bombers joined in, dropping bombs with perfect precision, an exact match of the routines' rendering.

Screams from engulfed enemies as they rolled onto the dry grass, spreading fire. Half the organic wave continued. He marked another line at four hundred meters. A squadron of VEN-SEC Star Cutters. Rockets flew from their angled wings, creating an incinerating trail along the front of quickly advancing enemy.

Hundreds of them screamed, falling over, and rolling in the flames. One even managed to sit up and throw off most of his burning clothes, except a pant leg that stubbornly clung to an ankle.

But hundreds continued the stampede, giving a chilling rebel yell in brainwashed unison. Their faces now visible without the zoom routine. The sea of dirty exiles opened a hailstorm of plasma at the police line with blasts brighter than the sun.

The rhythm of Eva's nearby sniper rifle changed from a chill bass to a frenzied guitar solo.

Three hundred meters.  The routine clicked-back with a *DANGER CLOSE* warning.  Enemy slugs pelted the ground in front of him.  Mayfleet's machine blaster turned silent as a slug blasted her head off.  Eva lowered her head under the ridgeline to reload.

MAR-SEC God of War attack ships from Aries Squadron split the sky, moving so fast their hulls burned as though they were starships re-entering the atmosphere.  Their wide wings puffed trails of smoke with car-sized missiles and bombs.  Even at a high altitude their screaming engines pushed trails of brush and grass flat against the trembling ground.

"Peter, that's too close!" Eva screamed.

"Abort mission!" He screamed into his transmitter while trying to use eye movements to call off the bombing run.  He was too—

"Too late."  Eva jumped at him, knocking him over and they rolled down the ridgeline, cursing as twigs broke under their armor, finally stopping as they struck a small tree with a small cloud of dust.  "Are you okay?"  Explosions and flames erupted over the edge like several of Dante's circles combined.  Burning bodies fell over the edge, one of which rolled down the hillside and landed on Eva's leg.  She quickly kicked the smoking bones off, lifting a cloud of dust.  A sub-routine rang with a KIA chime over the skeleton.

Officer Boothe.

"Oh no."  He stood and looked over the remains.  Boothe was hardly more than a teenager, reduced to charred bones.  The constable indicator by her name faded into a time of death: *14:22*.

"Peter," Eva whispered, somehow audible over the un-ending rattles of battle.

"I promised I would never do this again."  Something wet on his eyes and face.

"Peter," Eva said again. Her hand was interlocked with his now, though he didn't see her take any steps. "You are keeping more of us alive."

"A minute ago, she was fine," he said. Eva pinched his forearm. "Ouch."

"Snap out of it handsome. We can feel guilty if we live that long." Without asking she twisted his emotion dial to some setting, turned him by the shoulders, and shoved him one step up the hillside.

At the ridgetop, the field had turned into a burning plain of corpses and craters. A memory pill could sweep away this sight, and the accompanying stench of death. Two more waves of the enemy charged through gaps in the walls of fire.

He tapped and dragged a line at 200 meters. Star Cutters and Gods of War on parallel flight paths trimmed the plateau into something less level by the second. Another line at 100. The outcasts screamed through the immolation until finally the remainder turned, though their brief dream of a retreat was quickly extinguished by fire.

Turrets from the higher walls of the Sandcastle locked onto the ground support squadrons. Thick tracer rounds sprayed the sky and cracked the wings of a God of War. The elephant-sized ship spun out in random directions, fire coming from more than just its thrusters. The ship cut the air in a whirr, engines gasping for air in agony with increasing volume and pitch. More ground fire added insult to injury.

A line of shadow moved over the front, and he looked up. The Zeus weapon platform slowly encroaching the sun. The shade ended on the horizon by a blue signal. Lyon. This must be why Delphi predicted she'll die. Kyudo wanted me to keep her alive just long enough to die as a sacrificial pawn. Collateral damage.

Mayday signals over the wireless. A smoking aircraft tipped and rolled towards the police line, and him.

"Peter," Eva said.  "Look out!"

# The Sandcastle

Bright florescent lights flickered and buzzed on a concrete ceiling. Joan couldn't move her hands. She was in a reclined examination chair, like a robo-dentist office. Both hands tied to the arm rests. Her coat was missing, and her blouse removed. Just her sleeveless undershirt. Something tied to one of her biceps, maybe a sensor. Another attached to her forehead, though the wire was off to the side, brushing an ear when she turned her head.

"Officer Lyon," Wazzerman said, but he couldn't be seen. "I've always wondered, are you related to that golfer? What's his name?"

She fought the restraints in vain, groaning. "Forest Lyon."

"Yes, I believe that's the one." Wazzerman stood over her, eclipsing the overhead lights with an amused grin.

"Oh yeah. He's my wealthy uncle and he'll give you a year's supply of food if you release me."

His smile widened. "Indeed?" Wazz stroked his chin. "Whatever were you doing at that farm of mine?"

"Albright kidnapped my sister. She's been taken hostage."

Wazz paced, occasionally looking over. "And you didn't think to inform me of this sooner? Perhaps you forgot our agreement?"

"No. I remembered. You want Matilda's anchor point. She reset time or somethin'."

Wazz lifted a hand. "I know. We uploaded your mind and found what we needed." He turned towards someone behind him. "Would you get that gift for our guest?"

"You were lookin' inside my head?" She tried looking up or finding a reflection among the room's electronic equipment.

He rechecked the sensor on her forehead and then removed examination gloves with a smacking sound. "Don't concern yourself, I assure you it's a harmless process." Wazz slid over a rattling stool and sat next to her to remove her sentiment circle. He lifted it, rotating it between his thumb and finger. "You shan't rely on this indefinitely. Every technology has its limitations." He dropped it on a nearby table and it rolled like one of them old coins, wiggling flat next to my cuffputer and stim-pack.

My memories played on a pop-up hologram. Quick images on fast-forward. A strange sensation from my head, like someone had stuck a straw in there and was sucking. "My nose feels funny."

"Well, it's still a beautiful nose."

The replaying memories moved into the sheltering years, and I turned my head away, closing my eyes.

"I have seen the memories of everyone on this planet. Things you wouldn't believe," Wazz said. "What other people do is a reflection of their character and not yours." Footsteps and a clank. "Thank you." He must be talking to someone else.

There was a beep, and I opened my eyes, glimpsing from a corner that the memories were no longer playing. Wazz was bent over a brain scan, adjusting the zoom with both hands. "Is that my brain?"

He looked over. "Yes." He stood up straight, lifted a memory disc from a nearby metal table, and returned to the nearby stool. "Do you see the regions I've marked in red?" The image of my brain rotated slowly. Mostly pink but a few blinking areas of red. I nodded at him. "That's trauma." Lifting the memory disc, he tapped it with a fingernail. "And this is your original mind. The way you were before Delphi destroyed our timeline to enrich themselves."

I looked away and swallowed. Only air went down but it was like an invisible cotton ball was lodged halfway. "I doubt I'd be any different."

"Isn't this what you want for your mother? For her to turn back into the person she should be?"

"I ain't the one that needs to change."

"You are much changed, though not altogether better for it. A different past can make for a different future."

"And how long would the pre-war me survive here. In this world?"

"The person you're becoming might not survive long either."

"I need to remember who's dangerous, and who isn't."

Wazz took a deep breath. "You could walk out of here without a care in the world." He looked down for a few seconds. "The Settlements may not consider you human afterwards, but wouldn't that be a better life?"

I scoffed. "Out here in the wastelands?"

Wazz grinned but his eyes remained somber. "The cost of freedom."

"I'd never see my mom or sister again. That might happen anyway, but..."

"Pity. If only the world could hear you sing." He placed the disc in a canvas satchel, which he dropped onto my cuffed hands. I looked up at him with raised eyebrows. "You can always change your mind later."

Something on Wazz's forearm. "Do you have a tattoo?"

"Indeed, I do." He rolled up his sleeve. A man carrying a jar or vase of some kind. A bit like the Hapi water company logo but different. The water jar had knotted curves arranged like a triangle. Like the logo of the gym Mary works at.

"What is that?"

"A Celtic Trinity Knot." He moved it closer. "And it reminds me every day of someone that once loved me. And knew me."

I ran my fingertips over the disc's plastic enclosure and stared at the small light glowing within, like it held a human soul. If there is such a thing. "What about my mom?"

Wazz wrapped his hands around the back of his head and leaned away. Behind him, an old Atlantic Alliance transmitter on an equipment rack. "One of my associates will furnish you with that in due course."

"Sir, settlers have reached our perimeter," someone in the hallway said.

"Damnation. Do remain here Miss Lyon." Wazz stood quickly, knocking over the stool and storming out of the room.

***

It took 10 minutes of twisting myself in the chair until I could chew thru the fiber-ties around my wrist and untie the other. The room occasionally shook violently, pushing crumbling handfuls of dust from the ceiling to the floor.

Once I was free, I re-attached my sentiment circle, slung the canvas bag Wazz had given me over a shoulder, and stuck my head out of the room's only exit.

An unguarded hallway of concrete walls lit by suspended lights that shook with the vibration of distant blasts. Screams and yelling but it was at least a few halls away.

She followed the noise to an intersection of hallways, where a few support columns provided hiding spots in the dim lighting. Two large metal doors straight ahead, and a few rooms on each side. A quick peek to the right. The tunnel had collapsed after about 40 meters or so. The left hallway. Dark, with occasional flashes matching the sound of blaster fire.

Starting with careful footsteps she quickly accelerated. There's enough noise from the fighting to conceal footsteps. Hastened footsteps even. Maybe jogging? Nah.

At 50 meters it became obvious that the two large doors had a thumb-scanner. Bio-locked. On the left and right, small storage rooms. The doors left open. On the left a black and white sign next to a single large door. *Memory Bank.* So, this is it. Finally. Her lifted hand now seconds away from touching the latch.

Raised voices came from the opposite end of the hall. A large door, a mirror of the one leading to the memory bank, though it was halfway open. She bent her knees and took careful steps, then slowly tilted her head until one eye could see past the edge of the door.

Five outcasts in white jumpsuits, scurrying around arrangements of flat computers. Nearly pitch-black inside, until a computer beeped with a flash that formed into a hologram of the Zeus weapon platform. A dozen red squares formed around it, shrinking down into locking coordinates on its underside. Someone zoomed out until the planet dominated the moving image, reducing the platform to a satellite. Yellow lines connected points on the surface to the Zeus platform.

"Chris, check the connection to the targeting computer," someone said.

They're targeting Zeus. But with what?

Footsteps approached, and she quickly retreated 10 meters to one of the storage rooms, staying low and rushing to the end to hide behind shelves. Colder in here. Cold air behind her. A broken window with a unique view.

Descending hillsides of smashed and burning bunkers. Plumes of smoke robbing half the sky. Cannon fire sprayed out from the outcasts still fighting, some of it aimed at police ground forces but mostly at aircraft zooming by.

The satellite icon lit up on a lens function with static that turned into pandemonium on the police wireless. Somehow, she got auto-moved into a different channel with a beep.

Someone spoke but it was mostly interference with scrambled half words.

"Jo—repor—stat—con. Say ag—" It sounded like Troy.

"Troy? Is that you?" she whispered.

"Joan, can you hear me?" Troy asked.

"10-2."

"Kyudo is positioning the Zeus weapon platform to destroy the Sandcastle. She's ordered it to fire the moment it's reloaded. Janissaries are covering the retreat. You have to get out of there. Now!"

"Troy, Wazzerman is targetin'—" Both eyes twitched and gave her double vision as she stumbled into the nearby wall. A beep and warning message from her sentiment circle: *EMOTIONAL MODIFICATION FAILURE. PSYCHOSIS IMMINENT. DISENGAGE DEVICE IMMEDIATELY.*

I ought to warn Troy about Wazzerman targeting the weapons platform, she thought. But if I do, Kyudo will target that missile control room with airstrikes. And the memory bank. And me too if I don't get out of the way fast enough. Then Mom will be gone forever. But there's 10,000 people on that platform. Of course, one of them is that bastard Warner.

Her annoying sentiment circle beeped another warning message.

"Shut up you stupid thing." She smashed her cuffputer against the wall.

"Joan, say again?" Troy asked. He dispatched a remote lens function with a countdown.

*11 minutes, 22 seconds.*

"It's five kilometers for you to reach the minimum safe distance," Troy continued. "You have to get to one of the mercenary ships. Quickly. Joan, please."

She pressed and held the stim button on her cuffputer until it beeped with a warning: *You have exceeded the stimulant safety limit.*

***

*9 minutes, 51 seconds.*

The memory bank was a single, massive circular room, arranged like a pit, where each descending floor was a smaller ring. Countless memory discs arranged in a maze of shelves, Jesus there must be millions of them. A library of every human mind. Five stairways led to a datacore at the room's center, the lowest level. It was large, the size of a re-actor.

Bright sunlight from the ceiling. A glass dome with the blue sky above, interrupted by white clouds drifting by. And aircraft zooming past. Orange groundfire chasing each of them, sometimes successfully.

She scurried down the stairs, tripping and falling down several as the floor shook with the sound of an explosion close enough to hear but not see.

At the tall datacore was a chair and a terminal. An old one like in those hacker holo-films, a black background and green text you had to type.

How the hell does this thing work? Hmm. She typed *help* and pressed enter. Several pages of text zoomed by, probably too fast for even a robot to read. "Damnit."

*8 minutes, 41 seconds.*

She sat down and placed the canvas satchel on the floor, where it twisted open enough that her own memory disc was visible inside. Wait a minute. Someone was just here, getting that one.

Swiping led upwards on the terminal and to commands executed earlier. *Memlib -find "Lyon, Joan"*

That should be easy enough to edit. *Memlib -find "Lyon, Penelope"*. Enter. The terminal spewed digital gibberish but ended with something perfect:

*1 Record(s) found with criteria:*
*Lyon, Penelope*
*DOB: June 26, 2116*
*Disc location: floor 5, section 1.*

It's back near the top floor. Figures. She grabbed the satchel and ran up the stairs two at a time. A few more shocks from nearby explosions, she gripped the railing and didn't stumble this time. The shelves were labelled, and the disc was beeping with a blinking blue light. After gently pulling it from the row and turning the plastic encasement towards the light, she read the label. *Penelope Lyon.*

Mom. Time to take you home.

Another vibration on the floor. Though this time it didn't stop. No sound from an explosion, but a steady rumbling. A line of shadow moved over her hand, then Mom's name on the disc and the floor of the narrow aisle. She looked up.

The Zeus weapon platform slowly eclipsed the afternoon sun. A glow from its center.

*7 minutes, 31 seconds.*

She zipped the messenger bag up and clicked the transmitter on her cuffputer. "Troy." Static. "Troy?" The satellite icon changed to a flashing one with a red crossed circle. She ran for the door with loud clops on the floor. No time left for sneaking around. Throwing the door open, she froze. Three outcasts, all armed.

"A settler!"

"Blast her!"

With all of her body weight she slammed the door shut and pressed a button on that latch that hopefully locked it, then ran around the ringed floor toward the other exit. Voices behind her. A blast flew by, bursting half a nearby aisle of discs into shattering bits of plastic. Increasing her pace, the canvas satchel banging against a thigh with each rapid stride. A sign along the wall pointed an arrow in the direction she was running. *Hangar.*

At the far metallic door, bullets struck the surface around her as she pulled the latch and jumped thru the half-open threshold.

*6 minutes, 49 seconds*. (*Estimated)*

Yet another dark hallway with a bunch of open doorways on each side, all of them strobing with flashes and the rattle of automatic fire. At a full run she reached a 90-degree turn at the end, followed by another that was bright and open. The tunnel had collapsed, blown open by an explosion or something. She ran over the pile of concrete rubble and back into the dungeon.

Where she slipped and fell. Something sticky on her arm. Blood and burn marks covered the walls. The stench of death near and far, like what shelters used to smell like. A skeleton next to her with a blaster pistol in its bony grip. *I landed in someone's liquefied remains,* she thought. Dislodging the weapon was gross and it only had 12 rounds. But a nearby bandoleer held a single grenade. Worth dirty hands.

Back on her feet one of her boots now made a sticky noise with each running step. Her calves burned first. Then her abs before both thighs joined the pain party. At her top speed she slipped and skidded at the next corner into the concrete wall, then against the large doors marked *Hangar.*

*5 minutes, 31 seconds*. (*Estimated)*

She pulled one of the thick doors open a quarter of the way and peered inside. A dozen aircraft with refueling hoses attached. Circles of light around each of them from large openings in the ceiling. A dozen outcasts in oil-stained jumpsuits. One of which looked over and pointed, screaming something to the others while pulling a weapon.

Grabbing the grenade, she pulled the pin and tossed it at him. It bounced and made a thudding noise, like it landed against a barrel. Fuel barrels. "Oh shit."

She closed the door and ran around the corner. The hallway shook, the dim overhead lights flickered as dust poured from the cracking ceiling. The doors behind her crashed with a heavy clank. An alarm klaxon of some kind sounded farther away than it probably was. Kill chimes in both ears. The Kill-Count app works offline?

Swallowing, she choked on dirty grey fumes. Sweaty fingers turned her sentiment circle to Suicidal-Assault, 100%. A strange tickle took the back of her head, and a cloud of smoke engulfed the hangar. The explosion had destroyed half the aircraft and baked a fiery, blood-red bone cake. A figure emerged. She lifted her blaster. Flames shined on the polished weapon like a mirror as she pulled the trigger.

Another figure emerged, not stumbling but running and jumping at her, knocking both of them to the hot floor. The blaster flew off in some direction.

*4 minutes, 12 seconds*. (*Estimated)*

Back on her feet, she saw her attacker thru the smoke. A tall guy who was well built. She attempted to roundhouse him into a wall of fire. Blocked. She fell back and stumbled, but regained balance. A one-two from him sent her into a nearby wall, and he choked her from behind. Her legs used the wall like a Mobius strip and they both landed on the floor. She rolled off him, but not for long. His vice-like grip returned and she landed on her back.

A wrench nearby. She grabbed it to hit him but dropped it with a shriek. Red hot.

He started to choke her, and she twisted her head, but it didn't end the suffocation. Landing punches and kicks against Mr. Muscles proved ineffective. I'm dead, she thought. My dial is too high to live my own death. It's all going to turn black.

Something in the corner of her eye. The satchel had landed in one of the fires of burning fuel. Oh no. Her hands grew numb as something dug into her back. A familiar shape and weight. A blaster.

She bit thru the flesh behind her attacker's thumb, but his grip didn't let up while she kicked him in the crotch and twisted her body to reach the blaster. She lifted it and fired but only grazed his right ear. The dirty man's metallic blood dripped into her mouth and she nearly coughed.

Her bite tightened. Fleshy gristle passed between her teeth like floss as the man struggled to break free from her enamel. His other hand moved to the blaster. Her fingers turned white and red around the blaster grip.

Bending her wrists until they cracked well past the normal range of motion, she managed to line up a shot and fired. A skull graze in a red line thru his hair. Enough to knock him back. She emptied the blaster into his chest while spitting blood with a scream.

The outcast's blasted brains landed in fire with a sizzle. She found herself unexpectedly weeping as she brushed his remains off her. A kill-chime rang far in her ears. The hardest $30 she'd ever earned.

She leapt thru a knee-high wall of fire with a yelp, picked up the charred canvas satchel, and ran for the nearest intact hovercar.

*2 minutes, 14 seconds*. (*Estimated)*

*IGNITION SEQUENCE FAILURE* screeched in red letters on the hovercar's console. She leapt and ran to the next aircraft. A police hovercar flew into the hangar and landed a few meters away. The passenger door flew open. That damned Peter.

"Get in!" he said.

# 41
# Petrichor

The moment the Zeus weapon platform eclipsed the sun with a parallel horizon, a flash as bright as a nuke engulfed it with the sound of a falling anvil and a shockwave shook the hovercar.

"What happened?" Lyon asked.

"Something hit Zeus!" someone said on the panicking wireless.

The blue sky turned bright red as building-sized bolts cracked and burned into meteorites. Re-entry flames engulfed the city-sized fragments of the platform as they sheered and cracked away from each other.

Dashboard klaxons.

"Collision alert!" Lyon said. The volumetric of the splitting platform in front of her grew brighter as shadow grew from above.

"How long?"

"188 kilometers closin' at eight kilometers per second!"

A car-sized chunk of flaming metal flew by a few meters from the driver side window. "The time damnit!"

"20 seconds!"

He looked up. A flaming section of the destroyed platform grew exponentially larger. He threw the throttle forward and thumbed the red afterburner button.

"We gotta go faster," Lyon said.

"We're at max speed."

"It ain't enough it's gonna crush us."

He angled the hovercar away from the falling pie slice. "Prep ejection sequence."

"Um."

"All that time in the simulator and you don't know how to eject?"

"You don't DIE in the simulator!" Lyon said while gesturing wildly with her hands.

The line of shadow grew further away. "Cut the ventral thrusters." He pushed the pitch control forward into a near vertical dive more stomach-lifting than a rollercoaster.

"Are you crazy?"

"Bet your ass." He pulled the stick back as far as it would go yet the burnt ground only grew closer.

"We're too fast to pull up!"

"Re-engage all thrusters."

The horizon came into view no sooner than the sound of felled trees scraping the bottom of the hovercar. Straight ahead, one of the Sandcastle's towers tilted over. He angled the car diagonally between the ground and falling tower.

"The computer says this is bad idea," Lyon said.

"Then click on autopilot."

"Where's eject? Eject, eject." Lyon hastily searched dashboard buttons. Another dashboard klaxon. Instruments rapidly flashed. "Afterburners are redlinin'!"

"Override the auto-shutdown."

He threaded the narrowing gap between the ground and the falling tower a second before it struck the ground with an echoing thump of bricks and dust.

Lyon clicked a button and the afterburners automatically shut down. The crashing Zeus weapon platform chunks met the crumbling Sandcastle in the rearview mirror. "Can we never do that again?"

"Don't bet your ass."

The carnage in the rearview mirror faded and a windshield routine counted down kilometers to home.

"I know where Matilda is," Lyon said. "She has some stolen Delphi equipment."

"She wasn't at the Sandcastle?"

"Nope."

"How do you know?"

"Wazzerman was trackin' her, and I saw the coordinates."

Lyon could be a brainwashed mole. But if Albright is still around, my family could still be safe. Why didn't Albright show up at the Grove like she said? There was no sign of her in the barn or the farmhouse after the outcasts fled. "What did he want with you?"

"Wazzerman suspected a traitor in his ranks but didn't know who."

"And you told him about Albright?"

"He didn't give me multiple choices."

"Don't sweat it. He's dead now."

"Stone fuckin'."

The distance to the settlement continued counting down, several hundred kilometers with rapidly falling decimals.

"Attention all units," a voice said on the wireless. "We have confirmation of the destruction of the Sandcastle. No known outcast survivors. The Zeus Orbital Platform has also been confirmed as destroyed. All 11,000 personnel on the platform were killed in action, as was Councilman Warner and his staff. Ground personnel casualties are still being tabulated, tentatively calculated at 1,983."

"Goddamn," Lyon said.

"Albright's coordinates," he said. "Can you enter them into the dashboard computer?"

***

Crosswinds twisted the hovercar before the computer adjusted the flightpath. He looked up from the flight instruments. Sharp mountains pierced the edge of the sun, like teeth biting an egg yolk. A hangar and a mostly intact runway interrupted the surface of parched-yellow dirt. He landed on a crumbling helipad and powered down the engine in a zero-altitude cloud of spinning sand.

After 50 paces they emerged from the storm and continued towards the narrow black slit of the open hangar door. Another hovercar and a jeep were parked at opposite ends of the structure. He adjusted his holstered pistol underneath his coat and loaded a wrist-app to automatically inject stimulants at the first sign of adrenaline.

Parched ground crumbled under their boots until they paused in front of the structure. *ALL DEAD* spray-painted on the hangar doors in weathered red letters. One word per door, separated by the gap between them. Lyon and he entered simultaneously, each taking a corner with their drawn pistols.

Inside the cold black void descended into a dustless floor of a hundred suspended, white curtains, held up by arrangements of aluminum tubes. Three of them open, with hospital beds and medical equipment.

A makeshift hospital, hastily thrown together by doctors and nurses who didn't make it to a fallout bunker when the war ended just as quickly as it began. No skeletons, though the stench of death still lingered. One hushed voice carried from the labyrinth of curtains. Following it led to the back of the hangar, where the beds ended, and it was simply a large room.

Matilda Albright. A pistol in each hand of her hands, both pointed at the ground.

A woman behind her tied to a chair. Frazzled brown hair long enough to touch the glowing green ring on her wrist. Her mouth taped shut under eyes that nervously scanned the room.

Lyon and he aimed their weapons at Matilda.

"Are we interrupting anything?" he asked.

"Pete. You finally came." Matilda smiled.

"Who's that?" he asked.

"My sister," Lyon said.

"And where's my family?"

"Don't worry Pete, they're perfectly safe."

"Your family?" Lyon asked.

"I have—had, their minds on memory disks," he said to Lyon. "Wasserman is dead," he said to Matilda. "You don't need hostages any longer."

"Don't I?" Matilda asked.

"We had a deal," Lyon said.

"What about Gemma Overton?  What kind of deal did you make with her?" Matilda asked Lyon. "She's dangerous, Pete.  Who do you think is going to cheerfully arrest you on suspicion of war crimes the second you return to the settlement?  She'll betray you."

"Do you have a Delphi prediction of that too?  Let's see it."

"Peter knows you murdered Gemma Overton," Matilda said to Lyon.  "What will your kangaroo courts see when they upload his mind?  Do you want to join him in the recycling chamber?"

Lyon turned and aimed her pistol at him.  "I didn't kill Gemma. Ana did."

"How do you know?" Matilda asked Lyon.  "You took a memory wiping pill."

"I'm not a murderer," Lyon said.

"Murderess, bumpkin," Matilda said.

"Then don't point that at me," he said.

Lyon turned her pistol towards Matilda.

"A murderess?" he asked Matilda.  "You've been pulling everyone's strings, even your boss the Ventriloquist.  You manipulated the settlements into murdering him.  And you've managed to not only wipe out your fellow outcasts but killed 10,000 settlers when that platform exploded."

"Warner was a monster.  He deserved to die."  Matilda adjusted her grip on both pistols still aimed at the floor.

"Right. You murder thousands of innocent people to kill one guilty man."

"Riddle me this, Pete. Who's really innocent?"

"Those people were."

"People die in war. Did you forget that too?"

"I had orders. You chose to do this."

"Because I love you."

"Abducting my family is a strange way to show it."

"Forget about resurrecting ghosts. I'm flesh and blood. I'm real, I'm right here in front of you and I love you."

"And how many outcasts have fake memories?"

"This is real." Albright lifted her left hand and tapped a finger with an engagement ring against the grip of one of her pistols.

"Then why do you need a memory printer?" Lyon pointed at the device near the wall, partially concealed under a white curtain.

"Shut up," Albright said to Lyon.

"Peter, she's a psycho," Lyon said to him.

"Does shut up mean something different to you?" Albright aimed one of her pistols at Lyon.

"She doesn't love you," Lyon pleaded to him. "She just wants someone who can't say no."

"Don't point that at her," he said to Albright.

"Why are you listening to her?" Albright asked. "You don't even have a clue who she really is, do you?"

"I know she regrets the harm she's done. And the law will judge her. Not you or me."

"I did all of this for you. For us," Albright said. "If you're not man enough to fight for us—"

"Drop the gun," he said.

Albright took two steps to the right and Lyon took one step to the left.

"Don't move!" Albright said to Lyon.

"I don't got a clean shot," Lyon whispered to him. "Mary is right behind her."

"She's the last thing between us." Albright gestured towards Lyon.

"Don't do it," he said.

"Happiness is a choice, Pete. Choose carefully." Albright's pistol shook in her hand then steadied, aimed squarely at Lyon. "It's just one more life."

He pulled the trigger.

Blood sprayed over Lyon's sister. Albright fell to her knees and then over onto the concrete floor. Both pistols fell from her hands. He walked over and took a knee while Lyon kicked the dropped weapons away.

Albright's shaking hands gripped a small detonator. She clicked it several times, unaware it was broken in half by the slug that had continued through her torso.

He pulled her clicking hand away and held it.

"P—Pete." Albright coughed blood. "It would have been perfect..." Her eyes stopped moving, and her hand slipped away. A pool of blood spread from under her and around his knees. He gently placed her lifeless hands together on her stomach.

Lyon untied her blood-stained sister. "Go wait for me outside." They hugged and exchanged a love you of some kind, and Lyon's sister ran to the back of the hangar and through a door of blinding light that eventually swung closed with a clang.

He stood and turned towards Lyon. "Did Kyudo know Albright kidnapped your sister?"

"No." Lyon reached down to examine Albright's trigger device.

"You'll have some explaining to do when we get back."

"Mm hm." Lyon nodded.

He turned to leave, and a bang violently shook him as the world turned black.

# 42
## Upadhi

In a Hall of Justice interview bulb Joan spun a story about Ramsey and Albright. Star-crossed lovers that betrayed everyone else for each other.

"Unfortunately, my blaster was lost while escapin' the Sandcastle, so I could only stun him," she said. It was actually Matilda's stun gun. But it's not like anyone else will ever know.

"It's likely his validation window will close before he can return," Kyudo said. "Nevertheless, it would be practical to file an A-P-B in case he turns up."

She nodded. "Yes Colonel. And congratulations."

"Thank you." Kyudo looked down at her own shoulders in turn and brushed each of the identical, shiny insignia with her fingertips. She ended the holo-recording with a beeping button on the table. "Off the record. Did you find or hear anything about a device? Other than the memory-printer, that is. Perhaps a remote trigger of some kind?"

Does Kyudo know about the time machine? Saying yes might lead to more questions. Questions that could lead to Kyudo finding out about her sister being kidnapped. Thank goodness Mary passed protocol 11 validation. She held saliva in her mouth, forcing herself to not swallow. "No."

"I already knew about Matilda and Peter. What I didn't have was intel indicating that she had turned him into a double agent." Kyudo tilted her head up in suspicion, paused for a few seconds, and lowered her head.

She gulped. "Um."

Kyudo smiled. "It's okay Joan. Peter's performance had deteriorated over the past year to that of a substandard detective. I had to keep him around because I knew Albright was still out there and their history could solve a potential issue in the future." She examined her flatputer. "In fact, I've submitted paperwork to award you with a commendation for bravery. I think you already have one, but after the loss of Zeus we need to give the public images of success. Of our victory over the outcasts."

"So, the war—the war for Earth is over?"

Kyudo laughed. "Of course not. There are still pockets of resistance. And the newly elected council wants to set their sights on the colonies once the home world is secure. Eight corners under one roof." She stood with her flatputer. "I'm promoting you to full constable. Your salary adjustment will be reflected in your next pay period. Congratulations." She held out a hand and they shook. "Jack Orange, your new partner, will be transferring up from Settlement Ten next week. He's completely green, and a little cute."

They both grinned.

***

The glossy-blue dome of the upscale neighborhood coated everything with a strange hue that grew darker with each passing minute, like the world itself stubbornly wearing tinted sunglasses even at dusk.

Mary was late as usual, but it didn't seem annoying. It's just a relief that she's safe. She would have been on time if she were told about the memory disc, but she would have gotten her hopes up.

She decided to stop waiting and knocked on the front door of her parent's house. No one greeted her, no human anyway, just the servant robot, who took her coat and canvas bag.

Maybe he isn't here. Maybe—

"Joan." The voice startled her enough that she leapt, the hairs on her arms raised in a pointless defense. An invisible force gripped her spine like a coiled snake. He was standing in the shadows, an outline of darkness. "Come help me in the kitchen."

Samael.

In the sink was a stack of dishes dirty enough to attract real flies. The cleaning robot stood in the kitchen corner, standing ready for commands it would never hear. She turned the familiar knobs for water almost hot enough to burn her hands. Her father's breath ran up and down the stiffed hairs on her neck.

Her body tensed as two hands wrapped around her, low on the waist, before she ignored him and continued to clean. Moving her hands up and down dirty plates while he did the same to her with the invisible version of filth.

Between plates she risked a brief glance up at the street-facing kitchen window. The moon was rising where the sun used to be. It looked lonely without the Zeus platform to keep it company.

It grew dark enough that their reflections were now visible. He was grinning with his big teeth. She forced herself to not react when his forearm bumped her holstered blaster. She didn't dare to think of reaching for it, or even looking at her sentiment circle. She repeated the mantra in her mind. He doesn't affect me. He's doing it to someone else. My reflection. That's not me. Eventually he'll stop. When Mary arrives, he'll put on his mask. The loving father who could never harm either daughter.

A beep drew him away. He released her and she was temporarily free again. When she heard the front door close, she turned off the water and approached another window. He was walking back to his shop, 88 meters away.

Mom was in her room, where the only window faced the neighboring house, and an exterior light painted the always-drawn blinds a shade of pale yellow. She was sitting in her comfy chair, watching the news-feed.

Riots on New Eden. Complete with burning trash cans filling the sky with grey smoke. Lines of Janissaries in riot-shields versus clones with Molotov cocktails and small arms.

Up next: an interview with a crazy woman who threw a goat off the roof of her apartment building.

"Hi Mom."

"Hello." Mom looked over and smiled. There was always that split second where she might show recognition in her eyes, but it passed. "Who are you?"

"I'm your daughter."

"Mary?"

"No. Mary's the tall one. See?" She pointed and tapped on the two still images mounted on the wall, labelled with names.

"Oh, goodness. How long has that been there?" Mom moved some clutter from the other chair in the room, placing it on the small table next to her. A disassembled Matryoshka doll. The smaller, child-like layers were broken, with dried glue on the edges of the cracks where she had tried and failed to fix it years ago.

Joan sat and lifted her canvas messenger bag to unzip it. "I found something that belongs to you. Or at least, I think it does. Mary and I have been lookin' for your lost memories. For a copy of your mind." She pulled the memory disc from her bag and placed it on her lap. "We were hopin' it might cure you. Bring back your old memories and maybe even help you create new ones."

"I lost my memories?" Mom asked.

"You took a whole bottle of memory pills. Mary always wondered why but I never told her." She sniffled. "I used to tell myself that you were selfish. Like you hated yourself more than you loved me. I was helpless back then, and you knew what he was doin' to me and you did nothin'. And—" She paused to wipe away tears and twist her mood away. "When you forgot, all that did was make me feel even more alone."

"What happened?" Mom asked.

"I used to think guilt and shame were the same, but they sure taste different. I mean, I always figured this forsaken world was nothin' but a shitshow. But I never imagined I'd be the one makin' it worse, haunted by guilt and its lantern of damnation keepin' me up all night remindin' me of everyone I killed."

Mom's mouth fell open, aghast. "You've killed people?"

"I'm a cop." She tapped a fingernail against the badge on her removed coat.

"Oh, it's okay." Mom held her hand. "It's your job, right?"

"Right," she said, sounding more like Peter than she cared to admit. "You know you forgot some good moments too? Like one time, our shelter neighbor, Mr. Galveston, fell down the stairwell, and Mary and you and me were all laughin' like it was the funniest thing in the world."

"Did he slip on a yellow light bulb?"

They both laughed.

"You remember him?" she asked.

"No, not him," Mom said. "I remember someone falling down a stairwell."

"What about Mary or me?"

"No." Mom looked away briefly. "But I love both of you. I knew that when you walked in here. Before you even said a word to me."

Mom was tearing up, so she hugged her. She picked up the memory disc from the floor where it must have fallen. "I wish I could give you your old life back, but if you put these memories into your mind someone like me would be ordered to shoot you. That's how fucked up things are. The only way to help you was if I could change—" the past.

Mom reached over and lifted the disc up to the light. "Oh, could you bring me my water? And purify it before you add the salt?"

For some reason Mom gargled with salt water every night before bed. A strange little ritual she inherited from Grandma.

She wiped away the last of the tears and sniffled. "It's okay Mom. I always remember."

In the kitchen the holographic menu that wrapped itself around the faucet beeped as she twisted it to *Human Consumption*. A pull gesture popped another ring menu in front of it, which she rotated to *salt, 3.5%*. Bubbles formed around the rim of Mom's glass tumbler as she set it down without a thud.

What happens when the order is reversed? She pulled the holographic rings off the sink and switched the order. An error message: *Purifying salt water will reduce the lifespan of your biofilter by 50%*.

She tapped her fingers against the counter for several seconds. That scumbag Paul said Matilda requested twice as many filters. That must be why. "Son of a bitch," she whispered. The little lakes and ponds are all fresh water up there. And the Sandcastle was far from the ocean. So was that hangar where Mary was taken.

Matilda must have a hideout or something near the coast. That must be where she hid Delphi's time machine.

***

After Mom fell asleep clutching the memory disc, Joan covered her in a blanket and left a written note for Mary. A warning to not upload the contents into Mom's brain, along with a doodle of a Celtric Trinity Knot.

Outside it started to rain, a drizzle that grew into a steady pour by the time she reached the dark alleyway across from her father's robot brothel.

He had put up a holographic sign about all services being discounted to celebrate the settlements victory over the outcasts. The news feed playing at the adjacent shop re-played the destruction of the Sandcastle in an endless loop.

Rain drops partially sheathed the rounded lines of light falling from the street's tall lampposts. She checked her cuff-puter's chronograph. 8:12 pm. A message from Mary.

*Sorry Lemon I fell asleep. I'll take Mom breakfast tomorrow morning.*

The neon sign finally changed from *Open* to *Back in 30 minutes*, and her father's Wall-Thru signal left the shop. He always takes the back door to navigate the back alleys to Agatha's Sandwich Shop several blocks away for a night owl's lunch break.

As usual, he had left the back door unlocked. The son of a bitch is too arrogant to think anyone will ever rob him. With a switch the bright lights came on and when her eyes adjusted, she walked over to the ancient map mounted on the wall.

White tacks marked every node in the Atlantic Alliance Com-Network. The outcasts were using Atlantic Alliance transmitters in the Sandcastle, so they must have found a way to use the defunct, pre-war communication nodes. Most of the dots moved thru mountains where the map was shaded brown and the wartime nukes didn't take them out, but a few uplinks emerged around cities.

She ran a finger along the coast, past the mountains east of Settlement Five and thru the Northern Wastelands. Nothing within transmission range and near the ocean. With a sigh she tried again.

One of the tacks, pressed into an island on a lake north of the Jefferson Coast. A large inland lake called the Puget Sea. With a lens function she looked up the body of water. Salt water.

Another function beeped an alarm. Her father's Wall-Thru signal approaching. He's bringing his lunch back to eat it here.

She flicked off the light and carefully walked towards the front of the shop. She collided with someone.

"Sorry," a woman's voice said.

Cat-Eyes brightened the darkness enough to see the robot companion up against the nearby wall.

She ran to the front door, turned the lock, and ran out into the street.

Outside the sulfuric rain had grown into a downpour. Heavy drops pelted her for an entire block until she reached her car. Slamming her car door shut, she frantically sped down the street, hyperventilating and shaking. Her sentiment circle blinked with an error. A sight blurred by tears.

Turning up the heat vents didn't warm her, and her shirt peeled and stuck to her skin. Soaked to the bone from a dirty downpour incapable of washing away her shame.

***

In the morning she nibbled on a muffin and sipped steaming coffee while updating her will. Everything was left in Mary's name, including a note she was writing by hand. She used her right hand, Matilda's cursive ability was fancy and impressive, but the ability was fading, and her fingers were cramping up after every sentence.

On the kitchen counter the news feed played a press conference. Colonel Kyudo hailed Councilman Warner as a brave hero who died for the cause of humanity. She descended into a diatribe regarding cowardice and betrayal as images of Matilda and Peter lit up.

She used eye movements to dismiss the feed.

I could take Mary with me to find this time machine, she thought. Mom can't be left alone though, and the wastelands are still dangerous. But so is staying here. She looked at the two memory discs on the table and tapped one of her feet on the floor. Which one should Mary be left with? I haven't examined the one Wazz gave me. My own mind backup has the truth about Dad. She rested her chin on her palm.

If I change the past, everything should be made right. But if I fail, Mary has to know about Samael, even though it will break her heart.

A bowl rattled in the kitchen. Slippers scarfing down wet food. After three cans he's still hungry. She smiled and put the disc with her real memories in a box for Mary. The Wazz disc went back into her canvas messenger bag.

After breakfast she cleaned up and sat on the couch, putting her feet up as she stared at the phone app. A rotary dial with a repeating tone. With a sigh she took a deep breath and looked up at her view of the settlement, her abdomen tightened until it hurt to move anything. Just get it over with.

A sudden jolt sank in the sofa cushion. Slippers took paw-to-paw strides before licking her bare arm in a storm of purring.

"There you are." She stroked his head and he meowed. "I'm going to miss you, you little shit. You're gonna have a new Mama soon." She kissed the top of his head as he curled up on her lap.

After a few minutes she activated her holographic bird, a birthday gift Mary bought her last month. Slippers chased it. She lifted her wrist and dialed.

"Mencken News. This is Rrrrrobie the Robot Reporter," A robotic voice immediately answered.

"Hello Robbie."

"Why, you are Officer Lyon, Joanna, are you not?"

She looked down at her validation cylinder on the coffee table. I haven't run protocol 11 since I returned from the wastelands, she thought.

"Officer Lyon?" Robbie asked.

"That's me."

"How can I assist you today?"

"I'd like to talk to you," her voice cracked. "About the murder of Gemma Overton."

"The police have already solved that case and transmitted a public statement. What would you like to add?"

"The truth."

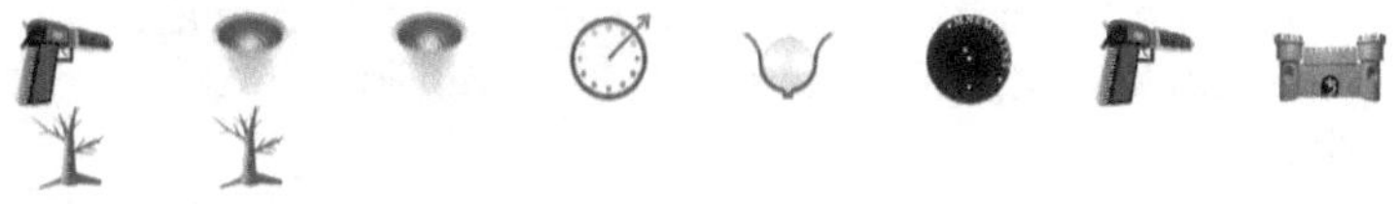

# 43
## Coming Forth by Day

A single line of light ran along the hangar ceiling, and something was cutting into his back. Stun prongs he pulled from his shoulder blade. The metal pinchers shined as he held them up and turned them, his other hand clutching the wound.

Son of a bitch. Well, Lyon is the last half anyway.

He picked up his pistol and searched Matilda's cold body.

The trigger mechanism she had was nowhere to be found. Small volumetric text spun from the diamond of her engagement ring. *Pete & Tilda Forever*. The pockets of her jeans were shallow but narrow and scraped the only two fingers that could fit inside simultaneously. A keychain with two ignition cylinders and a key. *Kyle's Storage* etched along the edge. He closed her eyelids and searched the hangar for an hour, looking for the memory disks of his family. Nothing. Nada.

The hovercar outside wouldn't start but the jeep engaged.

Backtracking the tread marks in the dirt led to a road of broken pavement and onramps leading North and South, marked on blue signs for old Highway Five. He parked and leaned his head against the steering wheel, accidentally beeping the horn.

A subroutine scrolled a reminder: *Your validation window will expire in 22 hours.*

South is the way back home. Unknown coordinates blinked on a volumetric emitter pressed onto the dashboard with suction cups. He used both hands to try to adjust the angle to read it. Which caused it to fall off the dash, bounce off the console and onto the floor mat beneath his feet.

When he reached down to pick it up something else was loose under the chair, a firm edge against his fingertip. A tableau of him and Matilda kissing. A mirror behind them led to endless reflections, smaller squares of them, alternating between the backs of their heads.  He flipped the creased corners to find a note written in ink.  *I Love you Matilda.*  A heart drawn under it.  His own handwriting.

He placed it on the passenger seat, where a previously unnoticed satchel was camouflaged.  The same color as the seat fabric.  Only one memory disk inside and his name was on it.  Another version of me, he thought.  No.  There's only one version of a person.  One Caramel Ramsey.  And one Ariadne Ramsey.  If only there was some way to bring them back.  Not as temporary knockoffs but the originals.

Setting the volumetric computer right-side up, the map coordinates blinked along with an arrowed line, North from McMartin Airfield through the Oregon desert but short of the sprawling ruins of Seattle.

He turned onto the highway and floored it.

***

After the great leviathan of the Pacific lifted dark claws around the Sun and selfishly ate the orange yolk, he drove through the night until the rising orange shield returned to valiantly fight away the darkness.

A bent green sign labelled *McNeil Island* pointed a white arrow towards a vehicle bridge, where one of two lanes had collapsed into the churning waters below.  He parked and walked onto the bridge's intact lane.

Bright fog enclosed it like a white tunnel.  Visible mist spiraling above waters on either side of the rusted support beams, which were spotted with spiked mussels and barnacles.  Some splashes and movement other than waves.  Mutant sharks, or whatever else had managed to mutate and survive in that cesspool.

Halfway across, the bridge started to lean with a loud sheer. Violent splashes from the water below. Tentacles wrapped around the railings.

Peter ran as the bridge tilted. 20 meters left. He pulled a muscle in his leg but kept running. The bridge listed nearly 30 degrees as he dove for dry land. Cracks and clanks as whatever lied in the depths consumed the metallic passage in a vortex of spinning water and pointed teeth.

The road to the prison was a two-kilometer walk bordered by thick trees and dancing fog. Branches moved, either by the wind or mutation. Twigs cracked and pebbles crunched under his boots. He checked his pistol. 11 rounds.

At the end, a field with the prison at the far end. Walls stretching from intact to broken into clumps of brick. A dome of latticed glass off to the side. New, or at least clean enough to be. A chain-linked fence by the rotting pier held up a tilted sheet-metal sign that swayed front to back in the wind. *McNeil Penitentiary* printed in large letters, partially covered by patches of grime and bound human remains.

The prison's entrance was a reinforced hatch within an archway of blinking control panels. Too absent of rust to be the original doorway. He ran his fingertips over the heavy, locked door, but stopped at the sound of an approaching turbine.

Hovercar lights cut through the fog, and the craft glided over the field with a slowing tornado of dirt, landing on filthy cobblestone by a dry fountain of shattered stone. Its door opened and Lyon stepped out.

She approached as the turbines turned silent and froze when he drew his pistol.

"Did you come to finish what you started?" he asked.

"Peter."

"Don't Peter me."

McNeil Island
Prison
ONLY GOVERNMENT
BOATS PERMITTED
ALLOWED
PA

She slowly parted her coat. An obvious move to eventually draw her weapon. "Maybe—maybe instead of killin' each other we can figure out how to undo all of this."

"We?"

"Matilda used her time machine earlier. More than one person can use it."

He held her at gunpoint in a minute of awkward silence, until sonic booms drew their attention to the sky. A dozen attack ships cracking the atmosphere with rings of glowing-orange flame around the re-entry side of their hulls.

"Friends of yours? Why didn't you shoot them in the back?" he asked.

"I didn't tell no one I was comin' here."

"They must have tracked you by satellite. An orbital drop. So their approach couldn't be seen on radar."

"If either of us is gonna do this we both have to work together."

"Right."

"Please, Peter." She moved her hand away from her holster to point at the doorway, and she ran over to it, randomly pressing buttons. "How long do you figure we have?"

He rechecked the sky. "Five, perhaps ten minutes."

"What is wrong with this fucker?" Lyon grunted and ground her teeth while attempting to turn the locked hatch wheel.

"I already tried that."

"Shut up and help me."

They both tried. And failed.

"Do you have a grenade?" he asked.

Lyon nodded upwards at her hovercar. A drone mounted to the top with green-tipped missiles.

***

Once the hatch exploded, they waited a few seconds before charging in with raised weapons. A klaxon of some sort resounded with flashing red lights mounted high on the wall, where auto-turrets fell from the ceiling and opened fire. Lyon and he ran into open doors on opposite ends of the hallway. They emerged and blasted the turrets into shrapnel. Attack robots crawled through the smoke rapidly, like giant roaches.

Lyon blasted them before he could.

It was a narrow hall when the smoke cleared, and it ended with two swinging doors into a tall, dome-shaped room made of fused-glass panes. 100 meters in diameter and certainly not an original part of the prison.

A web of cables and luminous tubes ran across the floor from a circle of a dozen human-sized glass cylinders to large computer panels stationed on lab tables. An adult-sized clone embryo of Matilda grew in one of the chambers. Some large computers, old mainframes, next to water-filled vats.

"Hey, Peter." Lyon was standing by a blue tarp draped over something large at the opposite end of the dome. She pulled the tarp by one corner. A barrel-sized datacore on its side, held a meter above the floor by metallic support beams. Smooth and glossy-white with the Delphi logo of swimming dolphins embossed in black.

"Delphi's time machine." He walked over for a closer look. A small computer panel on the side next to a tube with a trigger in it, identical to the one Matilda had earlier. "You can bet your ass that's Delphi out there coming for it."

"You can bet a whole lota asses on that." Lyon picked up the trigger device. "We both have to hold it for this to work."

He grabbed a piece of the device beneath her grip. Lyon clicked. And absolutely nothing remotely observable happened. Lyon clicked again, several times like a young child pushing an elevator button. Nada. Zip.

"Give it a rest," he said.

Lyon squatted down by the large machine's panel. "It's chargin' or somethin'." She pointed to a yellow light with 94% in flashing digits and looked up with raised eyebrows. "How long do you think it's gonna take?"

The glass ceiling rattled, and he looked up.

Three VEN-SEC troop ships. Janissaries poured down long combat ropes while others used jetpacks to quickly land. Some of them opened fire but the slugs couldn't pierce the thick glass.

"Peter!" Lyon was already at the room's entrance, pushing a nearby mainframe with the groaning pitch of metallic skids.

He ran over and helped her push it over, blocking the doors. Footsteps echoed from the hallway. Dozens of blasted holes burst from the metal doors as he and Lyon ran laterally away in opposing directions.

Sparks flew as the computer on the nearby worktable blew into countless pieces. He continued to run around a curved water tank. Slugs slowed and cooled to boiling-bubbles inside the liquid-filled cylinder. Water leaks leveled and changed to letting out steam.

Gunfire sounded but nothing landed nearby. He leaned around the water tank. Two mercenaries were pushing the toppled mainframe while a third covered them, exchanging fire with Lyon. Peter aimed at the Janissary's neck and pulled the trigger. Red blood sprayed and gushed. The entire scene turned sideways as Peter's ear slammed onto the tiled floor.

Sitting up in a freshly formed puddle, he turned back towards the time machine as it hissed, as though it was decompressing. *100%*.

He ran and slipped, almost falling but regaining his balance before stumbling again and sliding into the machine. Using his bruised hand, he pinched the edge of the trigger from its tube. A few slugs flew by. Indiscernible commands muffled by respirators from outside the dome. Mercenaries planting charges on the other side of the glass walls.

He looked back at Lyon, who was still exchanging fire as he looked at the device.

Should I wait for her? She left me to die yesterday. But she didn't abandon me a few days ago when we raided that house. "Lyon!"

She started to move towards him but edged back behind one of the mainframes. She's pinned down.

He stood and aimed at the mercenaries, who had cleared the blockage and were flooding the giant room. He fired until his gun clicked. Huh.

Glass shattered and flew through the dome.

He ran through the cutting debris. Lyon stood as he collided with her, shoving both of them into one of the towering computers.

They both gripped the trigger, and he clicked the red button. White light engulfed the room.

# 44
## Zervan Akarana

The sky was a shade of blue he had nearly forgotten. A dozen aircraft high in the sky, flying in different directions. As he sat up, real grass tickled his palms, songs of chirping birds filled his ears, and a pleasant breeze brushed his face while rustling the branches of trees. Lyon was next to him, and she sat up and looked over with her mouth hanging open.

"What happened?" Lyon asked. "Did it work?"

He stood and looked up from the shadow of the nearby building to the relatively pristine brick structure. Clean and shiny windows instead of dangling shards of glass. The chain link fence 20 meters away stood upright by a sign over a wooden picnic table. *Employee Lunch Area. NO IN-MATES.* "Something worked."

"How far back in time did we go?" Lyon brushed grass off the time machine trigger.

No signal on his wrist-computer, and his tracker ring slowly blinked dark green. Sat-enabled subroutines all returned the same error code: *Service Unavailable.* He clicked the Geiger routine. "There's no background radiation."

"The war hasn't happened yet?" Lyon quickly stood. "That's like, 16 years!"

"Right."

"How will we get back?"

"No idea. Didn't that thing come with instructions?"

"No."

"Why would Albright come back this far?"

"Wazz said the war wasn't supposed to happen. Maybe they've been tryin' to prevent it?"

"Albright and Wasserman? Their interests diverged."

"Maybe this is Wazz's trigger. Matilda's broke. Remember?"

He opened his mouth.  Something on the tip of his tongue and he rubbed his temples.  "Wasserman used a lab key to access a stasis lab under the mess hall at Chiron."

"A stasis lab?  Why?"

"I don't know.  But while we're here, we should probably prevent him from continuing his loop of violence."

"We're not settlers anymore."

"Wasserman is responsible for thousands of deaths."

"Fine."  Lyon sighed.  "What do you wanna do?  Blow up the lab?"

"No.  He's going to steal the security officer's key.  We just need to steal it first."

"How do you know that?"

"I found the key Wasserman used.  At Chiron.  Your father's fingerprints were on it."

"My father?"  Lyon grimaced.

A human voice from a nearby open window: "The Pacific Coalition has resumed negotiations with the Atlantic Alliance.  Peace in our time."  A volumetric news feed in his line of sight. *11:11 am, Monday, September 20th, 2147*, scrolled underneath the smiling anchor.

"Son of a bitch."

"The war's gonna start tonight."

"Right.  We better go."

***

They stood in a parking lot half a kilometer from the side entrance to Chiron airbase and the squad of robots guarding it.

"Once we're past the gate, we split up," he said.  "I'll get my family, you get that key, and we meet at the playground. Then we'll figure out our next move."

"How are we gonna get past the gate?"  Lyon asked. "Won't they think we're clones or somethin'?"

"Doubtful.   Last time I was here the D-N-A scanner barely looked beyond telomere fraying.  We're not clones so we'll be fine unless there's something you want to tell me."

"Weren't you at sea for like, a year before the war started?"

"A few months.  So what?"

"So maybe they changed it or somethin'.  Maybe they'll figure out you're AWOL or whatever it's called."

"The robots don't check that."

"Why don't we sneak in?  There's that broken section, somewhere by the softball field I think."

"Walk around the fence line looking for a hole?  That won't draw any attention."

"Fine.  But let's go one at a time so both of us aren't caught."

"Right. Ladies first. Give me your service weapon." He held out an open hand.

"What?"  Lyon took a step back.

"They'll scan us for weapons.  I was active-duty military back then—now. Since the computer records have you listed as a four-year-old it might raise a question or two."

Lyon pulled her weapon and handed it over.  "I better be gettin' this back."

"The moment it isn't too soon." He pocketed Lyon's pistol.  "That too."  He pointed to the time trigger on Lyon's belt.

"You're kiddin'."

"I can't remember the last time I shot someone in the back.  Can you?"

Lyon handed it over, walked to the gate, typed her name, and pressed her hand against the DNA scanner.  It beeped red and the robots raised their weapons.

He hastily reached for the time trigger and accidentally clicked the button.  "Son of a—"

***

"What happened?" Lyon asked. "Did it work?"

They were once again outside the McNeil Island Prison.

"Lyon? Are you okay?"

"I guess."

"What's the last thing you remember?"

"Mercs shootin' at me. Why?"

"I'll tell you on the way."

At Chiron Lyon led them through a rattling hole in the fence line by the baseball field.

"Okay. See you at the playground?" Lyon asked.

"One last thing. Give me the trigger."

"What?" Lyon grabbed the device from her belt. "Why?"

"You're going to break and enter into a house. The base MPs have a two-minute response time. Of course, your dad worked—works security, so perhaps you should tell me?"

"I remember where the hideaway key is."

"But your family doesn't know what you look like as an adult."

"Peter, I know how to not be seen."

"This isn't some dim bunker. This is broad daylight."

Lyon's mouth twisted, but she handed over the trigger and walked away.

The white colonial on Cedar Street was a perfect match for his memories. Two tall trees lifted intertwined branches high above the black-shingled roof like an archway. The biometric lock clicked, and the red door turned green as it opened.

"Caramel? Ariadne?"

No one answered. No one in the kitchen or media parlor. No one in his study. No one upstairs in the master bedroom. No one in Caramel's room except her toy ponies and model lighthouse between the dark curtains and bright window. Nothing but the echoing names he called out.

He sat on the pink blanket covering Caramel's bed. Perhaps an earlier version of me was here and took them to safety. He scratched his neck and chin and looked out the window. No car in the driveway. He stood.

Ariadne hates parking in the garage. She's always nagging me about my toolboxes taking up too much space. But if Ari left, she'd take things with her.

The master bedroom was arranged differently from what he recalled. Tableau albums and experience disks were arranged along a short bookcase across from the bed. He poured them into suitcases in the old closet and topped them off with clothes. The house robot walked by with a puzzled expression.

When he huffed his way down the stairs and reached the landing, the front door opened.

Ariadne and Carmen walked into the house.

For a few seconds nothing appeared real, as though it were a memory from a disk being replayed, but the sound of his wife's breath, her smile, the twinkle in her eye as she looked at him and moved hair away from her face. "Peter."

His heart skipped a beat, then made up the difference with a jolt that shook him enough to throw out his back.

Caramel let go of her mother's hand and dropped her giraffe plushie. She ran towards him with a smile so wide he could see nothing else. "Daddy!"

He fell to his knees and caught her in a hug. Her little heart thudded against his chest.

"Daddy, you're squishing me!"

He released her. "Oh, I'm sorry baby."

"Are we going on vacation?" Ariadne raised her eyebrows at the two suitcases behind him.

He opened his mouth to answer but froze. His smiling wife ran one of her own hands over her curved belly.

"You're pregnant?" he asked.

"20 weeks. I was going to surprise you when you got back. I thought I'd be further along."

"I got a liberty pass." He kissed her, having nearly forgotten what it felt like.

"I need to sit down." Ari said. "Sunflower, go watch your cartoons," she said to Caramel, who scurried off to the media parlor. "Are you okay?"

"Yes, I'm fine."

His wife ran a hand along his face. "You look like you haven't slept in a week."

"I'm alright."

Ari followed him to the kitchen, placed her purse on the kitchen island, and sat on the stool next to him.

"Is it a boy or a girl?" he asked.

"Another girl." Ari smiled.

"Oh boy. How's work?"

Ari sighed. "Hectic. Ever since the memory bank rolled it's just been one bug after another. And I have to meet with a psychologist who's flying down from Washington this afternoon. He's been studying all 11 steps of the verification process and its long-term effects on prison inmates."

"The memory bank? It's done?"

"Didn't the guards at the gate scan your mind?" Ari's eyes narrowed.

"Uh, yeah."

"The Pacific States have clones nearly indistinguishable from their original hosts. Testing D-N-A isn't enough anymore. In fact, it's almost meaningless."

"Yes. I remember now. The head scan the Navy had me do before I went to sea." And the disks that she gave him. He scratched his neck.

Ari's eyes bulged. "What model arm computer is that?"

"Oh, it's um, a new one. Just came out."

His wife grabbed his arm and examined the wrist-computer. "Aren't we budgeting for a bigger house?"

"I got a deal from a guy. When we docked in Pearl."

"Oh."

He played with the end of his wife's tied-back hair and ran his fingers along her neck.

Ari's shoulders tensed and she looked away. "I'm tired."

"Why don't I take Carmen back to the playground?"

"Oh, um." Ariadne frowned. "I can go with you. I'll just sit on a bench."

"Are you sure?"

Ari nodded.

***

At the playground he pushed Caramel on a swing while Ariadne sat on a bench 50 meters away.

"Higher Daddy!" she said.

"Any higher and you'll be a bird."

He looked over at the bench where Ariadne was sitting. Empty.

"Huh." He lifted a single finger and moved it up and down as he said to his daughter, "This little piggy says standby."

Caramel giggled.

Ariadne was standing behind a thick tree and didn't notice him approaching. "Yes, I need base police," she said into her wrist-computer. "My husband is here but, oh God, I don't think it's him. He looks haggard, like a clone. It was trying to steal experience disks from my home."

His stomach knotted, and he staggered to a nearby tree.

Popping sounds. Gunshots. Parents and children screamed and ran across the playground. He found Carmen standing by the swing set. "Daddy!" He quickly set her down on the ground and covered her with his own body.

More gunshots. Closer this time. Someone running along the adjacent roadway, exchanging fire with base MPs.

Lyon.

Blaster fire struck her down.  She crawled briefly but fell flat on the pavement.

He got up, took a few steps away from Caramel, and used the Zoom routine.

A trail of Lyon's blood moved away, up the street to the lost horizon.  Two MPs stood over her smoldering corpse. Something drew their attention.  Ariadne.  She shouted something to the police and pointed in his direction.

"Son of a bitch."  He took the time trigger from his belt and pushed the red button with a pronounced click that echoed inside his ears.

# 45
## Sekhmet

"What happened?" Joan asked. The sky was blue like the holo dome.

"I'll explain on the way," Peter said.

On a jump-ship he quietly explained how they had looped back in a time circle a few times but unbelievably, only he remembered.

At Chiron he asked about the old hole in the fence by the baseball field and they snuck thru.

"Give me the time trigger." Peter reached out with an open hand and made a gimmie gesture.

"Why?"

"I'm your failsafe."

"Why would I need a failsafe?"

"Base security shoots first and ask questions later."

"Did somethin' happen last time?"

"No. Of course not. Why would something happen?"

"I don't know," she lied. But was it a lie? She had no trouble supposing what probably happened but didn't recall either.

"You're breaking and entering into a home, and your family has only ever seen you as a toddler."

"Fine." She handed over the reset trigger.

"Perhaps you should give me your pistol too?"

"No fuckin' way."

"If security confronts you, don't provoke them."

"I'll be nice."

"First time for everything."

"Yeah, whatever." Jerk.

***

The sun was hotter than she remembered so she hid her removed peacoat in one of the neighbor's bushes.

The hideaway key was hidden where she remembered, in what looked like a rock, and tapping it against the back-door unlocked it with a beep and blinking greenlight. She slid it open slowly, knowing the speed at which it would loudly rattle, and closed it just as quietly behind her. Careful heel to toe steps moved her silently across the carpet with her drawn blaster in a two-handed grip.

A putrid smell from the kitchen, where flies buzzed around an overflowing wastebin. The house was dim, with drawn blinds colored yellow with sunlight.

Behind the white vented doors of the coat closet, she reached one hand onto the high shelf. Where Samael always kept his home laser pistol, inside a metal box. She carefully tucked it into her waistband and closed the box and closet.

No one in the family room—

"But both sides are still committed to the negotiations."

She turned her blaster at the corner. A news-feed had turned on automatically. Feel-good optimistic bullshit that played up until the moment nukes fell like rain drops. She pressed a beeping button and the hologram deactivated.

Her feet met each stair one at a time as she carefully shifted her weight. The bead of her weapon sweeping between the left and rights sides of the stairway.

The bedroom was filled with clutter. The bed wasn't even made. How did the asshole ever make it thru bootcamp? The lab key was among a pile of rusty coins, books, and discs on top of his dresser. She tucked it into a front pant pocket that was barely large enough to hold the small key.

No still images anywhere of Mom or her, or even of Samael. No still images of anyone actually. The whole house was funky and absent of Mom's relatively agreeable fragrance. And not a single one of her houseplants in sight.

The squeaking sound of the front door opening and slamming shut. She froze. Footsteps downstairs and the echoing of the news-feed turning back on. A male voice from downstairs sighing and loudly plopping on a sofa.

She slowly descended the stairway and at the landing stared at the front door for half a minute.

In the family room Samael was sitting on the couch. She aimed at him.

He looked over and did a spit take with the bottled beer he was drinking. "Who the fuck are you?"

"Where are they?" she asked.

"Who?"

"Your wife. Your daughter." Her rapid breaths landed on the upright hairs of her shaking arms. Both legs trembled and she almost lost her balance.

"I'm not married." He lifted his left hand. No wedding band.

"Bullshit. Where are they?"

"I've got a rare coin collection upstairs. Why don't you take it and go?"

She flipped the safety off and raised the barrel towards his forehead. "Last chance. Where are they?"

His eyes grew large. Dad leapt and grabbed the blaster. They each kept a hand on it, the barrel pointed at the ceiling. He threw a punch, and she blocked it with her free forearm, though the room still spun as she crashed into the wall, cracking the nearby visual feed into polygons. He tried taking the blaster away with both hands.

Five kicks to his groin and a punch to the face changed his mind, and his body fell back with agonizing groans. He took a few seconds to stand up straight again. She used the time to move away from the wall, a few steps away from him, and aim the blaster with two hands again. Her heartbeats pulsed in both ears.

Dad ran for the closet and grabbed his metal box, but quickly dropped it when he discovered it was empty.

"Lookin' for this?" She held up Samael's laser pistol for a few seconds before returning it to her waistband. "Come get it. See what happens."

Samael stood still, his bottom lip quivering, both bloody and bruised hands raised in a pathetic surrender. "Please."

Her teeth chattered together as she stepped towards him and beckoned. "Go on. Do it. Come on."

But dad didn't move. He sobbed while the tip of her finger moved up and down the cold metal trigger. A thump from the floor interrupted their heavy breaths. My fractured sentiment circle rolled across creaking floorboards towards the sofa. Could he be genuinely afraid? He might not be a monster yet.

"I can see it in your eyes." Dad smirked. "You don't want to hurt me."

I wiped the tears away with one finger before regripping my blaster. "These tears ain't for you."

Pulling the trigger disintegrated Samael's head and splashed red across the cream-colored walls. Dots of pink brain slid down at different speeds, leaving streaks of red that all together looked like a wide red comb. The image might not have been out of place in an art gallery.

The sound of sirens grew.

"Shit."

I ran to the front door but paused. Peter said the MPs were trigger happy. I closed the door, locked it, and ran out the back, thru the backyard where I retrieved my coat and put it on to cover the blood stains on my white shirt.

The adjacent backyards all had the same pattern of white fences and equally sized, manicured green grass sloping slightly upwards to a horizon of infinity. I leapt over each fence, chased a few times by dogs, one of which was rude enough to sink its teeth into the edge of my coat.

Finally, the endless yards ended at a corner lot with a swimming pool that smelled of chlorine, and I emerged from the tree line at the edge of the playground. I stopped to catch my breath.

A blonde toddler ran around a bush several times, then spun in circles until she collapsed from dizziness. The child sat up and stared, and after waving I froze too for a moment. It was not at all like looking into a mirror, and yet that was the only comparison looping in my mind.

"Joan?"

The child's eyebrows went up. With each step the face looked more and more like the one I had seen on old still images of my family. It's me.

"Joan?" I asked again.

"Huh?" the child asked.

There was a sound of small pebbles crunching, and without any surprise I turned to find that damn Peter approaching with a small caramel sundae.

"You're early Lyon." He pointed at the snack stand 100 meters behind him. "They've got hover cream if you're hungry. Need any contemporary currency?"

My younger self ran over to Peter and eagerly took the sundae with a hug. "Caramel!"

"It is," Peter said to young Joan while handing her the paper bowl of ice cream. "It's you. You're eating yourself."

"Blah." The child crossed her eyes and stuck out her tongue.

"Blah." Peter mimicked until the child giggled.

"Peter, what are you doin'?" I asked.

"Oh, I'm sorry. This is my daughter. Carmen."

"WHAT?" I stepped away from them.

"Hi!" young Joan said while scarfing down the ice cream.

"Peter, that's me!" I said loud enough that nearby parents took notice.

Peter squinted. "What are you talking about?"

Police vehicles skidded across the road at the far edge of the playground with sirens at full blast.

"You did it again, didn't you?" Peter walked over and looked under my coat, examining the blood stains.

A dozen armed MPs spread themselves across the playground and park. Peter pulled the time trigger.

I took a step toward him, wrapped a hand around the trigger, and pushed the button.

# Gaslight

Peter opened his eyes to the now-familiar sight of the blue sky above McNeil Island. Only empty grass next to him. "Joan? Joan!" He sat up and looked around.

"What?" She stood at the fence with her fingers wrapped around the chain-links. Her face half-turned back towards him.

He studied the profile of Joan's face and mentally compared it to what he remembered of Caramel. "How? How is it—how can you be Carmen?"

"I can't be." She turned towards the fence and checked the bottom edge of her coat.

"But you said—"

"I was mistaken."

"You remember what you looked like as a child, don't you?"

"It must have been the lighting or somethin'. It's been a long time." She looked back at him. "If it was true, we woulda known by now."

"Not necessarily." He stood and walked to Joan. "Privacy protocol. Our D-N-A has never been compared."

"Mary and I compared our D-N-A once. With our mom too."

"When was your sister born?"

Joan looked at him and blinked. "February 7th."

He tried doing math in his head. Ariadne is 20 weeks along. "What about us?" He pulled his handheld scanner from his belt and clicked the knob to *genetic*.

She swatted his hand away. A crazed look in her eyes as though she were a rabid animal. "Don't you fuckin' touch me! I don't need some gadget tellin' me who I am. I know who I am."

"He could have brainwashed you before the DOLOS validation system was built."

"Samael reprograms robots, not people. He's too dumb to figure it out."

"He told me, well he implied, that he's reprogrammed people."

"You talked to him?!" Joan's face turned red.

"I was following up on a lead."

Joan crossed her arms. "You still think I murdered Gemma, don't ya?"

His eyes drifted over her nose and high cheekbones. She resembled Ariadne but wasn't the same. She was uniquely herself.

"What?" Joan asked.

"Nothing," he said. Joan looked down. "Why don't you come meet my wife? She works with memories. She can tell if you were reprogrammed. Besides, you might recognize her." He loaded a volumetric portrait of Ariadne on his wrist-computer. "Is this your mother?"

Joan stared at it but not at him for several seconds, then she walked along the fence, away from him.

"Joan, give me the time trigger."

"No fuckin' way."

"Why do the base police keep chasing you?"

"It's nothin'."

"Carmen."

"You're not my father," she said. "Even if ya are, I ain't your daughter."

His chest tightened and all breath left him.

***

In his home he sat on a stool by the kitchen island and stared at the empty glass and bottle of wine he had placed there, adjacent to his shaking hands. The chronograph on his wrist-computer clicked. Carmen, the young version, and Ari will be home in a few minutes.

How can I make Ari believe who I am?

The only chance is to come completely clean. Tell her everything. Even if she sees my involvement in the war. Adult Carmen isn't interested in the truth. If her mother also doesn't, what else is there?

*Labyrinth Winery* on the bottle's label. One of the wines Ari uses in her pasta sauce. He twisted the cork off the end and filled the glass halfway with red wine.

One of Carmen's drawings hanging on the front of the refrigerator. A large cat playing in tall grass. A form hanging next to it. Do-not digitize paperwork, filled in with his wife's name.

Silhouettes at the glazed glass of the front door. It opened.

Little Carmen ran to him with her innocent enthusiasm. "Daddy!"

"Peter?" Ari glanced at the bottle of wine in front of him.

"Did you bring your memory reader home from the office?"

Ari hesitated. "Yes."

"I have to show you something."

***

In Peter's study Ari threaded through the volumetric maze of his scanned memories and sank back into the executive chair he normally used. "So, there is going to be a war." She rested her chin on her hand and said nothing. Only the sound of Caramel's cartoons a few rooms away.

"And a time machine," he said.

"Oh Honey, these memories are so strange they rule you out as a clone spy."

They both laughed, and looking over his study he noticed Ari's spider plants and sunflowers by the window, her thick neurology books tightly packed along each shelf of his bookcase, and a crayon drawing of a giraffe standing in a field of sunflowers next to a lighthouse push-pinned to his wall-mounted bulletin board. His home office had transformed into hers, and perhaps Caramel's too.

"What's wrong?" Ari asked.

"You saw how I'm involved in what happens tonight, right?"

"Right Honey."

He interlocked his fingers and raised his hands in front of his face. "In the future using weapons of mass destruction is a war crime."

Ari stared at him for what seemed like a full minute. She leaned over and gave him a peck on the lips. "It's not one today." She looked around the room. "What should I pack for the shelter?"

"The shelters don't remain civilized for very long. There's a ship on the civilian tarmac scheduled to depart for the colonies."

Ari ran a hand along her belly. "I can't travel in my condition."

The sounds of the rustling branches outside, their shadows cutting the glaring sun along the windowsill, and the breaths of his wife all seemed to slow down and nearly stop. "I can't stay." After a pause, he explained, "They'll sweep the bunkers for anyone with duplicate D-N-A. My younger counterpart will match me, so one of us will end up dead."

"Would that create a paradox? If the younger version of you dies?"

"I don't know. I mean, I've heard of time traveling paradoxes. But you can't believe everything you hear."

Ari shifted her weight in her chair and briefly squinted at him. "Goodness gracious, is Mr. Chain-of-command questioning what he's been told?"

"I suppose I am."

"Hmm." Ari scratched her chin. "What if you bring that time machine device?"

"Joan—Carmen, has it."

Ari sat up straight, scrolled to one of his memories of Joan in her patrol uniform, and smiled. "And this is Carmen now?"

"I believe so."

"You think so, or you know so?"

"I would bet my ass."

Ari giggled. "She's beautiful."

"She takes after her mother."

Ari blushed and looked back at the image. "She looks very serious. Intense, even."

"She is."

"She didn't come with you?"

"Apparently she's been brainwashed."

Ari's mouth fell open. "Someone replaced her identity?"

How much Carmen is in Joan? She asked me to be her training officer. Saved my life when I was wounded. Did some piece of her intuitively know? How come I didn't? "I'm afraid so."

Ari regained her composure and rechecked all the dials of each neuro-device on the desk. "Bring her here. I can help her."

"I told her but she's stubborn."

"I wonder who she got that from."

They chuckled.

"Where'd she get her artistic abilities?" He pointed to Caramel's crayon drawing on the bulletin board.

"Oh, you should have seen her. She said she loves drawing because it's the same picture today as it was yesterday."

He scratched his chin. "What hand does she draw with?"

"She's left-handed. Like your mom."

"Huh." Even if she was brainwashed there are things about her that haven't changed.

Ari smiled. "You never noticed when she ate?"

"Doesn't she just use her face? That's where most of it ends up."

Ari laughed. "Does she slow down when she grows up?"

"No. She still eats like it's going out of style."

Ari looked at one of his memories of Joan when she wore a jumpsuit. "How does she stay so skinny?"

"She says she goes to the gym a lot. Her younger sister works at one."

"Mary?" Ari scrolled on another volumetric computer to a book of baby names. "I was also considering Matilda."

"Mary sounds much better right now."

"Okay." Ari dismissed the volumetric book and stretched her shirt over her belly. "February 9th."

"Can't wait?"

Ari sat down and briefly pursed her lips. "Peter. What happens to me in the future?"

"Carmen said her mother is alive, but something happened to her. To you."

"What happened?" Ari blinked. "I mean, what happens?"

"I don't know. I should bring her here so we can find out."

"Where is she?"

Can I tell her about Joan's revenge quest?

Ari scrolled to his most recent memories.

"No, don't look at that," he said too late.

Ari had found his memory of Joan being shot dead by the base MPs. She covered her mouth with both hands and teared up. "Oh no. My poor baby," she sobbed.

He moved his chair next to hers, kissed her, and held her. "It hasn't happened yet. It's just a memory right now."

"We can change it?"

"We can." He wiped the tears away from his wife's face.

"How?"

"I'll stop her from getting into trouble."

"Why is she in trouble?"

Huh.  He had trouble imagining Joan being caught by anyone.  She may have murdered Overton with hardly a sound. My daughter is a killer, he thought. "Whatever happened, or happens to her, it's because I wasn't here, or there, for her."

"Can you be there now?" she asked.  Before he could answer Ari kissed him with enough force that his neck cracked, and it felt as though she was trying to find the back of his head by going in through the front.  "I love you, but you're different.  Your eyes keep telling me.  I belong to my Peter.  The one that's at sea right now, when he should be."  She stood and picked up a leather messenger bag.  "I'll get little Carmen to the shelter.  You can protect our little girl's future, especially since she's so big now."

"Maybe we'll meet again someday."  He held a strand of her hair between his fingers.

"We better."  She kissed him again for the last time.

***

He had run halfway to Mr. Lyon's house when he heard the gunshot.

No one at the front of the house but the front door swung open and closed with the wind.  He pushed the door open. "Joan?"  A headless man's corpse on the floor of the living room. A metallic smelling, blood red circle growing around it.  An identification badge on the bloodied body's short sleeve oxford shirt. *LT Samael Lyon.*

More gunshots from another street.

Joan has the time trigger.  I need to reach her before she gets herself killed.

He ran as fast as he could towards the sound.  The cuffs of his shoes cut into his heels as the suburban horizon twisted left and right.

Joan was on the ground, surrounded by dead MPs.  She struggled to crawl for a few seconds until collapsing on the bloody pavement.  Several gushing red holes in her wool coat.

It was like an invisible knife had disemboweled him.

An MP stood over Joan with a gun pointed at her back.

Peter drew his pistol, shot the MP in the head, and ran to his daughter.

"Joan."  He took a knee, gently turned her upright, and held her.

"Peter?"  Her voice was faint and hoarse, and her eyes moved erratically.

"I'm here."  He pulled the time trigger from her belt and wrapped her hand around it.

Her brave heart surrendered, and he clicked the time trigger.

# 47
# Anamnesis

She gasped as she awoke and gripped her chest. She screamed but nothing left her lungs. No pain in her back and torso. No bloodied holes in her blouse or body after rechecking a dozen times.

"You're alright. You're alright," Peter kept saying.

She sat up and tried to catch her breath.

"What happened?" Peter asked.

She closed her eyes for a few seconds and tried to think of anything else. "Nothin'."

"Right. If you know where Samael's going to be, how can he catch you?"

"I don't know," she lied.

"I never could get you to tell me."

"Get me to tell ya?" She stood and checked the time trigger on her belt. "You been circlin' without me?"

"I'm your father, Carmen. Tell me what's wrong." He reached for one of her hands.

"You don't get to control me." She walked away and towards the fence.

"I'm trying to help you."

She turned back towards him. "Now? You weren't here when it mattered!"

Peter walked up to her. "What we do now matters," he said quietly, and his eye were all somber-like.

"That's what I'm doin'. Makin' a choice that matters." She checked her holstered blaster and walked away from him.

"Carmen!" Peter said. "Every time you kill him you die."

She stopped cold in her tracks.

"And it won't change who you are right now," Peter continued. "It won't change *your* past."

She looked back at him. "You gonna put me out of my misery like that bird we found? Cause I'm never gonna fly."

"No. I'll never leave you again."

"There should be some version of me that grows up without—" she looked away, towards the brick walls of the prison and dialed her emotions away without bothering to check the mood selector. While wrapping two fingers like the claws of a bird around adjacent holes in the chain link fence, the pattern of galvanized wires reminded her of an infinity symbol.

If I grew up normal, she thought, I wouldn't be here to stop Wazz's time loop. Which means Samael ends up living longer than he ever should. And my younger self meets him again. And my soul dies again. And I end up here again.

"I'll get the keycard," Peter said, suddenly close enough that she took a step away from him. "Why don't you go see your mother?"

She shook her head. "She and I ain't the people we once knew."

"She's a memory engineer. She can help you remember."

"You mean change me into someone else?"

"No. It's not like that at all."

"Forget it."

"Right. Then how about I go with you?"

"You make more noise than a pavin' robot," she said. Though Peter did just sneak up on me, she thought.

"At least give me the trigger so I can be your failsafe."

"You mean so you can control me."

"Carmen." Peter put one of his hands on her shoulder.

Matilda's dormant feelings became somehow even more gross. She stepped away from him. But those aren't my feelings, she thought.

"Sweetie, give me the trigger," Peter said.

"I'm not your sweetie."

Peter reached for the trigger.

She drew her blaster. "Get the fuck away from me."

"Don't do this. Just walk away with me."

"Walk away?"

"Forget about Samael."

"What do you mean forget about 'em? Let him walk away like nothin' happened!?"

"You have your whole life ahead of you."

"My life ended when I was eight years old!" She tossed her handcuffs at Peter. "Cuff yourself to the fence."

"No."

She pulled back the hammer on her blaster.

Peter fumbled with the cuffs and threaded them around the nearby fencepost before clicking them closed. "I love you, Carmen."

"Yeah, well." She paused to think of the best way to insult him. "You're just another man to me."

"I'm nothing like him. You think I don't want to rip that monster's arms off and beat him to death with them?" Peter violently wriggled the cuffs against the fencepost, ending with a flail that bent it and left a red gash on one of his wrists.

"Peter, you're bleedin'."

"You're already free. You're your own person now, aren't you? Whatever he did to you, it doesn't control you."

"I already told you, I ain't walkin' away."

"You already did. We went to the colonies. You, your younger self, and me. Your mother wasn't happy, but she let you go."

She scoffed. "The colonies?"

"On the last ship to leave Earth tonight. *The Corvis*."

"Then why don't I remember?"

Peter's eyes teared up. "I lost you on one of the loops."

"If we went to the colonies, why the fuck would we come all the way back here?"

"We came back for your sister."

"Mary?"

Peter nodded. "If you're not here to protect her, then whatever he did to you, he does it to Mary instead. She can't live with it the way you can. Not when she has to face it alone."

She found herself sitting on the grass with a tear on her cheek for company.

"You've done it once already. You can do it again." Peter sat down. "Help me convince your mother to come with us."

The gears of her mind turned in vain to create a comeback or something about how her life is her own and she would do whatever the hell she wanted with it.

Her hands trembled as she silently stood and walked away from him.

"Carmen! Wait!" Peter kept saying until she was out of earshot.

***

She picked Samael's key off the messy dresser and pocketed it. A small notepad and pen next to the small clean space the key previously occupied. Trying to write on the paper the way Matilda could only produced a mess of scratches. She pocked the pen and paper next to the key.

After chambering a round in her blaster, she checked Samael's laser pistol, which she had taken from his coast closet. If I shoot him the MPs will hear me so that's a no go.

The sloppily made bed was comfy enough to sit and think for a minute. He's going to drink a beer. Maybe I could poison him.

Downstairs in the kitchen none of the cupboards had Rat Croaker or any other brand of poison. The beers in the fridge were all capped. No way to add it without opening them up, which Samael would probably notice.

The eyes of the half-assembled robot on the kitchen table lit up yellow every few seconds, like it was blinking or something. The dirty plates next to it were at least several days old. Four sharp kitchen knives but they were dirty. That would mean getting close, which would only be safe if he were taken by surprise. Not to mention the conspicuous mess it would leave on her clothes.

If only I had brought my stun pistol or baton, she thought. A baton.

Her chronograph beeped. Two minutes until he comes home.

Where would he keep a defense baton? She ran up the stairs and rechecked the bedroom, finding an expanding baton in the nightstand behind *Modern Hypnosis*, a wide book with a thick cover.

Exactly where I keep my baton at home, she thought. Maybe it's just a coincidence. Or maybe my own mind isn't entirely mine. I just plotted a murder. Even though that piece of shit Samael deserves it, that's kind of fucked up of me. It's what I'd arrest someone else for. And if I die trying, Peter will lose me again. He sort of has already. He remembers me from long ago, but I don't. Kind of like how Mary and I lost Mom.

She turned her wrist and read her sentiment circle.

Syntonic-7.

The chronograph beeped. 30 seconds.

At the bottom of the stairs, she ducked into the powder room and stared at her own reflection.

The sound of the front door opening froze her in place. When shoes clopped on the floor one by one, she stepped into the hall and struck him in the head with the baton.

He slammed into the front door as she continued striking him in the back, but he turned and grabbed the weapon, wrestling it away and immediately swinging at one of her arms and abdomen.

She yelped and staggered backward, clutching her arm which now throbbed like a mother fucker. Samael lowered his stance and ran towards her. She drew her blaster. He leapt to the coat closet and rummaged thru his weapon box.

"It ain't there dumbass."

Samael stood there with the empty box in his hands and looked over, glancing at the cuffs on her belt. "Are you some kind of cop?" Samael dropped the metal box with a loud clang and ran a hand along the back of his head, coating his palm with blood.

Both her hands trembled, and she was unable to keep an aimed bead at Samael.

Samael took a step towards her with a grin. "You can't do it, can you?"

She aimed at his groin. "Ya want me to kill you? Or make ya wish I did?"

"If you shoot, someone will hear it." Samael's grin fell and he took a step back.

While still aiming she carefully stood. Her finger tickled the trigger.

Peter burst thru the nearby door. Sweaty and heaving. "Carmen. Don't do this."

"Keep outta this," she said while looking at her target.

"If you pull that trigger, your sister dies. And your mother."

"The fuck you talkin' about?" She looked at Peter but kept an eye on Samael.

"He's the only reason your mother reaches the shelter in time."

"Bullshit."

"No, it's truth. Why would I lie?"

"You're—you're tryin' to control me. To stop me from doin' what I have to. You don't get to decide for me."

"Fine. Don't let him decide either. This is you right now. Do you want to see your mother's and your sister's face every night you won't sleep, knowing that you could have saved them but didn't? I hope you don't want that. I know I don't." His steady gaze had an openness and seriousness, some kind of sincerity she hadn't seen before.

"You're gonna meet a little girl named Carmen," she said to Samael. "Don't touch her. Don't fuck with her mother's head."

"Fuck you. I'm going to call the real cops," Samael said.

"Go ahead, mister big man. Tell them a little woman beat you up."

Samael lunged at her.

Peter tackled him. "Get the fuck out of here! Fucking go!"

She cracked the door, and a gust threw it the rest of the way open. She stepped backwards onto the porch and the creaky door swung shut. Halfway to the road she turned and ran down the street of Tudor houses to the playground.

At the edge of the park along the lines of trees she slowed. Out of breath, sweaty, and gross. A subtle thud on the ground.

The time trigger, but it looked smaller. Reaching down and picking it up, it was only half. The other was still on her belt. It must have snapped in half while fighting that asshole. "Fuck!"

Against a thick tree she leaned and teared up.

"Are you okay?" It was a woman's voice, familiar but with a high tone, youthful and carefree.

She discretely holstered her blaster, wiped the tears off her face, and looked back.

Mom. She pulled her large shirt around her pregnant stomach. It was strange to see her face painted young and full of life, so alert and in command of her faculties. Completely and not at all the person she remembered.

"What happened?" Mom asked.

"Oh, nothing, I'm okay," she said out of habit.

Without a word Mom walked right up and hugged her.

She rested her head on Mom's shoulder, but it didn't feel safe like it did long ago. Maybe those memories weren't real. Or maybe Mom's not the only one who's changed.

Mom beckoned her to a bench with a clear view of the playground.

"Carmen! Stay where I can see you!" Mom said to the giggling little blonde girl climbing on a jungle gym.

Should I tell her I'm her daughter, she wondered? It's too weird to believe. Even if she did, what would that change? Without Samael, she won't reach the shelter maternity ward. She could die in labor. Mary too.

Her younger self ran to the swing set.

"Not so high!" Mom said to young Carmen. "I'm terrified she's going to bump her head," Mom said to her.

"It's thicker than you think."

"She does take after her father," Mom said. They both laughed. "She found a baby bird the other day that fell out of its nest. She stayed with it until one of the preschool teachers came over and put it back in the nest. Carmen's going to be an amazing big sister," Mom said while stroking her belly.

"When are you due?"

"February."

Mom's words didn't seem real. How could she be so open with someone she just met? And her smile, so carefree, and with two naïve eyes like Mary. She doesn't have a working concept of evil. Yet.

It's not something Mom could ever give to me, only something I could take from her, she thought. Telling her who I am, or the ambush fate has for her, would only take away her last moment of true joy.

Toddler Carmen walked over to two older schoolgirls pouring out a water bottle to make a sandcastle.

Taking her away from here, to a place she'll never go hungry, would doom Mary. Peter—Dad, might have a point. The fate of others is the only thing I can change.

"Peter." Mom stood and walked over to the tree line.

Peter leaned against a trunk. He waved with a ring of dried blood around his wrist.

She waved back and looked at the playground.

Young Carmen was continuing to build the sandcastle by herself.

She walked over and took a knee next to her younger self. "Hi."

"Hi," Carmen said.

"I'm, um, Joan. Are you Carmen?"

"Mm hm."

She took out the notepad and pen she had pocketed earlier and started writing. "Can you come here a sec? I gotta talk to ya."

"That mean girl called me ugly."

"I'm sorry," she said. "That mean girl will be a radioactive skeleton by this time tomorrow," she mumbled.

"Hm?"

"Nothin'. You'll understand when you're older."

"Will I be ugly?"

She hugged the child. "No sweetie. You'll be beautiful."

"Like you?"

Tears tickled her mouth as she laughed. "Just like me." She released Carmen from the hug and held her by both shoulders. "You're goin' to have a new home soon. And a little sister. Whenever something bad happens, tell your sister to hide. Tell her it's a game. Hide and seek. You'll know what I mean later." She rubbed Carmen's shoulders. "You're stronger than the things that will happen to you. I wrote it all down, so you won't forget. Try not to lose it, okay?"

"Okay."

"Carmen!" Mom called out from the edge of the playground and they both looked.

She wiped her face clean. "Go on. Run home," she choked.

The toddler ran across the playground and jumped into Peter's arms. After a few minutes of talking quietly, Peter set Carmen down. "I *will* see you again."

She sat on the bench. Her heart and stomach strangled each other in her throat, and her arms trembled.

Peter sat next to her. "You finally made a different choice."

"What can I say? I'm unpredictable," she said hoarsely.

"Perfect," he said, but not in his usually sarcastic tone. "We should go back. We're out of time."

"Right." She pulled the broken time trigger and handed it to Peter. "What were you and Mom talkin' about?"

"I gave her a memory disc that will help her."

"You didn't tell her who I am?"

"You didn't, so I thought you had your reasons."

"Mm."

"Were you talking to yourself?"

"Yeah. Literally." She sighed and ran her fingers thru her hair. "I don't even know who I am anymore."

"I do." He reached over and wiped away what was left of her tears.

Far on the horizon, waves of heat rose from spotlights arranged in a circle under an upright starship, tall enough that it looked like a skyscraper. Over green grass, red scaffolding contrasted the true-blue sky and tapered to the pointed top, which shined like a lighthouse over the shadowing mountains behind it. The name *CORVIS* arranged vertically.

"It's gettin' late," she said.

"A storm's coming." He leaned over the edge of the bench. "We should go."

"Where? The colonies?"

"Yes. We've been there before. It's not Earth, but this garden isn't for us anyway."

"What about Mary and Mom?"

"I don't know. But we can work together again. We'll figure something out." He set the broken trigger on the bench and stood. "You'll need to leave your pistol and mood dial."

"For real?"

He opened a flap of his coat to reveal his empty holster. "There's a security checkpoint. And dials mess with the stasis serum." He lifted his wrist. No orb in his cuffputer.

She pulled her blaster.

"Unload and safety it," Peter said.

She complied and walked over to the slide. The gun slipped away, plopping on the sand, like the Earth reclaimed it. "When you're right you're right, right?"

"Right."

She groaned while removing her emotion-orb.

Peter was waiting at the edge of the playground. "Come on, Lemon."

"Alright already." As I approached, he held out his hand. I hesitated for a moment before taking it. "Okay Peter."

"You're still going to call me Peter?"

I smiled. "Bet your ass."

***

The sun is slowly falling behind the mountains on the horizon, and lights from the base and suburbs pop up one at a time like little bright dots.

Peter stops holding my hand at a holographic kiosk where he buys two tickets to New Eden.

*The Corvis* is a wide ship, and when I look up, I see storm clouds circling around it. The top is a blur. Everything is hazy. Without my sentiment circle my mind leaves me gradually less disoriented, like a bright fog that the sun is gradually thinning.

The door of the dark elevator closes, and I don't remember walking inside. It's large but Peter and I are the only last-minute passengers. Our reflections strobe on the huge window as the metal scaffolding interrupts the bright lights growing farther below.

Peter hugs me like a bear.

"Peter, you're squishin' me."

"Sorry."

"It's okay."

Inside the ship a robot tells me to change into a white jumpsuit and guides me to a row of empty stasis-chambers. Another robot makes rounds with a tray of glowing-red liquid in tall shot glasses. 70 milliliters of Hathor Serum, according to the label. It tastes a little gross, and I must now concentrate to keep my eyelids open as I enter a chamber.

The chambers seal with a hiss and there's a repeating tap. I look around the white floors and black cables running along the ceiling until I find Peter looking over, his fingertip pressed flat against the inside of the glass of his stasis chamber. I match it with my own, and a smile conquers my face.

The room darkens, but thru a distant round window the bright sun is reborn as a star.

Both eyes fall farther with each increasingly heavy blink. My fingertips fall along the slippery glass of the stasis tube. As the gentle vibrations of distant thrusters rock me to sleep, the Earth's star fades, and all I can cling to is the hope that it will shine a little brighter for someone else.

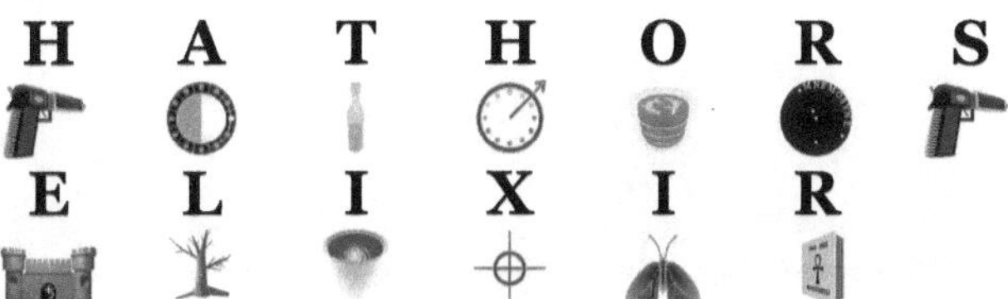

H A T H O R S

E L I X I R